U.S. Department of Justice
Federal Bureau of Prisons

WARNING — All persons entering this Federal property are subject to a search of their person and/or property (including vehicle).

AVISO — Todas las personas que entren a esta propiedad Federal serán sometidas a una inspección personal o de su propiedad (incluyendo el vehiculo) o ambas.

LOVE, HELL OR RIGHT

Copyright: Shakim Bio
Cover Concept: Shakim Bio
Cover Design: Cedric "CKillz" Killings
Typeset: Pam Quigley
Book Design: Greg Martin

Published with permission by Mikahs 7 Publishing
736D St. Andrews Rd. PMB 143
Colombia, SC 29210

Mikahspublishing@yahoo.com

ISBN # 978-0-9846596-6-1

LCCN: 2012932374

All poems/song lyrics by Rita Book a.k.a. Oceasia D. True Earth were quoted in this novel with permission from Rita Book a.k.a. Oceasia D. True Earth.

Acknowledgments...

Peace to the Nation of Gods and Earths, every God or Earth I ever built with, peace to my enlightener Lord Shaheen Wise for giving me K.O.S. over thirty years ago. Peace to The Power Paper Staff and Allah's youth center in Mecca, the Five Percent (Power Paper) Newspaper. Peace to my Ol' Earth and my whole family, to my Mikahs 7 fam for staying in my corner when everyone was praying I fail. G: Ali a.k.a. G: Millionz (true comrade), Sonya... love you for believing in a fella and taking a chance. The Tanner fam, mad love... Oceasia/Tamekia 9.12.21... love of my life. Evher Peace, my seeds, Far Rock, Farmers Blvd, the whole Queens, N.Y., the whole N.Y.C., all my true comrades (you know who you are), Ab God, Wise, The God Rahmega Shabazz Allah for your powerful build, I can never forget our builds!!! Brother Conrad X for the beautiful build (D.C.), Devin X for capturing my vision and putting it on paper. Ced Killings for bringing it to life like he saw it through my eyes. Plex, from Badland Publishing / Book Gang Media, Seth from Gorilla Convict, Al Monday, all my people from past, present and future.

Yo, I refuse to scream everyone out on this one but I must salute all the haters who wanted me to lose and wanted me to fail, you know who you are but guess what...

Next up... "The Omega Jon Christ – The Last Illest"

Mikahs 7 about to be worldwide!

You know my motto... I don't shoot guns no more... I shoot ink!

PEACE!

"Love is the highest elevation of understanding...

Hell is the trick...Right is to be right & exact."

This novel is truly dedicated to the real ones of the struggle and the women who understand the struggle, therefore, they continue to roll with us. They know and understand the meaning of true love...

NOTICE

All persons entering this Federal property
are subject to search of their person and belongings
(bags, boxes, vehicles, containers in vehicles, jackets, coats, etc)

AVISO

Todas las personas que entran en esta
propiedad Federal estan sujetos

CHAPTER 1

Terre Haute, Indiana
United States Penitentiary
Nov. 1999

I was sitting on the concrete, slab bleachers in the recreation yard, observing convicts of all colors, nationalities and sets, convicts from different states and countries, all either indulging in some sort of sports activity whether it was basketball, putt-putt golf, tennis, throwing a football or softball across the grass area, spinning (walking) the running track or on the free weight pile lifting weights. Not to mention the weather was getting cold. I was in the middle of Indiana in a town called Terre Haute, which, according to the 1998 almanac, had a population of about 61,125.

Terre Haute USP also known as "The Hut" was the first Federal Prison I was sent to as I began my sentence of 480 months for a 9 state drug conspiracy to distribute crack cocaine and cocaine. Terre Haute is the town in Indiana, where the Boston Celtic's Legend, Larry Bird went to college at Indiana State University. I had never even heard of Terre Haute but there I was, lost in thought, sitting on the cold, concrete bleachers, which were equipped to seat about 100 – 175 convicts. I was sporting my brand new crispy, white Nike, Air Force Ones and dressed in my prison issued, beige, Khaki pants and my personal grey Russell sweatshirt with the prison issued green jacket. This attire wasn't even built to keep a person warm during a fall breeze, let alone the winter cold. I was sitting up on the 7th of 8 rows, looking at the whole yard but in reality my mind was beyond the prison grounds. My thoughts were back on the streets, which is something I still do every now and then. I had been gone going on 6 years, 4 of those years I spent there at the Federal United States Penitentiary, Terre Haute.

The Terre Haute Federal Prison population consisted of close to 1600 convicts. The prison was old and dirty, there were mice, roaches and rats as well as pigeons and the ground squirrels that over populated the yard. I even saw a few cats walking around. "The Hut" been open since the 1930's or 1940 something but looked like it was over 100 years old.

"Recreation move, 10 minutes activity move opens now" was announced through the prison's loud speaker and the intercom heard by the prison's population. This gave us the opportunity to move around the prison and go place to place within the institution every 10 minutes of the hour. We could go to the yard, the inside gymnasium, school, law library, the chapel, inside Rec. to play pool, the barber shop or hobby craft shops. It isn't much to do in prison but sharpen up and become a better person, better criminal or worse individual than you already were.

As convicts moved about, going and coming on the 10 minute moves, I was sitting back enjoying the late afternoon, early evening sun. It was 8 minutes to 6 o'clock p.m.

"PEACE to the GOD!!"

I was greeted by Elbar, as he climbed up the steps of the bleacher slabs on his way up to where I was sitting. Elbar was from Albany, N.Y. He was brown-skinned with a mid-muscular build, 185 pounds with shoulder length thin and clean dread locks. I stood up to give him dap (a handshake) and embrace. We stood the exact height, 5'10" and he too was dressed in Federal Khakis, green jacket and Fresh Butter Timberland boots.

"What's the science Shakim Bio?"

"Nothing much Elbar, just sitting out here lost in thought" was my response.

In case you didn't know by now, my name is Shakim Bio-Chemical Wise, "Shakim" or "Shakim Bio" for short. I was born in Brooklyn, NY and raised in Queens and at this time in my life, I was 29 years old, a general in every sense of the word but this was not the reason why Elbar addressed me as "GOD".

Elbar was / is my A - Alike - Be - Alike - See - Alike. We are both God bodies, Five Percenters also known as the Nation of Gods and Earths and we address each other as God, Lord, Son of Man or original black man. I met Elbar on my first day at USP Terre Haute, while being introduced to all the New Yorkers by an elder NY convict. Once my name was mentioned, I was asked: "What, you're God body?" From there I was directed to "Elbar Powerful Science Allah". I was 25 years old at the time and Elbar was 31 with the swagger of a city dude, which surprised me, knowing that he said he was from Albany, N.Y. Me and "Bar" connected from there and he introduced me to the rest of Gods residing at the prison, which was only about 8 but Elbar was the one who was still true and living, showing and proving. There were other Gods there like Prince, Nyheim, Shabazz, Kasheem, and brothers who claim to be God but still addressed themselves as Broadway, Dap, Tone Rome, Action, Dirty, etc. etc.

Elbar was an older God like me. I mean, I was only 29 years old but at the time, I'd had knowledge of self for almost 20 years. I was enlightened at a very young age; during a time when an explosion in New York City's five boroughs produced a new generation of poor righteous teachers. I will give you a very, very brief history of who and what The Nation of Gods and Earths a.k.a. The Five Percenters are. We are a nation of Universal Builders; men, women and children, who know who and what God is and we bear witness that the original Blackman is God. We know and understand who the devil is and the objective of the white man is to keep Black people oppressed, poor, blind, deaf and dumb while worshipping their white god and white Jesus as one way of making the rich richer and keeping the poor, poorer. As Five Percenters, we are given our history of where we come from. We are Kings and Queens from the motherland. We are taught / reminded of the fact that we were the universal builders of all the science of the satisfied and dissatisfied. We are enlightened as to how the devil was grafted and made from the original man, which is the science of Yacub, who is the Father of the devil. We are given the science of everything in life, love, peace, and happiness. The Five Percenters teach Islam.

I self, lord and master for I sincerely live Allah's mathematics. We were taught self – love and knowledge of self to be a wise and civilized person. Our duty is to teach all human families of the planet Earth, which is the home of Islam. We do not consider ourselves Muslims, Muslim sons, an organization, a cult, a gang or any other fake labels the white man loves to label people. These teachings of the Five Percenters were not new. The "Father" of the Nation of Gods and Earths is Clarence Smith, who was born February 22, 1928 in Dansville, Virginia and later relocated in NYC in 1946. Clarence Smith later joined the Nation of Islam under leadership of the Honorable Elijah Muhammed and became Clarence 13X at Temple 7 under Minister Malcolm X. At Temple 7, Clarence ascended through the ranks, quickly being promoted to the position of lieutenant. Clarence 13X studied his lessons hard and soon became very proficient in them, the lessons developed in him a fiery wisdom.

In 1963, there were discrepancies as to what caused the disagreements that led to why Clarence 13X could not teach in Temple 7. Some say it was his marital problems or his love for gambling that led to his leaving the temple. None other than the "Father" himself knows exactly why but Clarence left Temple 7 taking with him an individual named "Justice" (Abu Shahid [John 37X]) and other brothers who understood the reality of his teachings. Those teachings brought a realization that would shake New York City and be felt around the world forever by taking the lessons with him and teaching Islam to the people in the community. Clarence 13X knew from his lessons while in the temple that the original man, the black man was/is the Supreme - being God.

"Supreme"- means the most high.

"Being"- means to exist.

"God", therefore is the name given to the highest form of existence: the black man.

Clarence 13X also knew from his lessons that eighty-five percent of all people were mentally blind, deaf and dumb, while ten percent of the people were devils in that they knew the truth but kept the eighty-five percent ignorant. He knew that the remaining five percent of all people were the righteous people who would lead the people from destruction. He focused his attention on the youth and developed the science of Supreme Mathematics as the basis for his teachings and the key to unlock the minds of our "black" youth. Supreme Mathematics is the ten principles that correspond to the number system zero through nine and the Supreme Alphabets correspond to the twenty-six letters of the alphabet that Clarence Smith and Justice created together. He taught the young how to break down and form profound relationships between significant experiences within life. Clarence 13x took his message to poor, delinquent and hardcore street youth; many of whom were drug addicts, school dropouts and in corrigible black youth, who society had long since failed and given up on. Using the Supreme Mathematics and Alphabets, he taught them the meaning of their names, ages, why life was so hard for the black man and other significant facts of life.

Clarence 13X was called "The Father" because many of his students were the products of broken homes and he was the only father they knew. His teachings and influence in Harlem spread throughout the city's five boroughs and became very powerful, attracting thousands of more powerful and dynamic young men and women, who became known as "The Five Percenters." By 1967, "The Father" and his Five Percenters influence caught the attention of NYC's mayor John V. Lindsay, who in return and with his aide Barry Gotherer, requested a meeting in which "The Father" requested the city provide buses for the Five Percenters for a picnic and a building to serve as a school where he could teach. This manifested positive results, for the mayor was interested in working with them and early that summer, Allah's Street Academy opened at 2122 7th Avenue. Clarence 13X (Father Allah) was the "The Mayor's Man" in Harlem.

In 1968, "The Father "received public and media praises for his participation in maintaining peace and order in Harlem after the assassination of Dr. Martin Luther King Jr, which sent shock waves throughout black communities across the country. "The Father" rose to become a very powerful figure within New York City. Even after his death in 1969, he remains alive, healthy and strong living within and through Five Percenters, who in the 1960's, '70s, '80s, and '90s grew to different parts of the world from every element of Hip Hop music, to movies, to every aspect in life. The Five Percenters are strong and active in every walk of life such as doctors, police officers, nurses, lawyers, mechanics, store owners, CEO's, to top entertainers, politicians, drug dealers and the common thief.

I had had knowledge of self for about two decades and was able to quote my lessons verbatim from Supreme Mathematics, Supreme Alphabets, twelve jewels of Islam, student enrollment (1 – 10), English Lesson C (1 – 36), Lost and found Muslim lesson number 1 (1-14) and 2 (1 – 40) actual facts (1 – 13) and solar facts (1-9). I was true and living, walking mathematics at one time in life. That's what I dug most about Elbar, he was still showing and proving. I was too but keep in mind, I could not be living my way of life right and exact if I was in Federal Prison for selling drugs that led to the destruction of my own people, families and homes. I shot guns, flooded communities with drugs, took over towns, abused my power to negatively influence others who would then carry out my schemes and I took advantage of women. Yes, I did all of this while knowing and understanding the meaning of civilization, the duty of a civilized man and if a civilized man does not do his duty what must be done. My knowing this and still falling victim to my environment was crazy. No one is perfect but how can one say he is God, yet say he is not perfect? I am still striving to correct my wrongs.

"Shakim, we need to build God" Elbar said as he brought me back to reality.

"What's the science?" I asked as I turned to face him, looking him directly in his eyes.

"You're being a little hard on the newborns."

I started laughing in Elbar's face.

"Too hard, how so?" I asked as Elbar joined in laughing as well.

"Sha, you too hard on the newborns. You got on some straight drill sergeant shit earlier with Y-Born and Sha- Prince."

Y-Born was Elbar's student from Kentucky, a reformed Gangster Disciple. Sha-Prince was my student from Boston. One thing about me that will never change is no matter where I am, anyone who is around me will be exposed to mathematics. It happens all the time. I have close to thirty to forty students that I gave knowledge to in my lifetime. I had three students there in Terre Haute.

"El, brothers gotta act like they want knowledge of self. I don't just hand out no lessons. When I first got K.O.S. (Knowledge Of Self), I was given Supreme Math, one at a time and I had to come back able to quote and add on before I got the next one."

"True, True"

"You got your ass beat if you didn't know your math. That's the era I come from. I come from an era of showing and proving, representing and living it out, even when I was caught up in the negativity."

"True Indeed" Elbar responded.

"I respect the fact that Brothers want to be conscious and know and understand self but just like they make time for Rap city on B.E.T., sports and all that other shit, they can make time to study their lessons. I too, was caught up on TV for a second Born U Truth (but)... I got hit with way too much time not to manifest positive results, El. I don't have to spend time trying to repair or reform broken men, I got wisdom seeds on the bricks that need their Old Dad. I know my duty as a civilized man, righteous man. I gotta make it back home."

"Sha, in or out of prison, your duty is still the same. True indeed, you know I know that you're true and living. You just a little bit too hard on the newborns but anyway God, what's the science with the Power Paper?"

"Sha-Born should be bringing it out to you in the morning when he comes to work."

"That's what's up. I need to do the knowledge in the paper."

"True Indeed, there are some real good articles in there" I responded.

"The Power Paper" is the name nickname the Gods in prison gave to the Five Percenter newspaper, which is a twelve page, monthly publication that is dedicated to its Nation's members. The paper is our voice, it gives the Nation of Gods, Earths and children around the country and worldwide, information dealing with our nation's affairs so brothers and sisters can add on to their understanding of our lessons and their show and proves. The Power Paper also touches on worldly topics, poems and even has the centerfold pages of photos of our elders, the new generation and new generation's family. Gods from

13

prisons write letters to Earth's understandings, which are then published in the paper. I've been reading the Five Percenter newspaper since the late 1980's, early '90's. I remember when I was out of state back in my crack hustling days, how Gods used to come through and drop off old and new papers at my crack spots so I could read them.

Sometime in the early '90s, the Five Percenter paper fell off and was no longer being published until 1995, when an elder God by the name of G. Kalim, who not only knew "the Father" but walked with him, took over and made the paper more productive, more knowledgeable. He put together a writers staff of hard working Gods and Earths, who took being editors, writers and journalism seriously and made them vocal through the paper. G. Kalim's motto was "S.O.S." Save Our School and he did a magnificent job keeping Allah's Youth Center in Mecca (Harlem, N.Y.) alive and active. Power is the truth and G. Kalim along with his staff brought it. So Gods and Earths in the prisons called The Five Percenter Newspaper "The Power Paper".

I started getting the paper at the end of 1997 when I came back from Ohio on my second trial; One being federal in 1995 in Norfolk, Virginia, the other trial in the state of Ohio. At first, the papers was being handed to me from other "God bodies" who were also in the same prison but I figured that I should have my own subscription so my sister Maxine, who is one year older than me, took care of the subscription fees and then it was a line of brothers waiting to read the paper once I was done with it. Once the last brother was finished reading my copy of "The Power Paper", it was returned back to me. These are newspapers that we don't throw away; a jeweler never throws away precious jewels. He stores and keeps them in the best condition possible. The Power Paper is serious like that.

"Shakim, before I forget, the Chaplin reviewed his files and no longer sees the Nation of Gods and Earths as a security threat group so we can get a room in the chapel only on Tuesday at the equality hour to build.

Born u truth, he only agreed to limited copying a week, so if you could make it possible, order some copy cards so we could make our own copies" Elbar said with a smile.

"True Indeed El" I said, smiling along with him.

I recognized Elbar's smile as a victory for we'd been back and forth, at war for two years with the Chaplin department. They would not recognize the NOGE (Nation of Gods and Earths) as anything other than a gang and a Security Threat Group. In late 1997, I spoke with one of the chaplains, who was a real devil about obtaining a Universal Flag button from the Allah's Youth Street Academy. After the back and forth questioning and more questions, he submitted and called the school for verifications. At the time, I was in correspondence with an Elder God named Master NaGee. I was flowing with the God through mail by either writing the school or straight to his residence. So after the Chaplin requested to speak to "Mr. NaGee" (He refused to say "Master"), put me on speaker phone, asked a series of questions regarding the Nation of Gods and Earths and OBTAINING a Universal Flag, I built with NaGee, who then put G. Kalim on the line. Kalim asked me the history of the flag, had me show and prove the points, degrees in points, the sun, moon, stars, the colors on the flag, what I represent and also the Supreme Mathematics of the day. All this language was foreign to the Chaplin, he was as baffled as me, NaGee and Kalim dealt with high explosives. The Chaplin then rudely interrupted and asked was I qualified in approving others to obtaining and WEARING a flag, which the answer was affirmative. Once we hung up, the Chaplin requested a list of all known Five Percenters in the institution, had I not complied with his request, I couldn't get the Universal Flag button. The Chaplin's request was a problem for me because I refused to identify anyone other than myself. I went and built with various "God Bodies", who felt one way or another in coming forward to be put on file as a "Five Percenter". They came with so many weak excuses like, "I am working on my case", "I am trying to go to a medium" or "I'd rather be identified as NOI (Nation of Islam)" etc. etc. Me and Elbar pressed the issue the hardest with the Chaplin in order to be recognized and allowedto wear crowns with the tassel. Brothers was wearing crowns without tassels, so it was like they were wearing "Kufis". Mine needed the tassel, then we were pressing the issue for chapel space like the Moorish Science Temple of America, the Native Americans, NOI, Sunni, Christians and the Jews had. So to make a point, I got the Universal Flag tattooed on my upper left chest so I didn't need any chapel or Chaplin to approve of me wearing the Flag.

We started having build sessions on the rec yard two times a week, attracting crowds that sometimes brought C.O.'s to break it up. We started attracting Christians, Sunni's and NOI's, who came to listen or have open discussions and questionnaires. Me and Elbar earned awards and certificates from the Nation of Islam ceremonies and I was asked to address the masses at a Friday Jumah Khutbah at the NOI where I invited Rastafarians, Sunni's and all. I'm known to put cats in their feelings for I can take you to the Holy Bible and Holy Quran. I am built for the heated debated. I am walking and breathing mathematics, I don't need no Chaplin to approve me doing anything. Elbar on the other hand, would file paperwork from here to the pentagon. He knew and understood the rules, codes, regulations, policies and so on. The God was a beast when it came to that.

"Yo Elbar, word life... you did that G!!"

I was truly happy that that manifested. Now that we had a time slot in the chapel – we was gonna make use of that time. If I didn't, I knew Elbar was... most definitely.

Elbar lived on the east end of the institution and I lived on the west end. Other than the outside recreation yard, just about everything was on the inside except for laundry and the Unicor Factories. You didn't have to come outside for nothing other than the yard you just had to walk through the corridors and clear the metal detectors that was at every doorway area. The east end consisted of four units. Every unit in the institution was identified by alphabet letters…Units J, K, L and M was on the east end along with the gymnasium, which had a full basketball court, pull up bars, dip bars, inside weight pile area and a cd listening area. There was a Special Housing Unit also known as SHU or the Box: SHU was on the east end. Elbar lived in K Unit. Each unit held approximately 175 convicts. Units C, D, E, F, G, G1, G2, inside recreation where more pool tables, ping pong tables, hobby craft shops and commissary were all the west end. So was the death row unit (D-unit) that was separated. The chapel, school, law library and barber shop and the old movie theater was also located on the west end but the theater was officially closed down due to the violence in dark areas and blind spots. I lived in E unit.

The cafeteria, also known as the chow hall, was in between the east and west end so was the lieutenant's office, the visiting hall and the corridor that leads you to the rec yard right before you pass laundry, not to mention the old unit called "I-Unit" that was closed down but scheduled to re-open in a few months.We used to hold ciphers in the law library, inside rec, the gymnasium, the school area, the rec yard, even at the chow hall tables. Now we were headed to the chapel.

Me and Elbar spent a great deal of time in each other's presence. We worked at the same job detail, which was the chow hall in the kitchen area. We were part of the sanitation team that kept the kitchen clean. We worked together, ate together. We were tight, not including several God bodies that traveled with us in rotation. My co-defendants "Sha-Born Everlasting" and "Cee Reality" both lived in my unit. Sha-Born was from Belize. He was bright, light-skinned with curly hair, slim built and he was a hell of a cook. God could cook those exotic meals. "Cee Reality" was a brown seed, very muscular built and rocked a bald head. Son moved in a "New York State of mind" kind of way because he was accustomed to jailing in the New York State Penal System. Even though he had a bald head, he was still hairy and reminded you of a George "the animal" steel kind of dude. I always joked with him, telling him he looked like that wrestler.

Let me describe Master Equality (me). I'm a light brown-skinned seed with a bald head. You can see my Jamaican descendant features from my flat nose and full lips. I stand 5'10 and had just started working out so at the time, I weighed in at 177lbs, which was an improvement from the 160lbs I weighed when I first came in. I had gold teeth embedded with numerous diamonds on my top four teeth and six on the bottom with my eldest seed DaQuan's attribute engraved. I must be kinda handsome because I've never had problems attracting females in my lifetime.

"Shakim, how is your case coming along?" asked Elbar as he snapped me back to the reality of that moment.

"Everything is good Fed-wise. I'm looking into finding a gateway to produce the affidavits from my co-defendants, who've had a change of heart and on my Ohio ordeal, I'm awaiting results on my direct appeal. I'm still at war."

"That's right Sha, I'ma help you get up any gold that's needed to get the things you need done."

Elbar made moves in the kitchen with the hustling of food products such as vegetables, rice, noodles, raw meat, coffee or whatever. He averaged about a good $300 to $450 a month, which added up to a nice number within six months. It was an illegal hustle but he was upholding his responsibilities as a man by feeding his seeds and taking care of his family on the outs while he was in prison. I just started getting with the little moves in the kitchen. I was learning the ropes and I'm a real quick learner. My problem was that I didn't like playing Indian to some of the dudes who worked in the kitchen, who had access to what was demanded by the buying population. A lot of dudes working in the kitchen was policing (Police – ing) the government food like they wasn't stealing it too. I didn't have the patience to answer to some of these cats who probably couldn't stand next to me in the free cipher. Unlike me, Elbar was different and was on a mission to get HIS even if he had to play their game. The God got HIS and I was pulling in $200.00 a month on the move.

"Yeah Sha, I got my Earth up here for two weeks all expenses paid for compliments of the kitchen!!" proclaimed Elbar.

We laughed.

"I gotta hold my wiz down! She plays her position so it's my duty to come through for her and the seeds… like you told dem devils in Ohio when you got sentence Sha, the game don't stop!!"

"Yard Re-call! Yard Re-call! The recreation yard is now closed!!!" announced a voice over the yard's loud speaker and prison's intercom system; alerting the population that the yard was closing. It started getting dark about 7pm, in Indiana the time does not go back or forward, it always stays the same.

"El, I'ma head in the unit to take a shower real quick but at the build hour I'm traveling to the inside rec for our weekly build with the students so make sure your students are on point" I said as we started laughing, getting up to head back into the institution's corridor.

*****

CHAPTER 2

PEACE TO THE GODS!!

I went back to my housing unit and dealt with refinement, which consists of taking a shower and changing clothes. Then, I got decked in gray sweat pants, gray, long sleeved t-shirt, my crispy white "Air Force Ones" and made the 8pm activity move to the inside recreation room. It was kind of crowded in there. A lot of convicts were busy playing pool at the six pool tables or playing ping-pong at the two tables. There were ten, four seat tables to play cards. The table top had a board design so one could also play checkers, chess or backgammon games on there. A lot of the crowd was coming in and out of the bathroom, where a crap game was goin' down out of the C'O'S eye sight. The bathroom was built to hold about ten people but there were about fifty people in and out of there; betting books of U.S. postal stamps and packs of cigarettes, which replaced money. Yeah, stamps and packs of cigarettes are the currency in The Federal Prison System. You can be broke with no money on your account but be "Prison Rich" if you had large sums of stamps or cigarettes. Bets were made at the card tables, on chess matches, ping pong and pool. Bets were even made on the sports games shown on the five televisions, which was posted about seven feet in the air in different sections of the rec room. I gave head nods and handshakes to convicts I was cool with as I made my way through the crowd towards the back of the rec center.

Elbar was in the back playing pool along with Sha-Prince, who was a bright, light-skinned understanding seed. He was a husky 240lbs and he had the "three-sixty" waves spinnin' in his low haircut. He was in his beige khakis and black new balance sneakers. Y-Born from Kentucky was a brown seed with cornrow braids, a slim build and he was a little older than us. He had on his gray sweat suit, multiple gold chains and a pair of blue and white Air Jordan's. Cee Reality was playing the wall, along with Sha-Born. Sha-Born had the natural curly hair with a white patch on the top, which was hereditary in his family. He always stayed fly and on this day, he was rocking a money green oversized sweat shirt, with the Air-Max Bubbles. The colors were now considered contraband, for the only colors allowed were white or gray other than the Federal issued beige colored khaki shirts and pants. Some convicts still had colored clothing they kept hidden but only wore it on the weekends when the prisons administration staff wasn't there, which was usually on weekdays after five p.m. and on weekends but one still had to be careful, I got stripped numerous times for wearing contraband, colored clothing.

Cee Reality had on his beige, long-sleeved, khaki button up shirt with beige khaki pants and his prison issued boots. He was "G.I. Joe" dressed, which means he had on all prison issued, khaki gear from head to toe.

"PEACE GOD!" was heard as we all greeted one another with dap handshakes and embraces. We always greeted each other this way even though we mostly saw each other on an everyday basis.

"What's the science, Sha?" asked Big Sha-Prince.

"PEACE LORD!!!" came from Y-Born

Big Sha-Prince and Y-Born were two of the newborns I was accused of being too hard on. One of my students, named "Light" was in the box so I looked around for my other student "Black Justice" a.k.a. "Black Just", who was a knowledge seed from Akron, Ohio.

"Where's Black Just?" I asked, speaking to no one specific but I got my point across.

"The God said he had something important he had to do" responded Y-Born.

"Is that so?" I asked then I proceeded to address...

"It's all terrific though, peace to the ones who showed up and always stay on point. Now last week I received in the mail, a scribe from one of my a-likes I grew up with. He sent me a "National Statement: The Science of the Lessons" from Dumar Wade Allah, who has a title and is the national representative of the Nation of Gods and Earths. It is a culture (four) page document. I can't say its right and exact or a plus degree. It's his understanding. I made copies and Elbar, Cee Reality, and Sha-Born all absorbed it. I can't really say that I fully agree with it in it's entirely. The God speaks that we are not Muslims or Muslim sons born u truth we quote Muslim lessons that come from the Nation of Islam. He gives his understanding of why we quote Muslim lessons, saying that as time changes, we must change. He spoke on the "quoting fool", which refers to one who can only quote lessons but cannot show and prove or live out what he is quoting. Like I said… I do not agree with it in its entirety or bear witness that it is indeed actual facts. Next week I want Sha-Born, Cee, El, Prince and Black Just from their own understanding to add on as to what they've drawn up from this so called national statement due to the fact that they as well as myself, know one-twenty"

As I looked around at the brothers, they paid attention to my every word while they nodded their heads in agreement.

"True Indeed" came from Cee Reality

"I will add on to that next week born u truth as of right now, I want to add on to the importance of Supreme Mathematics." said Cee, as he took the spotlight, while Elbar still controlled the pool table, directing the balls to numerous holes as we came together in a cipher around the table.

A cipher is a circle consisting of 360 degrees of knowledge, wisdom, and understanding. A cipher also exists when the Gods come together to build which is adding on. Matter of fact, bear witness and see for yourself, what goes on in a cipher:

"Supreme Mathematics is the process of thought within the mind of man. The human is structured in such a manner that man is able to achieve any thought he conceives and he produces thought into a physical construction. Supreme Mathematics is the activity of the mind conceiving an idea or thought. Example: ice radiates cold, fire radiates heat is the mind of man thinking himself out in a positive/negative form by using the term of addition, subtraction, multiplication, or division. Allah mathematics is the basic foundation of the Universe. The entire universe rests upon the terms of mathematics, meaning that for anything to exist within the bounds of the universe, it must have a length, width and height. There is such a thing as invisible energy but this energy is the form of thought waves building and destroying through the Blackman activating mathematics supremely."

"Build on it... Cee Reality!!" shouted Elbar.

"I see today's supreme mathematics as Wisdom Understanding all being born to Power-Refinement for today is the twenty-third two being wisdom, three being understanding adding the two and three together which comes to five, which is power or refinement. Wisdom is the ways and actions one uses to make their knowledge known, such as speaking wisely to the Black man. Understanding is the mental picture one draws from knowledge and wisdom to see things more clearly through the All Seeing Eye, which is the mind. Understanding is also the child, which is the best part. Wisdom understanding is all being born to power refinement. Power is the truth which is to purify and make one mentally and physically clean. Truth is the power to resurrect the mentally dead from their present state of unawareness and ignorance of self... PEACE!!"

Cee stepped back and Y-Born came forward.

"Peace, I came in the divine attribute of Y-Born BE Allah and I see today's mathematics as being Wisdom Understanding borning Power-Refinement. Wisdom is the manifestation of one's knowledge. Wisdom

24

is the Black woman, who is secondary but most necessary to God's kingdom. Wisdom is the words you speak as well as being wise in judgment by knowing knowledge. Understanding is the key of life. Understanding is the best part of knowledge and wisdom, it is the Black child, physically born from that wisdom's womb. To possess third eye, this is the mind. Wisdom understanding is all being born to power refinement. Power is the strong, magnetic conscious of the mind. The truth is the light of life which God shines upon all those who misunderstand. The truth will be the guide to purification… Peace!!"

Big Sha-Prince came forward

"Peace!! I come in the cipher in the Supreme name of Sha-Prince God Allah! Today's math is Wisdom Understanding all being born to Power Refinement. Wisdom is the wise words being spoken by the black man, black woman and black child. Wisdom is the black woman, who is the moon, she receives light from her sun, who is the black man and shines light upon the star, which is the black child. Wisdom is the manifestation of one's knowledge. Understanding is the best of life. It is the black child, who is the star. It is the clear picture drawn up in one's mind through knowledge and wisdom. Wisdom Understanding borns out to Power Refinement… Power is the truth, which is the light that leads one into their true way of life. Refinement is to be clean and purified physically and mentally… PEACE!!!!"

"One – One" said Sha-Born as he stepped forward to represent.

"I am Sha-Born Everlasting Great Mind Allah. Today's mathematics is Wisdom Understanding being born to Power and Refinement. Wisdom is the supreme truth, it is the way of the wise; the intelligent execution of all truth and facts needed to build a right and just foundation for self which is righteous"

Sha-Born spoke with his hands, moving them as if he was speaking sign language with his hands and arms. All the God bodies was surrounding him and our powerful build was attracting a crowd.

"Wisdom needs no element outside of itself to born itself. Understanding is to see things clearly with the third eye which is the mind. Understanding is also when the Black Family of life has knowledge of their selves by giving brothers or sisters the key to knowledge. Wisdom and understanding, making understanding understood. Understanding the mind, it becomes in tuned with knowledge and wisdom."

Sha-Born's body was in motion with his arms and hands, expressing his self like a college professor.

"The Black man gives light to the wisdom and she gives light to the baby. That light is the knowledge of self. Understanding is the best part because that's when you see knowledge of self and start to manifest your understanding of self. It's a potential force of God's power. God is the force and power which compels all creation to act. All creation depends upon the original black family to maintain its existence for we are the primary force of all life energies. We are the center of all life's activities. Refinement is to be clean and purified mentally as well as physically. PEACE!!"

On-looking brothers started clapping and I've noticed, brothers are amazed at witnessing builds like this especially if they don't know who and what the Five Percenters are and what we represent.

Elbar looked at me and before I could step up to the plate, he beat me to the punch. It was always a positive and friendly competition between us because we both were great builders. It was like listening to a great song, for example: "The Symphony" where Craig G and Master Ace both got off and did their thing but everyone was waiting on Big Daddy Kane and Kool G Rap because they made the song "like that" so

26

that was like what was going on with me and El during the build on this day.

"Knowledge, Knowledge" said Elbar as he passed the pool stick to Sha-Born.

"I am without question Elbar Powerful Science Allah. Today's date is the 23rd making today's mathematics Wisdom- Understanding all being born to Power- Refinement. You see wisdom is a primary principle in the creation of life for she was secondary but most necessary because of the key element in her symbolism to water. Knowledge being first, which was a solid thought.

As Elbar said this, he pointed to his temple with his index finger.

"Giving birth to liquid, in turn bringing forth an understanding of gas which was needed to complete the best part of God's power in refining himself into matter".

Elbar's arms and body movement was on one million as he captivated the audience, which was now at about thirty.

"From power, the truth of Allah's existence was proven by exactly what five represented in Man. Namely him having one head, two arms, and two legs with each point having five notes of operation. One is seeing, touching, smelling, hearing, and tasting. He gave himself five fingers and five toes. The power generated by God was as bright as the first star, which have five points given rise to his justice which is Just eye see in her by raising her up into her fullest equality which is to knowledge the wisdom I give to her to better cultivate herself in being the best part chosen in being my earth. Showing her willingness to reflect God's power as the moon reflects God's light as a moon she represents her equality sharing the light which is God's rays planting the seeds of abundant life in the fertile womb of her earth. Doesn't she revolve around me caught in the gravitational pull of my knowledge being born

27

or does she have power over me by dominating and cultivating God through sex? I could hardly believe that unless I was blind, deaf, and dumb so the promise I made to my nation that I would teach her refinement and through her a new nation would be born unlike Jerusalem I would have found peace... Protons, electrifies Allah's creative electrons!!!! "

As Elbar stepped back with a smirk on his grill, all eyes were now resting on... who else? My turn!

"Peace to my A-likes, my attribute is Shakim Bio-Chemical Wise and I see today's reality as Wisdom Understanding all being born to Power or Refinement. Wisdom is the ways and actions one uses to make himself known by speaking wisely through the understanding of their knowledge. Wisdom is also the wise words spoken by a wise person. It is the manifestation and transformation of all persons, places and things, for it is that divine vehicle to transport that magnetic energy, which is knowledge in a form where one of my five physical senses can detect, thus utilizing that detected energy to only show and prove that I am the universal builder of life. Wisdom is accumulated philosophic or scientific learning of knowledge. Wisdom is symbolic to water for its flow and the many different ways words can be used. Wisdom is always second to knowledge. Knowledge is always first. Wisdom is the black woman, who is secondary, but most necessary. She is secondary for she is that lesson light. She receives all she can from her black man, who is God. She is necessary for she is my equipment to bring into existence life positive creation which is the black baby and keep it in constant elevation. Understanding means to grasp meaning of, to have thorough or technical acquaintance with. Understanding is the third eye which is the mind that sees things clearly for what is being presented. Knowledge is to know wisdom is the flow. Understanding is to show what you know. Understanding is the best part, the black child. Wisdom Understanding borns Power-Refinement! Power is the truth, the ability to act or produce an effect, forever energy used to go work, mental or moral vigor. Refinement means to be clean mentally, physically, and spiritually. My reality of Wisdom Understanding borning Power or Refinement is…."

I leaned on the pool table facing Sha-Born but not looking at anyone specific, I addressed the crowd, which was well over forty deep, I stretched my arms over my head and got back into spit mode.

"While applying wisdom, you understanding to show and prove your power to refine your mind and the minds of others. It is real easy to quote lessons. A parrot quotes what is fed to him but only one who is wise can show and prove through their understanding and show forth their power. This is why wisdom is today's math in the Supreme Alphabet. In the twelve jewels, it is just eye see for the total square mileage of the planet Earth is one hundred and ninety six million, nine hundred forty thousand square miles. My wise understanding shows our power as a whole and if you don't bear witness to that. I can hardly believe you unless you were made blind, deaf and dumb. This wise understanding to this power is the reason why we took Jerusalem from the devil and Sha-Born… tell me what Elbar promised this nation he would do in his build? This power makes us God of the planet Earth and we can show and prove every inch of it. Hills and mountains cover one million, nine hundred and ten thousand square miles and always remember the power planet is Jupiter, which is four hundred and eighty three million miles from the Sun.

"That build was real peace Sha-Bio" kicked Sha-Prince as he dapped me up as well as Sha-Born, Elbar, and Cee Reality.

"Hey!!! No Grouping up in the Back!! Break it up!!" shouted a white, racist correctional officer.

"Mandatory recall! Mandatory recall!!! This move concludes all moves of the day. This is a one way move back to the housing units!!!!" was announced over the prisons intercom and loud speakers

29

"Yo Sha...You coming out at Pill line?" asked Elbar as we all dapped up and embraced one another.

Pill line was the move for the convicts who took medications. A lot of convicts get real slick and use their move to come out to conduct transactions. Me and El used the move to check up on one another even though if we were caught in the humbug, we'd get an out of bound incident report.

"Now Cipher El, I'ma take it in. I got some scribes to write" I said as me and Sha-Prince dapped up.

"Ok, see you in the A.M!!!" responded Elbar

"Final Rotation"

"PEACE!!!"

"PEACE!!!"

"PEACE!!!"

We parted ways and went back to the housing units.

*****

CHAPTER 3

As days turn into weeks in prison, a brother must move and do what he has to do. One must keep his mental active so not to get caught up in the bullshit prison has to offer. It's bad enough we were already amongst the walking dead, my schedule was basically the same.

I worked in the kitchen clean-up crew, got off work about 11:30 am – 12 pm so I worked out 1pm to 2:30pm, some days between 4:30 pm to 6 p.m. it all depended on my law library schedule. I took a few adult Continuing Education Courses too and after I obtained my GED in 1997, I built with the God bodies daily but I kept my mind focused in the streets. I stayed writing scribes and networking on the phone, that was my thing.

A prison runs itself! I mean it's the all-day everyday cycle. They count every day at the same time, feed every day at the same time, the only thing that changed was our movements. When you moved around, you were either in one part of the prison or the next but no matter where you were you were counted for just like jeweler who keeps counting his diamonds.

A real convict moves accordingly. I mind my own business but always remain on point as to what is goin' on around me. No matter what facility you're in, this Federal shit is completely geographical. So when I was in Terre Haute, If a New Yorker got into it with a convict from Texas, it would spill over into a N.Y. verses Texas thing or whoever ran with whomever. So a fight could pop off and without warning a Texas convict would find an innocent bystander or known New Yorker to retaliate on and vice versa. So I moved accordingly, meaning, even going to the showers, I moved with my boots on… and yeah I kept that thing with me too. If you don't know what that is, keep wondering dummy but I'd advise you not to run up on me or get in my way. Normally, my days went smoothly. I had good weeks and sometimes bad weeks. That is prison for you.

31

In prison, a very important part every Monday through Friday is mail call, that's when the mail is passed out. Being confined is miserable at times. You are deprived of many things that we took for granted when we were out there in the free cipher (world). Trust me, when you're incarcerated, you yearn for the simplest things such as certain foods, women, children, family, being able to move around freely... the littlest things, which overall, boils down to your freedom. So being in contact with family, friends, and loved ones is MAJOR to someone in prison. I don't care how hardcore you are or claim to be, how rich or how poor. You could have been living it up like Donald Trump but when you're locked up, you get a good feeling when someone checks on you. Someone could just send you some words of encouragement or information from the hood or something from the courts, it means a lot and sometimes it means the world to a convict so everyone looked forward to mail call.

You had those who bragged about their love life, fan club, or whatever then you had those who were embarrassed when they didn't get any mail at all on Valentines, birthdays, Father's Day or Christmas. Some inmates got "love" like, pictures from the hood, pictures of family or the baddest chick or the baddest car, it all unfolds at mail call. During the Valentine's through Father's Day and Christmas Season, it was a hell of a feeling and look when dudes didn't receive mail. Receiving mail can control one's emotions and attitude and emotions and attitude can change the pace in a hardened and violent environment such as prison, where the strong survive and the weak perish or have to pay to survive or better yet, breathe easy. Sometimes the weak controlled the strong by playing on emotions and one's intelligence. Prison is a steel and concrete jungle where one has to know how to adapt and how to move accordingly or end up being broken, taken advantage of or victimized on various levels. Prison is a psychological game, where one has to remain strong and the strong can be defined a million ways but overall, the strong are not those who can overcome the people with physical strength. The strong are those who can stay in control even when

32

angered or off balance. Some convicts didn't seem to have a care in the world about mail. They claimed mail meant nothing to them and some were really that strong or appeared to be but it was a different story when they heard their name called for mail.

December 21st, 1999 marked six years since I had been on the free bricks. My bid started off where my mail flow was heavy. I got mail almost every day Monday through Friday. I was getting so many different letters but as the years passed by, the mail slowed down. Sometimes I didn't get a letter for weeks but overall I had family, loved ones and close associates checking for me every now and then. My street cats, various God bodies from different Federal and State facilities were circumventing mail to me too. I had a few students who stayed in tune with me, a few close comrades such as Daymond John, from FUBU the collection was getting at me sending me money orders and reflections of his success. I had a few cats involved in the industry sending photos, my family, especially my seeds, my eldest son at the time, was eight years old. I had a few female pen pals in the Ohio State Prison that I was corresponding with but my number one at the time was a female from Queens, New York, who I was acquainted with from running around. Me and shorty were heavy with back and forth scribing, sending photos and phone time. I had a few females that came and went but like I said, I was good overall.

I was still very popular and had a reputation in different prisons and from the streets of different states. I also had enough co-defendents to write. My co-defendant or "Co-dee" Al Monday was in the Ohio State Prison System and my Co-dee Kelly Blue was in the Pennsylvania State Prison system. My Co-dee Tislam was in another Federal Pen and another Co-dee Kamel was in a Medium Fed spot so we were networking regularly and I had three Co-dees; Spice, Cee-Reality and Sha-Brorn, who were all in the same institution with me. I had subscriptions to various magazines and that was the rotation of them when I was done looking at them, they went to my Co-dees. I was getting Vibe, Source, XXL was a Hip Hop magazine publication that came out every 2 months and I was getting the Five Percenter newspaper every month. After my Co-dees, the magazines were routed to several God bodies to do the knowledge then return the paper back to me. I strived to stay busy so I spent a lot of time with my Co-defendants, working on our case ordeal. I spent time in the library and with the Gods and I kicked it with my New York comrades a lot also, especially the ones who resided in my unit plus we shared the same tables in the chow hall. It was New York, New Jersey, Connecticut and the Gods who lived in different states from Virginia to the Carolinas. We had a total of five tables that seated six people to a table so it was more of a sit... eat and keep it moving so the next brother can have a spot when they came in. In the Feds it was so geographical that everything was divided into what state you were from.

My celly (cellmate) was a Sunni Muslim from Pittsburgh, Pennsylvania named Siddiq. Siddiq was a reformed Blood member, turned devout Muslim but he remained on that gangster shit. He was a muscular Brown seed, who stood 6'2", weighed about 200 lbs. and had long cornrow braids. He was 31 years old and he was in excellent boxing shape, son was real nasty with his hands. He was very conscious of what he ate and he spent a great deal of time sparring. Siddiq was incarcerated on a heroin conspiracy. On the streets, son was eating crazily on the money side and was still semi- caked up. He still had a barber shop, video store and hair salon operating while he was in prison. He was working a prison factory job in Unicor and was enrolled in the barber shop program learning to be certified barber. We stayed in religious debates at least three times a week. I'm talkin' bout some real good, heated debates that lasted for hours. He was dedicated to making his five prayers a day on the blood red prayer rug, that's the only time he wanted the cell to himself other than using the toilet. During those five times a day, he was sincere with his prayer as well as being a Friday Jumah attendee but other times, he was a thug ready to knock something out and talk about all his females, his businesses, his money and his crew. Siddiq was my dude; he knew his religion well and had a great library of books. What he didn't know was as soon as he left or whatever, I was in the cell alone, absorbing all of his religious books and I was able to quote the literature. I was also able to quote numerous Ayats (verses) from different Surahs (chapters) out of the Holy Quran and I knew the ninety-nine attributes of Allah by heart not to mention I was / am able to quote Bible verses. I love theology so a combination of a Sunni Muslim and a Five Percenter as cellmates was like lighting a match at the gas station. Overall we had a beautiful friendship and Siddiq was a good celly. He gave me good advice and was very generous with his funds because he had so much of it. He meant well, he just couldn't leave his past. I called Siddiq a "Thugslim" part Thug, part Muslim.

"What's going on Mr. God?" Siddiq asked as he lay on his top bunk bed trying to be funny and sarcastic calling me God.

"I'm laying back on my style" I responded using one of his favorite lingos.

Mail call was at 3:45pm, fifteen minutes before lockdown for the 4pm stand up count. Siddiq got a couple of boxing magazines and a letter. I didn't get no mail that day so being funny, he left the boxing mags on my lower bunk so I could have something to look at during the count.

"Yeah, one of my young girls got at me today and sent me a couple pictures"

Siddiq passed the photos down for me to see. Shorty was an absolute dime piece.

"Who this... Irene?"

"Yeah, that's her, my young girl" he replied as he reached back down for his photos.

35

"So no one wrote God today?"

"Nah, I didn't get hit today" I responded.

"How can God get locked up and he don't get no mail, what kind of crap is that, God?"

"Same way how you bumped your head praying for that letter you got today."

"You're going to the Hellfire for committing Shirk calling yourself God." Siddiq proclaimed.

I got back at him playfully...

"Yeah? We already in the Hellfire "B"! Your shorty sent you a scribe to know when you coming out so y'all can go flying on your bloody, red magic, prayer rug and remember Ack, no firearms allowed in the Jumah mosque, Gangster! And oh yeah... tell Irene she can't rock that tight Gucci jean suit... she gotta be garbed up Ack"

We laughed.

*****

Chapter 4

For some reason, Friday was always my day off from working in the chow hall and working out. I'd take off from everything. I'd say "Its fall back Friday." It all depended on what mood I was in as far as which religious service I would attend. Sometimes I'd go to Sunni Community Jumah Khutbah, where the Imam addressed the community of Muslims with lecture talk and reciting of the holy Quran in Arabic and then translated it in English. I am very fond of religious books such as the bible and Quran now but as a child, I was forced to read the bible and worship a white god and a white Jesus. Being forced to go to church made me rebel even more but after a while I became attracted to the influence that the preacher had over his audience. It was something about all the people agreeing, shouting, stomping and even falling out and shaking so I started paying attention to the words.

Sometimes I'd go to the nation of Islam services, where they addressed current events with the Quran. It was in the same chapel as the Sunni service but the Nations service was up stairs and the Sunni's service was downstairs on the main floor. Both services were held at the same time. Sometimes I would go to both, spending thirty minutes at one and thirty minutes at the other, it all depended on the topic. In the nation's service, you could ask questions and view minister Louis Farrakhan tapes but in the Sunni service, it was no talking, just listening. No questions could be asked.

Friday is a Sabbath day for Muslims. They got a Surah in the holy Quran titled "Al – Jumuah (Friday) surah 62" so Friday holds a great significant to both sects. I noticed that even though both Muslim Sects are different in ideology and belief, both of their prayer rituals are exactly the same for the NOI adopted the Sunni prayer customs.

There were some real powerful brothers in the NOI in Terre Haute. U.S.P., such as Eric X, Samuel X, Brother Soldier and Brother Minister Timothy X, the firey speaking brother from Washington D.C.

These brothers knew the teaching well and stood firmly on its principals. I had been to more than a few Study Guide classes. They had a brother who was in their ranks named LeOtis Daggett, a dark skin convicted bank robber, who stood 5 10', 170 lbs. with a semi- afro. LeOtis was from Akron, Ohio and from day one, I noticed that he paid attention to every single thing and asked a lot of question during the study guide and NOI service. He started showing up to the ciphers we held outside and when we were out and about, he always had a question to ask. He wanted to know who and what were the Five Percenters, why we were required to know the lessons word for word and why we had to have our own understanding of each lesson. Every time I seen son, he needed a minute with me to ask questions like "What exactly is Supreme Mathematics?" I even witnessed him going word for word with the brother minister Timothy X. Sun was thirsty for knowledge of self so me and Elbar took time to build with brother Daggett, who used to be all ironed up with thin creases and polished up shiny boots at the ciphers, listening to every word. He was at every build and before you know it, he knew basic mathematics and the history of the nation of the Gods and Earths.

Elbar came at me and ask me if I would enlighten Sun.

"Why won't you?" I asked EL.

"Tell you what, we both will enlighten Sun" was Elbar's response.

So both Elbar and I started feeding Son. Elbar gave him the attribute "Black Justice God Allah" and I slow walked him through the lessons along with another one of my students, "Knowledge God" from Richmond, Virginia. Both of them knowledged 120 lessons within six moons and Black Just was showing and proving to the point of making enemies among the Christians and Sunni. That was Black Just for you. He was working in commissary as a clerk and was also part of the barber program, my celly, Siddiq was in his class.

"Peace to the God!!!" said Black Just as he greeted me.

"Peace B.J! What's the science Sun?"

"Knowledge Born all being born to Knowledge-Cipher borning back to Knowledge" he answered.

I smiled at my work of art as I headed to the chapel.

*****

As I walked on the ground floor of the chapel, there were brothers from the Sunni Community mingling around, speaking among each other in small groups. They were all outside the main auditorium that holds roughly three to four hundred people. This was their last time to talk before they entered in for their religious talk. I dapped up several brothers and was greeted by many in return.

"Yo. Shakim, you joining as for Jumah today?" asked a brother named Salideen.

"Nah, Ack, I'm going upstairs to watch a Farrakhan video and hear the message the brother is giving today" I replied.

"The real message is down here brother but I already know that you are fully aware, especially being cellies with Siddiq" he said while pausing to look me in the eyes. 'You need to answer the call of Allah before it's too late my brother. I leave you with Ayat 102 from surah three titled "Al – Iman, the family of Imran "... "Oh you who believe... Fear Allah as he should be feared and die not except in a state of Islam as Muslims with complete submission to Allah!"

The calling of the Adhan was being called, letting the community know it was time to get prepared for congregational prayer and religious talk. With that, I went up the stairs to the second floor, open floor where the NOI held their services. I was greeted by Brother Soldier, who stood at

39

attention at the top of the stairs. A Farrakhan video was showing on the big screen. The second floor, open floor sat approximately one hundred and seventy five people. I was directed by another nation brother to an open seat. I looked around and spotted Elbar, Sha-Born, Cee Reality and a few other God bodies. It was about ninety or so people in attendance. For the next thirty minutes, I got in tune with the powerful build of the minister Louis Farrakhan. He was and still is such a great builder.

The projection screen went off and three members of the nation of Islam marched up front to the podium. All three men were creased up, suited and booted with the black bow ties. Two NOI members stood at both sides of the podium as the speaker addressed the audience. Above the speaker was the red and yellow crescent and star NOI flag.

"All praises is due to Allah. I thank all you brothers who made time to come down to listen to our minister, the Honorable Louis Farrakhan. I know time is of the essence so without further ado, I present my brother... your brother... our brother and great speaker... the brother minister... Timothy X!!

As everyone stood up clapping, Minister Timothy X swiftly made his way to the front, shook the speakers hand and then saluted him like they were in the Army. The two men bowed cheek to cheek on both sides then the minister - speaker did a military style turn in place, where the men switched positions. Now the minister stood at the podium with the same brothers still standing at attention on each side. As Timothy X looked into the crowd and smiled, he said "In the name of Allah, The beneficent, The merciful, who appeared in the person of Master Fard Muhammad, who rose one, most honorable Elijah Muhammad... If I was to live to see one hundred or even two hundred years of age, I could never thank Allah enough for leaving in our midst, a warner, leader, teacher and guide... I speak of none other than the Honorable

Minister Louis Farrakhan. I greet all of you in the universal greetings of peace as we say it in the Arabic language...

"As Salaam Wa Alaikum!!"

"WA Alaikum As Salaam" said the crowd in unison. Both brothers on post went into "At Ease" mode.

"How are you brothers?" asked Timothy X, who was a brown-skinned brother, who kept three-sixty waves in his hair. He was short in height, about 5'4" with a small frame but he was a fiery speaker, who carried himself like he was eight feet tall.

"Good!!!" The brothers responded in unison.

"That's Peace!! Today I was given the task of expressing why the black man must respect the black woman. Bare with me as I go straight in, to the core, no chaser!!!"

"Speak on it Brother-Minister!!" someone shouted.

"And you know I am!!" he replied causing brothers to laugh.

"Living in an environment where we are deprived of the companionship, love and affection of a woman, we should know more than most, how invaluable the woman is, especially the black woman here in the wilderness of North America"

Timothy x's voice roared with intensity, he was a physically small man but his voice was ferocious like a mountain lion. He continued...

"For the black woman has endured the harshest treatment of us all, while still given the task of carrying on the lineage of a broken people, under the cruelty of a whip... rape... and mental anguish of being torn away from her children... she still held her head up high and produced the giants who propelled us to the state we are in today!!! "

Brothers was clapping and rooting for Timothy X to continue.

"That's Right Black man!!!"

Timothy X hammered back in with his powerful voice...

"During the civil Rights movement... it was a black woman who produced Malcolm X, Dr. Martin Luther King, W.E.B. Dubois, Frederick Douglass, Paul Robeson, Carter G Woodson, Booker T Washington, Marcus Garvey and the list goes on and on... While we were still the focal point of concern for our slave masters during the height of chattel slavery. It was a black woman ... named Harriet Tubman, who went back and forth from the north!!!

Timothy X pointed up with his index finger to signify northern direction, then down...

"...to the south, to free those who sought liberation from the oppression and tyranny of Southern Slavery. Through her ingenuity and network in the Underground Railroad, she was able to free hundreds, maybe thousands ... her fearlessness gave hope to our people just like Sojourner Truth's Land Proposal , which gave way to the concept of forty acres and a mule for emancipated Africans ... The constant sacrifices the black woman has endured to make sure black men are strong and well enough to fight for our freedom must be honored and respect!!!!"

"True indeed Timothy X!!!"

"Even as we sit here today"... added Timothy X "There is a black woman that is in our lives who has given us her all, even when the world has vitally told her we are no good... she still believes in us brothers. Therefore... we should elevate her and give her the respect due. The most honorable Elijah Muhammad taught us "A Nation can raise no higher than its women" so we must hold our women in high esteem despite her faults, in order for us to once again, regain our position as dignified men and women with the rest of humanity... Instead of niggas and bitches... The Honorable Minister Louis Farrakhan said the key to heaven is the woman, therefore, if we want to enter paradise we must respect our women. I thank you for listening and coming out. I came to you in peace and I leave you in peace. As Salaam Alaikum!!!

As Timothy X threw both arms up, brothers stood up clapping and shouting.

"WA Alaikum As Salaam!!!

Minutes later, down on the chapel ground floor, me, Elbar, Sha-Born, Cee Reality, Black Just, Sha-Prince and Y-Born all greeted each other with a dap handshakes and arm embraces.

"Timothy X went in" spit Cee Reality.

"Word life... He always goes in like that" responded Y- Born.

"That spill on the black woman was real peace... so peace that I'm going back to the unit to call one" I said and everybody laughed at my remark.

"I hear you Shakim, which one you calling?" asked Elbar.

"I gotta hit my boo Tammi up G. Yo that's the rec move, I'm out.... Peace!!!

"PEACE!!!!"

* * * * *

Chapter 5

I'm a man who definitely loves my beautiful, black sisters. I love the Latino ladies too. I love women period. Sometimes, I get caught up with characters shown on the television and movies. I like watching the movie "Love Jones" with Nia Long. I felt that sister... She looks beautiful, seems intelligent and she is so fine so I automatically fell in love with her character. Sisters like her, Stacy Dash, Tamala Jones, Sanaa Lathan, Vivica Fox, Wendy Raquel Robinson (that fine chick who plays the principal on Steve Harvey show), Jennifer Lopez... there's so many that its too many to name. Foxy Brown, Lil Kim, Eve, Brandy, Monica, Tamia, Mya, Janet Jackson, Brownstone, SWV... These women are some of the beauty that I truly miss. At night I thought about the "what if's...?" "Where I would be's...?" I thought about my past girlfriends and chicks I used to deal with. I had female friends who I just hung out with on the clubbing tip or just runnin' the streets. I liked them then but after six years in prison, I missed them desperately. I'd go to sleep at night in thought, grabbing my manhood, wishing I could hold a woman. I still miss having a woman curled up under me or wrapped around me. I miss that scent. I miss everything, that's why I strive to hold on to the ones I communicate with and I hold tightly to all the great memories that are embedded in my mind. I remember how my beeper used to beep all day, all night and I'd ignored calls as woman used to check for me so much I had to change batteries every other day... But nowadays, as soon as I get a letter from a shorty, I'm responding within three to four hours... funny huh?

*****

Prison relationships can definitely make or break a man confined. A man is made to be with a woman, she is his counterpart. Life is recycled through man and woman, one can't exist without the other, for reproduction comes from them becoming one. It is only natural that one attracts the other and vice versa so even behind steel

44

and concrete, man still yearns for a woman and her affection. Some of these men in prison will do anything for the attention of a woman, some go crazy from not being able to be with a woman, some act other than their selves and go against nature.

Holding on by all means is very important. The mail call of letters, the countless phone calls, the photographs and the visits all play a part in the relationship of man and woman especially if they share a child or children. One's day in prison is crafted from a relationship just like a woman's world changes to certain degrees dealing with a man in prison. The thought of each other is always constant on his or her mind. She rushes home for his daily letter or phone call... he plays mail call religiously or can't wait until it's time to make that call. Prison can sometimes bring out the best in a man. He says and does things he never thought he was capable of. He becomes thoughtful, appreciative and a master of writing words of love. He finds out he is a poet and an artist. I've been told there is no letter like a love letter from a man in prison. He can analyze situations from all angles, replay them in his mind, he has free time to become skillful by studying and researching the woman's mind, body, spirit and history. Some men learn how to use this to advance in life and love a woman better while some use this to take advantage of a woman and some men are just too stupid to appreciate a woman. Me? Maaaan, I be going through it. I mean I never thought deeply about it while I was free. You gotta understand I was young and getting money fast from all angles. I was ripping and running the streets and I really only had one real relationship.

Outside of that one relationship, I had females by the thousands so my booty call flow was crazy, late night creepers, one night stands, the every now and then ones, jump offs, the this week, next week, last month, last year female... I was constantly moving around so I kept numerous females. When I got incarcerated, some came and a lot went as time went by. No one was obligated, even though I had two females

45

that had seeds by me. They too, moved on with their lives but occasionally came back and forth.

I had this one special female I met in queens. I damn near messed with everyone in her clique but me and her where special. She seemed challenging from the jump but she was in love with someone and shared a son with him. That still didn't stop our late night phone calls and attention from a far and as soon as the handcuffs came off my wrists, she was in touch. First it was maybe once or twice a month or every two months to every month to every week to everyday. From me being in county jails, collect calls and pages and pages of letters, she dove in head first. She called me "Pooh Bear" and I addressed her as my "Boo"... she still lived her life but just couldn't move on without me being a part of it.

By now, I was bidding crazily in the Feds and my "boo" was playing her part. She kept me laced up with mail, photos, all the magazine subscriptions, she was making all my necessary calls to my street associates, she was even stopping by businesses to pick up money to make sure it got to me. She was very crazy about me and what was even crazier is that I never knew she felt this way about me when I was out there running around free. Through our letters, we went on dates, vacations, made passionate love and experienced vicious fucks. Every day it was something new; be it a card, a letter, photos or something and this had been going on for five years and change already. We were already familiar with one another and pretty much knew the same people. I knew she was still somewhat involved with her son's father and she knew there were others who popped in and out of my bid but she didn't care as long as I came right back. We were cool and close, she played her position by holding me down and she'd tell me about the club nights or her girlfriend's nights out and I could tell her about me going out on visits. It was weird the first time she told me that she really did love me for me and not for who I was, what I had or what I was able to do. She said she was into me for me and I never really had someone tell me that before. I can't even count how many females I'd been with or lied to about being serious, she was one of the very few, if I can even think of one or two, who ever said she loved me and she said it at a time when my fortune and fame was of yesterday. I was now trapped in the belly of the beast that is the Federal System, living off of reputation and fumes and like everything and everybody else, she could walk away but she chose to stay down when on the streets, we had no kind of commitment or serious history, she stepped up and made a place in my heart.

You got the brothers in prison who are straight niggas or should I say "Destroy Powers". You got "Build Powers" and you got "Destroy Powers". Build Powers have the potential to build their power, while Destroy Powers are the ones who stay ignorant and super-unconscious. So a Destroy Power might always be miserable from not having a woman in his life, not even his mother, sister, cousin, old girlfriend, child's mother or pen pal and he can't get hooked up with a woman either so he can't relate and always want to throw negative vibes in the air about women. He swears he knows so much but can't hold a conversation through mail with a woman unless she is from the Philippines. You know a woman from the Philippines will tell you anything to get you to marry her and bring her to the United States. You could hook a "dDestroy Power" up with someone already trained for this prison shit and he'd still mess that up. He's the reason why so many women refuse to deal with a man in prison. He's lazy, worthless, ignorant, a beggar, brings nothing to the table and speaks on stupidity like he had no input on why he is even in prison. The same one to tell you "women ain't shit"; "she's a bitch", a "hoe", a this, a that. Every woman that comes on the television, in a video or in a magazine ain't shit. He coulda got her or how one of his girls favors her. You hear the stories every day, he's the same dude that wishes for a woman to write him. He doesn't know how to act when he sees a woman. If he's in the presence of a female correctional officer, nurse, counselor or teacher, he pulls out his penis and masturbates in front of her or disrespects her

47

verbally, giving all prisoners a bad name, got us looking bad. He's the same dude who can't attract a retard or lonely female on a pen pal ad on the internet...

Then you got brothers, who are too conscious, too religious, the God bodies who are too scientifical, the thugs who are too thugged out, brothers trying too hard to be things they're not. You have the dudes who refuse to apply themselves, the ones who deserve to be deprived of women as a result of being abusive, raping and / or killing women simply because they could. You got some dudes in prison who have all the right qualities, characteristics and gift of gab to razzle-dazzle a female, it's just that he is in the wrong place.

Too many of us hustled to stay way above water. We took care of ourselves as far as everything from our looks, gear, cars, houses and jewels to impress women. Some didn't start getting money. Some are still scraping up money to keep a relationship with a woman. You got men paying like they weigh... Brothers work out extra hard religiously, educate themselves or step their game up, keep their hygiene up to stay extra relevant in a female's life. It can be genuine love or can all just be a game, either way, in some way we men become suckers for love.

Then you have the women who take advantage of men in prison with words, ways and actions. They do things only because they can get away with it. They run away with all your money, got men whipping your cars, sleeping in your house. Some women play their part by holding their men down, some don't and refuse to. It doesn't necessarily depend on what caliber of man you were, its dealing with the caliber of chick you were dealing with. A woman is a reflection of her man so if all you was doing is sexing her, that's what she knows and is used to. If all a woman knows is being high maintenance and you can't sponsor that, what do you expect? But like I said, it is not always that way; it all depends on the female. She's either built for it (cut out for doing sticking by her man) or she's not.

I've seen some dudes with females and wonder "how the hell he got her?" He could be the most stupid, softest, brokest or ugliest, it's too many different degrees to think of one name but somehow, he has a Lisa Raye, Kenya Moore or a Gabrielle Union looking chick with him. Then you got the man who had it all on all levels and he got a Whoopi Goldberg, the biggest whale or the skinniest, crack head lookin', bumpy faced female that he is reppin' hard to the fullest on prison visits. Some men upgrade while some downgrade but a part or piece of a woman is better than no woman at all.

✶✶✶✶✶

CHAPTER 6

Everything was going smoothly, I mean, shit happens in prison every day but because it happens does not make it important unless it stops the movements of the institution. There are everyday problems like fights, drug deals, homosexuality, drug use, robbery, rape, sneak thievery etc. but with problems there are also solutions. There are also a lot of productive things/activities that go on as well. Just because Federal Prison holds some of the country's most cruel, violent, and sophisticated criminals from every walk of life all over the world, doesn't necessarily mean that they can't co-exist without mayhem. Most of the time the good outweigh the bad but nevertheless, time still moves on regardless.

I was moving with my daily routine and nothing changed but my moods. On Tuesdays, I had to fit in show and prove classes at the chapel from six to eight pm. That wasn't hard for me to do. The hard part was tolerating the racist ass Chaplin. The first week he gave us a hard time about what room we was getting. First he put us in a small room that could only seat about six to eight people. There was no room for our guests to sit. When that was brought to his attention, he had a story about how on his roster, it only showed "five Black Muslims" or Five Percenters on the sentry file and how they only give the room to study and not to hold no meetings or invited guests and Blah Blah Blah but after all that he gave us the second floor open space that is used by the NOI. The second week, he saw that we were staying on point and had guests from other religious beliefs coming to listen to our builds so he came with another story about how our time schedule was bumping with the Native Americans so our time slot was switched to seven p.m. to eight p.m. and really he meant eight p.m. meaning "seven fifty nine" eight and not eight o- one eight. Either way, the Gods showed up on time and kept guests attending and showing their support.

* * * * *

50

I bumped into Cee-Reality in the unit.

"Peace to the God!!" Cee greeted me with a pound.

"PEACE!!"

"What's the science Shakim Bio?"

"My reality is striving to give this time back and make it back to the bricks of North America in one piece."

"True indeed Lord."

"Is it by chance that today's reality is Knowledge Wisdom all being born to Understanding?"

"Nothing is by chance, my G."

"So why does the devil teach that a mystery God brings all this?" I then asked.

"I see what you're getting at Sha."

We both laughed.

"I just asked a question, even though the actual question, which is today's reality in the one through forty is … tell us why does the devil teaches that!"

"Answer – Because he desires to make slaves out of all he can so that he can rob them and live in luxury.

"I see you're on point."

"Always" responded Cee.

"That's peace! Yo, I just got the Power Paper today so I'ma go through it and give it to you before we lock in tonight."

"That's peace Sha. I saw that's not all you got in the mail today. You know I was also at mail call, my G."

"Yeah, shorty from Queens got at me today with some reflections."

"What's good with her?" asked Cee.

"We mad cool, that's my Boo, but... you know."

"I know what Sha?" inquired Cee-Reality.

"I'm saying as for now, she is rocking with a fella but the reality of it is she is out there and I'm in here buried alive. I can't stop her from doing her or living her life but as for right now…. she is rocking with the Best!"

"I salute you for that Sha, you stay real."

"I know no other way"

I gave him another pound (fisted handshake), we parted ways and I went upstairs to the second tier to go to my cell.

I was in my cell sitting in my hard, plastic grey chair by the small steel desk that was bolted into the wall. Both me and my celly had our own chair so we could sit in either the TV room or the ground floor. Each unit in Terre Haute had two floors, which was actually one floor and a second tier. We were not allowed to place our chairs outside the cells on the second tier because they blocked people from walking through, especially the correction officers. Again, I was sitting at the desk right by the cells sliding door, which was also next to the cell's toilet, yeah the cell was THATsmall, six by nine or some shit like that but anyway, I was sitting there reading a letter and studying the photos that I got in the mail from my "Boo"Tammi, she sent ten reflection shorty was looking so beautiful. One word to describe her at the time she took those reflections... STUNNING! She was maybe a shade or two darker than me, about 5'6" with chinky eyes, nice lips, shoulder length hair that she kept in all kinds of styles, she had nice breasts, a phat ass, mean long legs, small feet and she weighed maybe a buck twenty five or so. I can still remember how we met in Rochdale Village, Queens. I came through to link up with a shorty name China and just happened to bump into Tammi outside her building. We looked at each other and made it our business to make ourselves known. Later that night we found out that we both knew China. China wanted me far away from Tammi. I mean, me and China were tight, she plugged me with so many different females from her clique and even her older sister but for some reason she didn't approve of Tammi. Tammi was not the baddest chick I had encountered but she was real cool, had a great personality, she was fine, cute, and very smart. She wasn't as "street" as China and crew but we got crazy cool and that was what it was all about. Even when she found out about my past dealings with numerous females she didn't judge me based on that, she was semi-involved with her son's father, who in return was messing with a female that I ended up gettin' at however, we didn't get sexual we just went on a date. Me and Tammi on the other hand, was attracted to each other from the start. Everyone moved on with their lives when I got locked up. China got "saved" and gave her life to Christianity. She also did hair and was always talented; she started doing Missy Elliot and Kim Porter's hair. After a while we hardly talked but I'd still communicated with her sister Zena. Tammi stayed in my corner when I thought it would be China more than anyone. As I stared at Tammi's photos, "Reminisce" by Mary J. Blige, played in my mind.

*****

BROTHERS ON THE CORNER

That was the headline on the December issue of the Five Percenter Newspaper aka "The Power Paper". I unfolded the newspaper and opened it to read page two, which was the editorial page by 'G. Kalim, the God spits fire every time. I looked forward to his builds and reading other God's and Earth's understandings and looking at the two page centerfold photos. It usually took me one hour to ninety minutes max, to read The Power Paper. Certain articles I absorbed fully and some I just did the knowledge to. The paper was just twelve full pages and was always interesting and very enlightening. On page three was an article titled "A sister in the wilderness" that caught my attention. As I started to read, I found it very interesting. It was about a sister from New Orleans, who was striving to find herself and the truth about who and what is God. The article spoke on her struggles and travels to find this truth as she journeyed to Colorado, Philadelphia and New York. She was also a rap artist and was now the Mother of Civilization in New Orleans...wow...that story was peace. She was really on a quest to find answers and I could tell she was a journalist from the way she told her story. She left her attribute "Oceasia D. True Earth" and address at the bottom of the article and I considered writing it down so I got up to get a pen and piece of paper.

As I was writing Oceasia's information down, I thought back to the year 1985 when I was dating this female that wanted knowledge of self. Her name was Tracey, she had two older brothers, one named "Justice" and the other one named "Divine", their enlightener's name was "Love Allah" but we called him "LA" for short. We used to build and hold ciphers regularly all throughout Far Rockaway, Queens. Their sister was "off limits" but the attraction was strong and me being so knowledgeable and true and living, it was only right that we became acquainted. I was young at that time but I fed her the right mental foods. I was caught up in her beauty and her parents were Jamaican and way too strict, just like mine. She was their only daughter and didn't want her calling me "God". I can still remember Tracey in her Sergio Valente glasses, asking me to show and prove today's mathematics and how impressed all the Gods was because I had her quoting mathematics. I smiled as my mind traveled over these thoughts. Tracey became "Queen Asia" only to go back to Tracey once her parents told my parents to keep me away from poisoning their sons and especially their daughter. I let shorty go and she never came back but I wasn't trippin', I wasn't checking for her like that anyway because I was caught up in the streets and very busy building, rhyming and getting money. I can't really say that she was my earth. The earth rotates and revolves around the sun for light, heat and guidance. Tracey went out of orbit...

*****

I snapped out of my thoughts as my celly Siddiq came in the cell. I had to get up to move the chair so he could come in.

"Shakim Bio. What you doing main man?"

"Doing a little reading, you know"

"Yeah, I see you got your little ghetto version of the Final Call paper today" he said with a smile.

I paid no attention to his comment and I handed him the photos of Tammi. He looked at them one by one nodding his head in approval.

"Young girl looks good for real, all she ever do is send you pictures like she lives with a camera".

"I know"

"She must think you eat pictures in here. When's she gonna send some money?!!!"

"Get the fuck outta here!!!"

"Nah... You gotta get out... cause it's time for my Salaat (a Musliim Prayer)" he smirked.

*****

Me and Elbar had a thing at work where when we had idle time on our hands we would recite the lessons. One twenty, even though I always say it's one twenty two because two degrees was repeated twice. In the student enrollment 1-10, the 5th degree is the same as the 4th in the lost and found lesson number 2, and in the Actual Facts (1-13) the 10th degree is the same as the third in the Solar Facts (1-9). So adding the lessons 1-10, 1-36, 1-14, 1-40, 1-13, 1-9, equals 122.

I would quote a degree starting from the first of the Student Enrollment (1-10) question and answer then Elbar would follow up with the second degree question and answer. We would go back and forth until we completed the whole One Twenty. We was so swift that sometimes we only dealt with the One Twenty from the second set of numbers starting from the 1-10. So the 1st degree in the 1-36 was the number 11 in the one twenty. So if Elbar asked me the equality build degree in 120, I knew it was the build degree (#8) in the 1-40.

Growing up, that was how I was taught and given 120 and I had to be able to show and prove. So Elbar might have asked me a lesson or I may have asked him and once he answered, I might ask him to show and prove that degree. Everything we dealt with included the lessons and mathematics. We communicated in our language constantly. When Sha-Born first came to U.S.P. Terre Haute a few months after me, Cee-Reality and my other co-defendant Spice, he was a little rusty on his lessons but within months, he was on point and swift with his as well. I got my student "Knowledge" from Virginia super swift and Black Just was getting there. I met a lot of God Bodies in the Federal System later on in my journey and not many of them knew their lessons like that. It wasn't really important to know them by those second numbers but I was cut and groomed from a different type of cloth. As long as you were able to quote and show prove, it was all love.

*****

56

In one of our show and prove classes in the Chapel, we were going over lessons. We had some plus degrees, which were of other brothers' understandings that they typed up or printed. It was the show and prove of the 1-10, the 1-36, the 1-14, and the 1-40. It was a nice amount of brothers that showed up to the class. One thing about true Five Percenters, we never take anything on face value... or just because someone said this, that and the third or it sounded correct. We deal with actual facts, so we research to find out. If we read something we go to research and study, we show and prove what we find in our research to the best of our ability. One brother may go deeper in certain areas than another brother can, some understandings was not right & exact... they were misunderstandings.

Guests came to sit down and listen to these great builds and debates and it was an open floor to ask anything that was on your mind. I asked a question in the beginning of class and it still was a debate going on. My questions dealt with the first degree in the 1-40. When it said the Quran will expire in the year 25,000. That's 9080 years from the date of the writing, which was February 20, 1934. 1934 in our Asiatic Calendar was the year 15,020 adding 9,080 years makes it 24,100 year so 900 years was missing-where was those 900 years? And what Quran was we on? Some say it was a mistype in that degree, B.U.T. I corrected them with the next sentence after the 9,080 years. It said "The Nation of Islam is all wise and does everything right and exact". Black Just then took brothers to Elijah Muhammad's Theology of Time", where "Just" stated it said the first original man took 900 years to create or recreate himself. So all hell broke loose as brothers asked a series of questions and went back and forth with their theories and own understandings. Time flew and before you knew it, it was time to depart back to the housing units.

As brothers was leaving, I walked over to Black Just.

"B.J., you started a whole lot born u truth...that's you!! Yo let me read that Theology of Time, when you got time. I gotta do the one to that".

"True indeed Shakim, I got you".

Other brothers, along with Elbar giving pounds and embraces before journeying back to their units.

"Yo Shakim!"

"What's good B.J.?" I responded.

"I know you did the one to that earth that's the mother of civilization in Now Cipher, the one who did that article in the New Power Paper."

"Right and exact... I wrote her geographical mathematics down but I didn't scribe her yet".

"Yeah... that article was real peace! I never met or built with an earth before... I gotta civilize my wisdom or find me one to complete my cipher"

Black Just was looking serious.

"Right and exact... matter fact B.J., before the next class I'ma have a scribe at her"

We dapped up and parted ways.

✶✶✶✶✶

That night, I took 15 minutes out to re-read the article by the Earth / mother of civilization in New Orleans, Louisiana. The article was titled "A Sister in the Wilderness". After reading it again, I sat down and wrote her a quick scribe...

Peace Queen,

15,085

I trust these manifested thoughts find you in the ultimate sphere of strength and safety. I remain progressive without an end! Today's reality is Knowledge God all being born to Build or Destroy. Build means to add on, Destroy means to take away from. My name is Shakim Bio-chemical Wise and I just absorbed your article "A sister in the wilderness" in Five Percenter Newspaper, Knowledge Wisdom moon editions.

I commend you for your strength and courage, your struggle and strive to know the truth of self and history of whom and what is God. I really felt your article, so much so... I read it twice. I first came into Knowledge Of Self in the 15,065 year and acknowledged 120 in the 15,067 yr. Back then, growing up saying you were God, people use to joke and say "make it rain if you're God" and believe me we made it rain, hail, snow and we caused earthquakes! I was born and raised in NYC so hearing the black man is God was never unusual in the mid 1980's. I understand your struggle Queen because I traveled to southern states before and I know and understand how some minds be. That's peace that you are the mother of civilization in Now Cipher, <u>that's big</u>, that means you gotta represent to the fullest and you traveling to Now Why to Allah's Youth Center in Mecca was peace. You are a powerful minded sister and your article made me smile. Queen is number 17 in the Supreme Alphabet for she acknowledges God, God and Queen together make "He and Her" #8. Yeah you spit (rap)? I used to spit too. Unfortunately, I got caught up in hustling and now I'm buried alive in the Federal Penal System but I will be back... Nothing is impossible! When you spell impossible you're only saying "I am possible" (smile). The number eight is 2 ciphers on top of one another. A cipher is a complete circle containing 360 degrees of knowledge, wisdom & understanding. The bottom cipher is the lower self. The one on top is the higher self. One must be able to master both ciphers or be in tune with both ciphers.

59

Thank you for your very powerful story. We need more conscious sister like you; most sisters are caught up on fashion, TV and selling their souls for dead presidents.

Positive energy always crushes evil   -
Shakim Bio-chemical Wise

*****

I placed the letter in an envelope, addressed it to the Queen Oceasia but instead of journeying to the mailbox at the end of the staircase on the ground floor… I put the letter on top of my locker.

*****

The next morning at work in the kitchen, I was moving around. Elbar was making his moves with the Taster's Choice Coffee. He was breaking open the cardboard Taster's Choice boxes and taking the little one- serving packs that were supposed to go into the breakfast bags and on to receiving and discharge for convicts coming in or going out the institution. Instead, El was helping himself to it. They didn't sell Taster's Choice in The Hut, they sold a generic brand of coffee in commissary; that and Folger's coffee so Taster's Choice was some top of the line exquisite shit to all coffee drinkers. We collected all the empty Folger's bottles that we could find between the two of us and filled them up with Taster's Choice, breaking each serving pack open. It was hard work ripping open over a thousand packs but it was well worth it.

Elbar had down to a science how many packs fill up a Folgers jar (176). We sold each jar for ten dollars. Cigarettes and US Postage stamps were equivalent to money in Federal prison. We had ways to liquidate them back to currency (money) on either our prison accounts or we had the currency sent to the streets to our families or loved ones. Even in prison, moves was being made on all types of levels. Every now and then I had to put my "working" act on and mop certain sections of the back kitchen or pile up garbage bags by the dumpster door but in reality, I was only checking the kitchen supervisor's location because if we got knocked, we'd lose our jobs and have to do "hole time". Making up to five hundred dollars a month doing something this simple was worth it though, even though that was nothing compared to what I was averaging on the streets when I was free. Once we were done filling ten jars, Elbar went to put them up in a hiding stash until Sha-Born came in to send them out back to the units.

"Yo EL, I'ma go up front into the chow hall and see what's up."

"Ahite Sha-Bio but yo, don't stay out there too long G, keep coming through to keep up our front. I'ma see what I can get out the butcher shop!!!! As Elbar headed to the butcher shop, I made my way to the chow hall area, where convicts was getting their breakfast trays, after standing in line then going to their sections to sit and eat. The chow hall was crowded. They were serving pancakes and bananas, I made it over to the N.Y. section, where brothers was sitting, talking and eating. Cee-Reality was there talking shit as I dapped up all the brothers sitting with him and those at the adjoining tables.

"Shakim Bio... Look at the God with the kitchen white khakis shirt and pants... who would believe it took a prison bid to get Sun a working job?"

Brothers started laughing.

"Yeah, it's all good" I responded to Cee's joke. "It's better than cleaning these nasty ass showers. Who knows what's in them stalls?" I said and brothers cracked up at that one.

"It's all love Sha, plus it pays more so I can't complain"

"Yeah but at my job I eat good too" I responded.

"No doubt, no doubt... Yo, what they got for lunch?" asked Cee.

"Barbecue'd chicken"

"Make sure the sauce is tangy and the rice aint sticky... waiter"

"Cool! And make sure the showers is clean so I can use them when I get back" I shot back.

We kicked it back and forth for a few minutes as I got on my New York shit. We tried to make jokes and smiles out of a messed up situation. I moved on to the Sunni Muslim section where Siddiq was sitting with his Muslim brothers.

"Shakim Bio"

"What's good?"

"Nothing... I was just sitting with the brothers talking about the three aspects of Tauhid... Yo, I saw an envelope on your locker. I picked it up and dropped it I the box on my way out... that was cool?" he asked.

"Yeah... that was cool" I answered.

"Yo, I need some Taster's Choice Coffee, bring me three jars but I'm only praying for two!!!"

"I will see you later Ack" I responded being funny. "I don't do no seeing" He said with a smirk, being funny with that gang b.s.

CHAPTER 7

Chow mainline was over and the tables and floors were being scrubbed clean. There was a job detail for every element in prison. Our job in the back was done until the cooks were finished fixing the lunch meal. Our job was to keep the back clean. Sha-Born had started working, he wasn't exactly the main cook but he helped prepare the rice, vegetables and soup entrees. He was so fly that his kitchen whites stayed starched and crispy, he made work look so easy you would think that he didn't work. He took time out from opening the industrial cans of green beans to come build with me and Elbar.

"Peace to the Gods!!"

"Peace Sha-Born... what's the science?" asked Elbar, giving Sha-Born a pound.

"Constant elevation" was Sha-Born's answer.

"True indeed".

"What's good with you?" asked Sha-Born.

"Oh... before I forget, I'm not coming to workout after work. I got a one p.m. call out with my unit team."

"Is that so?" I responded.

"Yeah... maybe these devils will drop my points so I can journey to a medium and be closer to my Earth and seeds!!!"

"Word!" exclaimed Sha-Born.

Unit team consisted of your counselor, case manager and unit manager. Each inmate met with their unit team every six months. Your file was opened and read and an analysis was conducted on your conduct and job performance, If you took any classes to further your

63

education, living skills, If you had been paying your fine or restitutions imposed by the courts. Many aspects, such as crime offense to family ties to clear conduct factored into the analysis and these aspects added or subtracted to a bogus point system they used to determine your security status. If you still had high points, you remained in high security institutions but if you'd been "programing" and your points were average or low; you could go to a medium security facility, otherwise known as a "F.C.I." or Federal Correctional Institution where they had all the good conduct, education and job performance and programing. None of that shit did me any justice because my conviction in Ohio raised my points due to it being a consecutive sentence, meaning it was run wild to my present federal sentence. I got high points for a detainer so until I go that detainer off, which was to get the conviction overturned. I was stuck in high security, in other words, Federal United States Penitentiaries (U.S.P.).

Elbar on the other hand, was "programing" in the eyes of his unit team. He maintained good job detail performance and ethics, had classes and certificates under his belt, good conduct and was making an attempt to pay his fine. He was sentenced to twenty years on a drug conspiracy where out of twenty, one must do a little over sixteen and half years. Elbar, having a little over nine years in with seven years and a few months remaining, was striving to go to a medium, maybe Otisville F.C.I. located in N.Y. about forty-five minutes from the city or Ray Brook F.C.I. that was upstate N.Y. by Canada but closer to Albany than Otisville.

Elbar, Cee-Reality, Sha-Born and my other co-dee Spice all had points that would send them to a medium status institution. If it wasn't for that detainer I would too but I knew it was just a matter of time before all of them would be transferred.

"Yeah. I got unit team at the Knowledge hour Sha. Trustfully, I will be able to be put in for a transfer to a medium. "

"True indeed G."

"Yeah, I go to unit team next week. So does Cee-Reality and Spice" said Sha-Born.

"Word?"

"Yo, we may all be on the same bus." Elbar added in.

"True indeed!!!"

"Yo. Shakim… what's the deal with you?" asked Elbar.

"I'm stuck like Chuck my G… but I'm good no matter where I'm at, I'm Shakim Bio-Chemical, the Brooklyn fella from Queens!!"

We all got a chuckle out of that but deep down inside, I wanted to go to a medium too. All that going to the showers with my boots on and having to be on alert status was played out. I wanted to relax and do mine with ease. They sell dreams where you think the Feds got rich dudes and the swimming pools and all that other b.s. when in actuality, it's a menagerie of rats, homos, wolves, sharks, monkeys, gorillas, a few rhinos, giraffes, elephants, hyenas, a couple of whales and it was a million damn doe-doe bird ass dudes and ostriches throughout the Federal System. As I sat back looking at Sha-Born and Elbar engaging in conversation about going to mediums, I thought "Fuck a medium… I'm striving to get the fuck out of prison all together".

*****

"Shakim Bio… what's up Sun of man?" asked Sha-Born as I stood with the mop in my hand.

"Nothing much Sha, I'm waiting to get off work." I answered.

"That's what it is. Yo, what you doing later on?"

65

"Law library... gotta hit those law books for a few days and get a better understanding of how to proceed with my war for ultimate freedom."

Sha-Born was my co-defendant on my federal case and what's so ill is, we didn't rock like that on free land. We knew each other but lived on opposite sides of Queens. He was from the LaGuardia Airport side and I was from the John F. Kennedy Airport side. We never hustled, hung out or nothing together but we knew the same people and were linked through that. They called this link "conspiracy".

"Yo, what's good with Tammi?" Sha-Born asked me.

"She's good... I'm trying to get her up here and shit".

Sha -Born knew of Tammi because he knew China and her clique and China knew everyone in Queens who was getting big money. As I mentioned before, she did hair and most of her clique ran in the same circles so Sha-Born knew a little somethin' about me and I knew a little somethin' about him through these chicks. We just didn't know that we were linked until the government linked us.

"Yo, let me know cause I want Carlita to come up here to see me".

"Yeah I will do that" I responded.

"Any new cases you find, write down the cite so I can look at them too."

"True indeed", I responded.

"You got the Power Paper back? Cause I gave it to Black Just".

"Right and exact... I penned that Earth from N.O. last night. I felt her article".

"True...They got Gods and Earths all over the world now".

"That's peace!!!" I responded.

"Yo, Shakim... we gon' get out of here alive and laugh about this shit while we chillin'with our families."

"Shit's crazy how we went from generating crazy paper to selling stolen kitchen goods".

We both laughed.

"We gon' get back Sha-Bio".

"I know no other way but to get back G".

*****

To a convict in Federal prison, it isn't enough hours in a day. I was playin' the law library real heavy, trying to get a better understanding of the law on drug conspiracy, multiple drug conspiracies and buyer-seller relationships. Law is so complex, I would bust my brain cells trying to understand all that shit. I'd be re-reading cases and case laws on the two prong test of cause and actual prejudice dealing with ineffective assistance of counsel. Shit was stressing a fella out. I looked at my watch and saw that twenty minutes was left before the conclusion of the recreation moves for the night so I got up from my table to return the law library text books to the clerk. For the institutional count to be at about sixteen hundred, the law library was not packed with convicts working on their cases, striving to go home like they should be. There was a nice amount of people in there though, some were researching and studying but a lot of them was in there on some other shit, making copies of gambling slips and what not on the copy machine, being that that was one of the only places to make copies without submitting it to an authority. As I looked around, I saw that it wasn't even seventy people in there but back in the housing units, there was double that in the TV room watching B.E.T., sports or doing some other nonsense like playing cards. Half of those men were minorities, mostly blacks or hispanics and over half of them had life sentences, multiple- life or some astronomical number of years to serve due to a drug conspiracy or drug related offenses. Most of their time doesn't fit the crime. This shit could turn a drug king pin into a law professor. Don't get me wrong, it's nothing wrong with watching TV or playing cards... but all day? The courts just gave you all day to do... all day meaning, forever and you're lying down like that? Not me B... I gotta get some, if not all of this time up off of me.

✶✶✶✶✶

Weeks were flying by fast but at the same time, moving slowly. Elbar's unit team put him in for a transfer to an F.C.I. Sha-Born also went to team and got put in for an F.C. I. So did Cee Reality and my other Co-Dee Spice. They all were pending transfer and I was happy for them. We still built mostly every day and worked together. The pending transfer didn't stop Elbar from trying to stack his ones but he wasn't going as hard because a write up could shut that transfer down. An F.C.I. was a big improvement when it came to jailing, especially between a medium and a U.S.P.

✶✶✶✶✶

CHAPTER 8

The following week, I received a few scribes from various people. Tammi was a regular but I caught one from New Orleans, Louisiana as I saw the return was from Oceasia D. True Earth. The Earth wrote me back. I opened the staple from the letter, took it out of the envelope and read:

Peace to the God:

As the Earth travels at the terrific speed of 1,037 1/3 miles per hour around the Sun, I am trusting these words find you in positive energy.

I am in receipt of your scribe and I strive to reach back to everyone who took the time to write me with their supportive wisdom. I truly enjoyed reading your letter. It was peace to know my article is being felt like that. Thank you... Shakim Bio-Chemical? What kind of attribute is that? How did you get that name and what does it mean? Yeah, I rhyme or as you say "spit". I go to college, majoring in performing Arts and Journalism at a Community College. It feels great being the mother of civilization.

Can I ask you something? How did you come up with the years 15,065 and 15,067? I was trying to decipher that...so help me out.

New York is an exciting city. I would love to live there. That city definitely never sleeps, I have family there.

Well I must travel now, I'm at school.

You can scribe me back so we can 8.

Peace

Oceasia D. True Earth

*****

I went to inside rec to meet up with the gods. I couldn't wait to tell Elbar about the scribe I got from the Earth. When I got there and greeted the gods. Elbar had an announcement to make. He was packing out in the morning to go to Ray Brook F.C. I. Everyone gave him a pound as we saluted and built with him as usual. He left me his address and told me to stay in touch. I was so busy building on so many things that it slipped my mental to tell him about the Earth's response.

*****

Cee-Reality and Sha-Born were getting ready to transfer also. Sha-Born was going to Ray Brook F.C. I. and Cee, to Cumberland F.C.I. in Maryland. Spice left for Ray Brook with Elbar... within 2 weeks they were all gone.

*****

The Earth Oceasia surprised me when she wrote back to me so after a few weeks I wrote her back... One/15,086

Peace Queen Oceasia!

Happy New Year to you!! I trust this year brings you many successes and happiness. I am striving for perfection.

I was surprised to receive your scribe. I wasn't expecting a response from you. I felt you deserved to be commended for being mother of civilization and for your journey to get K.O.S.

My attribute is Shakim Bio-chemical Wise. The original attribute given to me was Lord Shakim Wise Allah but I changed it to Shakim Bio-chemical Wise Allah in 1983/84. Bio means life. Bio-chemical is the science that deals with the composition, structure and properties of substances and of the changes they undergo... it's the chemistry that deals with the chemical compounds and process occurring in living things. I took Allah out of my attribute in 1986.

Now about the Asiatic calendar – the culture degree in 1-14, in the answer it says at the end that "Musa was a half-original man, a prophet who was predicted by the 23rd scientist in the year one, 15,019 years ago. Add 1 to 15,019...15,020. 15,020 was 1934, we just traveled to the year 2000. Subtract 1934 from 2000, which leaves 66 years. Add that to 15,020 you get 15,086. That's what year this is in the Asiatic calendar.

Yeah I love N.Y. but I like traveling to see how other states move. I got a question for you. I caused a great debate in our show and prove class so I would like your input. It says in the knowledge degree in the 1-40... "The Quran will expire in the year 25,000, 9,080 years from the date of that writing which was 1934... if you add 9,080 to 15,020 it comes to 24,100. Where or what happened to the 900 years? What's your understanding of that?

Anyhow, I'ma close for now. Thank you for responding.

Knowledge - Knowledge

(12 Jewels of Islam, Knowledge – Knowledge degree, get it?)

Shakim Bio-chemical Wise

*****

Again, Oceasia wrote back to me, her scribe read...

Knowledge – Knowledge!!

I trust that this angel finds you well.

I received your thoughts and as you cee /see I am responding back to you again!! That was real peace how you showed me how to calculate the years of the Asiatic calendar. I am learning so much...and to speak (or communicate) with someone who had K.O.S. since I was a baby girl is amazing.

To answer your question: that was a great question.   added up those years. I think that it might have been a typo with the numbers or lie, the degree states that this lesson is "very near correct" and was a questionnaire quiz given by W.F. Fard and answered by Elijah Muhammad.   I am going to look into that. You can recommend what history to read or research if any?

Do you have any seeds? And if so do they have K.O.S.?

Well I gotta go. I have to study for these final exams but feel free to write back. How often do the Gods have Show and Proves in there? Do you get to 8 everyday? There aren't too many people with K.O.S. here in New Orleans a.k.a. the Big Easy. So don't let my questioning make you laugh.

Gotta Go

Peace & Love

Oceasia D. True Earth

*****

It was peace hearing from the Earth again but what wasn't peace was where I was now resting at. I was in the box, under investigation behind some drama that popped off in the unit that I had no knowledge of. However, them people (C.O's) found an eight and a half inch sharpened, steel weapon with a handle in my cell and I owned up to it belonging to me because it was mine and it didn't make sense dragging Siddiq in it with me.

*****

CHAPTER 9

As the years of doing federal time passed, so did the institutions I served my sentence in. I travelled from U.S. P. Terre haute, Indiana to U.S. P. Marion in Illinois, which is a Super-Max. I didn't stay there long but my presence was felt and I left an impact before traveling to U.S.P Lompoc in California. Without an end my presence was felt there and again so was the impact. Shakim Bio showed and proved no matter where I was at as I traveled the country through federal prison... I was transferred to U.S.P. Lee County in Jonesville, Virginia in March 2002. I was sent there because it was a new Federal Pen and it was close to the eastern seaboard where I was convicted. They transferred almost one hundred east coast convicts from U.S.P. Lompoc to U.S.P. Lee County to open up that pen. I was the eighty-eighth convict processed there. Lee County was the first institution I went to where everything was outside. We had to come outside to go or move around the institution such as chow, commissary, the yard, the gym, law library. You had to go outside and walk to the building where shit was located.

The housing units were in three buildings, each building held four units. It was split in halves where each side had 2 units, one on top of the other. There were three buildings, making it a total of twelve units. The prison was built on top of a mountain where it looked like they blew off the top of the mountain and built the prison inside of it. You could see the curves of the mountain by looking up. The architecture was crazy. Each building was connected by tunnels from the units to the west corridor buildings to the east corridor buildings so if it was raining too hard, if it was too foggy or snowing too badly, we traveled thru these tunneled hallways/corridors. It was the first brand new spot I was ever in and the C.O.'s were new and green. I was already a seasoned convict; coming from three previous gladiator pens made me move more skillfully so I progressed off of their stupidity and believe me, they were some slow hillbillies in training; a lot of them had never been around Federal inmates.

There was a gun tower in the middle of the yard and that was new to me. I'd never seen or heard of a prison with a gun tower in the middle of the yard before. They fed us good, the cells were huge and we got to pick our job details, cells and all. It wasn't even three hundred convicts in the prison yet but every day they had a bus coming in, bringing more convicts from other federal pens like U.S.P. Atlanta, U.S.P. Lewisburg, U.S.P. Allenwood, U.S.P. Leavenworth... convicts were coming in from all over. I started meeting convicts from all over, some, I was already familiar with personally or from reading or hearing about them or their cases and many of them was already familiar with Shakim Bio or heard of me. Everything is so geographical in the feds so we started clicking up and marking our spots; where we sat in the chow hall, the rec. yard, etc., etc. New Yorkers was linking with each other andI bumped into brothers I hadn't seen in years. I bumped into a cat named Supreme, from Queens, N.Y. Supreme ran around the same areas and same circle as me but he was a little before me. Son was from Laurelton, which was a suburb section of Jamaica, Queens. He had a crew called "Boom Bash"' that made noise in the eighties and nineties throughout Queens. Supreme was like 230lbs, brolic (huge, muscular) with super big arms, light skin and very athletic. Son hit homeruns in the softball field easily, he ran cats over on the football field and was a bully like Charles Barkley on the basketball court. When we saw each other we bugged out. He knew just about everyone I knew in Queens and he was linked to industry cats like I was. "Boom Bash Preme", as he was known, was still remaining strong. He just gave back twenty-five years of his sentence, he was still looking young and was just as arrogant as he was when he was in the free cipher (free world).

Supreme no longer showed and proved. He still greeted the Gods and knew basic mathematics but he was rusty on his lessons and didn't care about sharpening back up. You already know in due time he did, especially now that Shakim Bio was there. Sincere from Hollis, Queens was there. I was familiar with the young God from two previous institutions. Sincere was a little small version of Puff Daddy and was

74

very swift with his math. Sincere from the Bronx came there also. I was also familiar with him. He was a dark-skinned seed about 5'8" in height, 170lbs with a bald head and full beard. He too, was very swift with his math. Then you had a brother from Virginia named "My Lord and Prophet Allah" but was called "Prophet" for short. He was a brown seed, husky cat who was swift with his. It was my first time meeting "Prophet". Victorious Allah, who was a tall brown skinned cat from Washington, D.C. came in as well as C-God, who was from Harlem and another tall basketball playing God I was familiar with. There was a Spanish looking God named La-Sun from Brooklyn, who wore his hair in two long braids like he was from the west coast. He favored the rapper Mack Ten and from our first encounter you could see that it wasn't going to be any peace between me and him. Then there was Ramega Shabazz Allah, a brown seed with long dreads from Connecticut but the God caught his case in Richmond, VA. The brand new U.S.P. in Virginia was quickly filling up and I wasn't surprised cause that's what they build them for… to fill them up with Gods, even if the convicts don't know that Gods are who and what they are.

Everyday all the Gods would meet up and we built like crazy. The thing was, it was more of everyone trying to feel each other out and see who was the swiftest and it came down to me, Ramega and La-Sun but me and La-Sun wasn't seeing eye to eye. It was something about him that I couldn't put my finger on at the time but of course, in time, things become clear…

Sophomoric = Being over confident of knowledge but poorly informed and immature.

Coward= One who lacks courage or shows shameful fear or timidity all equaling = <u>LA-SUN</u>.

La-Sun was giving different brothers knowledge of self and powerful names but none of these students were able to build without him being present. They were told not to build with me, which I found very amusing. It was like La-sun was building an army of Gods just to keep around him. His response was "I'm doing my duty as a civilized and righteous man". We stayed debating on numerous different things about the lessons and giving brothers K.O.S. Things were very different being that we were in the feds and cats were joining different groups for different reasons. One very common reason was to hide and be protected.

So I felt that brothers should show their paperwork and why they were incarcerated to prove they wasn't a snitch and in their own words, tell me why they wanted K.O.S. Some brothers were turning Muslims just to hide. I don't hide or protect no rats, homos or cowards. La-Sun was giving lessons out like it was nothing. Every time I seen him he had four or five students with him and he carried his book of life everywhere he went, no matter what, he had his folder under his arm. He was a real character and I felt he was hiding from something. It was always one thing or another with him. He held ciphers in the yard every day at the God hour (7 PM). Many times, I couldn't make it on an everyday basis. I had other things to do like, go to the law library to research my case issues. I showed up but not every day. So La-Sun being La-Sun, used that opportunity to talk about me and the others... how "we wasn't doing our duty"... we "were faking"... we "wasn't showing and proving"... but when I came around I brought topics that sparked the mind. Dealing with today's reality. I built on today's events... then La-Sun would always want the spotlight so we went head to head with the words. Outside of quoting lessons, La-Sun was a dummy and I knew he was a coward so I picked on him... everything he said had to be shown and proved.

One particular day, the Bloods showed up. Now I'd been in jail since 1993 so it threw me off balance to witness N.Y. embracing the gang lifestyle and rep it like that. That Blood thing was all over N.Y. and N.Y. being N.Y., had its way of representing with its N.Y. appeal attracting so many young cats and a lot of these young cats came to prison, Federal prison that is. I came to jail at 23 years old and I'm a General in every sense, so a lot of young cats were / are influenced by my words, ways and actions, my character, my strong morals, principles and I talk that fly shit too. I'm not with or against this Blood culture shit or any other gang shit. I would build with some to try to understand the mindset of our youths. I look at the ones with the potential of force and power and I might build with him once or twice and invite him to the cipher to witness the Gods build. He might come and bring a few of his Blood friends and they felt our energy. A few Bloods wanted K.O.S. or had K.O.S. and wanted to renew their history. My influence was powerful like that.

I built everyday with Ramega, me and him was like how me and Elbar was. We ate together, went through one twenty and law work daily, we worked out and walked together. Another brother who I was familiar with went by the name of Wize. Wize was a young, 190 pound, light-skinned cat with dreads from Newark, New Jersey. He was one of the highest ranking Bloods from NJ. We built a lot because he knew his math and occasionally showed up to ciphers or wanted to start a build when we saw one another. Wize was also a subscriber to the Five Percenter Newspaper. He was too intelligent to be gang related in my opinion. We used to build on all kinds of things and I sometimes asked him what made him turn Blood. His whole family had K.O.S. and his first government attribute was Walik. He was conscious on several levels but stood firm with his Blood movement. We remained close never the less and he addressed me as "Ole Head" even though I was only six years older than him.

As weeks turned into months, it wasn't long before the other cats was coming to U.S.P. Lee County with scribes buried in their property addressed to me. A couple cats form N.Y. were looking for Shakim Bio and had kites from several associates they left in institutions en route to U.S.P. Lee County. I had to wait until their property came before I got the kites, which sometimes took a few weeks. All the scribes was concerning a God Body, who was allegedly not right and exact and was now residing amongst us in Lee County. There was black and white (paperwork) showing that he was a rat. Sound travels at the rate of 1,120 feet per second so when sound got in the air that scribes was sent to me exposin' a rat who was God Body, La-Sun got shooked and started acting real funny. The ciphers wasn't being held every night at the God hour no more. I showed up to find him missing but a few of his students were outside mingling around doing everything but building. I asked any student of his I seen "Where is La-Sun?" No one knew so I relayed a message, "Let him know Shakim Bio is looking for him".

I will never forget this one Friday... I received a scribe from another Fed Pen that was circumvented through the mail via third party. It was mostly dealing with the new arguments pertaining to the crack cases in Federal courts but the last few lines was the killer lines... "Jeffery Mitchell on your end from medina... his case issues is on the way... pork chops smothered with gravy, heavy on the green peppers and onions... swine". I'm like, "Who is Jeffery Mitchell from Medina?" Medina Being a name for the borough of Brooklyn, Mecca was Manhattan, "P-lon" being the Bronx, the Desert or Oasis was Queens and I didn't remember a name for Staten Island until Wu Tang started spitting Shaolin. I used to just call it S.I. or Saviors' Isle. I asked the God Ramega, "Who is Jeffery Mitchell?"

"That's La-Sun... why?"

"Is that so?"

"True indeed!"

* * * * *

The next morning I went to the chow hall, I saw La-Sun sitting down in the NY section... before I could get around the crowded chow hall to make it over to the tables... he was gone.

"Peace!"

"Peace Shakim"

"Where La-Sun went?"

"He just left"

Before I could make it back out the door, I saw him speed walking to the lieutenant's office. This was the first time I ever saw him without that folder under his arm.

"Yo, La-Sun!!!" I called out to him.

La-Sun ran like his life depended on it.

A few days later, a lot of his students went back to their government names and old habits.

It was time to tighten up!

*****

The next day, all the true and living Gods was asked to show up in the gym on the first recreational move after chow. Word was delivered to all La-sun's students to be there. Gods like C-God, both Sinceres, My Lord and Prophet, Kinetic Energy, Victorious Allah, God Far-Sun, The Blood Wize showed up... and to my surprise Boom Bash Preme was there as well as Remega and me. Out of all La-Sun's students only three showed up but I figured from the jump that that would be the case. We sat on the gym's bleachers as other convicts ran a full court basketball game and others was working out on the treadmills and bike equipment.

79

"PEACE to the gods!!" I said, addressing the fourteen brothers that took time to show up.

"PEACE GOD!" was the response.

I stood in front of everyone and said...

"I'm glad you brothers took time out to come together. This is a very necessary build. I know some of you took chances by skipping out on job details and school to come through so I will make this short so everyone can get where they supposed to be by next move. By now y'all heard the science about La-Sun... that was yesterday. This is today... we gotta keep it moving ... each of you as civilized, righteous men, have a duty to teach civilization. Not only your mathematics and lessons must be on point but also your ways & actions, morals & principles, conduct and all. WE ARE NOT A GANG!! WE ARE NOT SAVAGES!! If you are in this nation because you are a rat or hiding for protection... we don't want you here!! That's emphatically, mathematically, scientifically, Knowledge-Culture, Knowledge-Power, in other words "<u>HELL NO</u>!!" So leave immediately, because if I find out, you will be dealt with accordingly and will be picked up off the ground to be sent up top... and I'm not talking about going to New York when I say up top."

Brothers started laughing.

"Seriously God, I don't expect a cipher each and every day but at the same time, I expect everyone to be on point with their lessons. I expect everyone to be able to show and prove, be able to hold their own. Those that need help or need lessons... I am here... Ramega is here.... Both Sinceres know One Twenty... Prophet knows One Twenty. Our duty is to teach civilization to all human families, the knowledge of themselves and the science of everything in life, love, peace and happiness. It is not to walk around with all these powerful and colorful names, carrying your lessons like you can't be exposed."

I looked at everyone and everyone was looking around at each other.

"At the same time, we got brothers who need to be in that law library. We don't need God in prison... we need God on the streets! Brothers who understand the laws need to help those who don't.... Brothers who can type need to help those who need motions typed... its each one, teach one."

"True indeed!" shouted little Sincere.

"So we are showing and proving from here on out. Every last Sunday of the moon, we will get together to build on all aspects. Ramega will do the cooking, everyone will bring sodas, water, juices, cookies, chips and whatever mega requires so he can have a full meal ready while we have snacks. If we can't do it outside, we will find a spot inside... With that, I leave in peace and give Ramega the floor to address the newborn – PEACE!!!!"

"PEACE!"

Ramega stood up and made it down to the gymnasium floor with ease as he turned his back and bent down to fix his pants cuff over his fresh "beef and broccoli" Timberland boots. He stood back up and fixed his dreads by tying them up, removed his glasses, cleaned them off and returned them back to his face.

"PEACE to all true and living!!!"

"PEACE!"

"I enter the divine cipher as Ramega Shabazz Allah... Ramega meaning man of great character... Before I leave to go to the law library on the next move, I wanted to spark your brain cells on who and what is God... for brothers walking around the compound claiming to be God but have no idea or clue to what makes him God. Who is God and what is God"

81

Ramega smiled, showing his bottom row of gold teeth.

"God is supreme intelligence, which is the energy and life force from which all was and is created. It always has been and always will be. God is the "all" from which everything manifests. Negative and positive, both are needed to create balance in the universe. One does not exist without the other. No matter how dominant or docile the other may be. Supreme intelligence is that which causes the heart to beat and the blood to flow within the body without having to be told because Supreme Intelligence (God) created the body to function in accord with its will. Some say that God is only positive and has no negative... born you truth, if everything in the universe is a reflection of God and in everything there is a negative and positive, then how can there not exist these dualities in God?...The science of mathematics cannot be denied because it always reveals truth. One and one is two... which means you have to do the knowledge twice to get to wisdom... the original black man is God by nature. Nothing makes the black man God. He is... everything that exists within the universe exist within the black man. The science of the universe is the science of you!! The original man, the Asiatic black man is the true and living God, supreme being, there is no mystery God for the mystery of God has been revealed to the blind, deaf and dumb to be within self by the righteous man, who has knowledge of self knows who the true and living God is"

Ramega folded his arms in the universal square and continued.

"It is said... man was not always here as man... yet man was always here. The universe gave birth to man. The universe was man and man was the universe. Supreme intelligence which is Allah, gave birth to all. The universe has no birth record for it always existed as the black man has no birth record because man is the universe which is supreme intelligence, which is God, whose proper name is Allah-peace!!!"

"PEACE!!"

Brothers rose to their feet and started dapping up Ramega, patting him on his back, pounding his fist and embracing him. That's what I like about Ramega, not only did he love to build like I do but he also showed and proved. He was very swift & changeable, he reminded me of myself. We both thought outside the box (I still do) and can be seen going to the NOI, the Sunni Muslims, the Moorish Sciences and sometimes Christian services. We could be seen in the library digging for those legal jewels and could still play the yard with the guerillas/gorillas of convicts with ease.

As I think back to Ramadan, me and Ramega both participated in the month of fasting. We used to build and break our fast together and took turns going to either the Sunni or NOI services and certain brothers in each community were talking reckless about the other sect when they both honored the same Holy Quran and fasting month of Ramadan. So Ramega and I had a debate with members of both NOI and Sunni Muslims. I took them to their doctrines quoting Ayats from the Quran. When asked about the Nation of the Gods and Earths and the differences between us and both the NOI and Sunni communities, it was like Ramega had been waiting for this topic to surface cause he went in and shut everyone down. Peep how the god went in...

"On the difference between the Five Percenters also known as the Nation of Gods & Earths, the Nation of Islam and the Sunni Muslims, first and foremost let me say that for the Five Percenters, Islam is not a religion, Islam is one's culture and one's way of life. For the NOI and Sunni's, I feel they look at it as a religion, which the Merriam-Webster Collegiate Dictionary defines religion as (1) the science and worship of God or the supernatural. (2) A personal set or institutionalized system of religious attitudes, beliefs and practices. The Five Percenters do not worship any God because we know and teach that the original black man is God. So there would be nothing to worship other than self. The

83

Sunni belief is that God is some mysterious being outside of self that will only be seen on the Day of Judgment after you die. Emphatically Now Cipher! For we know that God can and is seen and heard every day in the black man here in the wilderness of North America and all over the planet earth... another factor between the three is discipline... I must admit being God; I see more discipline within the ranks of the Nation Of Islam, as well as the Sunni community. All three have divine orders, laws, rules, general orders, protocols, doctrines, hadiths or whatever you want to refer to that should be followed and adhered to. Born you truth... I see with my brothers that these laws and rules are rarely upheld because number one, most members don't know or practice them, they receive one twenty degrees and knowledge that. After that, they feel they are free to roam the land without a standard of how to properly represent the nation as far as appearance, how to act and speak in public and anywhere abroad. All of this is very detrimental when viewed by others because everywhere you travel in the universe, you are looked at as a representative of your nation, your culture and at all times you have to show & prove being God by your wisdom, which is not just your word being bond regardless of whom or what born you truth also your ways and actions!"

"Another difference is that the Sunni community has to believe the entire doctrine of Sunni Islam without question. There can be no question as to any part by any Muslim. As a Sunni you don't have to know or even ask "why" all you have to do is ... "Do!" Only someone in a blind, deaf and dumb state would want to follow something that they can't question if they have doubts about something they feel may not be right and exact. Not saying that Sunni Islam doesn't have good principles and ethics that should be followed because they do... but the Sunni facet of Islam was prescribed for a certain people during a certain time and that people was not the original man. The original man is God. The Five Percenters teach that and the Sunni call this teaching, "shirk", which is associating partners with Allah. We know who the true and living God is, while they believe in a mystery God... something other

84

than self. The original man, Supreme Being who is the author of the Holy Quran, The Nation Of Islam, which is the foundation of the nNation of Gods and Earths, know who the true and living God is because they both study the same lessons. Born you truth... God is in the universe and not the university and must teach those members of the human family, who are blind, deaf and dumb, the true reality of God and Islam. The Nation of Gods & Earths also known as the Five Percenters, travel the universe while the NOI remains in the university. This is how Ramega sees the difference between the Five Percenters, NOI and Sunni Islam."

Brothers had to agree with Ramega's understanding for he produced facts which couldn't be questioned and when truth comes, falsehood vanishes. This was Ramega 's exact understanding, I was there sitting in the front row. Me and "Ra" constantly built together, debated, fasted, worked out, spoke on numerous aspects of things from personal dealing with wisdoms, family and money schemes and the God used to cook God Degree (food) for me. Me and Ra were close like how me and Elbar were, we used to sit going back and forth with the One Twenty lessons daily. He would quote one degree and I would quote the next and so on and so on... we kept each other on our toes.

Ramega was definitely true and living.

*****

"Yo, what you really know what a Thug about/locked up in the bing with no grub about/on your block doing his thing slinging drugs about/ tell me what you really know what a Thug about."

-Beanie Sigel

CHAPTER 10

There are many different circumstances that led to me ending up in the Special Housing Unit (SHU), also known as "the hole' and "the box" or "the bing". Like I said previously, Lee County's Federal Penitentiary was new and most of the C.O.s was new and green so I was moving around in circles making little moves. You know you got your haters amongst the convict population, "yeah a rat is always a rat". Anyhow, a lot of things led to me being locked up in SHU but I eventually resurfaced five moons later only to get indicted. I really don't want to get into details but yeah the Feds indicted me in 2003... But I was acquitted. My being indicted made me more arrogant to the point that even under the microscope of the prison's investigation personnel, I was still indulging in making moves. This led to me being locked up and put under investigation again.

Like I said, I can't quote in detail, words of destruction as to what was what, just know this! I manifest power and force amongst the convict population... a fella had to eat... The SHU, the box, the hole, whatever one wants to call it. It is actually administrative segregation, where one is cut off from the prison's population. At first, I was on "house alone, Rec alone" status, meaning I couldn't have a celly and wasn't able to be put in a rec cage with other convicts. The cell was as big as the ones in population but there were no lockers or moveable chairs and there was a stainless steel shower in the cell. I was in the cell 23 hours a day and got 1 hour rec Sunday through Thursday. Other than that, I could only leave the cell for a haircut every 2 weeks or if I signed up for the law library, in which I got one hour by myself to research cases and use the typewriter. They changed clothes every other day but sometimes twice a week and I was fed hot meals three times a day. The food came through a slot in the steel door, packaged in a small plastic tray with three sections, one for the vegetables, one for the main course and one for rice. There was another tray consisting of salad, dessert, two slices of bread and a juice packet. You really had to be a real move maker to make moves in the box for you are in the cell 23 hours a day. They had inmate orderlies who worked the tier, cleaning up or helping the C.O. pass out clothes or supplies. The orderly who was a real convict would help pass something for his fellow convict who is locked down in the box without hesitation but not at all orderlies believe in this code... Not all orderlies were on convict time.

Prison is nothing to glorify, there is nothing fly or outstanding about being locked up. Prison is a horrible and fucked up place... but even some of the most precious jewels come from horrible and fucked up places. I was doing real well for a man who was in the box. I had extra clothes, towels, access to the phones on certain days and hours, I had kites coming from convicts in the SHU being passed by the orderlies and certain C.O.'s. I was networking and communicating with comrades on the compound through scribes and convicts coming in and out of the SHU returning to population or coming in to be boxed up their selves. The SHU held convicts in all categories, the ones who couldn't be controlled, the unruly ones who wouldn't follow the rules, the ones who sought protection from being victimized or the ones who were victims of assaults. There were convicts who ran up prison "bills" and couldn't pay them, convicts who were run off the compound because they were rats, other's had other discrepancies within their "car". The aggressors were the ones who were under investigation. There were a million reasons why a person was placed in SHU. They also had a disciplinary segregation part where convicts were sentenced for violations of breaking prison rules. So it was like you was in the jail of the jail, you wasn't allowed no personal property in the disciplinary segregation (D.S) part but in the administrative part you were allowed your Walkman radio and headphones, a certain amount of commissary and personal property like photos, law material and it all depended on how long you were in the SHU before one started accumulating more property. Believe me when I tell you this: In 2003 USP Lee Country's SHU was <u>sweet</u>. They had XM Satellite radio where you could tune in on your personal Walkman and listen to non-commercial music all day – all night. I was stacking up on commissary to the point I had too much shit. I had a pipeline where convicts was sending me packs of tobacco and illegal shit that wasn't supposed to be in the institution so I was generating new books of stamps and was reselling them for commissary or sending them back out to the compound to the ones who was sending me the goods. It was a great network that lasted for months. Even when it was exposed, we came up with another method of getting it to the SHU. Everything was utilized to get it back there such as the laundry carts, food carts, even human mules. The N.Y. car, Ramega and the Gods and Wize and his Bloods all contributed to make sure I was good while residing in the SHU. I had my cell looking like Trump Plaza. I was so laid back, if someone came to the SHU and mentioned my name to the SHU officer, The C.O. came to my door with the convict's I.D. print out so I would know he was there, that way I could put together a little care package of soap, toothpaste, deodorant and shower shoes and get the package passed along. I had a little networking thing going on regardless of being under double lock and key in the box. The Game Don't Stop!!!

*****

To a convict in the box, mail was even more important than it was to those in general population. Being in the SHU was even more miserable than anything. If you didn't have no people as arms and legs for you, you were hit, all your movements were very limited. The SHU was designed to break you down. Convicts went crazy in the SHU with Broken spirits.

I was getting every magazine either by subscribing or trading the ones I had for different kinds or newspapers. Knowledge is a range of information so I was writing people I wouldn't usually write to just to burn time and stay busy. I would write maybe six to eight different letters a day. I had a workout schedule which started in the cell. I did fifteen hundred push-ups, six days a week. When I went to the rec yard,

I did pull ups in the corners of the cage's gates. I had a fifty pound water bag that I used for the one arm curls. My day started out at 6a.m., by 10:30 a.m. I was already showered, reading and writing. I was a writing machine so focused that I started penning a novel. I was getting a lot of mail and magazines and was in tip top shape mentally, spiritually, and physically.

My biggest goal other than trying to get out of prison was now trying to get out of the SHU. I was still under investigation, the prison sent it to the Feds and was waiting to see if criminal charges would be pinned on me but the prison staff wasn't telling me nothin'.

*****

Ramega and Wize were shooting urban street novels at me rapidly; all Terry Woods books from her catalog, Triple Crown novels, Nicki Turner and Wahida Clark. I was also into the James Patterson, Dean Koontz, Jackie Collins and Malcolm Gladwell books. I was reading books; knocking them out. Every week they shot something at me, once I was done, I let a few comrades read then I shot the books back to general population. I showed my appreciation and honored Ra and Wize's realness for holding me down so whatever they sent, I sent back with brand new books of stamps when I was done. Then Wize did something that surprised me. He started sending me the Five Percenter Newspapers every month, everything from the old news I missed to the up to date ones and that was definitely peace.

*****

I was going back and forth to court and I had two co-defendants on this new beef plus I was still pending investigation that got referred to the FBI. Shit! On the new beef, we were taking it to trial, they didn't have much on us and what they had wasn't tied to me anyway. I was caught up in someone else's spider web, so off to trial... I went.

90

*****

My court date came up again and the U.S. Marshals came to get me. I got searched, dressed, handcuffed and shackled to go to court, which was two hours away. In court, I got acquitted! The judge honored my rule 29 motion that the prosecution did not present reasonable doubt that I was guilty as charged, so I beat the Feds.

When I came back to U.S.P Lee County, I was in R and D when some Sheriffs came to pick up a dude named Pierre on some state charges he had pending in Dansville, Virginia, which was a few hours away. We saw each other and he asked me what was up and I told him I got acquitted. Pierre congratulated me and asked me what's up with me and the investigation. I told him they still had me buried alive. He said he was going to Dansville to take care of an old charge but he would come right back so I should get at him so he could contribute to my struggle, meaning, put him on to the pipeline.

"Good looking out" I responded.

Pierre also told me to shoot my name and register number and he would do something for me. "O.K" I responded. Pierre was from the Bronx, N.Y. I met him when I re-surfaced from a five moon vacation in the box before I got indicted. When I went to the SHU back then, the prison population count was a little over three hundred. When I returned to population five moons later... it was over fourteen hundred and there was a lot of new faces. A lot of convicts thought I was new and just getting there, only to find out that I been there... I was just coming out of the SHU.

When I went to the chow hall, got my food and came to the New York section, I was greeted by the ones I knew and was familiarized with and I met the ones I didn't know. One cat was sitting at the next table staring in my direction. I peeped him and automatically sized him up. Seated, he was about 200 lbs., light brown- skinned and bald headed. He was sitting with his back hunched like he had a cobra back. I don't know if he was trying to intimidate me or what but if he was, shit was not working. He had "DAMU" tatted in big red letters on the side of his neck. "Damu", means "Blood" in Swahili. He also had three cuts shaved in his right eyebrow; some back in the days 1989 shit. So we locked eyes for a second and I asked my manz who was sitting with me at my table..."Sun... who's this?"

"That's the Blood homie from Bx."

"Is that so... since when Bloods sit with us?" I inquired.

"Sun, the Bloods are crazy deep and most of them are from the town (N.Y.)"

I glanced back towards Duke and he looked my way... First thing that comes to my mind is a Jay-Z line so I sang the shit in "Blood Homie's a.k.a. Mr. Damu's" direction as I got up with my tray to leave the chow hall...

"I seen the same thing happen to Kane / three cuts in your eyebrow / trying to wild out"

Then I exited the chow hall.

*****

The next day, I saw Wize at the smoker's section, where convicts were allowed to smoke their cigarettes and cigars. I saw Mr. Damu with the three cuts in his eyebrow dude with Wize. Me and Wize conversated and dude was standing there smoking, I said to him...

"I'm Shakim Bio."

"Yeah... I'm Bloody Pierre."

"God body from Queens."

"Blood from Bx."

Me and Bloody Pierre got cool from that day on and always joked about that first day we saw each other in the chow hall. We use to walk the track on the rec yard and build on all kinds of aspects. Within time, Bloody Pierre was learning basic, Supreme Mathematics and Alphabets from being around me or in the presences of me and the Gods building in a cipher. We linked up and spoke on his relationship with his girl, who he was marrying in a few moons and we built on family and the importance or realness. Real always recognized real... Even from a distance.

*****

CHAPTER 11

<u>13 Moons in the box</u>

Time was flying but at times it seemed like it was standing still

I was communicating with a lot of wisdoms from my past and some new ones. Convicts in the SHU would hook me up with their girlfriend's friends, their sisters or cousins plus I was a hot item on the internet (LOL). I was also off of "house alone, rec. alone", so now I had a celly; a brother I knew when I was in Lompoc, California. He was a Black Guerilla family Member from Detroit, Michigan. He was cool but his story of why he was in SHU was real shaky. I let him stay in the cell with me cause I knew he wasn't a rat or homo, we was semi-cool and stayed out of each other's way.

I was still living good and had the pipeline on smash. I was a writing machine, penning this novel titled "The Omega Jon Christ – The Last Illest", which is a "Street Hop" joint about my life in the streets and involvement with Hip Hop... I'm releasing it after this one... the shit is BANANAZ. I was able to type up a lot of pages in the library. Ramega and Wize were still blasting shit through to me, I had a few other cats on board and Pierre was staying true to his word. I had been on the disciplinary tier a few times to do D/S time for little infractions I caught while back there. The C.O.'s didn't really fuck with me too tough but there was a few assholes. It's all good cause whatever they confiscated, came back triple. I was God back there... matter of fact, here they come with my mail right now.

"Room service... where my food at?"

"Funny Edwards... real funny! Here is your mail"

Shit... for real it's like they were room service, they brought my hot meal three times a day, brought me clean clothes, took the dirty ones, delivered my mail, and picked up the letters I was sending out...

Shit... What you call that? They cuffed me up and escort me to wherever I had to go, so they were my escorts too. There was even a button on my wall that made them bring their asses down there to me whenever I pressed it and if I didn't like their services, I could protest until their manager came to my door to see what was wrong. The manager was called the Lieutenant or "L.T." They usually want to play hardball but he knew I'm a tough cookie so the L.T. always wanted to compromise and negotiate. A few times, they geared up and ran down on me with the business. They didn't want that, I didn't want it either but I was not telling them that or letting it show.

You room service to me.

And I'm God

"Lights off mothafucker!!!!"

*****

A new warden came to U.S.P Lee County and with a new warden came changes. The SHU lieutenant was replaced by a real hardened hillbilly and he brought his goons with him. They came and tore the SHU up. They did a universal shakedown. We were only allowed to have what the handbook said, so all that accumulated property was confiscated. No longer were we allowed to have the Big Koss headphones in SHU. Believe me, those headphones sound like car speakers, if you put them in the window or in an empty box. Them people took them and any radio that wasn't clear / see through. I got hit up for a lot of shit but I came back and recovered quickly. I ordered a clear Sony radio and a pair of earplugs from commissary. It took two weeks for the SHU lieutenant to sign off on my order and when I got it, the earplugs were cheap and broke easily but the XM satellite radio was off the hook, so I needed that.

My celly was looking sad cause they took both his radio and Koss headphones. So he was without music. I thought to myself "I can't help you son, get your money up, call or write home… better yet, get on the door and find out why your ass is still back here!"

Oh… gotta go… Fifty Cent's "Many Men" just came on.

*****

Damn B, they put memorandums under the door of every cell in the SHU. We were only allowed one fifteen minute call every thirty days. No more using the phones regularly and the phone system was electronically operated so once you used your fifteen minutes you couldn't use the phone again until you revalidated in thirty days.

Where the fuck this warden come from? Bitch-ass Hillbilly

*****

That new phone shit put a dent in my love life. I used to call Zena at least twice a week, called Tammi three times a week and hit up my comrades. Zena was ready to come see me and everything. Last time I seen her was the last time we slept together… Damn…

*****

I was sharpening up on my lessons building back and forth with the Gods in the SHU and building with a lot of God's in the free cipher. Wize was still sending me the Five Percenter Newspaper also known as "The Power Paper", which is what we call it in prison. The papers were a few moons old by the time I got them but they were keeping me in tune with what was going on within the Nation of Gods and Earths worldwide. I got two waves to read, the January 04 issue titled "Improper Food" and the February 04 issue titled "Hidden Empyrean Ancestry"

I read every article back and forth and absorb as much as I possibly could. I noticed an article titled "Mental Wars" by Rita Book. It was like a song or poem. I read it and moved on to the next article.

*****

In the next Power Paper I read, there was another "Mental Wars" article. It was part two of the "Mental Wars" article from the previous issue. The article was about a sister who had K.O.S. but was ready to give it all up after experiencing so many losses and pains; I read along and FELT her pain. At the end of the article she gave her info: Oceasia D True Earth/Rita Book with an address in New Orleans, Louisiana.

In my mind I was like... "Hold up... wait... I think I know this Earth"I started wondering "is this the same Earth I was scribing and didn't answer the last scribe she flew me in 2000? Nah, it can't be her" so I moved on to read another article... born u truth (but) it kept popping back in my mind that it could be her so I got up, grabbed my pen and pad and scribed a short scribe.

Eternal PEACE and LOVE

I trust my thoughts find you in the ultimate sphere of Love, peace, and happiness. I remain true and living.

I just read an article in the Jan and Feb 04 issues of the Power Paper titled "Mental Wars" and saw your attributes. I'm not sure but I think we built before... this was back in Born Born/Wisdom Triple ciphers year... My attribute is Shakim Bio- Chemical Wise.

The Asiatic Calendar God?

Your attribute and your geographical being in New Orleans is what caught my mental. Are you the mother of civilization in N.O.?

97

Love, Hell, or Right

If I'm mistaken and we share no brief past, disregard this letter and thank you for the build in the paper.

One - One.

P.S. You still spit (rap)
Shakim Bio

*****

"I Keep Poverty in a chokehold, suffering under extreme pressure, I drink pain and oppression and piss struggle" –Shakim Bio

CHAPTER 12

After I mailed that scribe, the Earth Oceasia from N.O. hit me back in less than a week. I was kinda surprised as I took the staple out of the envelope, took out the letter and began reading...

Peace

It's funny how I am just walking through the door to the only piece of mail with my name on it. So before I go any further, let me make it known I'm thankful for your scribe.

Mathematics don't lie...You know something? I do remember you and hearing from you is perfect. I have been bottled up inside and really haven't been talking/building too much with people. Don't get me wrong...I get a lot of feedback from my articles, and I appreciate all of them. B.U.T I don't answer all of them. Sometimes I don't even open some of them. So do know that ur power and the strength of your essence from your scribe made my day...

Ok as far as my music (spitting) I'm still working hard, writing and doing shows. I go to the studio a lot and do lots of tracks. Maybe you can help me get some legal things taken care of. I don't have a manager B.U.T. all my material is copyrighted. I'm learning how to play guitar and soon drums. I have both I changed my named to Rita Book (Stage Name) for various reasons and I'm in the process of making book marks and book covers to be distributed into public schools.

So where have you been? Why you stop writing? What happened? I thought you went home and forgot about me. You checking for me is a relief to know you still care about a Queen. I can fuck with you on some serious levels of business and some mental pleasures as well. I was very motivated and inspired by you. We been 8ing back and forth and still don't know what each other looks like, so send a sista a reflection...

Be peace and we will build again. I'm preparing myself for the studio.

PEACE

Oceasia D. True Earth

a.k.a.

Rita Book

*****

No question I wrote back, inquiring about her and the fact that she had K.O.S. I put the scribe in a card, addressed the inside of the card "Breathing Diamond", put a reflection of myself inside and mailed it off to her. It took about 10 days or so for me to get another scribe from her... I responded and she wrote back then we went back and forth, back and forth. I got to know her through ink spots, here are some of her scribes...

*****

Peace 7

The card was sweet. I've never been called a "Breathin' Diamond" in those words before. I like that. The reflection was straight. C.U. aight !!! (Smile) I'm wisdom God and my physical is God/Knowledge understanding. I was attending Delgado community college majoring in both Performing Arts and journalism. I didn't finish though cause I got caught up in what we call "life". I'm single for a couple of reasons, for 1 thing, these fake dudes don't know what to do with my caliber of intelligence. You gotta have more than cars and clothes to impress me, plus right about now I need to be more focused on me and my career. Don't get me wrong, I dun fell victim to men before, you know how that is. I've had knowledge of self for equality rules so far... right now I'm rusty as far as quoting degrees b.u.t. I know the science. I know 120 you have 1 of self for a very long time. How did you end up in Federal Prison? Where are you from Brooklyn or Queens?

Of course I know Marlo – Big name in my hood – The calliope projects, 3rd Ward... How do you know him?

A lot of my life story is published in the Five Percenter Newspaper Dec 99, Jan 05 and Feb 04

I'm in and out of the studios working on some new material for my album and some stuff to go on mixtapes. I'm already on one mixtape. This D.J. from down here (The Best) Dynamite Dave Soul. We really jammed, we do shows together.

I have a song I'm featured on with a God name "Truth Universal" called "New Orleans Finest" that's on his album and we shot a video for it about a year or 2 ago that still comes on the local video stations.

I get a lotta mail from Gods and Earths. I truly feel supported and that keeps me going strong and working hard.

Ur scribe was powerful and stood out that I had to respond

U was the one that almost got away (smile)

I gotta go, I got an appointment wit a dude named Beck Beats so I'll get with u later

PEACE + LOVE

PS I'll send copy of my bio and a portfolio picture from my modeling book next time.

*****

We were going back and forth strong with the scribes. The Earth was smellin' a fella and I was definitely digging her style.

*****

It was after 6 p.m. and a C.O. was picking up the food trays. Mail call was in any minute. Another C.O. came on the tier and passed out the mail. Even though I was, I didn't want to appear to be on the door awaiting mail so I laid back on my style and played it off like I was on some other shit while my ears was on alert, listening to hear if the mail man hit the tier yet. My celly was on the door sweatin' because he needed to know if he got any mail. He was expecting a money order so he was on that door. "Fuck that!" he said. I put my headphones on and tuned into the rap station. Nas' "Made you look" came on... that was my shit, I zone out...

"King of the town-yeah I been that/ you know I click clack where you and your menz at/ Do the smurf. Do the wop, baseball bat/rooftop like we brining 88' back"

The C.O. stopped in front of our cell with a cart full with mail. He looked at the face and name tags on the door then opened the mail slot on the door.

"Edwards, you have mail"

The C.O. passed the mail to my celly, who passed it to me. I lifted my headphones up to look at the return addresses. There was a big manila envelope that had a little weight to it and some regular envelopes. The big one was from the Earth, a regular envelope was from my boo Tammi and I got one from my street comrades. I put all of the mail to the side and zoned back out on Nas.

"I'm a leader at last, it's a Don you're with / my mine spits and N___ lose consciousness"

On the real, my mind wasn't paying attention to Nas no more. I was wondering what was in the big envelope and what was in there that made it so heavy so I reached for it and peeped the "DO NOT BEND!!! Photos enclosed" on the envelope. This was the moment I'd been waiting on. All the back and forth scribing with me baring my soul to shorty cause I was really, really feeling shorty and I didn't even know what she looked like. She had me playing the door for mail, had me scribing her back a.s.a.p., she was asking me a lot of questions too and I was answering them too... Shiiiiit. She better look like something. As I opened the manila envelope, I saw like eight or nine photos on three colored print out photo sheets. I studied each one. "Damn, shorty is tatted the fuck up crazily", I thought to myself. I was expecting to see photos of her all garbed up in Earth attire, three fourths of cloth. WOW... she looked like shorty from the movie "Baby Boy" but with dreads. She had the big bingo locks too, long joints. I thought "Damn, what's shorty name from Baby Boy?" I dug deep in my thoughts, trying to figure what that fine shorty from the movies name was.

"Yo Mark"

"What's up Sha?"

"Check out this shorty who flew me these flicks" I said as I passed a photo sheet over to my celly.

"OH Shit, she look just like that chick Taraji P. Henson but with dreads, damn she favors her".

"Yeah that's her name"

"Who?"

"Shorty from Baby Boy"

"Yo... who is this?"

"That's my Earth Oceasia... yo give me that sheet back"

I examined the photos carefully, staring at Oceasia's features. There was one pic that was real mean, she was wearing tight jeans with a cuff and what looked like a tight wife beater. She was sitting on a Yamaha R1 red, white and black, maybe blue. You could see the tats on her shoulders, she had a fisherman's hat pulled down over her eyes, lookin' like she was about to peel off on the bike with her pouting lips. That shit looked so mean; I was really feeling it so I showed it to my celly.

"Damn Sha, she is killin' it in this joint, she rides bikes?

"Stop sweating my piece B" I said with a smile, I couldn't help it.

*****

CHAPTER 13

Peace 7

Chocolate covered strawberries? Taste really Good!! (Smile)

Hey! Why you didn't tell me you were running for V.P. of the country?

You got my vote.

Your "Beautiful Breathing Diamond" wants you to know that I be thinking about you too. You got hit with a lot of time – True but the way you talk with levels of high energy charisma and your positive way of thinking really is an inspiration to me. In many ways, it's helpful to me in my life situations and teaches me to look at the bright side of things no matter how bad or ruff shit gets. When I read ur letters, it sounds like your always smiling and in a good mood, that's peace! I love you for that, you a strong dude.

I also read about your case – wow!! You can call me, my cell number is 504-762-XXXX. You can't call me by my government name. Ok I guess I'll jump out the window and tell you B.U.T usually never discuss that it's Ta-me-ki-a. 4 syllables not 3.

No one calls me that. Not even my ole Earth.

I'm thinking about cutting my hair (why) because I hate to wash it, it's too much work 2 wash (what you think)

Besides my model photos and bio (make sure you give me feedback) I enclosed a special lil' gift that I hope you like as much as I do. I had so much fun making it and playing with it. I wanted to keep it for myself so I almost didn't send it to you. Instead I made one for myself (UR lucky)

OH, I got a name for you. Just "minez"

I just made it up now. Do you like it? Or is it corny?

How did I come with this name? Well for 1 it's the place where beautiful diamonds can be found and 2 your mine (Get it?) and these gives the 3 the understanding from knowledge and wisdom (Cipher complete)

We'll build later. Remain just and true.

Love is Love

Oceasia D True Earth

*****

The next day, at the same time as the day before, another manila envelope came from my N.O Earth. There were four photo sheets inside and one said "Ms. Book got looks" It was different photos of her dressed up in dresses, bathing suits, photos of her on stage at her shows, one pic of her on her drum set, there was one of her and her cousins titled "Revolutionary but Gangsta", there were photos of her and Fred Hampton Jr., some modeling shots. Enclosed with the photos was her short bio and flyers of a show she did that said "KUMMA Productions – Till we Free"

They had the revolutionary rap group "Dead Prez" on the cover.

Contemporary Arts Center 900 Camp St   DJ Dynamite Dave Soul, Blackout Poets, Rita Book, Truth Universal, Staher the Femcee. Free Parking!

On the other side was a blown up article from the New Orleans newspaper "The Times Picayune". It was the Sunday Feb 29th 2004 Page E5 a newspaper clipping from the show showing hip hoppers EF Cuttin', Rita Book and Truth Universal, "Dead Prez" didn't show up. Shorty was about her business and serious about that rap shit. As I looked at another thing that was between the photo sheets I said ... "Oh Shit Shorty's ill". I peeped that she blew up a photo I sent her of me with my arms out, she cut me out the photo once she blew up and took a photo of her sleeping on a couch, she put my arms through the photo to look like I was holding her while she was sleep. She took two photos and made one, very, very creative. On the photo it said:

Wish no more, Concrete and steel got nothing on me. Now we will always be together. You get to watch me sleep, sleep with me, hug and kiss all the time.

Wow... I really dug Shorty's style.

*****

I picked up my pen and pad and wrote 2 poems dedicated to her, I also had time so I went to the law library, typed the poems and put them in the mail that night... peep these words:

"Some things I do and say are beyond comprehension to limited minds"

Peep the Uniqueness

Supreme Mathematics

With Godspeed thoughts I travel through penitentiary walls / you my Beautiful Breathing Diamond, who cried joy as I penetrate your sugar walls/ it is not all sexual, Nah ma, we have a bigger cause.

Me loving you is not the issue/ we just met and I already miss you/ can't stop dreaming about how I'm going to kiss you/ and all the ill positions that I'ma twist you. So caught up as your body mental and physical reflects/ is it really mind detects? / or is "mine" so complex?/ is your brain cells sparked yet?/ cause I want to bomb your heart next.

You keep the God amused/ I want to be all over your body like those tattoos. I'm knowledging your wizardly wisdom and understanding, your culture/ and how can I utilize my powers to rope ya.

Did you catch that? Mathematical Metaphors / dealing with supreme equality and this God wanna be "yourz".

Come build and destroy, lets born this completed cipher/ my love is eternal, and I'm sentenced to you to be a "Lifer"

108

When you recover, holla back!!

＊＊＊＊＊

I used the Supreme Mathematics in that poem to her, that's why I titled it Supreme Mathematics. I used knowledge all the way to cipher. She was so open, she told me her first government name so I did one titled "Tamekia" and made love with the words   peep it.

Tamekia (Ta-Me-Ki-a) :

1: <u>To be completely cherished appreciated and loved</u>

2.) <u>Precious gem</u>

What can I do to bring that beautiful magnetic smile to your face? What can I say to grasp your mentals, to make you put down my letter and fall in deep aspects...? Mentally physically, emotionally, spiritually, mathematically, lyrically, etc. etc... What must I do?

Show me... Teach Me... Step by step... Walk me... undress your soul... Bare it <u>ALL</u> to me...

There are 12 trillion, 478 Billion, 118 million, 400 thousand inches of our planet Earth.

I will carry you... Hold You... Caress you...

<u>Love You</u>

<u>Never   Let   You   Go</u>

＊＊＊＊＊

There were lots of letters between me and Oceasia that I keep in a "treasure box". We were back and forth with the scribes regularly. I was always looking forward to hearing from her, reading her thoughts and I knew she was looking forward to hearing from me too. I had it down to a science, knowing if I flew her scribes Sunday night she would have it by Wednesday and if I sent a scribe by Thursday night, she would have it by Monday so like clockwork, she was waiting for Mondays and Wednesdays.

Me having nothing but time on my hands and on my side, I could bless Oceasia with six, seven, eight and sometimes ten page letters. What was ill was that she was returning the pleasure. We were getting more and more personal and with every scribe, she was telling me about her hard work ethics. She was working as a manager at a boutique in the Oakwood Mall on the west bank. The boutique sold African art, oils, incense and T-Shirts. She also had a second job at the Mushroom Record Shop on Broad Street, where they sold rare music and albums by underrated artist and local New Orleans musicians.

Not only did Oceasia juggle two part time jobs, she was going extra hard when it came to writing songs, doing tracks, being featured on mix tapes and doing songs with others. She was doing little shows here and there but she didn't have a manager and needed to fully understand how to receive her royalties. She didn't own her publishing or know how to go about getting it. She was constantly in the studio. In every scribe she went in deep...

*****

Peace 7

First of all the vice president thing was a joke. The democratic candidate for VP name is John Edwards (get it?)

I'm waiting on you to call me!!!

I'm glad you enjoyed the flicks. You'll have more coming your way in a minute. The one of me on the bike I was frontin'...I can't ride.

I love tattoos. I have 17 of them all over my body. I also have the universal flag tatted on me right above my left wrist.

What part of Florida does your ole Earth rest? You can send me a visiting form… like right now.

I was making moves to get into my personal property thru the SHU officers to get photos out of my album to send to the Earth (Oceasia).

*****

I am the mother of civilization down here. I am the first born Earth from New Orleans. I got knowledge from Philly. Well, I got my lessons from there, my history to my strive is in the Dec 99 article. The first real Gods hugging me B.U.T I thought you was…what you think I made that picture of us for? I have your flicks all over my studio but I like keep them close for certain reasons. Why do I have your middle name "Austin" on the hush? What's wrong wit that? I like that name cause Austin powers, that's how I see it so that's peace.

We were building on her music…

"I don't have publishing right now cause one time I sent some stuff to BMI from a letter I got through the library of Congress and they told me I needed to have a publishing company or something and I didn't know what to do about that. However, I do have © for my material. I have recorded "the Birth" song already. I just needed to get "Flying Kites" recorded…

In lessons…

"They used to have rallies down here. I don't know if they still do cause the Gods down here is fake to me, they be one some other shit and I don't agree wit that b.s. cause I didn't get knowledge from down here like there was new Earths, so they can't come in my cipher with that weak nonsense"

And on me of course…

111

Boy, I get hot every time you start talking about your workout. I wonder why cause that kind of stuff usually don't affect me. I guess it's just you and the fact that I'm feeling you. Literally, I would love to just be there to watch you work out then work me out afterwards. I am waiting on some photos of you and I got fresh batteries for that!! (Smile).

* * * * *

Me and the Earth built about everything from our different environments, our childhoods to our culture. What had me so absorbed in her thoughts was her love for the hip hop culture. At one point in my life, I thought no one loved hip hop more than me, especially the rhyming element of it and Shorty could spit. She sent me so many of her songs, just sharing them with me and asking my input and opinions.

I told her about the books I read from "Everything you need to know about the music industry" to this "This business of Artist Management", told her my ideas, even told her about how I was penning my "Street Hop" novel. I was also telling her about my past associations with certain music industry peoples. Oceasia had a real love for rhyming, she did her own CD cover and was selling a 5 song cd for five dollars a pop. She wanted to do more shows. She had fifteen new songs recorded, not counting her old cd or the unrecorded stash she had ready for the booth. She really bragged about her skills too.

"Everybody who hears my music says "I'm ready". Everybody who sees me perform says "I holds it down". I strongly agree, the look is there, the skills are sharp, - The presence is felt, the style is original. The name is Rita Book (sick!). The chick is raw – she is "like that". I have one weakness… Free stylin', I'm not perfect with that, but I express myself better when I put time into searching for words that best describes my thoughts. I'm happy wit my formula of creativity. I'm an expressionist. "

I did the knowledge on Oceasia's own words and stored them in my mental. I could use that when doing her "Bio". She had tracks she spitted with "the Brave Hearts", she spitted with "C-Murder" and I was

112

feeling her thoughts musically. I was striving to find a way to make shit happen for her. I respected her for her and I respected her grind. She repped herself hard and was proud to do so. She was from the Calliope Projects in the third ward of the city of New Orleans; home of Master P and his brothers, down the street and a few blocks down from Baby and them from Cash Money. New Orleans... the worst city in the U.S., worst in everything, poverty, education / school system, the most rats, very bad drug and HIV/AIDS epidemic, most corruption in politics and police. Shit was twisted out there but that is where I found my Beautiful Breathing Diamond, my star in the "Dirty – Dirty". I was willing to wash her off and give her polish even if it had to come from my own spit.

*****

I don't know exactly when I exposed to the Earth that my parents and whole family on both sides were full blooded Jamaicans but I was a New Yorker, an Americanized Yankee, even though I didn't like being identified as such. At the same time, I didn't like being called a "Jamaican". Growing up in the 70's and early 80's, being teased and taunted by the American kids made me a violent Jamaican youth, who was very Yankee-fied.

The Earth went berserk when she learned that I was "Jamerican". She told me how she got a song done in Patois-style and she sent me the lyrics. It was ill how no matter what, she felt so comfortable with me and wanted to share her thoughts, feeling and music with me.

*****

YUSH!!

DREADLOCK RUDEGAL,

De time has cum fuh eye n eye mek yu know fuh sure dot mi ah rude bwoy, dat keep everiting, <u>crisp</u>! Mi tink yu fi redi done know dat, so mi don't to chat fuh mek yu know dis. B.U.T. still in all, sum tink cuz eye n eye is dem sugah dat mi goal focused to be womanizer & tingz pin dat nature, which iz <u>not so</u>!!! Eye n eye ting iz nuh to mek yu skin out yu panti fuh eye n eye. Mi pon sum next ting. Mi won to luv you <u>totally</u> and <u>completely</u>. How yu eva hav man to luv yu <u>totally</u>? And yu luv him back <u>totally</u>? Nun hold bar type ting Luv dis de highest elevator of overstanding. Luv know right nor nuh wrong, fuh it obey itz law of its own. Beauty – dem all mathematics. Beauty hides faults fuh people dem so busy luking at wrapping of di package dat dem fail to see whatz inside or not inside – <u>SEEN</u>?!! Eye in Eye luv is <u>wicked</u>, mi staartress, mi sistren mi will Fuhever big yu up everitime – seen!!! <u>Yu Mi Beautiful Breathin' Diamond</u>.

Love and Respect

"YOURZ"

✳✳✳✳✳

Peace 7

How are you feeling today?

You want to know more about my mom and dad…

Oceasia gave me the history of her closeness with her ole earth and non-existent relationship with her ole dad, they just know each other. She told me about her brother, who died while her mom was pregnant with her and about her brother, who was murdered in Feb 2000. She was close to him and his death took a lot away from her. She shared everything with me, told me all about him. His name was Tyree and she spoke very highly of him. He was one year older than she was and she missed him very much. She is now her mom's only living child…

114

I loved to the two poems you sent me, they were real precious and on some higher heights – thanks

And don't worry I won't call you "Whoadie" when you call.. can't wait for that call... I don't have a manager. I need one. I have been doing shows, I don't even get paid for some of them...

As for the dreads, I don't know, I'm still thinking about cutting them. I'm ready for a change. I've been wearing them for equality miles, to some that's not a long time, however if I do cut 'em I'm sure u'll like me without locks just as much, if not u'll have to get used to it. I can't braid my dread cause they are too fat, I got bongo locks, it's hard for me to wear all them different kinds of styles, they're too thick for that. I'm glad you enjoyed "our" picture. The pictures you sent me where satisfying. I really like them especially the "can I live" joint and the one wit you on the amp (I can't live without my radio either) and I finally got to see your teeth in one of the pics cause I was gonna ask you when you gon' send me on wit you smiling or showing your teeth, that's peace you must've read my mind. I got the three b-day cards. They were cute – Thanks

I just recently finished working on a piece for the august issue of the Five Percenter Newspaper. Make sure you cop that!!

I'm your "Beautiful Breathing Diamond" and your "just mine" that's what's up. Get at me! Hugs and Kisses

P.s. I would like to see your kids. Do you have any reflects of them?

*****

My phone day was coming up and I couldn't wait to call and speak with Oceasia. I even wrote a short poem to build up the hype of our special event.

"I wonder what you sound like...The things that you will say... what you will be like... your laugh...ur accent... will you like the things I talk about? Will you enjoy the God behind this pen, who religiously sprays ink to his

Beautiful Breathing Diamond? The God who you see in those reflects... Will I say the right things? Say the right words... for you to say... Please call me again... we will find out when we speak..."

*****

Flying Kites

-written and performed by Rita Book

Chorus[I'm flying kites 2 my pen pals – who's locked up in Belly sending me mail and that's why I'm flying kites 2 my pen pals who's locked up in the Belly – sendin' me mail cause they got something 2 tell me]

Verse 1

Thru ink spots communicate

Keep 'em up 2 date 2 what's going on this side of the gate

We keep each other informed, we keep our pages so warm

We keep each other strong, until the day they come home

We keep on keepin' it real

I know how it is – to deal with being alone and no one knows how u feel

Cause it aint easy for me – although I am free

I still need what I want and I still want what I need

He told me he dun came close 2 losing control

Instead he just go grab a stamp and envelope

Is what he wrote in his notes, he wanted 2 know

Would I hold him down – I said I'll hold u 4 sho (cause ur... my pen pal)

Chorus

Verse 2

We can mend as friends, even if ur in the pen

Doing a serious bid, longer than five to ten

I won't turn my back on u, I'm not like that

I'm too true and one day I just might need you

I might be coming to visit or write and say I miss u

Or how about a kiss sent on the back of the picture

Whatever the case/u'll have a smile on your face

And these thousand words/I know u'll never erase

23 hours of solitary confinement, an hour a day it really aint enough time to do the assignment so just deal wit refinement and break out the chains they think they're keepin' ur mind in

Don't let down ur guard/Doin' that labor that's hard

Whenever u want hit me wit a collect call

If it'll make you feel better/cause we're in this here together

The sky is the limit we're flyin' kites like they're feathers (me and my pen pals)

Chorus

Verse 3

We only live once, but do u understand

That life sometimes hands us a 2nd chance

I wanted to say, thanks for the birthday card

I see u been lifting weights by the muscles in ur arms

Ur lookin' good there, but it aint fair

I keep askin' myself, why u had 2 be in jail

How is your family doing? Is everybody ok

Like me I know they can't wait/ can't wait 'til ur release date

And all ur boys in the hood/they said u know it's all good

Cause they'll continue 2 hold down like u know they would

U stay on my mind I write u like I write rhymes

Including – truly yours each line, then I sign it to (my pen pal)

Chorus

Dear Pal

I hope this letter finds u in the best health/as for me well I'm taking care of myself. I can't complain I received the mail you sent me just the other day but I been in the studio so I couldn't write back sooner. Oh and by the way Happy Late Birthday. I didn't forget I just been doin' a lot of shit **(Fade Out)**

*****

Shakim

Peace 7

Yes indeed! U got the right voice, just right

I'm send u a rundown of my tats. I'll try to take a photo shot of each one with the meaning and description.

Am I emotional? – sometimes

I'm glad u liked "Flyin' Kites" cause parts of the song was inspired by U. I'm glad we finally spoke to each other, believe it or not, I'm still open –

cause I can still hear u – especially now when I read ur kites…it's like ur talking to me instead of me reading off paper.

I don't drink or smoke no more and I stopped eating red meat and chicken in 1997. I want seeds. I'm wisdom build and don't have one seed yet. I was pregnant once when I was 19yrs old but I had an abortion. I will never do that again for no one. After I terminated my lil' one, I haven't been pregnant again since and that was in 1995. I really want kids. Why u have to be just kidding about your nice big lips? U better kiss my tulips cause both of these flowers need watering (smile) Am I feeling you? YES!! What kind of question is that? Picture my big juicy lips on u.

Kiss me.

*****

CHAPTER 14

Believe me when I tell you, I like to keep shit real and funky at all times and for some reason I felt I had to tell Oceasia about Tammi. I kept it thorough and told her how shorty was there when a lot of females bounced. Told her that we were crazy tight and I addressed her as "my Boo". Why did I do that, is what you're probably askin' right now, right?

I don't know but all hell broke loose when Oceasia absorbed that scribe!

*****

Ur Beautiful Breathing Diamond? – Please!

What's up "friend"

How could u say u trust I enjoy readying ur scribes and it must be meant 4 us to connect like this "then turn around and say "Who knows? By next month I may be tired of u –"

Well if she's ur boo – who the fuck am I? That scribe was an emotional roller coaster by Vivian Green. That made me mad, made me laugh, smile and everything in between except cry. So I had to dig in my crates and pull out this poem I wrote in 2003. "He makes me" it's a perfect response to this drama. However above all that – I have to tell you that we really think a like because like a day or two before I received ur kite I wrote kite to you. B.U.T I hadn't sent it out yet and when I got the kite from u I saw that we were kind of saying the same exact thing and thinking about the same songs and everything (only thing is I'm referring to "my boo" as U). Anyway I was going to send u a very sexy picture of me – but I changed my mind. It's a lot I want to add on to about that kite u sent but I rather not right now. Maybe a few days from now I will. That is after you get over "U and ur boo" shit. ¬NO I wasn't feeling that at all. She's ur boo and I'm just a friend with a so called special name – that's that BULLSHIT though I am glad you opened up and told me those things BUT shit didn't sound right and exact. Don't call me your beautiful breathing diamond anymore and u better be glad u didn't call me cause u wouldn't have like what I would've said to u. Trust Me. But who knows? After I sleep on it tonight, tomorrow I may have a better understanding. Once I read it again for the 2nd and 3rd time.

I still got mad love for you. My feeling don't change overnight like my emotions. U might be a little too much of di dem gal dem sugah for me to handle all that sweet talk. Is it pure sweetness or is it sweet and low artificial sweetness? Am I ur beautiful breathing diamond only when ur talking to me or just a friend when ur talking to others and mention me?

Oceasia was seriously jealous when I told her about Tammi; she enclosed the poem, peep it:

HE MAKES ME   By: Rita Book

He makes my day cause he makes me smile

He makes me dance like I didn't know I knew how

I mean he makes me move – he makes me feel so - OOOH!

He makes me laugh- he makes me relax like a warm bubble bath

Over all makes me feel like a natural woman

So I'll make him breakfast in bed after I make him my husband

Then we can make babies, one after another

Cause we'll be making crazy long lasting good lovin'

He makes me want to get in shape, get my tummy flat

But he makes me sure I know in more ways than one

He aint worried about all that

He makes me feel lifted like a cloud in the distance

He makes me cry purple rain drops when he calls me his princess

121

He makes me what I am and

He makes me do things like I'm under his command

But I'm not

I'm just caught up in the man that's inside a confused spot

GOT DAMN HE'S POWERFUL

Look at all he can make me do

Without even forcing me to

But that aint it

He usually makes me feel good, but right now...

He makes me...   SICK

*****

I was laughin' out loud... so loud my celly stopped what he was doing and looked at me.

"Sha... what's up over there?"

"Nothin' B, I'm just bugging out on this scribe I got"

"Oh...ok then, I thought you were losing your mind"

I ignored him and continued reading page 4...

Shakim,

This is what I wrote b4 I read ur kite

Too bad u won't get the picture that was gonna go wit it

U being dem gal dem sugah is an understatement

Ur the brown sugar, the honey, the high fructose corn syrup, the maple syrup…

Ur "Just" Pure Sweetness (For real)

My mouth waters to taste you

The only thing I would rather more than u

Just calling me back – is to not hang up in the first place. I can talk/ listen to you all day/night long. U do things to me, u get me HOT… I want to make love to you in (slow motion). I want to feel you. Your voice caresses me like a gentle touch on any part of my body cause it all gets weak for certain hands. That's right If u got my mind. U got my P_SSY thumpin'.

Ur work out description sounds like a good fuck.

Sweat drippin', ooh and aahs, talking dirty, work me daddy. Dick me down good cause I like it ruff especially when I'm ruffed up right .

The best thing about a good fuck is it don't have to be long cause time is not a factor as long as the banging is on point. (Therefore it all adds up). I already love you. I've already seen and heard you, now I need 2 smell, touch and taste u. I'm <u>sensing</u> that I found the tenth jewel in "Just mine" does this mean I'm rich?

✳✳✳✳✳

That shit was so powerful, I sat back, closed my eyes and zoned out for a good ten minutes. I picked the letter up and read it again, got my writing tools and responded.

✳✳✳✳✳

<u>MY OATH</u>

<u>NOTE: My heart is looking straight into your heart as my oath is being quoted</u>.

123

I promise 2 never do anything to hurt you, never try to take advantage of, violate, disrespect, use or misuse you.

Oh, I'm "just running game?" or... you "heard all that shit b4" is what you're thinking? What is the knowledge - knowledge degree in the 1-14? Take heed cause I take that <u>seriously</u>.

I want 2 B what causes your rain, hail, snow and earth quakes .

Know <u>me</u>   understand <u>me</u>   Believe in <u>me</u>

Am I a mystery God?

The answer is, emphatically, mathematically, scientifically HELL <u>NO</u>. Let's take this potential energy and turn it into kinetic energy, which is made thru force and motion. <u>Let's manifest that.</u>

Everything is mental first, the seed of thought is planted, watered and given light... then it grows. B.U.T. it must be cultivated or else it won't produce properly. Let's not be left in darkness. The God is here for you. WORD LIFE

I put that on our unborn seeds

"Super friends" to the end...

...Lovers in between.

4ever loyal is our beginning

I'm "<u>Yourz</u>"

＊＊＊＊＊

Hey U

What's happening?

I can't stay mad wit you even if I wanted to but your ass is on probation right now.

I got two kites from you today

I'm going to do a show in Cali at the end of the moon.

I'm gonna stay out there for almost 2 wks. Take this address, it's my Auntie's.

I'm doing "Rhyme Night" at a club called "1650"

You better not act up while I'm gone and I'm looking forward to ur scribes while I'm out there.

Peace & Love

Oceasia D. True

UR EARTH

*****

Soon after that scribe, I received another letter from Oceasia but from a California address. I opened it and it was a one page front and back, I began reading …

Dear John,

I'm not gone – only "missing U" way too much, still wishing we were kissing as I listen to u build.

Watching as our foundation starts to appear

I feel a sensation cause ur medication heals me in ways

Sweeter than a sugar cane glazed with honey

Your eyes got flame that numbs me

Ur scent is my sage it smells so lovely

My body's calling for ONLY YOU to touch me

When I listen to ur voice, it's like reading a page

Of my favorite book made, the way ur words display

My attention is urs – so just hold me

I got sight now – my visions used to be blurry

When u touch me – u melt me

When u told me u felt me – u don't know how much u helped me

Start living again – turned my ugly frown into a pretty grin

And all my mental wars became wins

The heart I once lost now beats with in ur skin

Ur definitely the definition of a gentleman

My Ginseng and my cup of tea, peppermint

My raisin and my spice, my stick of cinnamon

My whispers when them drops of rain drizzle in

My winters and my springs, my summers fall again

My sentences of ignorance or innocence

Your mines – yes u are my every sense

U are my very strength – u are

U are by far my life ...I'm yours ... ur wife

So just alike ... therefore I write ...Dear John

Dear John, I hope U understand and see clear

I'm the lines in the palm of your hand – I'm right there

Closer than you think – I'm so near

Even though u blink – I won't ever disappear

And every time u drink – I got ur cup

Each time u pray we'll be together no matter what

I'ma hold ur head for u I'ma make your bed comfortable

Hold ur pen – every time u think of something new to write

Wash ur body down just right ... hold ur dick for u

In the middle of the night ... I'm a daily necessity

Anything u do is gonna involve me ... I'll never leave

I can't if I wanted to – if u lose ur voice

I'll speak languages for you - silent sounds of signs

Like fingerprints we bond ... closer than close

I'll be the diamond u find... held that toast ... every time

U committed a crime – physically approach everything expect ur mind

I strive to be urz and u be mine – everyday u wake alive

I wipe the crust out ur eyez ... I'm honest I'll ride til the day that u die

If u ever decide to forget – rewind this ... content and reply to

            I send kite   DEAR JOHN

9.12.21

*****

In case you're wondering why that poem was called "Dear John", John is my first government name but anyway, I seen she wrote the numbers 9.12.21 and automatically deciphered that immediately. 9 is the "I" in the alphabet. "12" is "L" which represents "Love" and 21 is the letter "U". So she said "I love you" in our language. You just had to be swift to catch it. Wow!!! The Earth is jealous and she loves me.

*****

I penned Oceasia back with a joint called "The Bridge" and sent it to her Aunt's crib in California.

The Bridge

I want you to teach me how to format a song, how to write it, compose it, space the bars and read the notes.

That way we can write songs together, sing the song together.

Ladies first

So do your part

Then I'll do mine

Then we can meet at the bridge of the song. Where we will be together, in tune, in perfect harmony.

There, I want you to teach me how to please u. So I know how to make you hit all those high notes. Show me what makes u cry and moan, what makes u shiver, so we could do it right there, at the bridge, on the bridge, all over the bridge...   Deep in our song.

Grab hold of me as I go <u>deeper</u>, we are dripping sweat from our love making right there on <u>the bridge</u>. Teach me, show me how to please you.

Where 2 touch, where 2 kiss, where 2 bite, where 2...!

So every time we do <u>our song</u>, I will know what to do once we meet at <u>the bridge</u>.

Once we get to that <u>bridge</u>, I want us to stay there. <u>Right there on that bridge</u>. Have u ever heard a song that gets stuck at <u>it's bridge</u>?

<u>That's the kind of song we're going to make</u>

I'm waiting on u to teach me...   show me

So I can practice to master that <u>bridge</u>.

*****

"MS. U" By Rita Book

I miss you so much, those lips, body, kiss and warm touch,

That scent, them days that we fussed, that way we used 2 finally make up.

After actin' like we aint give a fuck, how we played in the bed as we laughed and laid, the way u used to hold me and my legs, talking 'bout what we did on the first date. Da tears dat u gently wiped from my face, telling me to stop crying, ur sorry, u made a mistake.

How you made me breakfast and dinner, made me feel just like a winner when u would say u love me, the things u taught me, showed me support. Lifted my voice wit a effortless force, gave me ur heart, told me swallow the key and everything u had was also for me. Dr. feel good drugged me up w/real love, knew what my thoughts was and when I needed hugs when I

129

needed more attention than a baby does, always took time 2 listen, put up wit my wayz, drugz I was bitchin', every day, stunning w/every song ever sung to me, all the poems u wrote wit passion, in every shape, form and fashion, imagined every time I open my eyes 2 a surprise, larger than a life size story with 2 sides... I am never bored to death wit u, my heart, rather rest wit u till death do us part, anytime u sneeze or cough I'll be right here to say bless you or pat ur back soft, at ur rescue, whenever of course I'm gon' test u, not doubtin' u bein' true to me. Got u figured out so I'm letting off steam, cultivating, boss queen, they very dark dreams beamed overwhelmed on our face and still smiling, still together, still tell him I love him. Feel blessed, I'm his woman. He knows that I'm comin', see him up in prison, to kiss him and hug him. Tell my husband... I miss him

Enclosed was a form from the USP Lee County mail room saying they were rejecting a photo that was included with the correspondence and had to return it to the sender. "Specific material returned: one nude photo"

So Oceasia tried to send that photo to me after all...

*****

A few weeks went by and I hadn't heard from Oceasia nor could I catch her on the phone when my phone day came back up. I came up with an idea to help shop her demo; I was going to re-do her bio and all. I wrote to her and sent the scribe to her N.O. address so the scribe would be waiting for her as soon as she got home.

*****

Peace Love

I know it's been a while B.U.T...

Oceaisa told me about her journey to California and how her Aunt got an old flyer and had misinformed her about the show she thought she was supposed to perform at. The flyer was a year old so being that she

130

was already out there in Cali, she and her aunt went to Vegas and the photos were on the way...

When can I visit u and where? I miss you so much, u stay on my mind. Know that I'm right here. Shit is a lil' crazy on my end too B.U.T I'm still crazy in love wit u. I've been working on a couple of new songs and stuff. I have a cd for u and whoever u say u want to hear it the only thing is, I have some other joints that I wish was on the one I already have, which is a lil' fucked up. I would want to send somebody something a lil more crisp than that so I'm holding out 'til I finish this next demo – almost ready.

So how did u like the "Dear John" letter? That's a song u know – just for you.

Are the photos alright? I finally sent u the one I was holding back but u couldn't get that one anyway.

I need to hear ur voice, it makes me feel good –for real. It's not my voicemail anymore because after a while it automatically erases off. So give me my medicine (smiley face) I'm overdue so I need an over dose. What's up with "the bridge"? When are u ready to start working on that? Don't stay away so long baby! I don't like that – wide gap prolong let's keep it tight & consistent.

9. 12. 21

Mrs. Edwards

*****

I peeped how she was using my last government name so when I scribed her, that's how I addressed the envelope Mrs. Oceasia Edwards.

*****

Peace My Love

Guess what? My grand Ole Earth calls me Mrs. Edwards now. She peeped that on the mail and started callin' me that. Aint that cute!

U said u hear more from me when I'm mad, that's not true but when I'm mad I go on & on & on basicly tryin' to fix shit cause I don't want us beefin'. I want to make sure u know I aint going nowhere and that I'm not tryin' to run u away from me – cause I don't want u goin' NO WHERE. Home is right here – U are minez! I fuss & fight for my shit – what!

Sometimes when I'm mad at U, I get even madder that we can't fuck and make up. So me writing u a 7 to 10 pager is like me getting my nut off (I'm playing wit my power u now lol)

Song

Far away from here, far away from here, Far away from here lets jump in a taxi cab, pack a bag & get away fast – that's a married couple – I think their name is the Kindred Family or something like that – I hear their album is real nice – I wanted to get that cd too cause I heard like 2 songs and they were hot. When are you calling me? I keep checkin' to see if my ringer is on. I went and got a brand new phone and everything – Handle ur Biz

Visitation

Just say when

I'm ready! I'm trying to save up some money. U might have to meet me half way but I'm ready to roll out a.s.a.p.

I'll get back wit u, right now I'm trying to play catch up. I'm almost 31 scribes strong. I can't begin to tell u how much I love u. I rather show u.

Ur Beautiful Breathing Diamond

Mrs. Edwards

P.s. let them bitches know ur married now. It's official.

132

*****

We had been flowing for several moons and I was calling her, kicking it and even listening to some of her music. We were open off of each other, sometimes she would write a one pager saying "I Love you" that's it or maybe a poem or a free style rap. Think I'm bullshittin'? Check out a piece she shot me with...

*****

Peace my Love, the thug I wanna hold and hug...

Start each day I wake up wit thoughts of u to think of

Talk through lines and birth words from mind to mind, lost in time I searched to find, or be found first, every sound I whisper he's around to listen. I'm his conscience sister we be smiling while we kissin' between the miles of distance. I'm seeing now the difference. I'm free of doubts, I scream & shout, be dreaming bout commitment behind the bars he sittin', marry God in prison staring at stars. I'm wishin', he was home, I got a vision. In the physical form where he belong, beside me livin', he's keepin' the vibe between us strong. I'm drawin' up in him. So I sleep in his arms, his heat it warms me up like linen very sweet with charm, that keeps me flowin', blowin', blushin', grinin' & he speaks to me calm. Get freaky for him, suckin' his skin. Daddy treat me the bomb, he read me poems, I'm nuts over him. Every street he be on, the beef is on, don't fuck wit Shakim. Heavy deep in a song, my heart beats on, so much love for him, set me free in the dome and brought peace on, sho' nuff plugged me in

Love U

Mrs. J "5" Edwards

*****

Peace Shakim

Boy,

First of all, I want to tell you I love you because I didn't get to tell you before we hung up. I went and got Jesse Powell "You" song – BEAUTIFUL

I'm sending u these 2 songs. This song is one of my favorite love songs of all time by one of my favorite singers and now I finally have someone I can actually sing it with and we both mean every word.

"Nothing like this" by Rochelle Ferrell/F/Will Downing

"The best thing yet" by Anita Baker

9.12.21 Oceasia Edwards

*****

I sat down and read the lyrics to both songs and I can't lie, I felt exactly what she felt.

"To all my people I war for, blow the four-four for you know I gets... (Down)

even if we trapped standing back to back... I'll (hold... you... down)

No matter if you wrong or right you still right, for you I lay a man (down)\

I don't care if it's the president, I cock my heat and ...

(Hold...   You...   Down)"

Illa Ghee's verse from Alchemist's "1st Infantry" ALBUM

Song title "Hold you down by Alchemists featuring I'll Ghee Nina sky and Prodigy.

CHAPTER 15

"Hold You Down" is an ill song. I really feel and can relate to that and would you believe that Alchemist is a white boy? Son is nice on the music production as far as beats. He is down with the Infamous Mobb Deep and I like their music as well. Alchemist fit right in with Mobb Deep and them cause he had that grimy murder music sound. Him and Havoc was on the same page when it came to beats. The Nina Sky sisters got off on the hook too "even when shit gets hard, I'm gonna make sure that I'm around to hold you (down) will never leave your side until the day I die I'm gonna (Hold...you...down). Recognize that this game could be hard long as you roll with me we are (down). Here by your side always to (hold me down baby) (hold....you....down)

My N.O. shorty, who was also my Earth, was now singing this hook to me regularly and pledged to always... hold... me... down. We were scribing each other crazily, trading poems... and vibin' on the phone. My once a month call went to her now and in return, she made all my other necessary calls to my street team, comrades and mom... Oceasia was my secretary.

Oceasia was sending me the lyrics to a lot of the songs she was recording in the studio and me, with my pollyin' and networking moves, came up with some powerful ideas and set them in motion. One of my co-defendants, who was also one of my best friends, was in the State of Ohio Penal System. He was known as "Al Monday" and he had connections with various music execs. Monday was prepping up acts in prison and sending them to music executives to get on. Monday was also making beats in prison and started his own label titled "Black House Entertainment". He put out a compilation album comprised for the most part, of cats in prison spitting over his beats. I got one of my streets comrades' songs featured on the cd. One of Monday's acts was home and got on. His name was Lyfe Jennings. He was a smooth R&B

singer, who wrote his own songs and played the guitar. He was from Ohio and did ten years in the Ohio Penal System.

Monday sent him to another associate of ours named Irv Gotti, who was on top with his "Murder Inc" label but Irv was feeling himself and didn't want to fuck with Lyfe so Monday sent Lyfe to our other associates who owned FUBU and had the FB Entertainment label. They also declined to put son (Lyfe) on.

Lyfe Jennings competed on the show "Amateur Night at the Apollo" at the ApolloTheater in Harlem, N.Y. and Son won so many times that he ended up with a recording contract from Sony then Irv and FB Entertainment wanted to work with him but that wasn't happening. Lyfe, being a real dude, remembered the struggle and those who were down for him and he kept it real with his people, one of those he remembered was "Monday" so I threw an idea out to Monday. Now that Lyfe Jennings had a cd out, I wanted to get Oceasia on a track with him and put it on her demo package to shop around for a deal, I also wanted Monday to submit tracks as well.

Monday's baby mother, who I had known since the eighties, had a younger brother who I was cool with. He was now an entertainment attorney for a few established artists such as "Black Rob" and "Nature" to name a few. He wanted to shop my novel as a screenplay so I was going to go at him with this project, knowing he had rap and R& B acts who he was also shopping for deals for.

Before I was unexpectedly sent to SHU, I was striving to make moves with this Philly cat named Damon Meadows, who I had met while on the compound of U.S.P Lee County. Damon was a Muslim who went by the name "Amin", he was from South Philly and he had a lot of connections with industry people. I knew of him before we actually met because his co-defendant "Quadir" was a real comrade of mine so I was familiar with Amin when our paths crossed. He had a past relationship with author Terri Woods and was childhood friends with the basketball

137

legend Julius "Dr. J" Erving's children, one being Jay Jr., who then had "Jay Wonder Entertainment" and was managing the R & B group "Floetry". Jay Jr. had a partner named Troy Carter, who had something to do with several artists' careers such as Eve, Philly's Most Wanted and others. Amin also had connections with Patti Labelle's son Zuri Edwards (no relation to me). Amin used to give me numbers and put me on the phone to polly with heads. I was trying to get Monday's tracks in their hands as well as trying to get my Earth Oceasia a.k.a. "Rita Book's" career on and poppin'. I was sending scribes to Amin rapidly about my new move and within a short period of time, he was with it 100 percent.

I was really feeling Oceasia, she had knowledge of self and I was attracted to her mind; she was also smelling my struggle and style. I was going in, all the way in... so much so that I fell back from my novel projects and started focusing more on her music career. My team started bugging on how I just moved to a project no one knew about. That's how much I was feeling Oceasia so I started working on her project and deaded mine. First up, she needed her package a.k.a. "press kit" re-done cause the shit she had put together was trash so I had to revise it, come different and come hard. She was a female and a different kind of spitter plus her image wasn't matching her skills. She had the long Bango dreads with more of an Afro-centric look. She wasn't showing skin like Little Kim, Foxy Brown, Trina or Eve. She didn't rock the tight, tight pants or high skirts but her skills was over the top and she could spit better than the females who was already out. She sounded like a Young Eve while complex like a Rah Digga. Shorty had skills but the skills and her look didn't match. Her image was more like a Erykah Badu, neo soul type of artist but she spitted that street shit like Remy Ma. So marketing Rita was something I was working hard on. She and I was vibin' back and forth about it but I needed some photos to go with her Bio. My first pick was the pic of her sitting on a motorcycle with a hat and shades on. She was looking real sexy and mean in that pic. I picked another photo of her kneeling over a mic and I let her pick the third photo.

The next move was to put together a demo cd with five songs that would really stand out so I had to study her lyrics and rhyme patterns during those fifteen minutes when I called once a month. I had to listen to quick snippets of songs and beats.

I took the photos of her I had chosen and I re-wrote her Bio for her. Getting to know her as a person through vibing and scribing then reading her lyrics, poems and thoughts all through ink spots as well as seeing her in photos and learning her voice on the phone once a moon, enabled me to pen her Bio, it fit her perfectly. I flew it to her a.s.a.p.

Oceasia responded... but doubted herself once she read and absorbed it. I had to go hard on her to not only believe in me but believe in herself. I didn't want her to believe in only what I saw, I wanted her to see all that in herself.   Take a glimpse of what I put together in her Bio...

The underground, sensational Ms. Rita Book is already seeping from the swamp waters of New Orleans, like mists of fog attacking the music industry's mainstream sound waves and she's on her way to becoming the next big thing to spit on any mic device.

Ms. Rita Book has been ripping mics and stages in half in and out of the dirty south for the last 10 years and she's well known in numerous underground spots such as "The Neighborhood Gallery", "The Blue Nile" and "The Dragon's Den" amongst other hot spots on the underground scene. Rita Book received rave reviews in the Times Picayune as she saved the day performing when "Dead Prez" was unable to show up and perform at their own venue at the Contemporary Arts Center.

This Hip Hop / R& B "expressionist" spell binds her audience with picy, Cajun lyrics, riding Tabasco beats with lyrics as political as Angela Davis with the social consciousness of Maya Angelou. She has the direct delivery of a Sonia Sanchez, with the voice like the militant

139

Sista Soulja. This Jazzy, Beautiful Breathing Diamond has more versatility than Lauren Hill, a sprinkle of Jill Scott with the raunchiness and sex appeal of Millie Jackson. Rita has numerous featured appearances and Freestyles on mix tapes and studio tracks by "The Best" DJ Dynamite Dave Soul, Beck Beats, other producers include Block Boy, Tut, Patrick, Lou and up and coming Beatsmiths Al Monday and G Millionz.

This sista is hurting the game something awesome!! Sharing the same birthplace as the Jazz Music Genre itself, Ms. Rita Book grew up on the means streets of the Calliope projects, uptown in the 3rd Ward. Vocally, her Bayou Roots are evident, her tone moves second lines making it known as she's not just another rapper; she is an "expressionist"

"I am an expressionist! I express what I feel at the time I feel it; be it Jazz, spoken word, Blues, Cajun, Hip Hop, R&B, whatever! Experience and Imagination is expression of Life. There is no beginning or end, therefore, I have no limits when I write" Rita Book proclaimed when asked to elaborate on why she refers to herself as an "Expressionist". Her almond eyes mesmerize you, almost allowing you to see her soul. She claims the name "Rita Book" because she says : "At one time in New Orleans and across America, my people were not allowed to read books so I think it's important that we read more, teach and encourage our children to read more. This sista is very deep! On top of Rhyming, she's currently taking guitar and drum lessons. Look out for Rita Book as she spits the real on tracks such as: "My Type", "The Birth", "Flyin' Kites", "Hooka", "Grapefruits", "SistaHood/Hoodsista", "No Idea" and "Nitty Gritty".

People are very tired of the fake shit, the "sex sells" approach, lyrics with no real contents in lyrics bullshit and the screaming designer names, "Bling - Bling" nonsense. Rita Book has more to offer than the usual, that's already been said and heard flow.

<u>Rita Book brings the real with creative and inspiring street, club and soul bangers!!!!</u>

<u>Don't judge this Book by its cover…</u> <u>Get ready for Rita Book</u>!!

Once Oceasia typed up the bio I wrote for her and had her music on disc, we went with the following five joints. 1) No Idea 2) Hooka 3) SistaHood, which is sick… (in the middle of the song the beat changes and the song flips from "SistaHood" to "Hoodsista") 4) Nitty Gritty and 5) My type. We also included the three photos, a copy of the flyer that promoted her opening for the rap group "Dead Prez" and the newspaper article that reported how she saved the day when "Dead Prez" didn't show up for the show. We had done it, Oceasia and I had put together her "press kit". Everything was on smash.

Amin sent us Jay Jr. from Jay Wonder Entertainment's info so we sent the press kit to him as well as Monday's wife and the Entertainment Attorney then we sent Amin and Monday the press kit without the cd.

The first feedback I got was from Monday; he was the coordinator of programs in his institution. He had outside guests like Lyfe Jennings and Triple Crown publications CEO Vickie Stringer show up to the institutions programs. One of the guys who put one of the shows together happened to see the press kit and wanted my shorty "Rita Book" featured in their next program. Monday's wife liked the tracks and played them for him over the phone so he was excited about working with her. He was inquiring about what kind of equipment the studio she worked in had as far as pro tools etc. so he would be able to submit some tracks he had. We was also waiting on the Lyfe Jennings collaboration and to hear what Amin and his folks at Jay Wonder Entertainment had to say.

Amin got at me and wanted Rita Book's press kit, demo and all, sent to his peoples at Versatile Music in Philly. They were managing a cat name "Alpha Mega", who did Fed time and was crazy nice on the spitting tip. He came home and had a lot of things going on since Amin plugged him in with Versatile. Alpha Mega had opened shows for Diddy, he did tracks with rapper T.I and every southern rapper out. He was from Atlanta, Georgia, I can't take away from him his ability to spit but it was a known fact that he was allegedly a rat and was run off of several prison compounds in the Federal System. He turned Muslim for protection and that's how he met Amin. I was like "My shorty aint doing no songs with this rat rap cat... is you crazy?" I shot a kite back at Amin telling him we couldn't fuck with his dude "Alpha Mega" cause we knew son "Nuh right"

*****

Rita Book

I open by calling you to learn and then accept Islam as your way of life! By baring witness that nothing has the right to be worshipped except Allah above and Muhammed is the messenger of Allah. My man at Versatile said that Jay would know how to market you better than he can because of "Floetry"

After I pumped you up to Jay Erving Wonder, he wants you to call him a.s.a.p.!! (261) 328 – 9602. You make sure you send your Demo a.s.a.p. because I'm going to stay on him! Let Jay know everything you have done and what you are doing to this day!

Handle things on your end and I'll handle things on my end.

Tell Shakim to stay progressing   (212 – 763 – 2XXX ext. 9121) Jay's office number.

Amin

*****

Bay

I wanted to tell U that I finally got a chance to get "Lyfe" cd and I like it — it's peace.

I'm sitting in here right now trying to put the cd together (the five songs for the demo) but I still haven't decided which 5 of the 11 recorded songs to put on the cd. I also have other songs that I'm really feeling that I haven't yet recorded so maybe I'll be able to record those joints on some trax I get from ur menz dem. I'm thinking about putting 1. No idea 2. Hooka 3. SistaHood 4. Nitty Gritty 5. My Type possible: Judge me and the birth

What U think? Get back at me with ur run down

I'm having thoughts of writing a song called "Mindz" and I came up with the idea for the song from us — for one, we are connected on some mind detect mind and for two, U are mindz. I don't have words for it yet only the concept. It's metaphoric because some of it'll be about mindz (meaning U and everything else that belongs to me) and some of it'll be about the mind (the usage and the power of)

Anyway, I was just kyting to let U know I'm thinking but U and missin' U all day, every day (24-7)

I can't wait until the Love, truth day

Love U

Mrs. Edwards

PS — All I want for Christmas is to sit on my husband's lap and tell him how much I love him, that's all I want from Santa Claus.

*****

SHA,

Peace! Yo, my wife got that cd from your peoples and is really feeling it. I heard a few tracks over the phone... Maybe we can do something with her. My dude Lyfe Jennings is supposed to come up and speak to a group in here. I can run a few ideas by him just to see what's up.

Until then send me her number and another bio and photo. Glad to know you are doing something constructive and positive.

Tone told me that you got an ill novel. Watch what you say. We still fighting.

One... Monday"

*****

My Earth got at me, she was in "Now Why (New York)" networking, trying to make moves. She was supposed to do a joint with the "Brave Hearts", which is Nas' little brother "Jungle" with Wiz and them from Queensbridge projects.

She was supposed to live there with some of her family who live in "The Bridge". She knew Nashawn and Wiz and had Wiz just called her, asking why she didn't call him back and why she left NY without doing the track? Then she told me... don't trip, he live with his girl don't trip? N____ lives with his girl? What the Earth on? Then she touched up on a few things...

"U asked me how I feel 'bout people questioning me about claimin' a jail N_____? Easy… He's the one for me. He won't be in jail forever and besides… why would I deal wit a dude just because he's not in jail, knowin' he don't have what completes me, what it takes to deal wit me and nothing long term overall. Instead of spending time trying to change men every so often and still ending back at square one wit no one, I could be building a foundation wit someone I do see being a permanent part of my life. I love U, miss U, need U, want U.

I received the Bio… its cool. I think I need to read it again or let someone else read it and see what they say because me reading about myself is kind of crazy since it aint for me to read, it's to inform other people about me. U know how sometimes U may feel like DAMN! A little overwhelmed because reading that really makes me look like a real powerful person, not sayin' that I'm not B.U.T. I wouldn't have written that about myself. However, knowing that other people compare me to some great names, really makes me work harder on perfecting my craft, learning more about politics and writing more things that those great names would enjoy listening to. The part where u said "I have more versatility than Lauren Hill" it may be true but I don't want to sound like I'm dissin' cause I like "L-Boogie (Lauren)". She is an inspiration to me and I would love to work with her. I don't know if I can go with this bio. I got a poem I wrote for you, I didn't know it was so short but it's short and sweet. I decided to title it 375 degrees and 30 minutes later because that's the temperature to equality and the 30 minutes is usually how long it takes to bake so understanding the cipher, which borns understanding, added to equality borns born. So I see that together we born; peace (of cake), love (is love), happiness (smiles) to the celebration of birth (being born) days. Now I can even appreciate my physical day a little more now that I see it like this because I had got to the point of saying it was nothing but another day and that celebrating it was the point of saying it was nothing but another day and that celebrating it was a kid thing. U learn something new every day or U get a better understanding on some of the things U already know. I hope it does something for U as well because I was thinking of U when I wrote it.

Listen to that song by Amel Larieux called "For Real" peep it out that's my shit.

9 – 12- 21

*****

"375 degrees and 30 minutes later" by Rita Book

What am I?

I'm cake batter.

Ur the pre-heated oven my substance is gathered upon. As I rise

I Bake at a

Time based on size of the pan inches

U make me delightful and delicious

My taste be a bite full of mouth watering drooling drippings

When all trimmed wit – icing

Enjoyed by millions and millions armed wit gallons of Ice Cream,

Special on any occasion

Weddings Birthdays

Sometimes it's made for selling – but either way.

Even when homemade colored in a rainbow of shades as shapes are displayed cupped, upside down, with 7 up or rum for some laced with candles to make more wishes than they could handle. Anyhow or any case, I brings to the face of any adult or child, an amazing amount of decorative smiles. This is true but it wouldn't be possible without the warmth of U.

*****

Bay,

Your peoples Al Monday called me via 3 way. He spoke to me about that 5 song demo and how he heard it and was feeling it. Didn't y'all say that Irv is y'all people too? He asked me what kind of equipment they use in the studio I go to 'cause he got a Triton and a Motif. So I gotta go look into that. He said he needs to know cause even if he send me tracks on a cassette tape it won't be no good all dealing with what equipment they got... we will figure something out. so, basically he was telling me to just keep doing my thing, keep writing doing shows and start sending material to some of the record companies and he's most definitely gonna see what he can do on his end. Ya boy Greg called, he was on his way to FL to some kind of function where a lot of industry cats be at every year. He wanted some of my material so he could try to make some moves /connections. Now that's what's up. U know I miss u right? I think about U all day no matter what I'm doin'. When I'm writing, eating, taking a bath, in the studio, looking in the mirror. Putting on my clothes or taking them off. I wish u were here "physically". I really do need u. I love u. Big time...

Sometimes I go deep off in a Fantasy world and the mind is so powerful. It's like u actually be here wit me for real. Mind detect mind. I know u be thinkin' about me too so ur energy already be here wit me, touchin' my mind. I just take it to the supreme extreme... I can see us together as God and Earth, husband and wife, King and Queen, man and woman.... I know good things come to those who wait so I'll be right here. However, what happens if u decide to go in another direction after I wait however long for u? That would mean I was waitin' for a mystery and we know what a mystery is. Or what if u get out and we're together, whatever, whatever... then u find u a lil' sweetie that ur feelin' and u stay married to me or living wit me but (only cause I didn't walk away and turn my back on u) but still be cheatin' on me wit this new bitch... Not saying that's gonna happen but ... I trust u. I don't think u'll fuck me over like that, matter of fact I'ma say I know u wouldn't do me like that. Everything here is <u>Genuine Supreme Understanding</u>. I'm not doin' anything for u to owe me something, it's to show u <u>pure feelings</u> I have for u <u>no beginning</u> or <u>ending</u>. So I wouldn't even want u to just be wit me because I was there for u. I know that's not the case with us. I'm just talking because I know I'm able to

147

talk to u about any and everything "homie, lover, friend (R. Kelly song)" and u'll add on letting me know how u see it. I had a dream about u last night. I don't remember too many details all I know is that it felt good. We were together and I never wanted it to end. We were happy, smiling, holding each other, it just was the best and of course u know I woke up wit an extra moist power u.

Love u

The official Mrs. Sha Bio chemical

*****

I'm just sharing some of Oceasia's thoughts to show where we were with our feelings for one another.

*****

Bay,

Can't wait to talk 2 u – can't wait. Miss u so much. Love u so much. I wrote u a poem a couple of weeks ago, I need to find it and send it to u. I forgot the name of it, but its tasty. I hope u like sweets (no. its not nasty) by the way, what u think about the wet dream I had? U can't be doing that to me – just poppin' up in the middle of the night playin' wit my power U like that then leave before I wake up.

I probably have like 43 letters from u so far

Do you love me for real? How much?

Ur wife

Oceasia Edwards

9-12-21

PS – I got that Lye Jennings cd. It's banging, they aint ready for that brother yet. They are sleepin' on him. I was listening to number 10 (stick up kid) but I listened to the whole cd and really do like it. It's like a run down of his life from the pen back to the streets. I'm just happy every song is not about sexing a female like most of these singers are doing on their cds. He talking about real shit on each cut. Son is deep, straight to the point. He's like a rapper but he sings. U can tell he's a street dude, not a pretty boy soft singer. I would love to work wit him so if you can hook that up, that'd be peace.   9-12-21

*****

CHAPTER 16

Whatz up Daddy?

I'm just here thinking about u on this Thanksgiving day. Missin' u like crazy its funny cause I be thinking 'bout us, our relationship, our communication, our supreme understanding and to say we never physically met or done anything physical. I get excited when I hear ur voice, read ur scribes and view ur flix all because the "mental" connection we share is more than amazing. However, I do get lonely to the point of being a little upset sometimes because even though I feel u from so far away, I long to feel u up close and personal so we could go to rest together every night and wake up to each other's faces. If we think we love each other now, just imagine that!!!! I can see it now I have visions of our future.

SOLID – AS - A - ROCK !!!!

I know we make a perfect team because not only are we both street wise but we're also intelligent and civilized as well. I fantasize of u being here, us doing things and going places, making love and babies, working out, sick days, holding hands, etc…

Wanting U is one thing

Needing U is another

Having U = Priceless

(to be continued)

＊＊＊＊＊

Knowledge wisdom/knowledge equality

Peace my God,

On this same day knowledge-understanding rules ago, I had my virginity broken…

Oceasia went in and told me the story of how she was pregnant and went from playing sick to staying home from school to the actual event. We shared things like that. Shorty told me everything about her, the high and lows of her life. She held nothing back either. She knew how to say some ill things to me that kept me going too.

"I got that fire for real staar… and I'm saving it just for u for true cause I have no problem keepin' my legs closed, my thigh muscles are strong. Grab ur dick for me. I wish I could do it myself then put it in so u can hurt me on ur way in… OOH that feels so good. Don't stop!! I like it like that. Get it from the back. I don't know how to act… slow motion for me…

Her talking to me like that made me turn on the quiet storm on XM radio, grab my manhood and go to rest thinking about my Earth.

✳✳✳✳✳

I was laying on my bunk listening to XM Satellite Radio. DJ Cam was spinning the hottest rap joints when a C.O. came and banged on my door…

"Edwards"

"What's up?"

I got up taking my ear plugs out as I walked to the door.

"We just got someone from off the pound, he's mentioning your name so we need some place to put him"

"What's his name?"

"Hall"

"Hall?" I brainstormed, then thinking to myself, I remembered..."Damn that's "Unique" from Harlem's last name, I wonder what the fuck he did".

"Waynesworth?" I asked the Officer.

The C.O. looked at the photo tag card "Nah" and showed me the card, it was Pierre...DAMN!

"You know him?" the C.O. asked me.

"Yeah... that's my dude, give me a second to find a spot for him"

"O.K. guy" said the C.O. as he walked off the tier.

I was fucked up behind receiving this news. I thought "Damn, what Pierre done did?" I didn't hear the deuces go off. I was buggin' out as I hollered down the tier.

"Yo Freeway!!"

"Yo!" "Freeway responded back.

"Yo I need a cell for my dude who's coming off the pound. You know he may have something for me, you know???"

"It's all full over here Sha" Freeway hollered back.

"Damn" I look at my celly and off top, he felt the vibe.

"What's up Sha?"

"My dude is up in this piece... gotta make room"

Moves were made and they put Pierre on the tier right around the corner. I sent him everything he would need plus some smoke and a kite telling him to play rec. early tomorrow.

The next morning as I was brought to the rec yard and out in the rec. cage I left an open spot for Pierre. Once he came in and got the cuffs off, we dapped up and embraced.

"Good to see you but not under these circumstances" I greeted him.

"Yeah God… Damn you got crazy brolic (Buffed, built, diesel, muscular) back here" he acknowledged.

"Yo, what they got you back here for?" I asked, cutting to the chase.

"You gonna be heated God" he responded.

"Nah…" I replied.

"Yeah son… they got "Betsy"".

"Damn!" I was sick.

"Betsy" was the name I gave to this weapon I had. It was a solid iron rod, about eleven inches long, sharpened to a point tip that would go through any material. "Betsy" was a bona fide bone-crusher that was considered a murder weapon. Wasn't nobody trying to get stabbed with that shit. I nicknamed it "Betsy"… she was so beautiful, yet deadly ugly. When I came to the SHU, Betsy was hidden in my property so well the C.O.s didn't find it but I knew if I was to be transferred, they would x-ray and find it so it took me over fourteen moons to figure a way to fool the property officer to allow me to go into my property to "retrieve some legal work". He went through it and didn't realize he just gave me "Betsy", my eleven inch monster, which was hidden and disguised in my legal work so I was in SHU with a vicious murder weapon. I had it for about a month waiting to attack someone with it but I couldn't find no one who would jump out there. I felt that sending it out to Pierre was much better than letting the C.O.s find it or someone who didn't deserve it getting it so I put it in a shampoo bottle from commissary and gave it to a convict who was returning to general population, instructing him to give the shampoo to Pierre.

Pierre sent word back that he did indeed have it. Barely 3 moons passed and here he was face to face with me in the box cause they found "Betsy".

"You think they gonna hang me over that shit or what?" Pierre asked me.

"Death Row B" I said.

"Fuck it then" he responded.

"Damn, they got "Betsy'" I stressed again.

"Yo, I got that 'Purp'." I know you tryna blow"

"Motherfuckin' right"

*****

The next few days Pierre and I met up at rec. but I made a few moves and got moved off my tier to his tier two doors down from him. Five C.O.s came carrying me and my celly's shit, then here came the God (Me) as I transferred tiers. So now we had to catch up on prison events and on my investigation, which had been dropped by the FBI and was being dealt with on the prison level of things again. I told Pierre about Oceasia, how we met and lost contact and how we linked back up thru the "Power Paper". Sun seen how open I was...

"When is she coming?" Pierre asked.

"Imperial's wife lives like 4 hours away so I'ma link them so she can fly there and drive up with her."

"Nah God... have her fly to my Ruby Red. She will bring her up son"

"Word?" I asked.

"Word Sha, make that happen"

"No question."

*****

I was on top of that. The only thing was Oceasia didn't send the visitor form back to my counselor so she wasn't approved on my visiting list yet. It was two weeks of back and forth cause I was spitting at her through ink spots at Godspeed rate but it was landing in her mailbox at the mailman's pace. So until I got my monthly call, I had to build with her, letting her know that we were switching lanes, instead of going to the God Lord Imperial I was linking her with one of my comrade's wife, who will journey and bring her to see me but she had to re-route to Charlotte, North Carolina. At the same time, Pierre had to put his wife on point with our plans and make sure everything was everything with his Ruby. My Earth definitely hit me right back with questions and attitude...

"I'm trying to make some extra money and figure out a plan for this visit thing because I have to make sure that once I purchase the ticket, I'll be able to get there. U said someone will have to drive me there after I get off the plane – right? So if I don't have a definite ride, the rest of the way, then I'll be stuck out there and can't visit u anyway. First of all, what part of VA would I have to fly to?" Where would I rest for the two nights and who would or how would I reach U? These are things I need to know before I purchase and lose money on a round trip ticket. I also gotta take sick days from both jobs in order to come out there. Ruby Red has not contacted me so I don't know what's up wit that and the only other plan we had was Lord Imperial and if he don't come through, what am I gonna do? Because I don't know where I'm goin' and u don't know where ur at directions-wise. So we have to be dependent on someone else just for us to be together and that's fucked up!! But what can we do? It has to be another way, we gotta pre-meditate another plan a for sure, for sure, not an

155

unknown so I will see when Ruby will call and I hope she don't call at the last minute. See u in my dreams"

I was striving to manifest force and power by pushing my pen. I was spraying ink rapidly, shooting 10 pages and better. I had to re-route my thoughts and actions to the God Lord Imperial. I had to build with my manz "G", who was in N.Y. navigating my newborn movement. I was building with a lot of people through mail.

Me and Pierre stayed on the door. He was 2 cells away so I made sure he was good with the cigarettes, food and I even had weed. We played recreation every day and built, I stayed on him to make shit happen so the visit from our queens could manifest. He saw that I was serious and open over shorty. Pierre knew me and how I operated from him being around me on the compound, he seen my photo album and what caliber females I was messing with so he knew I used to be that dude...

"Yo. Pierre!!"

I hollered down to his cell.

"What's popping', Sha Bio!" he answered back.

"Yo, did you get the horn since you been in the box?"

"Nah big homie, I aint get it yet, why, what's up?

"If you want, I'ma get it for you, that's what's up."

"Make it happen then God" was his response.

"Yeah I'ma do that"

"Yeah Sha. I already know you want me to get on my Ruby!"

"You already know then Blood!"

We laughed.

*****

CHAPTER 17

My counselor "Torres" came through making his rounds early in the morning while I was doing my daily 1000 push-ups in 34 minutes. He banged on my door barking my name...

"Edwards!!"

"Torres, what you got for me?" I asked.

My counselor wasn't a bad dude at all; he was more of a convict's counselor. He testified in my trial when I got indicted. He helped me more than he helped the prison's allegations and he knew I was involved a lot of shit too.

What's goin' on Torres?"

"Same shit... you are still under investigation but the FBI kicked it back so you don't have to worry about bein' indicted again... but you got an incident report coming real soon."

"For what?" I asked.

"Nothing should be a surprise to you whatever it is... OH... I have something for you, it's an approval of visitor... here's your copy"

Torres slid my copy of the visitor approval form through the crack of the door.

"Good looking!"

"Ok Edwards, get back to getting your push-ups in. You're gonna need all that muscle and strength to keep this investigation from crushing you"

Torres walked off laughing; he was being sarcastic because he knew the investigation was all bullshit. I looked and seen my Earth's government attributes on my approved visiting list.

"Shakim Bio… I heard that B!" hollered Pierre.

"Yeah… Yeah… Make sure you play rec. when they come on the tier!!" I hollered.

"No question homie!!"

Yeah so now Oceasia was approved on my visiting list so I had to get her there to see me.

My celly was eyeing me from his top bunk.

"So now you got her approved, I know you about to get her up here."

"Of course playboy, you know I'm on top of that" was my response.

*****

Now that my shorty was approved, I stayed workin' out even harder. I went harder with the pull-ups outside on the corners of the gates in the rec. cage. I'm a monster.

*****

The day I got the phone, you know I was on it heavy.

Oceasia was very excited to know that she got approved on my visitor's list, she was ready to make reservations. A little later on after dinner and mail call, I asked a C.O. to come back to my cell when he was free, he came an hour later.

"Edwards, What's up?"

I explained to him that I had nearly seventeen months in the box and I been chilling out, not causing havoc or influencing others to pop off so out of respect due, he should take the phone on the tier at 9pm and deliver it to "Hall", who was just two cells down. He said...

"Ok. It will be done."

"Cool"

I hollered down to Pierre.

"I already know Sun" was his reply.

*****

Shakim,

I really enjoyed speakin' wit u today, U definitely made my day. I wish I could talk to u more often or even better, wish I could hold u for days at a time. I can't wait till I'm about to let u touch this hot p___y like u touch my warm heart. I listened to u on my voicemail and kissed that facial (photo) before I went to rest.

I got a new song I recorded the night before I talked to u. I really like the song, however I need to re-record it or the engineer needs to handle his business because it sounds a lil' thin but it's still banging. It is untitled right now but the first verse of the joint is the verse I let your manz G hear. He said he was feelin' that shit..

Hurry up and get that visitation thing together fuh mi redi fuh sum of dat rude bwoy love from di gal dem sugah, who happens to be Oceasia's husband zeen?!!.

9 – 12 – 21

*****

160

Saturday, 01 /15/05 was a very important day. It was the day that my Earth Oceasia, who I now addressed as "wifey", was coming to see the God. I was up at the power hour {5am} doing 1500 push-ups, back arms from off the wall and one-arm curls with the water bag. I was getting it in Early. I made moves and had a brand new orange jumper and brand new slip on shoes. If I was out in population, I could grace the visit with a Fresh Federal Khaki outfit and either my Timberlands or brand new sneakers but due to my being in the box, what I had on was what I was required to wear. The barber didn't come to the box until 8am Saturday so to make sure I was on point, I had the magic shave that I bought from commissary and some vitamin E pills so I could pop them and use the gel on my facial. You couldn't tell the lad (ME) nothin'. I had the gold polish rag to make sure my teeth was gleaming and diamonds was sparkling; the God was in there like swimwear.

Pierre didn't get up and call me until after breakfast was served and that was after the God hour [7am].

"Yo Sha, that's you down there making all that noise early in the a.m."

"What you talkin' about P?"

"C'mon God, I hear you moving around. What... you working out?"

"No Question. I thought you knew"

"Sha, your arms aint gon' get no bigger"

We started laughing.

"Yo, Pierre!"

"What's good Sha?"

"You think they gonna be here or what?" I asked.

"I don't know about yours but my Ruby will be here, homie".

161

We laughed again. Shit was crazy because I couldn't call to see if Oceasia left, landed safely or if her and Ruby was on their way... couldn't call to see if everything is ok. All I could do was wait and trust that everything was everything...

By 7:30am, I was in the shower getting my refinement in order. By the time I came out, got oiled up, put some Egyptian musk and the vitamin E on, I was ready but I brushed my teeth again.

I heard C.O.'s on the tier. They stopped at Pierre's cell and told him to get ready for a visit. By the time they made it to my door, I'd been ready. I snatched up my photo tickets, checked the mirror again and popped two peppermint candies to make sure the breath was in order. Once we were handcuffed and secured, the guards had to close the whole prison compound down in order to transport us through the tunneled hallways that led to the visiting room. We were still allowed contact visits with the regular population but we was seated upfront with orange jumpers on. As we walked through the tunneled hallways, I was looking through the windows at the prisons' yard and compound, shit was crazy. Once we made it to the visit, we had to be pat searched and the rules was explained. Even though a fella like me already knew the drill, it was mandatory that the rules was given to us again verbally.

When we came out to the visiting floor and had to report to the front desk, they told us where to sit and warned us not to get up and mingle with population or visitors or else our visits would be terminated. "Yea , yea- right, right" I thought to myself as I scanned and seen my Earth cheesing like a 2 year old. I made it over to her on my N.Y. shit, she ran to me with open arms. When we stood face to face, Oceasia wrapped her arms around my neck and we kissed each other like it was no tomorrow. Then she stopped me to suck on my bottom lip. I just knew she wanted to do that. I wrapped my arms around her waist and hugged her tightly and she buried her head in my chest inhaling my aroma. We hugged and kissed for at least five minutes then

I released her and spun her around. Even with heels on, she was shorter than what I expected. She stood 5'2", in heels she was maybe 5'5 – 5'6. She had on a knitted yellow sweater with two bottoms on the top and a hood, some fitted jeans with a big belt buckle. Her bango dreads was tied in a ponytail that flowed down her back. She smiled that big radiant smile as she held me by both hands and looked up at me in my eyes.

"PEACE to my God Shakim Bio-Chemical Wise"

"PEACE Queen"

"I look the same as the photos?" she asked.

"Nah… you look better"

"Can I kiss you again?" she pleaded.

The answer was no but I told her…

"yeah, so come here"

We engaged in another quick kiss.

Oceasia sat across from me as we held hands over the table during the whole visit. It was truly all about us. She unbuttoned the two buttons of her sweater where I could see her cleavage of her breasts.

"Ma, what are doing? I asked her.

"It's hot in here… I'm unbuttoning my sweater"

I observed the rose petal tattoo between the top of her breasts.

"I see your tatt."

"Yeah, it goes all the way down to my stomach, passed my navel, where I have the roots and all."

"That's peace. I see your universal flag too"

I looked at her left wrist as her hands were in mine.

"Let me see yours" she requested so I opened my shirt and show her the flag tatted on my left chest muscle. Oceasia raised up and leaned forward to look in my shirt and snuck a kiss. We was laughing...

We had so much fun and was so comfortable around each other. It was like we'd been with each other for decades. We got the checker board and I beat her in so many games I lost count. We were loud in the visiting room too. Oceasia went to the desk and came back with a deck of cards so I spanked her again. Pierre and his wife had fun watching us act like little kids. I met Pierre's wife on a previous visit when my mom and sister came up and Pierre was out there too. Oceasia said...

"Boy, Ruby got photos of Pierre all over her car and the color red is everywhere. What the hell is he a NY Blood?"

"Yep" I answered.

"For Real?" she asked as she looked over at Pierre and his wife then she continued...

"I like her, she is really cool. When I landed last night, she picked me up from the airport, took me out to eat, showed me around and refused to let me get a hotel room. We kicked it hard last night, talkin' and havin' fun"

"That's my man'z Ruby"

Oceasia held my hand and looked me straight in the eyes...

"You so fly... and you are arrogant as hell too. I know you were a mess out there in the free cipher"

We continued to laugh it up.

She walked to the vending machine switching her ass up a storm, putting on a show for a fella. It was packed in the visiting room and more convicts was coming in. A lot of them stopped by my table to salute a fella and ask me how I was doing. Oceasia came back with chicken nuggets and some fruit salad.

"So everybody knows Shakim Bio huh?" she asked as she hand fed me chicken nuggets.

"They are not important right now Ma. It's all about you "

"All about me?" she asked while smiling from ear to ear.

"Yeah... you" I assured her.

We spoke on the lessons and she asked me a lot of degrees within One Twenty from the second set of numbers.

"Yeah I gotta make sure you're sharp Bay" she said in her southern drawl... I laughed at her.

"What's so funny?"

"You sound so sexy and country" I responded.

"So?" she snarled...

We laughed like crazy, it wasn't a dull moment on that visit. It was all about me and her in our own world. No one existed outside of us as we built and enjoyed our very first visit. She massaged my hands then worked from my hand to my forearm then up to my bicep and she squeezed it.

"Damn Bay... I didn't know you was big like that..."

As she squeezed my arm with both hands, the touch of a woman felt soooo goooood to me, especially since it was MY woman. No joke, I looked her in her eyes and let her know.

"Everything about me is real big... except the legs"

We laughed a lot and when it was time to take photos, we really, really showed out. I had ten photo tickets and we were out of the C.O.s vision as the convict camera man waited for our pose. I wrapped my arms around her, she did the same and at the same time her hands was exploring my upper body as I smirked knowing what she was doing. "So you want to play like that?" I asked as I squeezed that booty of hers. We had so much fun as I held her in front of me hugging her up for the camera. The photo man took pics while we laughed and smiled and eventually, she felt that iron in her back area. She put her hand behind her back to cop a mean squeeze to see what the tools size was. We really got our laugh on then. I was so glad that she was happy. It made my day to know that she enjoyed the visit as much if not more than I did. We definitely had that chemistry, that lust and we truly enjoyed each other.

Dem people cut our visit short by 30 minutes, ending it at 2:30p.m, which was thirty minutes earlier than general population's visits ended. Me and Pierre's visit was cut because we were in the SHU and the C.O.s had to strip search us, shackle us, secure and lockdown the compound in order to walk us back through the tunneled hallways back into the box. When I was told that we had 10 minutes left, My Earth's eyes started tearing automatically. She hugged and held on to me for dear life. Our kiss was so passionate, it told a story of true love and again, she stopped so she could suck my bottom lip.

"I love you forever Shakim"

"I love you too Oceasia, I mean Tamekia"

166

"You the only one who calls me that"

"I know"

"I love you for real Bay."

"I do too"

We kissed again. It was time for us to leave so I looked at Ruby and thanked her for looking out for me and my Earth.

"No problem Sha!" she responded.

I turned to walk away, took two steps and turned back around to wave bye but Oceasia ran back to me to hug and kiss me again.

"Nine – twelve – twenty one"

"Nine – twelve – twenty one" I responded back.

*****

On the way back I was all smiles as Pierre kept looking back at me. Although we were shackled up in leg irons and handcuffs, we "strolled" back to the box. I had that smirk on my face.

"Yo Sha. You was a big kid out there, I'm glad you enjoyed yourself"

"No question. Good looking out for showing love like that" I said, thanking Pierre for seeing that his wife played her part in bringing Oceasia to see me.

"Realness "B". It's Realness" he responded.

"No doubt" I shot back.

"Yo I want to ask you something when we get back, Sha."

"Ok."

*****

I was still on my high as I lay on my bunk and replayed the visit in my mind.

"Yo Sha" Pierre called out to me.

"Yo, whats good?" I asked.

"Yo sun, what did that "nine – twelve – twenty one" mean? I heard the Earth say it to you and you said it back to her. Show and prove that" he asked.

"Supreme Alphabets Sun... nine is "I" ... twelve is "L", which is Love and number twenty one is Universe, which is "U" and I verse" I answered.

"Wow!.... Now that's ill... y'all said "I love you" with numbers. I respect that right there, how you broke it down. Write that down for me Sha"

We started laughing.

"Yo Sha. I need a bigarette. You got any over there?"

"A what?" I asked jokingly.

"You know what ... A BIGARETTE!! ... Yo send your line. I got some of that Redman and method Man!!

"No question... it's on the way!" I responded.

*****

The next few days passed and it was back to the same shit. My eldest seed's physical born day was 01/14, on which he turned 14 and I got at him with a few cards that Oceasia sent to me to sign. They were sent late but...

The big issue now was that the investigation was over and I beat the incident report. It was going on 20 months I'd been sitting back there in the box. They had to decide what they was gonna do with me, the options were to let me back out into the prison's population or ship me to another Fed Pen. The prison's captain, the associate warden, the S.I.S Lt. and S.I.A. all got together to do another b.s. investigation on me. They came back saying they were "considering" releasing me back to the prison's population... so I was awaiting results.

*****

My Earth sent me a few cards and I got a scribe that was mailed before she came up for our visit. She said she sent me a surprise so I was trying to figure out what it was because I didn't see no photos or nothing in the envelopes of either the letter or cards. I sat wondering what she was talking about.

*****

The next day... I didn't get no mail but I got a receipt in the mail, alerting me to $200.00 that had been sent by mail to my account. The sender's last name was "EDWARDS" so it was either my sister, who is one year older than me or it was my eldest son DaQuan who sent it... they are the only "Edwards" I know... wait a minute... unless... yep!

The next day I received a scribe from my Queen, it was the first time she wrote since our visit...

*****

169

CHAPTER 18

Know/knowledge God borning Build or destroy.

Here's to u my dear. Poppin' open a bottle of Moet, smoking a black and mild, listening to Janis Joplin. The "Love Janis" cd. It's real groovey on some 60's, rock type blues/jazz. I got #10 on repeat, it's called "Summertime" from Porgy and Bess. That's my shit! I'm in a mellow mood, I'm real laid back right now, thinkin' bout my baby... I LOVE U SHAKIM!!

I have to say I was so nervous for days even before I got up there and also while waitin' for u to come into the visiting room from the back... Then after that, I was cool and at ease as if we had been together for years. I could tell from the way u kissed me that you were a bit nervous yourself. I didn't know what to get for u to eat. I was hopin' I made the right choices cause even though u didn't specify, I figured I should know my husband's taste. I think I did good for a first try. Those lips of urz are even more irresistible in person. They are so juicy, I couldn't help but want a kiss every time I looked at u but I had no intentions of getting u in trouble or putting our visit at risk. I just know what I was feeling and going off that alone, I wish I could move right next door to the USP so I could visit u every day. I miss u so much. Next time I come up there I promise u I'm gon whip ur ass in checkers so be ready! I really had a nice time bein' wit u all day Saturday. I wish it could've been forever. I be laughin' to myself, thinking 'bout when we were up takin' our pictures, we didn't know what to do or how to pose with everyone watchin' and at the same time we were trying to sneak our lil' feels, getting our roll on. That was so funny, especially those last 3 pictures when ur divine eye cee king got... hmmmmmmm... I loved it for real. I can't wait till the pictures come back... Anyway, I'm glad u got to c my hair cause I've been holdin' on to it so u can c it before I decide to cut it off. Yes I'm still thinking about doin' that, think I should? Now since u've seen me in person, do u still feel me and still think I'm beautiful? Less, more, or the same? I never knew u had that many golds in ur mouth. I got to see my baby pretty smile even though u were trying to hold back. Ruby is so cool. I spoke to her like 5 times since then. I left her with some current for being so nice to me. I want to come back up there a.s.a.p.! Don't act like u don't want me to but keep in mind ur not across the street. I work and have to make sure I got enough current for shelter and to bless whoever transport me from point A to point B and so on and so forth. However, I want u to know by any means necessary, I would sacrifice whatever to be wit u. I'll go hungry and sleep in the airport (cuz I'll be so full of u, I'll be able to rest easy anywhere) so if I get just enuff for my ticket and gas money for Ruby, I'll make that move – Believe that!! I know u want to c me on a regular. I wanna c u too, plus I gotta snatch that title from u, let u know who the true champ is in checkers. I want u to hit me off wit some album titles. I have some and I keep comin' with more. I'll send u a list soon.

We build later tonight so keep my spot warm and don't be hoggin' all the cover.

PS – I sent u wisdom double ciphers   9 – 12- 21

*****

Early in the morning, while the C.O. was picking up the breakfast trays and I was doing my push-ups, I heard the C.O. at Pierre's door.

"Hall, pack it up. You're going back out to the compound… be ready in about thirty minutes!"

"Ok" was Pierre's response, he was still in a sleeping doze.

"Yo Pierre…   I heard that shit!"   I hollered.

*****

The Feds needed room so they was kicking people out the SHU, even convicts with pending incident reports would just have to go to their hearings from the compound. The C.O. passed my door so that killed all hopes of me going back to the compound at that time.

*****

171

It was Valentine's Day but still just a regular day in prison, especially since a fella was in the box going on 21 moons and was still sitting back here. I'd been shot down for a disciplinary transfer and for Marion Super-Max so I was waiting to see what dem people's next move was gonna be.

I worked out crazily today for no reason at all, other than just to go super hard body. This was one of the first Valentine's that I didn't shoot Tammi a card or two plus she's a Valentine's Baby, her B-day is on the 13th. I didn't even send her a card. I hadn't been hearing much from her. My monthly call was going to Oceasia, faithfully and I guess Tammi was caught up in living her life or whatever... It was all good... I was good where I was at anyway and I was happy. I trusted Oceasia got all the cards I sent her with the visit photos enclosed and I was sure she enjoyed them just as much as I did.

Later on that evening

I received numerous scribes from different people but I was only looking for the one who was so important to me. I got three Valentine's day cards and two scribes from Oceasia. I also got a scribe and some reflections from my street team and a letter from this Jamaican chick, who I was penning from time to time. She was now living in the Crown Heights section of Brooklyn and was very open over a fella. I checked the time on my Sony Walkman Radio... I was waiting on the Quiet Storm on XM radio so I could get in my lay back mode and pen my Queen. It was something about those slow jams that did something to a fella. I zoned out into my own world to the point that I forgot that I had a celly... as I sprayed that ink.

It was 9pm and the Quiet Storm was doing its thing. I had until 3am to put a scribe out. I read the scribe from my street team and looked at the photos of them and what they were doing out in the wilderness of N.Y.C. I speed read the Yardie chick's scribe. She wasn't really saying much, even if she was... I overlooked it because my interest wasn't really there... I decided I wasn't going to respond to her anymore.

I picked up the three cards and opened up the first one. It said "For the world's best Husband on Valentine's day", it was a "Mahogany Hallmark" special. I opened up the four dimensional card, read it and observed the characters as they expressed its meaning of a couple deep in love. Oceasia signed off "9 – 12- 21... The Official Mrs. Edwards". I opened the second card and it was an ill joint. In big letters on the front it said... "ON VALENTINE'S DAY ALWAYS I LOVE YOU" The card was a connections Hallmark edition and it was real nice. I read the words on both sides inside and again, Oceasia signed off "9 – 12 – 21 The official Mrs. Edwards". See... that was what's up right there! I was definitely digging these cards so I picked up the last card. I noticed this card was a long one as I opened it up. It was another Mahogany Hallmark with a cartoon female on the front with a dress on. It showed the females whole body and said... "To my Husband, it's Valentine's Day and I want you to know exactly how I feel". I opened up the card up to read the inside, where it said... "So feel me already. Happy Valentine's Day Baby" and there were two photos taped on both sides of the inside of the card. "Oh Shit... No she didn't" In the photos she wore a white sheer (see through) lingerie top and she was pulling them up to show her stomach area. She was also wearing white lace panties with some brown Gator cowboy boots and in her panties, was an 8 by 10 blow up photo of my close-up facial shot. This was a photo I sent to her a few months before and now I see that she had it blown up. She had it in her panties as she held up her lingerie top and posed for me. In both photos, ma was looking very, very sexy. She really went there as the Earth went from three fourths of cloth to one fourth... well maybe it was less than one fourth but she let it be known that she was more than comfortable going that far to entertain my mind with a special treat. I stared into the photos of my slim goodie and wished I could hold her close and please her to the fullest... Damn... at that very moment "Just me and you" by Tony, Toni, Tone came on so I turned it up in my headphones.

*****

My scribe to her...

Tu eres my todo. Mi mundo entero

No puedo respirar sinti...

Tue res mi hermoso, brillante diamante.

El amar de mi vida, constant mente pienso enti...

Tu le das, mucha alegria a mi vida...

Estoy muy alegre de tenerte, como mi esposa...

Quiero suvir montanas contigo...

Un rey no es nada, sin su reina

Tequiero por vido...

<u>Siempre</u>

Translation (even though I didn't include it the scribe to her; I made her go find out what it said) read:

"You are my everything, my whole world

I won't be able to breathe without you. You are my

Beautiful Breathing Diamond, the Love of my Life

I think about you constantly. You bring so much

Joy to my Life and I'm so happy to have you as my wifey

I want to climb mountains with you

A king is nothing without a Queen.

Love you for Life

<u>Always</u>

* * * * *

Baby Daddy,

I received my Valentine's cards and reflections yesterday on Valentine's Day. We look cute 2gether. Did u get ur Valentine treat? How did u enjoy it? I wrote u a poem. I sent it yesterday 2/14. Tell me if u like it.

Do u need anything? Do u have money? I miss u. Call me soon and write me back. 9 – 12 -21 so very much. Did Ruby Red get the cards I sent to her thanking her for everything? I still haven't heard from her. Pierre must've told her don't call me anymore or something.

What ever happened to my song u supposed to send to me since like 2 moons ago?

9 -12 – 21

Mrs. J '5' Edwards

* * * * *

My scribe must not have reached her yet cause shorty got at me and went in kinda hard on a fella.

* * * * *

PEACE Sha! I called Cliff and he said to tell u that he still got love for u and he aint rich yet. He asked had I seen u recently? I said yeah, ur

175

doing fine even though ur in da box. He asked "he still in da box?? His cell #917-577-XXXX.

I also called Chris Gotti but his voicemail came on and I didn't leave a message. I called Jay for the demo and his sec gave me the address. I left my # with his sec also. I wonder if Amin sent him my photo and Bio. I'm going back to NY in a few days and gotta go to the studio before I leave too.

Anyway, now that I've taken care of some of ur business, it's time for me to tell ur ass about urself. Bay, I sent ur ass a lovely V Day gift and u didn't even acknowledge that shit that's fucked up yo!! I know I haven't been writing u like I supposed to B.U.T. that don't mean I don't love u or I'ma wanna say I love u and miss u and just send that every day but u make me feel like I have to write a whole chapter just to say 9 – 12- 21 cause no matter which way I say it or how many words I use. It's "Supremely Understood" that I love u. Isn't that enough? Mind detects mind. I know that u love me and u think about me every day. I can feel it, can't u detect the fine mist of gravity rotation around u? That's me!! Read that "Dear John" letter again cause u must not have comprehended what I was sayin' in that letter. That's like my "Oath to U" sometimes when I don't hear from u or don't hear what I expected to hear in some of ur kytes. I be mad B.U.T I automatically think about or go read some of the previous words u said because even though the scribes are old, does that mean that feelings expressed then are not fresh and as genuine as what's expressed now? At first I knew I understood U, meanin', when we met and started building, I saw U were just the type of man I need. Second, I spoke about understanding U, meaning, I let knowledge be known...

I started tellin' U how I felt and that I love U. Now my understanding is understood meanin' 1. I "3" why I love U + 2. 2. I show and prove I love u + 3. 3. U.N.I = Ly and Supremely © see it. Also, because I benefit from reflectin' U, we both have a lot in common true B.U.T ur more business minded than I am, and among other things, I'm learning how to be a more powerful person, inside and out especially under pressure... I really admire U. Mentally ur strength is immeasurable. U have zero doubts, zero boundaries, just a determines idea. U are invincible so I'm proud to be your Earth. I know I am swift and changeable, U are so equally intelligent, civilized, lovable, gentle, Big hearted, passionate, understanding, loyal, fair, just and true, inspiring, supreme.

All the above and all mine (smile)

I'm grateful to get ur only phone call every moon, trust me and I want to show u that I'm here to play my position as ur wife, secretary, Queen, business partner, best friend, night nurse (even in the day time) Don Diva, Everything, all the time, Pro-Shakim !!!

I must reflect U, so my impact has to hit N_____AZ wit identical strength as if U was here. I just wanna rep U right and exact baby so I be building myself up and preparing myself to maintain my emotions and focus only on what I need to stay focused on.

It's no question that I love U all the way Shakim, no matter what.

9 -12- 21

PS I'm still waitin' to hear about the V-day gift N_____A!!

*****

"She said she got a man, but he's in the Feds/

And she miss him so much, that she peez in the bed"

Jadakiss' verse "Ryde or die Chick"

L.O.X. featuring Eve

CHAPTER 19

The Feds move real funny...

Thursday night I put in my commissary slip, I ordered food, stamps, the usual even though I didn't need it. I was extra heavy on everything and living very comfortable in the box. Friday morning, I was up a 5 a.m., layin' back on my style, not working out. I was just lookin' forward to the Friday night jump off on XM Satellite Radio. By 6am, breakfast was served. While the C.O.s was passing out the food trays, they let it be known that there was no rec that day.

"What the Fuck is going on?" my celly asked.

"A lot of y'all are being packed out!" was the response.

"Is that so?" I asked.

"Yeah Edwards, you are one of the ones being packed out"

WOW... just when I thought I was going back to the compound, they spun me and transferred me. A few hours later, I was taken to R & D to pack my property, which took another hour due to how much property I had in storage.

"Where am I going?" I asked the R & D officer.

"Not allowed to tell you Edwards" replied the racist hillbilly officer.

That night I was on the door shouting down to my dude Carlos from the Polo Grounds in Harlem. He caught his Fed ordeal in Baltimore, MD in the early 90s. I left him a lot of commissary food, he was in the box under investigation. He was a known move maker so we kicked it all night as I promised to leave him all the hygiene and food items I still had in the cell, which was a lot. He kept telling me "Sha, they're gonna move you tomorrow."...

"Nah Sun, Tomorrow is Saturday. I'm leave Monday or Tuesday"

"Shakim, Dem peoples is coming to get you about 4am Saturday morning"

I don't know how he knew but he was on point. About 3:30am, a C.O. turned my light on just as I was goin' to rest.

"Edwards"

"What?"

"Get ready! You're leaving, I'll be back in 20 minutes"

Carlos, who was 3 cells down, heard the C.O. say that and he called out...

"Sha"

"Yeah Son... you was right... I'm leavin' everything in here to you"

I instructed my celly to send everything down to Carlos then I took a shower, brushed my teeth and got ready to leave U.S.P. Lee County on a mothafuckin' Saturday.

*****

Three C.O.s escorted me to R & D. On my way through the halls, yells and shouts was coming from every range as convicts banged on the doors crazily, saluting and saying farewells to the God Shakim Bio-Chemical Wise... Queens' illest. I was slow walking in shackles and handcuffs, nodding my head to convicts, who looked out their cell door windows and I saluted those I left behind... 22 moons (22 months, just under two years) in the box was now over, a done deal... a wrap.

*****

There were eight of us on the bus to... I had no idea where we were going. I was thinking U.S.P. Atlanta, which to me, would have been a very good look. My manz "Slash K", from Irvington N.J. (but rep Newark/Brick City) was on the bus with me. He was an East Coast Crip from the Grape Street set. I taught him mathematics and he was doing well. He acknowledged Supreme Math, Alphabets, his new attribute was "Born King", 1 – 10, 1- 36, and he was ready for the 1 – 14.

Civilizing "Slash K" was hard and took about a year of long debates and discussions because he was a sincere, poison animal eater and very young, very wild and very ready for war. That's why he was on the bus with me. He was known to knock cats out.

"Shakim Bio!!" shouted Born King.

"Peace to the God!!" I responded.

"I'm glad to see a real one is coming with me." he said.

"Likewise" I shot back.

I was studying the highways and Interstate signs, nothing was really registering but I was also looking at the license plates of the cars on the highway. The bus driver was taking a lot of back roads and short cuts so I remained on point throughout the whole journey.

*****

After riding for about three hours, I realized that most of the cars had Kentucky license plates so we were somewhere in Kentucky. I went through my thoughts to pinpoint where they were taking us. There was a new U.S.P. in Kentucky called "Big Sandy". It was in Inez, Kentucky, a town not even in the almanac being that they didn't have more than 16,500 or more inhabitants. The prison had been open about 18 months or so and most of the town's population worked there. It was the only place out there in that unknown town that was exactly two hours from both Louisville and Lexington, Kentucky. "Big Sandy" was more close to the state of West Virginia than anything and was built the same way as U.S.P. Lee County but instead of being built inside of a mountain, it was on top of a mountain. We arrived and was processed, after that we were "Fed dressed" and put in their SHU so I was in a new spot but back in the box.

*****

Me and Born King were cellies in the box, we were waiting on Monday for the captain's review. A captain's review is when the captain pulls you out and interviews you one on one with his executive staff to see if you're eligible to walk his compound.

About 2pm, an orderly came up the tier sweeping the floor; he also was looking in the cell windows and checking out the I.D. bed cards to see who the new arrivals that landed on a "Saturday" were. Arriving on a Saturday transfer was unheard of to many. The orderly stopped at our door and peeked in.

"What's up?" asked Born King.

"Anybody from New York or Baltimore come with y'all?"

Seeing that Born's number ended with 050, which is New Jersey and mine ends with 083, which is Virginia, he automatically thought that that's where we were from.

"Why? Who's asking?" responded Born King.

While Born was at the door, I was sitting on the iron stool attached to the table.

"Nah there's a kid named Universal on the next tier, he's asking if he had any homies from N.Y. and I'm from B-more." said the orderly.

181

"Universal?" I say to Born "Yo ask him if "Universal" is Andrew Johnson."

"Yeah" responds the orderly.

"Well tell him that I'm Shakim Bio from Queens, he knows who that is but before you go, what part of B-more you from?" says Born, who is now playing a game.

The orderly looked shocked to hear this, he said...

"I'm from Cherry Hill"

"OH yeah?" asked Born.

He looked at me so I'd know to go along with his game and give him some streets and names being that I was in Baltimore real deep in the early 90's so I said...

"Tell him you was on Emondson Ave, North Ave and Warwick, all over West"

As Born relayed what I said like it was him who was in the know, the orderly said he would be right back and left the tier.

*****

Me and Born was laughing

"Yo, you shoulda seen the look on his face when I said that" chuckled Born.

I was laughing because Born King a.k.a. Slash K is 6'2", weighed about 230 lbs and was dark skinned with braids in his hair. He also had tattoos of grapes on the corner of his left eye. He had "Grape St" in bold letters shaded in on his neck in the front on his throat area. So I could only imagine what the orderly dude thought seeing Born and hearing he was from Baltimore.

Thirty minutes later the orderly came back to our cell door.

"I got a care package for you in this bag and later on I'ma bring some cigarettes" said the orderly as he slid an envelope under the door.

The envelope was addressed to "Shakim Bio, Queens' Illest". As the orderly left the tier, Born picked up the envelope and passed it to me while asking...

"Damn Sha, who you know on this end?"

The envelope had a scribe in it to me from "Universal". I knew him as "Drew" because he was in Terre Haute U.S.P. with me like five years or so before I got there to Big Sandy... He was also from Far Rockaway, Queens; a hood I know so very well. I answered Born...

"Yeah, this Kyte is from Universal but I know him as "Drew". We were in the "Hut" together back in 98' -99' plus Son is from Far Rock."

"Word?" said Born, who was looking on as I read the scribe...

"Peace to the God!"

I'm happy to know a real one is here in Big Sandy. This pound is off the chain but nothing to someone like you. N.Y. is strong here and so are the Gods. As you can see, I have Knowledge Of Self now. I'm on my 1 – 40. I sent you a care package, I'll send cigarettes and stamps later thru the other orderly, who is a homie named Raheeme and he has K.O.S too. I'm back here (in the SHU) for eating this kids face, left him with 300 plus to remember me by. He stole from me so I told him he forgot something (smile). I been hearing about you too, I know you still rep hard. Far Rock is in the building. Shoot a

71

scribe back through Rah. Let me know what's good. How come you landed on a Saturday? Must be some heavy shit. I'm on D range, cell Wisdom-Cipher-Understanding.

One – One Universal

I told Born that our new spot, Big Sandy may be "Big Candy" for us but the only way to find out was to see for ourselves. I penned Universal a kyte in response and left it until the new orderly came up around 7pm.

*****

At U.S.P. Big Sandy, they served food to convicts who were in "the box" like how a king is served; shit was sweet. The food portions was huge, the food was on point and the kool aid tasted like a black person made it. The cells were built the same way as they were in Lee County (spot I just left). As the COs picked up the dinner trays, the pm orderly came up on the range, I heard convicts calling him...

"Yo Raheeme, come to cell 217!"

"Yo Big New York... come see me at 227!!"

"Hold the fuck up! I'ma make it down there Baby Pa".

As Raheeme pushed the broom and looked into cell windows as he went by, I could tell by his accent he was an Old School New Yorker. He made it to our cell, slid an envelope under the door and kept it moving down the range with his broom, stopping at other cells, doing drop offs, picking up kytes that were to be passed to other convicts, passing off magazines, newspapers and so on; he came back to our door again and looked in. Raheeme was brown-skinned with a bald head and a full but low cut, graying beard. He was like 6 feet tall, looked like he weighed 220 and he was type brolic... brolic meaning, it wasn't hard to tell that he took good care of himself and worked out. He also had a very ugly scar on the right side of his face that went from his temple to his chin and another one going across like he had a cross on his face. The scars appear to have healed well but they still told a story of a rough and grimey individual. Raheeme asked...

"Who in here from NY and which one of y'all is Shakim Bio?"

Before either one of us could respond, we both started laughing at this character at the door.

"What the fuck y'all find so funny? Y'all the funny ones, coming here on a Saturday" Raheeme said as he sized us up through the door window.

Believe it or not I was already familiar with Raheeme's case and story. The fed system was big yet small so I knew he was a goon from the 1980's and he was still caught up in that era in some ways. He was now serving a life sentence for a drug conspiracy, which he was actually innocent of because he wasn't a part of that organization. He was pressuring and extorting some dudes and they was paying him to stay out of their way. Raheeme was the only black dude on his case, the rest were all Hispanics and the only reason they didn't kill him was because it was better to just pay him to stay out their way but when everything came crashing down on them they turned around, lied and implicated him in their wrong doing.

"Knowledge - Knowledge Raheeme! I'm Shakim Bio-Chemical Wise" I introduced myself while sizing him up on the other side of the window.

"PEACE GOD! I'm "Raheeme Forever God" but for now I'm "Big Raheeme the orderly and nothing moves unless I'm in".

Before you knew it, Raheeme ("Rah") and I became acquainted and we gave each other a quick briefing of our histories. He told me his circumstances of being in the box and later that night slid the paperwork along with postage stamps and he left some extra cosmetics at the door for me and Slash a.k.a. Born King. That day, Raheeme came to our door every time he came out on the range and slid us some cigarettes. He told us...

"Yo... by Monday you will see the captain and he's gonna let both of y'all out"

"Ra" gave me the spill about how the compound operated, which was just like any other compound I been on. This United States Penitentiary was the fifth one I'd been in since 1993.

*****

CHAPTER 20

That Saturday and Sunday, I wrote letters to my Earth Oceasia to let her know my new whereabouts, even though my calls were gonna beat the letters. I wrote her because that was our daily routine and she looked forward to reading my thoughts through ink spots. Sunday was the same, we worked out, ate and slept through the afternoon until "Rah" came after 4pm with a kyte from "Universal", telling me I would see the captain and be out of the box tomorrow. Me and "Rah" kicked it for a few hours and I gave him my word that I would see what was up with the Gods and N.Y.ers to get him back out in population. I also told him where I would leave the hygiene and stuff if I went to the compound before he came out to clean up because I wouldn't need any of it once I touched the pound. I knew I would hit the commissary and buy everything I needed. So with that, "Rah" said his peace and trusted that I would be out and about on the compound moving around. He also gave me a kyte from "Universal" letting me know who from N.Y. I should build with when I got on the pound. I made sure I had two five page letters addressed to Oceasia and stuck them in the crack of the door so the C.O. would pick them up on his routine walk.

I took a shower and went to rest early so I could get my mentals prepared for the upcoming day. The next day, which was Monday, made exactly Wisdom-Wisdom (meaning 22 months) that I'd been in the box.

Monday morning both me and Born King were amped up. I didn't do my work out, push-up routines or nothing. I was up pacing the floor. The C.O.s brought the breakfast trays up early. We didn't ask no questions, didn't want to seem like we were new to this, only true to this. 45 minutes later they came door to door asking if we want "rec", we both accepted. The rec. yard in the SHU was incredibly bigger than Lee County's and it had so many kennel style cages to provide recreation to convicts who were on SHU status. I looked on as other convicts were brought out and placed in rec cages across from, on both sides of us and behind us. Shit was serious. It was a lot of small talk goin' on as some convicts asked me and Born King where we were from, where we came from and so on. Once the hour was up, we were cuffed and escorted back inside where they used a handheld metal detector to wave against us and under our feet and then we were taken back to our cell.

After a few hours of doing nothing but either pacing the cell or lying on my bunk, lunch was served. Those bastards fed us good in the box; it was a splendid meal but it didn't taste nothing like momma's. Born King was now pacing the floor as I sat on my bunk. As the C.O.s picked up the food trays, one of them said...

"Palmer... Edwards... get ready for captain's review! Back in 15 minutes!!"

The C.O. slammed the food slot in the middle of the door and turned the key, locking and securing it. I got up to brush my teeth and Born dropped down to do push-ups.

"Born King... what you doing G?"

"Getting ready and in Blast" he responded as we started laughing.

15 minutes passed and two C.O.s came to get us. We were cuffed up again, scanned with the handheld metal detector and escorted to a holding cell somewhere downstairs.

"Palmer!" barked one of the C.O's. as they came for Born King a.k.a. Slash K first. They re-cuffed him through the cell grill and took him down the hall through a door.

I sat down on the iron bench and waited my turn. I waited a good ten minutes before Born King came back with a serious look on his face. I went to the grill to be cuffed up so they could open up the holding cell to let Born King in and take me out.

"What's good?" I asked.

"I'm good" he replied.

"That's what's up." I said as I put my game face on and was escorted to see the captain of the "Big Sandy" U.S.P. ship.

*****

As soon as I came in the door, all I saw was the back of the captain's head and shoulders because he was facing the windows.

"Have a seat" was all he said to me.

I took a seat across from him. When he finally spun around in his chair, we locked eyes.

"Where do I know you from?" he asked as he looked at me knowing my face but was unable to place what U.S.P. he knew me from.

I smiled... I hadn't seen this piece of shit since I was in U.S.P. Terre Haute, where he was a lieutenant and straight up racist, cracker. Back then, we convicts called him "Lt. Dickhead".

"You know me from "Terror Hut" I said with a smile.

He looked at the stack of files piled up on top of each other on his desk.

"What's your name?"

"Edwards... John Edwards, just like Senator John Edwards"

"Almost Vice President" he said, laughing at his own dry joke. "here we are..."

He went through the pile of files, taking about a good five minutes, which was a long five minutes at that. He read some of my file aloud.

"John Edwards a.k.a. Shakim; Brooklyn, NY; drug conspiracy; big shot; Virginia number; detained in Ohio for murder; ran numerous states for the Gillins Enterprise; Ohio; Baltimore; the Carolinas; in custody since 1993; 40 year sentence; five years in U.S.P. Terre Haute; Marion... Super-Max? ...Yeah I recall you and that incident... Lompoc and Lee County... hmm.... indicted for drug possession... acquitted... several investigations.... you are a Five Percenter... ok... ok... my question to you is... is there any reason why you shouldn't walk my compound... any Issues?"

"None" I responded.

"Big Sandy is not like Lee County. You've been around so I know you will find your spot and fit in very well. Just need to let you know something... This isn't Lee County so you won't be calling any shots in my pen. I'm going to give you a clean slate here but the very moment you act up, we are coming to get you and you will spend another 2 years or more in the SHU before we decide to ship you elsewhere. I was "Lt. Dickhead" but I'm captain now. I'll give y'all space to move around as long as no one gets killed and none of my officers get hurt... so go do you're thing... but as soon as your name comes across my desk..."

Captain Dick Head stared at me...

"Yeah I know" I responded.

"Welcome to Big Sandy U.S.P. where Captain Dickhead is the boss".

At least the Dick Head knew nothin' had changed but his rank.

I was escorted back to the holding cell.

"What's good Shakim Bio?" asked Born King.

"I'm waiting to be kicked out to the compound" I smirked.

*****

While we were being escorted back to our range, the C.O.s told us to pack our stuff; the captain would be signing off on us and kicking us out to the compound so we were on the a.s.a.p. kick out list that quick.

"No doubt!" replied Born King.

*****

We were dressed out in the R & D khaki bus pants, dingy white t-shirt and blue karate shoes that was the new jack attire until one made it to laundry clothing issue. I knew Raheeme would find the scribe I left him along with the stamps and hygiene items I returned to him, leaving them inside the cells shower stall. It was like twelve of us being released from the box, we were lined up and given a bedroll and I saw that the units was stacked up on top of one another just like Lee County; 3 buildings, each with 4 units but even though the prison was newer than Lee County, it looked very ghetto. We were taken to laundry, where we gave our pants, shirts, boxers, t – shirts, boots and shoe sizes etc. etc. Then, we were escorted to the housing unit's walkway and told what units we were assigned to and which building it was located in. Me and Born King was assigned to the same unit so we made our way down the walkway. There were convicts posted on the walkway stopping and mean mugging the new arrivals, some were looking for a familiar face... be it the face of a friend or foe.

"Yo, where you from money?"

"Where you came from?"

These were some of the questions being asked as we new arrivals in the front made our way through.

"Oh shit! Shakim Bio... Peace to the God!" someone shouted.

I looked to the side and seen the God "Serious Wisdom" standing with a group of convicts, who were all wearing oversized khaki, beige, winter coats, some of them wore knitted skullies pulled down on their heads. I was right, "Big Sandy" was a straight up hood spot.

"Serious Wisdom... Peace God" I said as I stopped to give "Serious" a pound and embrace him with my free arm cause my bedroll was under the other.

"What's the science Lord?" He asked as he looked me up and down. "I see you still look the same... but you need a haircut!"

We busted out laughing. I knew "Serious" since we were in U.S.P. Lompoc, California together. The God was from Portsmouth, VA. He was brown-skinned, 6 feet tall, 220 lbs. He had the 360 waves but his front hair line was shaped up round with no point. The God was very swift with his math.

"Where are you coming from?" he asked.

"Lee County"

"Yeah, you left Lompoc to open up that spot" he remembered how we parted cause I left him all my food items.

"Yeah"

"What happened out there?" he asked me."

"Long story "G" but I'm good nevertheless..."

"No doubt, no doubt" he responded.

Serious introduced me to everyone standing there and I introduced him to my student "Born King".

"What block they got you in Sha?"

192

"C One unit"

"Come on, let me walk you that way and put you on point about this spot. Your N.Y. homies is real strong here. It was a little N.Y. beef when the God "Universal" cut this one cat but other than that, it's all love with the N.Y. car. The Gods here is very strong too. It's like wisdom-cipher of us but only half true and living... Yo! Hold the fuck up!!"

Serious stopped short, observing one of the new arrivals, who was walking toward us. We all posted up as Serious focused his attention on the kid as he bopped up the walkway.

"Calvin?" asked Serious, who was pointing his index finger at Dude.

"Yeah? What's up? Yo Serious, what's good?"

"What the fuck you think is good, Rat ass bastard"

Serious walked up on the dude Calvin and everyone surrounded the kid.

"I don't want no trouble Homie... I just got here and they ran me up outta the last spot... I been goin' hole to hole" the kid pleaded.

Out of nowhere someone pulled out an ice pick.

"It's either you leave by going back towards the SHU or you die right here!!"

With that being said, Calvin dropped his bedroll and ran full speed towards the directions of the SHU.

We all laughed.

"Yeah Sha, that kid was a rat from VA... he told on mad real dudes. He can't stay here. All cars is basically on the same page here as far as rats go but we know there are some hiding... let's roll out before Cee-ciphers pull us over"

We proceeded toward my new unit.

*****

There were convicts all outside the unit standing against the wall; some were on the staircase leading to the upstairs units. Some convicts were smoking cigarettes, some were outside just kicking the breeze and I saw a lot of convicts that I knew from other pens as they came to greet me and ask me what unit I was housed in. Serious introduced me to several convicts; I dapped and nodded my head in their direction.

"Yo, Sha, I'ma meet you up the walkway on the next rec move. I'ma bring you a care package, lay it all out for you, just make sure you come out on the move Sha."

"No Question Serious"

I gave him a pound with my free hand and stepped in the unit, which was built exactly like Lee County on the inside as well but there was no TV's in the TV room area. All the TV's was hanging in the air, I saw six 19 inch, color televisions as I made my way to the unit C.O.s office and knocked on the door. A small- structured white C.O. came out and said...

"Yes?"

"Edwards... I just came out of SHU."

"Palmer... just came out as well" Born said as he made his presence known too.

We were given the cell numbers we were assigned to and everyone was looking at us... When I got to my new cell, a big 6'6, 280lbs muscular cat with buck teeth was standing in there.

"What's up?" I asked him.

He looked me up and down and responded...

"Nothing much... I didn't know a bus came in today"

"Nah, I came in a few days ago... just got out of the box"

"Ok"

"I'm Shakim"

"Lawrence... but everyone calls me "Big L" or just "L".

"Ok" I responded.

"Where you from?"

"New York"

"I'm from Indiana" "L" said.

As big and intimidating as he looked, "L" wasn't only the biggest dude on the compound muscle- wise; he was also very smart and very humble. He offered me everything in his locker. I told him I was cool but he still went out his way to give me numerous items. He left them on my locker so that I would see it all later that night. Convicts in the unit came by the cell to be nosey and see who I was, being that I was the new dude and Born King was goin' through the same thing. I made my bed and went lookin' around the unit to see my new environment.

CHAPTER 21

On the next recreational move, I went outside to the front of the unit. I saw "Serious" coming towards my building with a small crowd; he was also carrying a net bag, which I knew was full of necessities and food, a radio and headphones for me until I got straight and my property arrived.

"Peace to the God!" I said as I came towards Serious to greet him.

"PEACE!"

"Peace God!" was said as I was greeted by several brothers who were with Serious.

"Peace God! I come in the name of Gifted Allah" said a brown seed, slim dude who greeted me and looked to be in pretty good shape for a man in his mid-forties.

"Peace to the God. I'm Universal Divine Prince God Allah".

"Peace! I'm Born Justice Allah"

"Peace, my attribute is Born Sun of Allah"

"Knowledge-knowledge, I come in the divine righteous name of Very True and Living Magnetic Allah"

"Knowledge-knowledge to my A-like, my attributes is and will always be The Infinite Al-Khadir Always God Allah"

"That's peace! My attributes is Shakim Bio – Chemical Wise" I said as I looked at the Gods whom I'd just met.

"Peace Sha! Yo, let's make this move to the gym... here... pass this bag off to someone in your unit"

Serious handed me a full net bag.

＊＊＊＊＊

The inside gym was located in the east corridor. Inside recreation was where the prison's gymnasium was located. They had music rooms, where musical instruments was kept, card tables with built-in chess / checkers and Backgammon boards. There were TV's, a room where you could watch dvd movies, a room to take photos with different backgrounds and they had a full size basketball court, numerous workout machines for the legs, stomach. There were bike machines, stair masters and a volleyball net on the other side for volleyball games. We went to the corner of the gym by the work out machines and formed a cipher. I learned that Al-Khadir was from South Carolina and was in his forties. "Divine Prince" was from Raliegh, N.C., "Born Justice" was from Akron, Ohio and "Born Sun" was from Mount Vernon N.Y., "True and Living" was from Brownsville and "Gifted" was from Harlem. What was ill was that all of them knew One-Twenty and built regularly everyday on one basis until they were able to show and prove. Parliaments was held every last Sunday of the month and all Gods must be there.

We built and I got more familiarized with the God bodies at Big Sandy and I learned the rotation of the Power Paper and in what order it circulated from one God to the next. I made Knowledge Born that I was to receive the Power Paper as well and after goin' over that day's math, I revealed that I had an Earth who was also a journalist in the monthly Power Paper.

"That's peace… How long did you know her and how did y'all meet?" asked Serious as I gave them the sciences that captivated everyone's mind.

"That's Peace… you said she knows 120? Does she stay in three-fourths?" asked Al-Khadir.

197

I learnt from being in Al-Khadir's presence for that hour that he was into specifics and details.

"Now cipher, she isn't in three-fourths" I responded.

"How come? The Earth is approximately covered under water over approximately three-fourths of her surface!!"

"True Indeed... but it will take time to get her back in time fully" I said giving the God a cold stare.

"She from N.O., huh? I remember reading a couple articles written by her. I almost wrote that Earth too... she got any Earth friends or sisters?' inquired True.

I automatically recognized that "True" was very scientific and very dogmatic; he carried it like a Brooklyn dude. He thought he was a lady's charmer with his light brown eyes and wavy low cut hair. "True" had a show and prove explanation for everything. I'd been around Gods like him and he was the kind who always wanted to take control of everything.

"No, she doesn't have any sisters, born u truth she may have some friends. You shoulda wrote her if her build in the article caught your attention. I penned her and now we official" I said, giving him the answer he wasn't looking for.

"I got pictures tickets so we will take reflections real soon." he replied.

"After the culture hour (4pm), come out to chow... I'ma show you the N.Y. homies, introduce you to everyone and show you around." he added.

"Ok... it's "True and Living"... right?" I asked again.

"Why equal self (YES).... but call me "True" for short".

"True Indeed".

We sized each other up and Serious, knowing me personally, caught on that.

Everything was peace so I brought up the Raheeme ordeal and it was agreed that the Gods would step up to get him out. We kept the cipher going until the move was called. Everyone said their "Peace" and we departed. Serious walked me back with the God "Gift" in tow.

"Shakim Bio. I'm glad you are here" admitted Serious.

"No doubt... I'm glad I'm here too."

"Yo, another thing... that's how "True" is God... I peeped how y'all was sizing each other up"

"It aint nothin', it was a N. Why (NY) / Brooklyn - Queens type thing" I said with a smile.

"Gift" being an older God and typical Harlem head butted in...

"Uptown is where everything is at"

"Yeah? Well Shakim Bio from Queens is where everything is at now"

We all started laughing as we walked towards C building.

* * * * *

After almost two years in the box, it felt good being able to move around again. I linked back up with Born King, who had already found the Crip car and was around them. I asked son where he stood, knowing that he had K.O.S. and he couldn't rep gang banging at the same time. I told him he had to draw the line and show and prove where his loyalty stood. I saw in his eyes that he wasn't built to be a

Universal Builder. No hard feelings "B" but I'm God Forever... the only two masters I can serve is "self" and "Truth" which is my true self.

*****

I couldn't wait until tomorrow because the computer would automatically have me programmed into their system as being on the compound. For me to use the phone or go to commissary, my numbers and account follows me throughout the Fed system; they transfer along with you, your register number and 9 pac digit code stays the same it just takes a day to be activated. So I couldn't make no calls or go to the store because the computer still showed me being housed in the SHU... I couldn't wait to call my Earth.

*****

After 4pm stand up count, we came out and I was a laying back focusing on my thoughts. I couldn't wait until my property touched so I could complete my "Last Illest" novel project. Chow hall was called and I journeyed outside leading to chow, which was in the west corridor. Outside it was like the projects; convicts was out there in scattered groups and the C.O.s wasn't even trying to let it be known that group crowding was not allowed. Convicts stood all leaned up on the walls of units, in the grass areas, all on the cement walkway and were leaning up on the yard's fence. It had that real ghetto project feel to it and all the groups were geographical or clicked up in some way.

After entering the west corridor and clearing the metal detector, I went inside the chow hall, which had about 200, 4 seat tables. It was a dirty egg shell white wall with a stainless steel, hot bar of rice, pans of beans and soup and a stainless steel salad bar with big bowls of salad and numerous different dressings. There were 2 lines leading up to where the main course was served with drink dispensers and soda machines. They had roast beef and gravy with a side order of mash potatoes. I didn't eat red meat so I went and got me a salad at the salad bar. "True" waved me over to where he was sitting; seated with him and at the tables on both sides of him, were convicts staring at me hard. I was now in the New York section.

"Shakim, this is where the New Yorkers sit and eat at" said True, who began introducing everyone around him one by one.

"Miz from Bk, El from Bk, Do Dirt from L.I., O-Dog from Bx."

True was pointing dudes out and naming names, I just nodded my head, acknowledging everyone. Not one of them offered me a place to sit as I stood with my tray. I made myself comfortable by placing my tray on the table so True then got up to let me sit.

"What spot you come from?"

"Lee County"

"Word? You know King Tut from Bk?"

"Who don't know Tut?" I answered.

"La-Sun from Brooklyn still there?"

"Nah... he went up top cause he wasn't right"

"Huh?"

"Yeah. Duke was pork chops smothered in gravy, heavy on the onions Duke" I snubbed and made sure that I was understood. After kicking it back and forth for a minute, "Miz" asked me what I needed. I told him I was good. My property should have come with me so I may get it tomorrow...

"but I need a shank".

"No problem... what else?"

"Nothing else" I answered.

"How long you been in?" Miz asked me.

"Since 93"

"Word? You been in a while then, what other spots you been at?"

"A few."

"You from where in N.Y.?"

"Queens!"

"You on Prince and them case?"

"Nah"

"You know this one cat named Bio-Chemical?"

I smirked and said...

"You're looking at him"

"Word?"

"Word!" I reassured him.

"You Big Tiz and them Co-dee?"

"True Indeed"

"Yo Sha, let me know what you need, whatever it is... I got you"

"I'm good. No doubt... but as soon as my property touches I'ma set my paperwork out"

Everyone looked at each other than back at me.

*****

5:30 A.M. THE NEXT MORNING

The next morning, as soon as the doors were opened, I was up, dressed and ready. I was waiting for the phones to come on, which was at 5:45am. I had 15 to minutes to wait so I went under the stair- well grills and did a few sets of pull-ups, where I was a monster.

5:50 A.M.

After doing close to twelve sets, I walked over to one of the right phones stalls, picked up and dialed 118, then my 9 pac digit to check my available balance, my phone account and how many phone minutes I had. Since 2001, they came with a three hundred minute a month per inmate thing. It was a whole lot of poli-TRICKS that played a part in what really made this plan go in effect but it affected everyone in the Federal System. Three hundred minutes wasn't enough for the average convict but we had to work with what we had and improvise to make ways like a real convict does and that's exactly what I do. I just didn't secure a way as of yet but in a day or two...

I transferred funds to my phone, hung up and caught a dial tone, then dialed my Earth's number. An automated voice spoke to me...

"Please say your name at the Beep"

Beep ... "Shakim"

My name would remain on the phone recording until I transfer again.

"Thank you" the automated voice on the phone said.

The call went through and the phone started to ring on Oceasia's end.

After 4 to 5 rings

"Heh... hello?"

Again, an automated voice spoke but this time it was speaking to Oceasia... my Earth.

"This call is from a Federal prison. It is a pre-paid call. You will not be charged for this call. This call is from… "Shakim"… To accept this call dial 5 now… to deny this call hang up now… to prevent this person from calling dial 7."

Oceasia pressed "5" and I said...

"Peace Ma"

"Baby… Peace! Where you at and how you get to call me so early?"

I explained to her that I transferred to Kentucky and that I was out and about moving around in population. She was very happy...

"You gonna to call me every day… right?"

"Of course… you already know and understand this"

"I miss you so much."

"I miss you too, Ma."

"I need you to call me every morning at this time too. I gotta hear your voice, that's how I gotta wake up."

"No doubt... You got that" I answered.

"You need anything? Money?" she asked.

"Nah, I'm good… I just need you."

"Find out exactly where you are and how far… matter of fact. I'ma go on the computer, I gotta come see you."

"Hurry up my Queen! I need to hug, squeeze and taste you."

"Hmmmm... I love that" she replied.

"Yeah... and I love you" I spitted back.

"I love you Shakim"

      We kicked it for the entire 15 minutes; it was all love. I was so happy to kick it with her and hear her voice and she was just as happy.

Then the phone beeped, warning us that the end of the conversation was approaching and the call would be terminated.

"Baby... when you calling me back?"

"In understanding Cipher" I responded.

"A month?"

"Nah, minutes ma... thirty minutes"

"Make sure you secure another love Islam now equal"

"You already know"

BEEP

"I love you Shakim"

"I love you more my Earth"

"Nine – twelve – twenty one "

"True Indeed"

"Word is Bond"

Click

Not only did they only give us a measly 300 phone minutes per month but we had to wait 30 minutes before we could make another call. From the time me and Oceasia hung up... it was a 30 minute waiting grace period. That was enough time for me to skate to Breakfast and come back in time to hit her back so that's what I did because I needed to do something to make the 30 minutes go by quickly.

*****

CHAPTER 22

Chow was called so I walked to the chow hall for breakfast. I'm not really a breakfast or coffee drinking kinda dude but I wanted to show my face and at the same time, see who the early birds were. Entering the chow hall, I got off of the line and went over to the tables where the New Yorkers sat. True God was sitting there with a few other cats I hadn't met yet.

"Peace to the God"

"Peace True God! What's the science with you?" I responded.

"Just getting a cup of coffee. Yo, this is Cat, Flash and Miller... This is the new homie, who just came from Lee County, Shakim from Queens'. I seen that "True" was a real character, always sarcastic and making sure to let heads know I was from Queens.

"You Tiz Co-dee?"

"True Indeed"

"Where he at now?"

"Otisville"

"Yo, Sha, I can get you a job detail in the corridor with me if you give me your government name and number" said True.

"Ok... we can do that... and by the way, no need to be funny, my case is on the computer down at the library"

The fellas at the table started laughing.

"I'ma make sure I bring that cop out too... which way to R & D? So I can check up on receiving my property"

"I'ma show you" responded "Flash".

"Aiight, I'ma see you peeps later.....Peace!"

I made my way to the door with "Flash" catching up to me.

*****

After being shown where R & D was and making it back outside towards the unit, I bumped into Serious...

"Peace God!"

"Peace! What's the science Sha?"

"Not much, on my way back to the unit to get back on that phone!"

"No doubt. Yo, we all steppin' to the captain at lunch time about Raheeme. You got his government – right?"

"True Indeed... Lonnie Redmon" I responded.

"Ok Gee, See you then"

We dapped up and I made my way back to the unit.

*****

Back to the unit, I went straight to the phones and dialed those numbers and my pac digits right behind it in one sequence"... Once again, the automated voice said...

"Thank you"

The phone rings...

On the third ring, Oceasia picked up and after the recording came on she immediately pressed "5".

"What took you so long to call me back?"

"Ma, Stop playing"

We burned another 15 minutes, renewing our vows and love for one another.

BEEP

"Damn Baby... when you gonna call me back?"

"Later on tonight... let me move around and do what I do."

"Ok stay on point and please stay out of trouble."

"No doubt"

"Can you please kiss me"

I blew her a kiss.

"I need another one"

I did it again.

"I love you Shakim:

"Nine – twelve – twenty one Baby Girl"

We ended our call.

*****

From that morning on, that became my everyday routine. Me and Oceasia spoke twice a day until I was able to buy another phone. There were convicts who didn't have money coming so they sold their phone minutes as a hustle. I needed three, sometimes four phone lines so I had to buy the minutes by sending money to convict accounts and they put the money on their phone along with adding the numbers I was calling on their phone lists. This was illegal business, if caught, I was

209

subject to catching an incident report and disciplinary action but I felt like "fuck it! Who cares?" This is how we move in these concrete and steel jungles... these are the chances we take...

*****

I was starting to get familiarized with the facility, my new surroundings; the N.Y. car; my A-likes, B-likes, and C-likes. I got my property, made it to commissary and secured 2 phones so I was good for the time being. I even secured the orderly job detail in the corridor in the mornings with True God, where we got to build on a one on one basis and he wasn't a bad guy after all. He was from the Brownsville section of Brooklyn but caught a gun case in Rhode Island. They "careered" him and gave him 24 years. 24 years? That's time you get for a murder... not for gun possession and they didn't even find the firearm on him or in his possession. How the hell was it even a Fed case? He knew his lessons real well and he was able to show and prove. "True" was peace, just real slick with the tongue and always wanted to take control in every situation and have some kind of say so. I let True, Miz and Dirt of the N.Y. car and the Gods all see my paperwork.

I was moving around mingling with the convicts I knew from previous institutions and meeting new ones. The Gods were real peace as well and kept me on my toes. We could be speaking on anything and it would turn into a show and prove of either lessons or the science of mathematics dealing with the current events of life itself. Al – Khadir was the mad scientist God, he was the type to put together his own understanding, type it up and pass it around claiming it was a "plus degree". He even went to the extreme of giving a white dude an attribute of "Sincere Understanding' and he was feeding him mathematics claiming that the white dude was really a "half-original" from Pakistan somewhere but the God "Serious Wisdom" wasn't having it. I also found out that Al- Khadir was Universal's enlightener... shoulda known...

Out of the convicts from N.Y., I was more in tune with a dude who called himself "Do Dirt". Do Dirt was golden brown-skinned, 5'10 about 180 lbs., semi-built with shoulder length dreads. He carried himself like a hardcore Brooklyn cat but was actually from the suburbs of Central Islip, Long Island. He was in and out of jails but was a bookworm. He was also part of the rapper Keith Murray's "Legion of Doom" (L.O.D) clique and was in the Feds for robbing drug dealers. Me and Miz kicked it a lot; what's so funny is as I got familiarized with these catz, we realized we knew a lot of the same peopleand Co-dees from Fed and state cases. The New York "Car" was a real nice tight knit car; dudes supported each other.

We all stepped to the captain after me and the God bodies spoke up for Raheeme. We even approached the "car" that got into it with Raheeme and came to a positive resolution. I got my work out schedule on point and I was workin' out twice a day plus I dedicated two hours a day to the law library which was computerized. I definitely found my place and was now plotting and scheming to generate and stack some currency.

Me and Oceasia were constant with the letters to each other, the phone calls couldn't interrupt that. We were each other's medicine when it came to that aspect. I was writing a lot of poetry to her, letting her know how much she meant to me. There were so many creative convicts, who were incarcerated and using their talents as hustles at Big Sandy. There were artists who could draw so accurate that they should be drawing architecture structures of buildings. I had portraits drawn so beautiful to the naked eye; drawn with so much meaning. I was getting personalized custom made cards with special drawings and I did my own poetry in them. I was surprising Oceasia left and right, she looked forward to my calls every morning and throughout each day. I'd place a quick call before 6 am to tell her that I love her. She was one hour

211

behind time wise so it was 5 am on her end... She was tired from working double shifts, managing the small boutique shop and making time to go to the recording studios. I was politicking and networking on the phones to make moves to have her music be heard. The entertainment lawyer wanted a copy of her press kit with bio and five track demo and I was still networking with my imprisoned partner Monday, trying to get Lyfe Jennings on a track with her. Things were slow motion but slowly coming together. I took a lot of focus off my novel project (Last Illest) but I still found the time to complete the street Hop story and type up the last remaining pages.

Every day was a busy, hectic day but I made time whenever I was able to move around and make moves that made a difference. Big Raheeme came out of the box and it was like he was running for mayor. I didn't know he was that much of a prison celebrity. Everyone from all walks of life came to shake his hand and acknowledge him. Everyone damn near came to show gratitude, even C.O.'s stopped him on the walkway to welcome him back and believe me, Raheeme was a real talkative person so he would stand there and hold court without paying attention to time. He lived in the unit on top of my unit so we stayed in the same section. Raheeme brought everyone together, he was that kind of person. Everything was peace, I used to walk up into his unit and kick it with him for several hours. He was very old school and game tight on some 1987 shit. He was showing me his extensive photo album of him in his glory days in East, N.Y., Brooklyn and in up-north prisons. He still had his pants straight legged at the ankles that he sewed himself. His sneakers were laced "back in the day style" and he kept his workout gloves (with the fingers cut off) in his back pocket. One time, we were going through his album and he showed me reflections of his children, family and different females he had in his life. I notice that a lot of recent photos with the same background was taken there in Big Sandy.

"Where this at?" I asked.

"This is right here in Big Sandy" he responded.

"Yeah... who's Shorty?" I asked.

"This cat in ATL plugged me with her and we started writing and feeling each other. Her name is Rita. She's from West Virginia, which is like two and half hours away from here. That's my Baby right there"

Rah started smiling as I looked at the numerous pages of her in his album.

"Yeah? My shorty name is Rita as well... I mean she spits under the name "Rita Books".

"Maybe we can link them and she can fly this way and parlay when it's time to visit" suggested Big Rah.

"I was just thinking about that" I responded.

"Yeah... Rita and Rita"

We laughed.

*****

"Slash K, what's good sun?"

I greeted slash, who was formerly known as "Born King" until he picked back up on his Cripful ways.

"Sha Bio... Peace! Yo, believe it or not my dude, even though you are not feeding me, I'm still gonna knowledge 120"

"I hear you Slash, you still my dude"

We dapped up and I kept it moving to my cell. I had to scribe my Earth two scribes and get this card in the mail to her. I met this one cat by accident, while I was in line in the chow hall. He was an older cat standing in front of me and I peeped him opening up an ill pop up card, when he opened it, a heart came out. It was amazing.

"Yo!" I barked. "Excuse me old head… but who made that card?"

"I did young brother" he replied.

"Yeah? How much would it cost for another?" I asked him.

"Hmmm… because it takes a nice bit of time to make it then put it together. I will need a book and half of stamps."

A book and a half of stamps equated to $7.50 black market.

"Ok old head. I need four cards done" I spitted.

"Four?"

"Yeah. I need four of them" I repeated.

"What's your name and what unit you in?"

"Shakim. Unit C-one… oh and the cards are all goin' to the same person so change it up a bit. I need one like that, one with a photo of me and my wife poppin' out, one with a diamond ring poppin' out and I'ma give you a photo of my facial. I need that poppin' out a card just for her".

"Ok, ok. My name is Charles, Unit B – 3"

Me and Charles shook hands.

"Bet… I'ma pay you now but bring me the cards one at a time, as soon as you complete each one.

"I need her name" he stated.

"Hold on… let me get a pen and write it out… the mailroom aint gonna beef about me flying out padded cards that pop-up, right?"

"Nah, they know I make them... it aint no problem."

"Ok then... Let's do this!"

I gave him the stamps up front... I walked around heavy in the pockets like that.

$$*****$$

I could be outside with the N.Y. Guerillas / Gorillas on the yard talking about anything; building with the Gods or sitting in the middle of a rap cipher but as soon as they called a recreational move, I was off to the unit.

"Damn Shakim – Bio, we out here kicking it and having fun, where you goin'?" They would ask me.

"Yo, I got to go call my wifey B!" I always responded.

That's how it was with me, I made time for all things but I put wifey first. It was like she was almost there next to Mom Duke. Sometimes I used to feel the jealousy, envy and hate from other convicts, especially when I spoke about my earth cause my face lit up and my attitude would change. I didn't have to mean mug or act thuggish, thinkin' of her and speakin' on her changed all that. Being in prison, some convicts don't have no females they can call, write to or get a letters and cards from. They have no one to send cards to, they're not fortunate to have a shorty in their corner who they can talk about the way I talked about my Earth. It's sad but very true...

When I picked up my first pop-up card from Mr. Charles and was coming through the yard back to the unit, I stopped to dap the fellas...

"What's good?" I greeted cats and gave them pounds (handshakes with closed fists).

215

"Yo, Sun... what's that you got?"

"A card... this old head makes them." I responded.

"Let me check it out"

I passed it to Miz and he checked out the front.

"This shit is real nice" said Miz as he opened the card and the heart popped up with "Shakim Loves Oceasia" carved out fancy.

"OH Shit!!" he said, opening and closing the card again and again to peep just how ill the card really was. He said... "This shit is bananas!"

Other convicts started circling him, wanting to see the card and play with it like it was a toy.

"Ahite, Ahite Fam... pass the card. Y'all finger fucking my shorty's card".

"Damn Sha, this is some fly ass shit Sun".

"Word!" agreed others.

"Yo, how much this joint cost?" inquired Miz.

"Like 2 books" I answered.

"Damn, you doin' it like that for her? That's like ten dollars Sun, you must love her. This the same one you be bouncing to go call when we be wanting to chill?"

"Yeah, that's my shorty" I replied.

"Damn, I wish I had someone special to send something like this" Miz said, handing the card back to me. "Yeah Sha, you a lucky dude to have someone to love who loves you back. I see the spark in your eyes and you smile about this chick".

"No doubt, that's my girl. Anyway I gotta get goin', can't keep her waiting, she got that phone in her hand waiting for it to ring" laughter erupted as I moved towards the unit.

CHAPTER 23

"This call is from a Federal prison... This is a prepaid call... you will not be charged for this call... This call is from..."

Oceasia pressed "5" before the recording could say my name.

"Peace!"

"Peace Sha, why you just now calling me? I been waiting all day"

"I know, I let time pass. I didn't know it was that late.

"Not you, you're always on time. What's going on? Where's your watch?"

Oceasia's line of questions had me laughing.

"What's so funny? You better not be calling another bitch!!"

"Chill ma, it aint nothin'. My watch just stopped working. I went and brought a new battery but shit still don't work. Don't sweat it ma... what's good?"

"You... always you" she responded.

"That's right"

We built for the whole 15 minutes, Oceasia wanted to come see me but for some reason she wasn't on my visitor's list no more. She had to fill out another visiting form and mail it in. I told her about Rah's girl "Rita" and gave her the mathematics so she could call and get acquainted with her.

"Make sure you give her my math too" she demanded.

"Ok"

"When y'all go to the store?"

"Tomorrow... I think"

"What you getting'?" she inquired

"You know....my favorite Hot Cocoa and I'ma cop a pair of Air Force ones."

"What kind?"

"The black lows"

The phone beeped, warning us that the call was coming to an end.

"Make sure you call me early!" she demanded.

"I got you, My BBD" I reminded her.

"I love when you call me that."

"I know... that's one of your titles"

"(sigh)... make sure you call early and order a new watch"

"Chill... I got you ma."

"No... I got you....check your account tomorrow. I'ma send you some current so you can get a new watch and another pair of Air Forces."

"Nah, I'm good" I told her.

"I'ma make sure you good... nine – twelve – twenty one."

"I love you too" I responded.

"You better call at the power hour"

(Beep)

"Equality" I kicked back.

"Well it's 'power' over here" she spitted back.

"Got you... Love you"

"Love you... front and back"

(<u>click</u>)

✶✶✶✶✶

One thing about my Oceasia... she loved to spend money nonstop and never seemed to save any. She had bank account and paid all her family's bills, being that she was now her mother's only child after her brother's tragic death. She had a lot of responsibilities in caring for his seeds so I always told her to save money so she could start her own business and expand the boutique. She was crazy generous but I'm not the type to accept handouts. I'm a "go getter" and I wanted her to start a music publishing company then start her own music catalog so she could sell songs and shit like that. I wanted her to see into the future, look at the bigger picture and not just live for now but she loved to spend her money just as fast as she got paid. She loved spoiling me too. It was all good but a fella of my caliber wasn't about letting no wisdom take care of me. <u>Nah</u>, I gets <u>BUSY</u>.

✶✶✶✶✶

Every day after lunch, me and Dirt walked the track and built about makin' moves out in the world. I told him about my Street-Hop novel and Sun saw my vision. He too, was a writer and spitter.

"My novel gon' change the game" I said as we spun (circled, did laps, walked around) the track.

220

"I feel ya playboy. I read the first chapter and was hooked!!" exclaimed Dirt.

"Yeah... If I can get you to have your peeps Keith Murray peep it and stamp it official... I could attract more heads" I added.

"True dat... but Son just lost his Def Jam push. He did some dumb shit and got kicked off the label. You know since he been home from that assault shit he been wilding out."

"Damn... Dirt"

"Yeah if I was home, I woulda took that case for him."

Dirt could spit... he sounded like a Lloyd Banks from Fifty's G Unit.

"I can't do no more bids my dude... this is it? After this, I'm goin' all the way legit."

"That's right" I responded.

"Yeah and your novel, "The Last Illest" is what's gonna put me on or in the door".

"Yeah... let's do that!" I said as I smiled and we kept spinning the track.

I told Dirt about my shorty's spitting skills and how I was tryna get her on by all means. He definitely saw my vision, my struggle and the moves I was makin' to make things manifest.

"I gotta salute you for your realness, my dude. I know whenever you touch you gonna shine and if you never touch, you still gon' shine" kicked Dirt.

"Yo Dirt, on everything, I'ma get my soul train Lifetime Achievement Award and I'ma walk up there with my bop and thank the haters. I love

221

the love and appreciate the hate and I'ma shout out all the real ones behind enemy lines to let them know it can be done" I spitted.

"You and Rita B?" asked Dirt.

"Yeah Dirt... me and Rita"

I was smiling my ass off.

*****

After 4pm count.

Out of nowhere, I received a letter and some photos from Tammi. As I read the letter and looked at her photos, I couldn't believe she looked me up and found me. She was lookin' good too... She left her number just in case I forgot it. I threw the envelope under my mattress with the rest of my junk mail.

*****

This call is from a Federal prison...This is a prepaid call... You will not be charged for this call... This call is from...

"Baby?"

"What's good my Earth?"

"I got a surprise for you!"

"What? You'll be here this weekend?"

We laughed.

"I wish I was on my way."

"Me too" I shot back... "What's the surprise?" I had to ask.

"If I tell you, it won't be a surprise!"

"Ok then... surprise me"

"You better like my surprise too"

"I like everything about you."

"You suppose to love everything about me."

"Stop it... you know what I mean."

We went back and forth having fun and I knew she was gonna bug out when she got that pop-up card in two more days. I was wondering what her surprise was, what if it was a pop-up card too.

"I gotta go to the studio and spit these vocals on this track I been workin' on these past couple days."

"Yeah? What's the name of the song?"

"Distance!"

"What is it about?" I inquired.

"Can't tell you cause its part two of your surprise."

"Is that so?"

"True Indeed Mr. Edwards"

*****

Me and Big Raheeme was coming down the walkway, returning to our section of units when I seen Serious Wisdom, Al-Khadir, True God and Born Sun. They were all standing in the B section unit grass area.

"Peace to the Gods!"

"Peace Shakim Bio and Raheeme."

"No, it's Raheeme and Shakim Bee O or whatever... You see Big Raheeme first... Sha's with me!!"

We all laughed at Ol' School Raheeme.

"What's the science Lord?" asked Al-Khadir.

"Constant Elevation" I responded.

"Yo, what's the hour God?"

I looked at my new watch and said...

"Knowledge Power after the Knowledge Wisdom hour, why what's the deal?"

"We were goin' to meet up at the Knowledge hour in inside rec. to go over 120 and add on. What you doin' at the Knowledge hour?" asked Serious.

"Was gonna be in that law library born u truth I got a hour to spare... I'm out at the Wisdom hour though."

"Me too." kicked Raheeme.

"Ok, see you then" responded Serious.

"Peace!"

"Peace!!"

We bounced.

*****

When me and Rah got to inside recreation, it was slightly crowded because there was an aerobics class being held in the gymnasium. We still went in there by the Step-master and exercise bikes. Al-Khadir, Divine, Justice, Born Sun‚True, Serious and Gift were there.

"Peace!"

"Peace to the God"

The nine of us went through 120 in no time, which was peace. There were very few rusty swords, nevertheless, everything was peace. As Raheeme came forward to speak...

"I would like thank all you brothers for comin' together and steppin' up to speak on my behalf, which led to me bein' here now. I thought y'all left me for dead. Bein' back there in the box for Power moons (5 Months) gave me enough time to regroup, reorganize, focus on my case more, re-new my history and workout just in case I woulda bumped into any of y'all in another spot. I was takin' it to you and whippin' that ass for leavin' me back there.

Everyone started laughing then Rah continued...

"Another thing... I would like to thank the God Shakim Bio-Energentic"...

Everyone started laughing again as Rah playfully messed up my attribute but then got serious.

"Nah... Shakim Bio-Chemical. The God came through showin' and provin' that his word is his bond so I wanted to thank him and y'all"

Rah extended his hand to me and I shook it then he said...

"Next time, I'ma whip y'all if I stay in the box that long."

Raheeme threw his hands up in some 1978 Fifty – two blocks fighting style. I said...

"That's peace. I'm glad to be amongst universal builders who constantly keep me on my toes, knowing and understanding the duty of a civilized man. Even though we locked up in these concentrating Federal spots, our duty is still the same, regardless of whom or what"

I looked around after making knowledge be born then I continued...

"As you already know, I got my property and y'all peeped my legal work. I'm at war for my ultimate freedom but don't take that as a dodging bullet cause I'm constantly movin'. I'm still walkin' and talkin' mathematics... I love to build and add on. You can catch me in the yard, law library, unit, whatever. Don't let the attribute "Shakim Bio-Chemical Wise" scare you. I also got a lot of degrees that I accumulated over the years; some are useful show and proves, others are ones that was just floating around. Whoever wanna do the "One" on them can do so. You know I'm in unit C-One... Anyway... (I looked at my watch), they about to call the rec move. I must journey to that law library so as I came, I leave you in Peace... PEACE!"

"PEACE!!"

We all dapped and embraced one another one by one.

*****

My day was semi-hectic as I read so many cases but none applied to me at all; doin' all that research can really burn you out. I went back to the block on the institutional recall at 3:15pm and as everyone came back to prepare for the 4pm stand up count, I went to take a shower before the shower stall line got crowded. It was five showers on the first floor and five on the second with 120 convicts to each unit. I was always gone most of the morning and day so I didn't really see my cellmate much. I would only see him in the chow hall or in passing so when he came in and saw me, he was smiling. Seein' this buck tooth, 6'6", 280 pound giant smilin' wasn't a nice sight to look at.

226

"L, what's good?" I asked him.

"These crackers got ten days to transfer me. I got 'em, my points is too low to house me in a Max Fed Pen. I'm supposed to be in a medium but my points is border line low status so I filed on them crackers. They can't justify why I'm here so they gotta do somethin'!!"

"I hear you Big L, I hear you." was all I could say.

"Yeah... but you aint gonna see me... watch! Ten Days!!"

As I looked at "L", he looked crazy... the look on his face made him look insane. I remember when I first came here and after a few days, I let him know I had a knife in the cell. It wasn't actually a real knife but a metal object sharpened to a point that was over eight and a half inches long. Big L damn near jumped on top of the lockers. He was so shook and excited, tellin' me I didn't need one of those in prison. He was a BIG SCAREY ASS DUDE.

And there he was lookin' crazy again...

"I'ma holla back at you big man... I need to touch this water before they lock us in for count"

I gathered my stuff and made my way to the showers.

They didn't pass mail until after we came out from count so I had time to take a ten minute shower and prepare a cup of hot cocoa to lock in the cell with.

*****

They released us from our cells like 25 minutes after count then it was mail call; I received three letters and a card. I looked at the return address on the card and seen it was from Tammi; Shorty was at me once again. Two letters was from my Earth and the other was from my street comrade. I noticed that both envelopes had "<u>DO NOT BEND –</u> <u>PHOTOS ENCLOSED</u>" on the envelopes so you know these were the ones I opened first. I went back to the cell and moved my chair over by the window so I could listen to the radio and read. Big Sandy U.S.P. had satellite radio too but it wasn't XM. They had Sirius Radio so we got to listen to Shade 45, which was owned by the rapper Eminem. That station was hot, they played all the exclusives. Cipha Sounds had the Morning Show Monday through Friday, Tuesdays was DJ Green Lantern's. On Wednesdays, DJ Kay Slay was killin' shit and throwin' bums under the bus. Thursday was DJ Clinton sparks and Saturday was G Unit radio so from 10 a.m. to 8 p.m., DJ Whoo Kid played all the ill shit from the G Unit Camp.

It was Friday and my radio was on blast as I opened the envelopes. Inside was ten photos of my Earth Oceasia on stage spitting under her rap name "Rita Book". She did a show in Gulfport, Mississippi and ... Oh shit! I noticed in the pics she was wearing a thick grey t-shirt with my face on takin' up the whole front with "Free Shakim Bio" splashed across it. Yeah my shorty was reppin' me hard, even at her shows. Seein' her on stage with the mic in her hand, I looked at her photos with admiration. The photos were close up shots too, sexual thoughts invaded my mind as I pictured her grabbing somethin' more serious than that mic and I caught a semi-erection looking at her luscious lips... man... I was missin' her as I read her letter...

Peace My 7

I know you better love my surprise. I'm reppin' you hard baby, lettin' the world know, even at a show in Gulfport, Mississippi that I love you and want you home.

Love you

The Official Mrs. J.A. Edwards

I thought to myself "WOW"... as I looked at the photos again and opened the other envelope. This time she had on another thick grey t-shirt with a full body photo of me and splashed across it again was the phrase "Free Shakim Bio". There wa a photo of both shirts spread out across a bed and a few shots of her rockin' each shirt, standin' outside her Denali Truck, looking sexy ass hell. The letter that came with these photos read.

Bay,

You better be smiling from ear to ear like I know you be. I love you, want you and need you home with me right now. Call me for part two of your surprise. Call me now!!

9 – 12 – 21

I was cheesin' like a little kid, vibin' to Jadakiss "Why?", which featured Anthony Hamilton... that beat was so hard and ill... Who would believe Havoc of Mobb Deep did this shit? Then out of nowhere, the remix came on... WHAT? With Common and Nasty Nas....shit was serious.

My celly came in.....

"You alright celly?" he asked.

"All the time!" I responded as I slipped the photos in one envelope and continued vibin' to that ill track thinkin' "why I gotta be locked up and so far away from my Earth Oceasia?"

I stared at the envelope from Tammi for a few minutes. I was deep in thought, wondering would it be wrong if I just didn't open the mail she sent me. I looked up and caught my celly lookin' in my direction.

"You good L?" I asked.

"Yeah... yeah... I'm cool... you goin' to dinner?"

"Nah... I'ma pass on that" I responded as I watched him change sneakers, grab his water bottle and head out the cell closing the door.

"Weird ass dude" I said out loud as I continued lookin' at the envelope.

"Fuck it" I thought ... it couldn't hurt to see what was goin' on in this envelope so I removed the staple and pulled out the card. It was a kitten sittin' on a wooden fence, holdin' and smellin' a flower and on top it said...

"The only thing better than thinking of you..."

Inside the card said "...is being with you. Miss you"

The card was signed "Love you! Tammi P.S. Please call me 34773691_ _."

     Tammi was comin' at me hard body, I looked at the card again, put it back in the envelope and got up, putting all letters under my mattress and goin' out the cell door on my way to the phone to call my wifey.

✶✶✶✶✶

I was still smilin' as she pressed "5"

"Peace Wifey, what's good with you?"

"Sha, what's good Papi?"

"You... sometimes me.... always us... but never them."

"Yeah, I hear you Bay"

She sounded so sexy and country

230

"Why you smilin'?" she asked.

"What?…. What makes you think I'm smilin'?"

"Cause I know my Bay… get your surprise?"

"Yep!"

"like it?"

"Of course I do… no… matter of fact… I love it!"

"I'm at work right now but I want you to hear the surprise…. hold up".

I heard her moving around and making noise.

"Ready? Ok… listen…"

I heard a beat come on and Rita Book's voice spittin'. I couldn't hear lyrics crystal clear but I heard them enough to hear her say that she loved her husband and was reppin', bein' Mrs. Edwards until the end of time. After the second verse, she picked up the phone.

"You like?"

"No doubt… but I couldn't really hear the lyrics crystal clear."

"I know… it's still rough… but… I'm re-doing it… it's called "Distance"; it's dedicated to you Bay. I'ma send the lyrics to you by next week. Look… customers is comin' in here left and right… Please call me back later before I lose my job.""

"Ok ma"

"Love you"

"Nine – twelve – twenty one"

*****

On the recreation move after chow, I went to the upstairs unit to holler at Raheeme. The C.O. at the unit door was cool so I walked in like I belonged there and went to Rah's cell. "Born Sun" also lived in that unit so occasionally I went by to holler at him too. Rah was in his cell reading a Federal law book, drinkin' a cup of coffee and smoking a cigarette; he stayed on some old head shit. I knocked on his cell door...

"Rah?"

"Peace Sha... come on in"

"What's the science?" I asked.

"Studyin' on some time tolling issues because they claim I'm time barred on my 2255 motion but I'ma prove otherwise."

"True Indeed... peep the photos my Earth just flew me"

I passed the envelope with the photos to him.

"Look at this... the Earth gassin' you up even more than you already are. What... she starting a Bio-Chemical clothing line or something? ...Yeah that's peace, someone is reppin' you like that... you are truly blessed my brother."

"True Indeed"

"The thing is... would you rep for her like that if you were in the free cipher?" he said, pointing his finger at me.

"Have a seat God"

I sat down in the chair.

"We are doin' some serious time. I got life, meaning forever. I'm lookin' at the reality of it, even though I'ma give it back. You got a lot of time and you will give it back too but at the same time that Earth is really into you. I know you are feeling her and all but know and understand she is really ridin' with you hard body and she met you while you were in. So she only knows you while you are in prison. She is reppin' you crazily Shakim so remember you owe her, not own her. You owe her, she loves you."

"I love her too G"

"That's peace... the Supreme Alphabet is the second lesson we get, when we are a baby and learned how to count... that was mathematics... then you learned your ABC's, that's the alphabets.The twelve degree is Love, Hell or Right. Love is the highest elevation of Understanding, Understanding is to know and understand, Hell is the trick. It's what we go through to get right as well as right and exact... So be prepared for those stages in this bid my G... Don't run her crazy, she's a keeper too.

"Yeah...yeah, no doubt" I responded.

I stood up and stretched.

"Yo, I'ma journey back to the unit on this move. I gotta scribe some scribes and get on the horn to network with my street team.

"Yo, you may be able to manage me when I get on" Rah proclaimed.

"Get the fuck outta here!!"

"I'm tellin' you Sha... Big Raheeme Supreme can shake the buildin'! I'm tellin' you."

"Tell it to your self" I said as I left the cell, laughin' at "Kool Moe Dee" Raheeme.

*****

CHAPTER 24

Everything was Peace, I mean it was always prison drama poppin' off but overall, everything was peace. Me and Oceasia was vibin' on the phones regularly and I burned minutes on both my personal and the other phone lines I secured. I even convinced Raheeme to let me put her number on his line so I could call her when I was up in his unit. I let them build a few times also. Raheeme got back in his groove and started goin' out on visits regularly. That old, 1980's shit he was on musta been workin' cause he was the only one from N.Y. who stayed on that "dance floor", which is what we called the visiting hall and Rah was reppin' hard out there too.

I was still networking over the phones and through letters, pertaining to havin' Oceasia's music heard or even better, getting' her either a music publishing or production deal. Even the entertainment attorney was inquiring about the "Street-Hop" novel I was penning. He wanted to shop it bad and had a few people already interested in it but I was tryna to do the music thing, pushing my shorty.

I was also goin' very hard body workin' out; doing pull-ups, dips, push-ups and usin' water bags to substitute weights. They had a cardio workout called "Burpees" or "Universal body builders", which is an exercise where you go down and do a push-up then you jump back up and repeat it in sets. Some do 2 to 3 to 4 to 5 push-ups and jump back up, do a 2 step and repeat until 100, 200, 300 some did 400 or better. How many I did all depended on how I was feeling, I would do 300 then do jumping jacks then go do 12 sets of pull-ups, sometimes 20 sets, all while bein' tuned in to Shade 45, getting' it in.

*****

"Yo, what's good?" asked Dirt as me and "True God" were comin' off the track, on the yard and goin' toward the yard where the basketball courts were.

234

"We just chilling" responded True.

"I thought the Sun don't chill"

We all laughed at that old saying. Me and "True" was discussing some moves and I was enlightening him as to how to generate some currency. He was with it but needed some training.

"Yo, I know where some vicious White Lightening is at" Dirt said, sittin' on the metal bleachers, me and "True" followed suit.

"Word? How much and where it's at?" I asked.

"White lightening" was a name for moonshine that was made in prison. It was the vapor of wine, cooked to a boiling point with a distillation process. It was as clear and as strong as Vodka or Smirnoff, Belvedere, Grey Goose type shit. To test its purity and potency, some convicts used the flame test, where one lights a fire on it and it will burn. If it didn't do that it was bullshit. Not only was "White Lightening" good... it was also expensive; forty dollars for a twenty ounce bottle. In a water bottle you would think it was really water due to it's clear appearance so we put in water bottles to pass as such.

"They got it up in Big Rah's unit, forty beans a pop. Why what's up?" asked Dirt.

"Yo True... you trying to go?" I asked.

"Nah G... I can't handle the effects of that shit... plus I like to stay on point."

"True that... true that but fuck that. Yo Dirt, we need two bottles my dude."

"That's what I'm talking about"

We started putting our stamps together.

235

Some convicts walked around with huge amounts of stamps in a 5 book block like how one walks around with a pocket full of money. Havin' that many stamps was illegal though, we were only allowed to have or carry 3 books of stamps. I kept several blocks on me even though my credit was immaculate. I had a convict "Black card" for my face was good.

"Yo Sha... on the move. You gotta go up there to cop it... the Baltimore cats got it."

"Yeah... that's my manz and them."

"Cool"

"On the rec. move, I'ma shoot up that way."

Now I'm not gonna to sit and front like I don't get my drink on... Brothers who know me personally, know I pops bottles like I win championships regularly. I get saucy with it too but I'm the laid back type... not the "rowdy, all the sudden got heart, amped up type"...Nah... that ain't my style.

I was gonna get proper with two, twenty ounces of White Lightening. I ended up goin' back to the yard on that same rec. move with three, twenty ounce water bottles of White Lightening. Once I made it back to the Basketball court bleachers, I handed Dirt his bottle, he said...

"Yeah... that's what's up"

We tapped the bottles like champagne glasses, making a toast and we started sippin' as Dirt took me on a mental journey to the streets during his stickin' up drug dealer capers and I gave him a few prison war stories.

Big Sandy was a hell of a spot, the Deuces Alarm stayed ringing as C.O.s ran in the direction of the drama daily and kept that rubber bullet semi with the extended clips and the long range mace sprayers with them. They were poppin' off just like us... on some shoot and talk later. What was ill about Big Sandy was everything was negotiable with the prison's captain.

I seen the illest knife fights between two convicts or groups. We might go on institutional lockdown for a few days or even a few weeks but once we rose back to normal and approached the captain, he would give us the opportunity to be escorted to the SHU, put on the yard in a separate rec. cage and have the comrade you were inquiring about brought out to the rec. cage connected to the one you was in so you could conversate, sort and try to fix the situation. The captain would also put you in a non-contact visiting room with a convict, I never seen no shit like that anywhere. You could damn near vouch and bond someone out the SHU all depending on the situation. The spot was off the chain, there were forced armed robberies, extortion, snitches being ran off the yard, rapes, a couples murders, it was wild but at the same time, it was also sweet in certain areas compared to the previous 4 institutions I'd been in.

We were slow sipping and kicking it about a little bit of this and that when Dirt asked me...

"Yo, what's up with wifey, big Homie?"

"Everything is peace." I responded but because we spoke about things on all levels, I told Dirt about Tammi getting at me twice and our history and all.

"Word? ... she tryna come back in your life?"

"Shiiiiiiit" responded "True", who was just sittin' back listening to our past stories. He gave his input...

"In these prison bids, Wisdoms be comin' and goin'… getting caught up with physical attraction and what not and they lose focus on a fella who's locked up then whenever somethin' goes wrong… they find their way back."

"Word!!!" responded Dirt, who was goin' through some drama with his wife, whom he married before goin' to prison… only to get divorced and later find out she got involved with someone else but recently she got back in touch with him. Dirt was playin' hard to get with his wife after that though. Due to the fact he was eighteen months or so "short", meaning his time was almost up. In eighteen months or so, Dirt would be returning back to society. He overstood very well, the reality of what "True" was sayin'.

True was goin' through drama with his seed's mom, who got into another relationship and had another seed for the dude. Both my seed's moms got married and moved on in life but they reached out to me a few times when their relationship went downhill or sour, their letters would pick back up, they'd send a little money and make visits.

"Yo Sha, you gonna get back at her with a scribe or what?" asked Dirt.

"Nah Son… I'ma just let shorty (Tammi) go." I answered.

"Shakim Bio…You need to get with her just in case the Earth falls off." kicked True.

"Fall off? I don't need her for no currency or nothing material."

"Yeah… but she is with you on the strength as of now… What about later on in life and she wants that physical? You can only provide for the mental, spiritual, emotional and mathematical aspects of her needs but she's gonna want to be comforted physically and you can't provide that need" kicked true.

"She still can get that and keep it apart from what me and her built." I responded.

"Yea right… that shit sounds good… women are weak ciphered men and too emotional. They get caught up in feelings, especially if the dick is on point right then… she's gonna trail off… that's how they do!" hammered True.

I thought about that cause I seen it too many times and been through it myself. Tammi fell off, Zena fell off, all of my shorties fell off… I thought about it harder.

"Yeah… it's all good… when that time comes I'll just have to adapt and keep it pushin'.

"Shit, you need to scream back at that shorty who tryna get back in" kicked True God.

"Word!!" agreed Do Dirt.

*****

On the institutional recall back to the housing units; so we could get prepared for the 4pm stand up count, I made it back to the unit real saucy. What True and Dirt said stayed in my mind because it made a lot of sense but I already knew the reality of it. Inside the unit, the younger generation was wildin' out in the recreational room, making noise, playin' cards and some rowdy convicts were in front of the B.E.T. TV. Watchin' videos, some were in front of the sports TV., watchin' ESPN, while some convicts was tryna make it to the showers to get that funk from off of them.   I saw my celly standin' in front of our cell… You couldn't miss him; again, he was the biggest dude in the compound as far as muscle-size. There he was with that buck tooth smile too.

"L, what's up?" we dapped up.

"Celly… They got me packing out and leaving tomorrow. I told you I got these peoples… I'm going to F.C.I. Terre Haute!!"

"That's what's up" I said as I walked in the cell with "L" following behind me. He continued…

"Celly… whatever extra stuff I can't pack and take with me, you get first dibs on before any of my fake homeboys."

"Aiiiight" I said, climbin' onto my top bunk.

"Yeah … I see you tipsy too. Before the night is over, make sure you put in a request form so you can get assigned to the bottom bunk before they put someone in here while you're outside."

"I'ma move to the bottom bunk regardless L".

I reached under my mattress and took out my Earth's envelope with the recent photos and Tammi's last card. I re-read it and put it back in the envelope then took out Oceasia's photos and stared at them hard. I was thinking… but the alcohol made my decisions too blurry as I started weighing shit out in my mind.

＊＊＊＊＊

After count, they opened up the cell doors and I left the room to give my celly space to sort out his property for his pack out the next day plus a lot of his associates were comin' by to either give him his farewells in case he left in the early morning or to see if they could get anything that he might not be able to pack. Dudes were low down, slime-balls like that… I didn't care if he left me anything or not. I was good regardless plus I wasn't into wearin' someone else's clothes or used material. If anything, I wanted to see if he had any triple X girlie magazines, which were illegal to have but very much needed… shit… and I was gonna have the cell to myself for a few nights? You know a

240

fella had to squeeze off and buss at least two... I couldn't wait until he left... feel me?

Mail call... I got another card from Tammi. Ma was definitely tryna get at me crazily... On the rec. move, I slid upstairs to Raheeme's unit... I knocked on his cell door and went in.

"Peace!"

"Peace to the God, Shakim! What's up, Blackman?"

"Nothing much"

I sat down in the chair. Rah was sittin' on his lower bunk with his reading glasses on, reading some case laws. He always stayed on his legal shit.

"Damn Sha. You smell like a wine brewery and shit."

"Yeah. I got right earlier today" I told him.

"And you aint bring me none?" kicked Rah.

"You wasn't nowhere to be found."

"Shit... I was in that law library" responded Raheeme.

"Look, I'ma go see if there's more"

I got up to cop another bottle.

"O.K. bet cause I got some sticky light green to go along with it"

"That's what's up" I said before I left his cell to go see the Baltimore cats.

Because I was still feelin' tipsy and my stamps wasn't on super, super-swole to spend $160 in a half a day like that... I copped two, four ounce shorty bottles and threw them to Rah when I entered the room. Rah, bein' so old school, already had two cans of sprite with the plastic cups and had already rolled two small sized joints. He made us two drinks...

"Yo Rah, I'm already good my dude so only put a few drops in mine... go ahead and do you"

"Alright... that's what I'm talking 'bout... that's why I fuckz wit you"

He made him an extra strong drink and passed me my drink.

We lit up and blew both sticks back to back. Rah chased it with a Newport cigarette. I stopped smoking Cee I germs (C.I. Germs =cigarettes) a few months earlier plus the Feds was talkin' about discontinuing cigarette smoking throughout the system, which would later lead to a major black market, that generated money crazily for those who had game and access to tobacco.

I told Rah about my celly packin' out and transferrin' to a medium and he said...

"Now I'ma come down and make your spot the new hang out spot!

We laughed it up and kicked it for a minute.

"Yo let me use your phone pac to call my Earth" I threw out there to Rah.

"I knew it was something!"

We laughed again, I was crazy high as we got up and made it to the phones, I dialed her numbers and let Rah put in his pac number, even though I already knew it.

"Thank you" said the automated operator's voice as the call was processing.

"Yo I'ma be in the cell... don't say nothing crazy to make them people come lock me up!"

"I got you Rah... chill"

"Alright!"

After three to four rings, my shorty picked up and after hearing the recording the first time, she let it play twice before finally accepting my call.

"Peace!"

"Who dis?"

"Who you think it is?"

"Oh... cause I heard the name "Lonnie Redmon" and I'm like... who the hell?"

"Fall back, Ma" I interrupted.

She took the hint, understanding that I was usin' another convict's phone line.

"What's good with you?" I asked.

"Nothing... I was getting' ready to go to work for half a shift, then go to the studio later on".

"O.K. I just called to hear your voice"

"I'm glad to hear yours"

"Everything good?" I asked.

"Yeah"

"O.k. then I'ma call tomorrow"

"Alright my God"

"Peace"

"What you mean peace?"

"What?"

"You usually say you love me first"

"Yeah... I love you"

"... love you too" she responded soundin' funny style.

I ended the call, I don't know if it was because I was intoxicated from drinkin' and smokin' but somethin' didn't seem right... I stood there playin' the conversation back in my mind.

"Yo Rah, I'ma journey back to my unit on the move"

"O.K. then... good lookin' on the drink-drink"

"No question... yo let me ask you somethin'. How you manage the relationship with your wife in "Now Why (New York)" and your wisdom Rita?"

"Hmmmmm... I just do me G... I keep one separate from the other."

Rah's thoughts showed in his facial expression, he dropped some game...

"We in here Sha and I got a life sentence so I can't control what goes on out there. All I can do is hold on by all means. I know my wife is doin' her out there so I'm doin' me with Rita... she knows about Rita and Rita knows I'm married but both of them know I'm in prison... Wifey don't know that Rita tears down those visiting doors on the regular though!"

We laughed.

"That's what's up Rah"

The recreational move was called over the loud speakers.

"Yo that's me... I'm gone"

I went out the cells door.

"Peace!" Rah hollered.

I took a shower and went to bed early.
■■■

CHAPTER 25

The next morning, my celly packed out and transferred to a medium and I moved to the lower bunk. I went to call my earth but the call went to her voice mail. I tried callin' a few more times only to get the same results so I did my usual daily routines and remained focused. The past few days were pretty much the same and I kept getting Oceasia's voicemail. It was all good. I was layin' back and burnin' minutes on the phone catching up with my mom and several street comrades. I was goin' in early too, takin' advantage of not havin' a celly for however long that would last. I was jerkin' off, releasing build up... believe me, I was getting' it in too...

They let this young cat from Charlottesville, Virginia, by the name of "Calico" out the box; son appeared to be laid back but in reality he was off the chain. There were a lot of young convicts, who were just comin' into the Fed system and they were real wild. They would be caught up in watchin' videos all day, gambling, drinkin', smokin', runnin' up in cells doin' strong arm robberies and all that. Calico was 6'3", husky, brownish with corn row braids that he was lettin' grow into dreads. He had two life sentences and didn't have no understanding after that. We had mutual respect for one another. I used to be wild too but age and experience slowed me down, especially when I woke up to the reality of how much time I had to do. One morning before lunch, when I came back from my orderly in the corridor detail, Calico approached me.

"Yo Shakim... let me holla at you"

I went over to him...

"What's good?" I asked.

"Let's go in your room cause it's kinda private" he said, lookin' at me with sincerity.

246

We made it over to my cell, he went in first.

"What's good Calico?" I asked once we made it in and I let the door close.

"Sha. I'm not tryna get in your way, I know you do you and you're real laid back... but yo... I'm in the cell with a real sucker duck ass cat... I was gon' get on some real Rambo shit and "D-bo" the cell from him but I can't lose no more phone or store time... Look, I know you gone all morning and most of the day... let me move in with you... I will stay out your way. I won't smoke in the cell, unless we locked down or some shit and I aint too big on company.

"Dig..." I cut him off... "Give me two more nights by myself cause it's already Friday... and bring the request form Sunday night so I can sign it."

"Bet that up... Sha... good lookin' out God."

"One"

I showed him out of the cell. Calico was a cool young cat and I knew I was makin' the right decision. I strolled over to the phone and dialed Oceasia's number again followed by my phone pac digits. After about four rings, she picked up as soon as the recording started she accepted instantly.

"Peace Bay!"

"Peace, what's good?"

"Nothing much... missing you"

"Yeah I been hittin' you up for a few days but couldn't catch you."

"I know I heard the recordings on my voicemail... I been managing the boutique full time now and I had to let go of the record shop job... So I been workin' overtime and all. I been accumulating bills and takin' care of my Ole Earth and Grand Ole Earth... you know?"

She sounded like she was really tired.

"Word?"... I'm making a few moves on this end... need a little current?" I asked.

"Now Cipher... keep that! I'ma do what I can... It's gonna take a minute to save up to get a ticket to come see you... plus I still didn't call Rita. I been so busy... I need to call your Ole Earth too."

We proceeded to build but I was getting' a strange feelin' for some reason...

"What's up with demoes?" I inquired.

There was a slight pause.

I had to say "Hello?" to see if she was still one the phone.

"Yeah... I'm here... I didn't follow up on everything like you said... Bay...

"Why?"

"I been losing focus plus workin' hard."

"you gotta stay on your hop Ma"

"I know Bay."

"You gettin' my scribes and cards?"

"Yeah... I just didn't respond back as of yet.. I know I'm fallin' off... but bare with me Shakim."

"It's all good...

The phone beeped, the call was about to get cut off.

"When's the best time to call you back?"

"I'ma be at my Grand Ole Earth's tomorrow so call before you lock in tomorrow night."

"Alright Ma"

"Love You"

"Nine... twelve... twenty one"

We hung up.

Yeah I aint been hearin' from her on the regular like I used to but it was all good, knowin' that I got to speak to her a lot, sometimes several times a day, even though it aint been like that for the past couple days.

After 4 p.m. count, I decided to go over to the BET TV to catch up on some videos and mingle with the younger crowd. I was still young myself; my cell was almost in front of the BET TV. First I had to go check on mail call to see if I received any love. It was a Friday and after Friday, wasn't no mail jumpin' off until Monday. I ended up with two scribes and the new XXL magazine.

I watched like thirty minutes of videos and after hearin' those silly, backwards young bucks debate about video vixens, what rapper was doin' it, countin' rappers' money but not havin' any money of their own, I got up and took my chair back to my temporary one man cell. I was ready to see what Tammi had to say to me since she'd been getting' at me even though I aint get at her since I got to Big Sandy. As I looked at the envelope, studyin' her handwriting, I took the staple out and opened the two page letter...

Shakim

Hey You!!

What's up Boo? I've written to you and sent you cards... I know you got them because they didn't come back yet. Thought I couldn't find you huh? How you been? I'm missing you Boo...I'm still here... and lonely... I completed the police training at the academy and I'll be transferring to Charlotte N.C. My mom is sick and I need to spend time with her. So I'ma give N.C. a try plus give my son a different atmosphere. He is running wild in N.Y. What's up with you? Why you don't write back? You don't even call me no more :(I think I know why... it's that substitute chick you was telling me about... isn't it? I know she can't make you forget me.

Oh yeah I seen your "old girl" (you know who) she messes with the rapper Loon now...

Tammi continued to tell me how her family and job was and if I wrote back, she would send me some photos that would "spoil me". She gave me the latest gossip from around the way with what was going on, who was still around and how she was lonely and missed me.

How is things going with your case? I can't wait until you come home. I gotta be your first (For Real).

How far is Charlotte NC from you?

Tell me you didn't miss me!   Call me 347-525-XXXX

She can't love you like me

Love Always

Tammi

*****

CHAPTER 26

Several days went by and I was still not hearin' from Oceasia nor could I catch her on the phone. I had to make sure I got the boutiques number. Calico moved in and was never in my way, never had company in the cell and he kept all his dirt outside the cell. During lock down, count or at night before we went to rest, we would sit and kick it, have building sessions, sometimes blow some trees and drink. Calico left an infant daughter, who was being raised by his mom out in the free world. His daughter's mom was absent and that took a huge toll on Calico, causing him to take his anger out on convicts. Big Sandy was his first pen, he barely had three years in under his belt and he had just turned twenty- two years old. He asked a lot of questions on how I kept it together after all my years incarcerated; he asked what exactly was the Nation of Gods and Earths and supreme mathematics. He caught a bad hand in his case ordeal and he ended up with two life sentences and nothing about the law but he knew so much about B.E.T. so I took time to school him properly. I started having him spend a hour a day in the law library reading case laws and cases similar to his ordeal. I had him goin' over his trial transcripts and getting' familiar with the pending issues in court; we use to build about that. I slowly started feedin' him mathematics and history on the blackman and he started exercisin' and eating better. He was gettin' his life in order, his family came to visit him quite regularly and he had an old flame from his past troopin' it with him too, she was a winner.

Everything seemed to be fallin' into place for Calico... but out of place for me. I wasn't gettin' no mail from the Earth Oceasia and I still could hardly catch her due to her new work schedule; whenever I did catch her, she was tired so I fell back and gave her space to take care of her shit. I remained doin' me, doin' what I do, workin' out hard body, building with the Gods... schemin' with the prison schemers and stayin' on top of my legal issues. I started drinkin' regularly as well too... I remained sharp and on point regardless.

252

The best time to catch Oceasia was Sunday night because the mall was open only for a half a day so after about two weeks, I got to hear her voice. She spoke on her job and how she wasn't fully in tune with her music as much but she did send her cards weekly and maybe a half page letter but she did feel my powerful energy. Everything sounded peace... but deep down, I knew it wasn't.

One thing I did as much as possible was / is call and stay in touch with my Ole Earth (mother). I am her only son and we are close, even though she doesn't approve of some of my life decisions. She knows and understands that I am goin' to remain true to self and remain a man, if not a gentleman all across the board even during times of war. I can call Mom duke and talk to her about just about anything. She listens so I spoke to her about Oceasia and what surprised and amazed my Ole Earth was how throughout my runnin' the streets of N.Y. to different cities and towns of other states, in all my old womanizer ways days, I never brought a woman home to meet my mom. Even with my two sons' mothers; different circumstances led to how my mom met them but still never on a real personal level. I kept my Ole Earth separate and away from the dealings I had on any level; be it streets, women or my complete lifestyle period. So me speakin' about loving a women (one at that), was a shock to the Ole Jamaican lady who gave birth to me. My mother and Oceasia eventually began to call and speak over the phone and got to know one another. It would be times, I'd call my mom and Oceasia was on the

other line or "O.E.. (a nickname for my moms; short for Old Earth)" had just hung up with her. If I called and was goin' through somethin', the Ole Earth could always sense it in my voice or would already know cause Oceasia already called. The Ole Earth knew I must have really had love for this woman since I introduced shorty to her... the one who birthed me.

* * * * *

The next week rolled in and I got a card and letter from Oceasia...

Peace my love!

I miss you much… I know u may doubt me from my ways & actions but you stay on my mental all the time. I'm leavin' you the boutique's number and my schedule so we can stay in tune the way we were and are supposed to be… Smile, I know you are smiling now. Your physical is comin' up, what is your favorite flavor? Don't write me back if you don't answer that question! I spoke to your Ole Earth the other day, she is a trip! Here's the math 504-235-XXXX I come in at the knowledge-knowledge hour and work until the build hour, call anytime. Sunday is the knowledge hour to equality, I'm missing u and always loving u.

9-12-21

Mrs. Edwards

P.S. Our 1 year anniversary for when we reconnected is comin' up!!

* * * * *

Yeah, my physical (born day / birthday) was approaching. June 7th, that's the equality moon, God day. I'm a Gemini but I'm not into that astrology sign thing. I wasn't really big on the birthday thing since I'd been locked up either. Can't celebrate it like I want to so it's just another day… but a special day… on the streets I celebrated it BIG… but in prison I may have a few drinks, smoke and call it a day. I usually got cards from family, seeds and friends. This would be me and Oceasia's first.

* * * * *

Our phone conversations started picking back up again. I would call her once, sometimes twice a day. I would still scribe her twice a week and there were still quite a few times I couldn't catch her at her job or on her cell but I never been the panicking type, she knew how to get at me... My math is always the same.

Everything was peace amongst the God bodies in Big Sandy, as well as N.Y. Big Raheeme, who was shining on the visits and still being Big Sandy's mayor. Me and Dirt put some moves in motion, he didn't smoke cigarettes and had a vision that he was trying to capitalize off of. All Federal facilities was banning tobacco use so they were planning to stop sellin' tobacco in all Fed spots. Dirt was buyin' all the tobacco he could and trading commissary to other convicts for it. He stored it until it became gold. No one took it serious until it was a memorandum notice put up all over the institution; even under the cell doors, stating the sale of tobacco would be discontinued within 90 days. By then, Dirt was sittin' pretty on mountains of cigarettes... Now his plan was to hide it.

My birthday was ten days away, I paid this Muslim convict to put a nice meal together for about ten people, then me, Dirt, Calico, Serious, and Raheeme put our prison money (books of stamps) together to buy as many bottles of White Lightening as possible. We was gonna eat, drink and kick it amongst ourselves in honor of my birthday. I was turning thirty five and I couldn't believe that I was finally getting' old. Me and True God had a few moves in motion that generated currency and Miz had his thing goin' as well and Dirt was putting up as much tobacco as he could in all kinds of spots.

Tobacco was a necessity in prison. It released stress for so many so how could you tell a convict who had anywhere from 10 – 20 years to a life or multiple life sentences that they couldn't smoke? It beat me but we knew by this time next year, a pack of generic cigarettes that cost $2.50 in the store was going to be worth $300.00 or even more so I was takin' heed to Dirt's investment and I started puttin' up a few packs up myself.

▪▪

*****

My physical day (Birth / Born Day) was peace. I hung out with Big Rah then my celly Calico. I got drunk with Serious and Dirt but I made sure not to get too tipsy so I could stay on point just in case anything popped off. The Muslim "Ack" cooked fried chicken, macaroni and cheese, fried rice with mackerel & baby clams, deep friend whiting fish and cheese cake and all of it was good and on point. I didn't call Oceasia because I was waitin' on a visit from her for goin' on two moons. All this workin' full time, overtime and she still wasn't showin' up. Even when I started getting' my currency up and volunteered to help finance the trip, she still hadn't made it up to see me yet. I didn't hold it against her, instead I gave her space and enjoyed mine. I just didn't use that space to get at anyone, that space was reserved for her, for I truly loved Oceasia.

I enjoyed the day; we built, had fun and even played spades. Everything was peace and by 3:00 o'clock recall, I was in the cell laid up. Calico came in with another bottle of White Lightening and held it up in the air...

"After Count Sha!"

"BET"

"Happy Birthday Ole Head"

"No doubt... good looking out"

After 4 pm count, we came out at almost 4:30 pm. I was by the BET TV with my bottle of Lightening, enjoying "Rap City"; Calico was at mail call and came back with a pile of mail for me...

"Looks like everyone got at you for you B-day "

He passed me about twenty or so cards. I looked and seen mom got at me, my sisters, seeds, aunt and my eldest seeds grandmother, who shared the same birthday as me. Tammi got at me again along with a few other shorties. I saw four big envelopes from my earth as I headed to the cell to read my mail; leavin' Calico with the bottle to enjoy. He tried to refuse, sayin'...

"It's your birthday my dude... so do you!"

"Nah... go ahead and get right... I'm straight"

I handed him the bottle and strolled to the cell. I sat back reading every card, enjoying and cherishing the love from family and friends. I still couldn't believe that Tammi was still getting' at me even when I hadn't responded to her yet... Maybe I was bein' too mean to Shorty. This was my twelfth Birthday in prison and Shorty been there thru most of it even though she dipped off, she always came back so I read her card again. I picked up Oceasia's cards and opened them. One had some very revealing photos of her, they turned me on instantly. One of her cards had the chocolate icing from a cake smeared on the card; I laughed now realizing why she wanted to know my favorite flavor as I looked at the dried cake icing smeared on the card. The other cards had photos of her wearin' the t-shirt with my face on it and she and her niece and nephews were all blowin' birthday whistles. A chocolate Birthday cake was on the table with the candles lit. There was a close up photo of the cake...

"Happy Birthday Shakim"

We love you .... "Wifey"

I was cheesin' like a five year old.

*****

Two Weeks Later

257

I'd been tryna catch Oceasia all morning and afternoon but couldn't, this had been goin' on for a while. I hadn't spoken to her in like two weeks and since I got the B-day card, I only got one short scribe from her, tellin' me to check my account because she sent me current. I didn't need any money to begin with, she's supposed to be savin' money to make the trip this way plus the entertainment attorney wrote me inquiring about the five song cd she was supposed to send to him over a month ago. My other manz was waitin' on her to call so he could email some beats for her to listen to and they could do a few tracks plus I was waitin' on her to let me know what kind of equipment they used in the studio she went to so my Co-dee Monday could shoot somethin' that way. We needed him cause he was the link to Lyfe Jennings and she was nowhere to be found.

One afternoon, I called the boutique and the phone kept ringin' as usual. Just when I was about to hang up... Someone picked up. I caught a man's voice but the recording came on lettin' the caller know that the call was from an inmate in a Federal Prison and he could hang up to refuse the call or accept by pressing "five" or to receive no more inmate calls, he could block it by pressing "seven". Whoever it was, pressed "Five"

It was a male's voice...

"Hello"

"Hello... how you? I'm callin' to speak to Oceasia, who manages the store... is she in? I inquired.

"Oh no... she isn't... I thought at first this was a collect call until I heard exactly what the recording said... Nah she isn't in".

"Do you know when's the best time I can call back and catch her there?" I asked.

"Not really my brother, I haven't seen or heard from her in three days".

"Three days?" I repeat.

"Yes three days... so your guess is as good as mine"

"O.k. then... thank you"

"Alright"...

- click

Shit was crazy; I hung up, picked the phone back up and dialed her cell number followed by one of the other pac digits I secured from another convict. Her phone kept goin' straight to voice mail.

■■■

"Yo Dirt, what's good with you son?

"Nothing my dude... just stackin' that paper for plan B"

"True that!! I responded.

Dirt's tobacco scheme was workin', they stopped sellin' tobacco but we was still allowed to smoke. They was bannin' smokin' within another ninety days but the memorandum didn't circulate as of yet. In other Fed Pens, they stopped the smokin' and the black market of tobacco skyrocketed tremendously. Dirt broke the hustle down...

"Sha, I'm telling you B... Put some packs up, at least fifty... that way you can make fifteen stacks easily. Fifty packs costs $125.00 you spend from the store, now they aint nothin' but 200.00 my dude. By next summer those joints gonna run $300 to $400 a pack."

"Yeah that's a hell of a flip" I said as I did the math in my mind... "I got close to twenty packs, woulda had more but my celly Calico smokes and Big Rah steams crazily. Dem my dudes so I can't tell them no, feel me? I kicked to Dirt.

"I hear you... but business is business... and friendship is friendship. You gotta capitalize off of this thing right here. In a few years, cats is gon' be paying $500.00 for two packs when it cost less than $5.00 in the streets. Cats is gonna be makin' hundreds of thousands of dollars a year off this shit."

"Yeah" I said, thinkin' about what Dirt was tellin' me.

"I gotta go home with some paper so why not some long paper-feel me? Dirt made himself clear.

"True indeed" I responded.

"What's good otherwise my dude? inquired Dirt.

"Nothing much...this Jamaican chick that was scribin' me back in Lee County got at me and flew me some paper... like $250.00... I'm thinkin' of sending it back to her"

"What? You crazy B... keep that shit!" demanded Dirt.

"Nah Sun, can't do her like that... I'm not feelin' her like that no more."

"That's the reason why you should keep it; use it to finance the fifty packs."

"True... true... but nah... I'ma send that back to her. I'm good" I said, stickin' to my strong morals"

"that's good to hear... an honest criminal"

"yeah"

We laughed.

"Yo, what's up with Rita?" Dirt reminded me of my current misery.

"Maaan... I aint hear from her in a minute!"

"Say Word!"

"Word!" I assured him.

"What's poppin'? Why Shorty got ghost like that?

"Can't call it… but you know my steez… she will be back in a minute."

"They always do… especially when they know they dealin' with a real solid thoroughbred… Shorty is smellin' your gangsta" Dirt voiced his concerns.

"yeah… plus I'm missin' her like crazy too." I added as Dirt got his laugh on.

"Yo Raheem, I need a favor G" I approached Rah on the walkway as he was on his way back from the law library.

"It all depends what the favor is… and if I am able to do it" answered Rah.

"O.k. dig… My Earth's physical day is coming up and I'm always getting' at her with cards and all that… I'ma flood her with some this year too but I wanna do somethin' different too.

"You mean Romantic?"

"Yeah, exactly"

"O.k. what you got in mind? asked Rah.

"I was thinkin', a fruit basket or floodin' her with roses or somethin'… maybe both."

"So what's the favor? I know you don't need no gold for that, the way you stuntin' around here buyin' crazy bottles of moon shine and multiple Air Force Ones" kicked Rah.

"Nah I'm good… but don't act like I don't show love."

Rah started laughin' and getting' on his old school shit.

"So what you need from me Sha?"

"Yo I need someone to order the roses and fruit basket. I'ma send the current up front. I just need your wisdom "Rita" to order it and have it sent to my wiz for me in my name."

I explained my plans to Rah

"Yeah?"

"I will cover all costs and throw in a little extra too." I announced.

"Alright… I'ma run that by her on the visit tomorrow… lucky I like you or I wouldn't do it for you"

"Yeah, Yeah, Yeah Ole head" I joked.

"But Ole head stays on that dance floor dancin' while the youngsters need Ole head to reach out and make things happen"

We laughed hard.

"Yeah, whatever… just make it happen Rah."

"That's Big Rah… Big money Shakim-Bio" he said as we laughed again.

CHAPTER 27

When my Earth's physical birthday came on July thirteenth, which is the knowledge understanding day of the God moon, I made sure I did somethin' BIG for her to let her know that the God Shakim Bio loves her crazily. I blew some trees and copped some bottles of White Lightening in her honor but on her side of the world, I flooded her with so many pop up cards, a fruit basket and white and red roses. If I was able to, I woulda sent a singin' messenger to her door step to sing a love ballad to her, leting her know how much I love her ass. I called her early that morning, wished her a happy birthday and made her day. I had to call her back on all my lines to keep the excitement goin' and I knew once the cards, fruit basket and roses landed, it was gonna be ON but before any of that could arrive, she kept tellin' me that no matter what, she loves me and always will. She kept repeating herself to the point that I asked her what she meant by that. Her answer was...

"I just want to assure and reassure you Bay"

I told her that I was going to call her back at 7pm because I knew all my surprises as well as the mailman should have touched on her end by then.

"Why so late? she asked.

"What you mean ma? It will be six on your side, trust me, I'ma hit you then... OK?"

"OK"

"Love You"

"Love you too"

Later, when I called at seven, I was juiced up from drinking; she answered and accepted my call.

"What's good ma?" I asked.

"Nothin'"

I could hear in her voice that she was cryin'.

"What's wrong baby girl?"

"Nothing... I just got the roses... and the basket... and those cards, wowwww... I know I don't deserve you Shakim... I'm sorry."

I was like...

"What?"

She said...

"I can't get my mind off that card"

"Which one?" (I sent her like ten)

"The one where when you open it, the bride and groom pops up, I love that card".

She started cryin' harder, I was thinkin' "what the fuck is wrong with Shorty? She's buggin'".

"What's wrong Oceasia?

"Nothin'"

We continued to conversate and she said...

"Shakim I can't take it no more... that card done it"

"What?"

"Do you really, really love me?"

"True indeed"

"For real?"

"For real!! I assured her.

"Truly?"

She started that cryin' shit again.

"Yes truly... I really do... why?"

"I gotta tell you somethin'"

"What?"

"I can't... I'm scared to..."

"scared of what?"

Silence... no words... but I could still hear her cryin'.

Something just hit me and I felt it so I just straight up asked her...

What? ...You pregnant or somethin'?

Silence...

"I asked you a question"

I was pressin' her for an answer...

More cryin'...

The phone beeped alerting us that the 15 minute call was comin' to an end and would be cut off.

"Hello?" I snapped.

"Yes I'm here... she responded.

"The phone beeped.. it's gon' hang up in a minute" I informed her.

"Shakim..."

"<u>Please</u>... <u>don't</u>... <u>leave</u>... <u>me</u>"

She cried her heart out and the phone call disconnected.

✱✱✱✱✱

I was still standing with the phone in my hand even though the call had been disconnected. I still couldn't believe what just happened... this Bitch... I mean... my Earth just told me that she is pregnant... No she didn't actually say it but she cried and begged me not to leave her... "What the fuck is goin' on?" I thought as my mental computed what my ears just heard and I hung up the phone not wantin' to call back on the other lines. I was fucked up completely; the look on my grill told a story within itself. I was totally thrown off guard. It was like when I got betrayed by several of my co-defendants, who took the stand in front of the judge and jury in Federal Court, pointing me out, identifying and implicating me in a thousand drug deals in nine states. It felt worse than that, I had to snap back to reality and observe my surroundings. It was like everyone was looking at me as I walked to the cell, closed the door and sat on my bunk, replaying the conversation back in my mind over and over and over again. I was fucked up totally and wasn't even drunk no more... my eyes got moist but no tears manifested. I hadn't shed tears in close to twenty years and even though I was close to it at that moment, it just didn't happen. I was hurt... at a loss for words, disappointed and I felt betrayed. There I was, lovin' this chick, puttin' my all into her, our relationship and strivin' to help her with her career... I was sharin' my life... my world... I introduced her to mom duke... put all my time and energy into her... I put my projects on hold for <u>HER</u>... I stayed true to someone who isn't true to me... I was loyal to someone who was disloyal, I gave my all... all for nothin' ... and what did I get in return? ...A"please don't leave me" story?

I couldn't believe that shit as I hit my stash and bust out a pack of Newports. Shit was real and had a fella stressing... <u>REAL HARD</u>.

* * * * *

I stayed in the cell all night and I didn't say a word. I was so tight-faced that when Calico came in he looked at me and automatically knew not to bother me as I lay up in my bunk. He climbed up on his bunk at lock down, turned on his radio and I could hear Keith Sweat crooning thru his Koss headphones. On some real shit, I used to love listenin' to slow love music, shit always had me thinkin' about moments with certain females but after lovin' Oceasia the way I did, every love song bought her to mind. Like Neyo, I was so sick of love songs cause every song kept remindin' me of this lyin' ass chick, who just did me dirty. As Maxwell's "This woman's work" came on, I thought... "Aint that a bitch"... and I closed my eyes .

"<u>Love</u>" By: Shakim Bio

Love is such a powerful energy. It is built on positive and negative forces. Love can be with you or against you; it all depends on how you use it. Love is built on so many different elements... trust, loyalty, honesty, affection, compassion, life, death, sex, greed, lust, envy and hate. These ingredients are all a part of love. Love can make someone lose their mind or find themselves. Love can make a person a better person or even worse person than they were.

I'm building my whole world around you – Love.

Love makes an independent person forget their priorities and responsibilities and they become a dependent of Love. Love can add on or take away. Loves borns Power/Refinement-Culture/Freedom all being born to Born. It mathematically defines itself... Can't you see that? Musiq Soul child sung it well...

267

Sometimes love is taken for granted and not appreciated, not honored or given its respect. Love can be more bonding than krazy glue. Love is sometimes real, sometimes fake, unseen yet seen, unfelt yet felt, unexplained yet very well detailed. Love has so many meanings, so many reasons, so many feelings, too many excuses... If love is God, I pray that it blesses me. If it was light, I'd ask that it guides me. If it is strength, I ask for it to get stronger. If it was the weather, I need it to rain on me. If it lives, I want to live with it... If it dies, I want to die with it. If you have it... share it with me... If it's a drug... sell it to me... If I have to pay for it, I will be paying you my whole life for I will forever be in debt for it. How do I get it? Do I ask? Must I get on my knees and Beg? Please love... and I mean please...

Come and Stay with me

Living   Off/Of   Veracious   Eclectic/Energy

CHAPTER 28

The next morning when the cell doors were unlocked... I was still in the bed, my schedule was off until who knew when. I started slacking in areas such as workin' out, law library and socializing. I barely went to my job detail and convicts started noticin' the change... I stayed away from the phone for a couple days. I refused to break down and call Oceasia. I wasn't present at mail call so Calico started getting' my mail and leavin' it on top of my locker. I was on some next shit and I started steamin' Newports, spendin' most of my fortune on moonshine, even regular jailhouse wine. Oceasia was writin' and sendin' cards that went unopened; they started to pile up. I didn't wanna deal with that shit; I was tired of her lies and her deceit so I started stayin' in the unit; watchin' videos on BET. Big Rah used to come lookin' for me, so did Dirt, who was sendin' messages for me to come to the yard. I needed a few days to myself to regroup and get my thoughts together so the messages went in one ear and out the other. Big Rah started comin' in my unit, checkin' for me...

"Shakim... what's up? You aint been in the library or nothin'. My G... what's goin' on?

"I'm on some other shit right now" I said before I gulped some jail house wine.

"Don't tell me that time is kicking that ass"

I could tell he wanted to joke but he was feelin' me out first.

"Nah... I'm good" I said.

"Yo, everythin' straight with the family?... the seeds?

"Yeah, shit is straight Rah"

"What you heard some bad news from the courts?" he asked.

269

"I'm just goin' through a little somethin' right now... that's all" I replied.

"Yo, you can always come upstairs and build with me... I'ma always be there for you"

He took the bottle and took a quick swig before passin' it back to me.

"Damn that's some strong mop juice"

I laughed at the Ole head God.

"Yo, I'ma scream at you later Rah"

"Peace to the God!"

"PEACE!!"

*****

It took about two more days before I was back to doin' pull-ups and socializing with certain dudes again. I kept my hurt to myself as prison isn't a place for one to open his self and share his emotions. Some convicts see that as a weakness and use it as a way to get over on you. Plus I didn't want to entertain those who were secretly hatin' on me and would love to hear what Oceasia took me through so I pushed her to the back of my mind for the time being; even though I was extremely hurt and couldn't get over her that easily.

Finally movin' around again and striving to put everything back on point within my cipher in prison... I caught up with Big Rah and we kicked it for a while.

"Yo Shakim"

"Yeah what's the science Rah?"

"I didn't know you smoked Cee I germs (NY term for Cigarettes)... when you started?"

"I been smoking cigarettes since the eighties. I stopped for a minute but recently, fell a victim... but I'ma stop again" I said in a smoke filled voice after takin' a deep pull of a Newport.

"Now the tobacco shit is dead and I was hittin' you up for squares... Then out of nowhere you smokin' like a Chu-Chu train."

"Yeah... it aint nothin'" I responded. "You got someone to smoke with now "

We both laughed.

$$* * * * *$$

Later on that day, while I had the cell to myself, I picked up my mail and started reading, tryna catch up. I saw that Oceasia had been getting' at me heavy as well as a few of my street comrades and there was a small envelope from Tammi. I took my time to read everyone's letters except for Oceasia's, I left her mail for last.

Tammi was tellin' me that she was movin' to Charlotte, North Carolina within two weeks and her number was still the same. She wanted me to call so I decided I would fill out a phone list with her number and turn it in so I could give her a call. I thought, "Why not? I might as well"... Then I picked up the three cards and two letters from Oceasia. I started with the cards first, which were all connections from Hallmark. That line of cards was specially made for specific circumstances and situations and after reading them, I saw Oceasia took her time selecting each card. The "please don't walk away" and "I still believe in you and always believe in us". "Please don't walk away....trust me" was written in all the different cards... I put them down and was really at a loss for words and emotions. I am not a man who wears his

271

feelings on his sleeve nor do I walk around like I'm tougher than nails. I am human... I have feelings... No one likes to get their feelings hurt or get their heart broken. Bein' in prison makes one even more vulnerable because one's guards is always up but defenses go down for a female more than anything; never expecting to be taken advantage of in such form or fashion. You expect more from a female, especially when she knows and understands your struggle and pain. You don't talk that gangster shit to females, you can bare your soul and expect the same level of love that you put in.... maybe more. In prison, a man's heart gets more involved than anything; when on the streets it was more of a just tryna to fuck type of thing with no real commitment. I opened the letter from Oceasia...

Shakim,

I can't explain how much I love u and how much u mean the world to me... I messed up. I know this. I can't have u walk away from me. I had to tell u I'm so sorry. I need u to understand that... I never meant to hurt u or take advantage. Everything I ever said to u is REAL. I'm real about U. I need u to give me another chance. I know u love me. Please call me. I sent u some current. I'm waiting on u.

9 – 12 – 21

Mrs. Edwards

I couldn't believe she still had the nerve to utilize my last government name like that after disrespectin' me to the fullest. I looked on the envelopes of the cards and seen she used my last name as hers in the return address too. I opened the other letter and it was a paper printout photo of me and her huggin' on our very first visit... I ripped it into pieces, balled it up, threw it in the toilet and barked "I don't want to hear that shit!!"

*****

"Shakim Bio, what's poppin' God body? I thought you were bein' held hostage up in that block!!"

Dirt greeted me with a hug and pound as I hit the yard.

"Nah Do Dirt ... I was in fall back mode for a couple seconds... smell me?"

"You don't do your dude like that though... plus, I heard you were buyin' the bar out over there too... poundin' on the table screamin' "BARTENDER" crazily."

We both fell out laughin' and I pulled out a bottle of "White".

"Look at you B!"

"It's all good" I assured.

"I see... I see... yo, what's goin' on in the town? You been on the horns pollyin' and networkin' or what?"

"A little somethin'... nothin' major"

I pulled a Newport out my pocket.

"What the...? Sha... when you started smokin' the product B? You supposed to be puttin' them up not firin' them up!! What's the deal homie?"

"A little stress mode but I'm good and getting' back on point." I responded.

"Not like that you aint... that's the start up paper you smokin' Sun." Do Dirt said, shakin' his head. "What the fuck is stressin' you....wifey?"

He hit the nail right on the head but me, keepin' my game face on and emotions in check on the outside, cleared that up quickly.

"Nah, my dude... everything is good on that end. I'm doin' a million years so I goes through shit every now and then." I answered.

"The whole world is waitin' on you to show them the blueprint on how you always shine Sha so you gotta stay sharp... you God right?"

"True Indeed" I responded.

"Bein' around you made me sharper mentally as well, it's been an honor to study mathematics and hear you build at the ciphers the Gods be havin'. You remind me of my uncle who was so swift before he got on the crack rock."

"Everything is good... trust me" as I puffed on a cigarette.

"Ok then... yo pass that bottle of "White", let me catch a buzz and put you on point to the empire I'm quietly building"

We spun the track on the yard, conversating.

*****

I like to use the same measuring stick on myself as the one I use on others when measuring their morals, principles, integrity, character, flaws, intelligence, habits, conduct, appearance, the way they carry themselves and their ability to do things. The same way I measure these things in a person, I use the same standards on myself. I was taught as a child to always do the "one" that means to do the knowledge. Knowledge is to know, look, listen and respect so sometimes I fall back and do the "one" on myself. There are times where I need to be tightening up on loose ends and flaws in character dealing with self; an analysis or inventory of oneself. By nature, I am very arrogant and sometimes obnoxious but at the same time, I am very charismatic and sometimes cunning. Overall, I'm positive, productive and loyal to the cause of the struggle of my people. I played very dangerous games to generate currency; I robbed and stole amongst other negative things

274

but I feel that my positive outweighs my negatives. I broke a lot of hearts and had mine broken a couple times but I'm very big on loyalty and sincerity.

I love real and I love hard and will give my all. What more could a female want. I'm focused, I refuse to lose, refuse to fail, I'm a provider for my family and seeds and I don't stand on the sidelines with my hand out, I make things happen. I go out there and I take control. I'm generous and very kind hearted; everything a real woman could want. The only thing now is my movements are limited physically because I'm buried alive in Federal Prison so physically, I cannot do a lot of things and that matter to a lot of women in the free world. I looked at Oceasia in a different light because number one, she had K.O.S and she knew and understood our culture, what we stand for and represent. I expected better from her; not for her to do the same as a "regular" chick. She was supposed to be more in tune and on her square. I mean, realistically, I didn't expect her to be celibate and not do her. I know women move off of emotions, I knew she would need the physical comfort of a man but damn, she couldn't wrap it up (use protection)? What the fuck they got all those commercials on TV about condoms for? That didn't mean to give herself to another man unprotected, leaving herself open to anything. It's too many diseases and things out there nowadays. We supposed to be focusin' on her career and gettin' her right, then gettin'"us" right. I put her in front of me. We made vows to each other. How could she break her promises to me like that? I exposed my soul to her, shared my inner most feelin's with her and she knew how dangerous I could be on top of that. It was like she was schemin' on a schemer all along... we were supposed to be a team; for each other; each other's motivator but she did me dirty. In this short time, she learned my history and knew when it came to bein' dirty, my nickname was "FOUL"...

*****

"Yo Sha, everything good with you big homie?" asked Calico as we were locked in for count.

"Yeah Fam, everything is peace" I answered.

"Nah, cause the past couple days or so, you been kinda distant. You know, not your usual self, not talkative and shit plus we aint been buildin' on our usual so I figured you was goin' through somethin'."

"Yeah but everything is good." I responded.

"Word… that's what's up cause I look up to you for keepin' shit together after all these years. You aint lose your mind, get all burnt out or institutionalized, you aint no rat or homo, dope fiend or any of that other shit."

"Yeah"

I smiled at my immaculate character.

"Plus I need you to give me some game on how I can keep my shorty ridin' like how yours is ridin'. You got a rider in your corner Sha"

"Yeah, sun… I sure do" I said as my thoughts shot back to how my "rider" just did me.

*****

As we came out after count, I went to the phones to try Tammi's number cause I submitted a phone list with her number on it earlier that day. The number wasn't on my line as of yet. I slid over to the crowd as the C.O. was calling out names at mail call.

I ended up with a Vibe magazine and another letter from Oceasia then I made it back over to the phones. It was about time I called her to hear what she had to say; hear her reasons for doing me dirty the way she did.

"This is a call from a Federal prison... This is a pre-paid call... You will not be charged for this call... This call is from..."

Oceasia pressed "five".

"Yeah" I nonchalantly greeted her instead of the greetings of love and concern I usually addressed her with.

"Shakim... Baby... Why haven't you been callin' me? ...I missed you so much"

I pulled the phone away from my ear, looking at it like... "this chick must be insane; askin' me some crazy shit like that? She gotta be smokin' somethin'".

"Hello?"

"Yeah... I'm still here... You must not remember the last time we spoke... on your birthday... remember?"

"Yes... Bay, I remember."

"So you don't remember what you said... pretty much told me you're pregnant?"

"Yes, I remember."

"So why the fuck you actin' stupid and tryna play with my intelligence?"

She was shocked because I never came at her like that.

"But Bay"

"Stop calling me that bullshit (Bay)... that's not my name. My name is Shakim Bio-Chemical Wise so cut the fucking jokes."

277

She started sniffing and sobbing ... playing the crying game.

"Look... I aint call to hear this cryin' bullshit."

I had to say that.

"So why did you call me for? It's already killin' me that I hurt and disappointed you. Now you bein' mean to me"

She started back with the crying.

Truthfully, I am not one to listen to a woman cry, it puts me in a state where I feel their pain and I sympathize. I hate seein' females hurt and cryin'. It touches a weak point in me but I can't let Oceasia know that I'm hurting as well.

"Look... I'ma call you back".

"Why? ...talk to me now!"

"I need a little bit more time to think first"

"Shakim, please don't do this to me... to us... I love you."

"I'ma hit you back later" I said.

"Ok... but first let me know that you still love me."

"What?"

"Shakim... do you love me? ...say it!"

"I love you" I responded and then hung up...

*****

Goin' back to that took a lot out of me. Havin' to explain how I felt and what I was goin' through was kinda tough. This was one of the lowest points I've had during my bid so as I write this now I am

278

reminded of the pain and think how I used to joke and clown others for bein' a "Sucka for love"; only to fall victim myself.

I'm not gonna sit here and try to fool you; frontin' like I took it like a champ... Believe me, during phone calls between Oceasia and myself, I said some real nasty, ugly, unbelievable shit about her and her unborn that I wouldn't want to repeat. I was very mean to her, only because I loved her and she hurt me so at the time, I felt I needed to make her feel how hurt I was by returnin' the favor. Sometimes we could talk and sometimes I would lash out and hang up... but she always accepted my calls anytime I called back. Sometimes I would call on a particular day then I'd take several days or several weeks to call again. At times I was only callin' like once a month but no matter what, she always pressed "five" (accepted the call), not knowin' what to expect from me lyrically. She was hurtin' too but still she continued to write and send me cards even though I wasn't responding. Sometimes I hated her because I loved her so much.

$$*****$$

I don't know what made me call Tammi but I did and she was very happy to hear my voice. She made me smile big time, we reminisced on old times and she put me on point with what was goin' on around the way; filling me in on her new environment in Charlotte, NC. A lot of times, when our conversation was goin' good, the phone would beep to let us know our fifteen minutes was comin' to an end; I always told her I'ma hit her back...

"Ok... in thirty?" she asked.

"Nah... fall back ma. I'ma hit you right back on another line... just press five"

I was now crossing that line.... the lines I had for Oceasia, I was now using to call Tammi. It was just as bad as fuckin' another female in the same bed me and my wife slept in. I crossed that line and kept it movin' like I did nothing wrong... shit, Shorty (Oceasia) gave up the goods to another "Scram Jones" and got pregnant... so I can't do no harm in talkin' and kickin' it, right? Shiiiiiiit... I was re-openin' doors that should've stayed bolted closed.

*****

"Shakim... you don't call me like you used to Bay... You know I need to talk to you" said Oceasia as she complained. This became her routine every time I called, which was very spotty (here and there).

"I didn't want to call and bother your baby's father or get in the way of anything"

I was being funny and mean towards her at the same time.

Sometimes I didn't even understand why she even put up with my shit. I was locked up, my only connection to her was when she pressed "five". Once she stopped pressing "five" our relationship was over but she kept pressing "5" every time I called.

"Bay... stop that... You are my husband! You're my soul mate! There is no other man. My baby father is only the sperm donor. I don't have no feelings for him. I love you and only you" she stressed.

"Hold up... How can you say that? You spent time with dude... gave yourself to him... without usin' protection, you got pregnant, you're havin' his seed and you mean to tell me you have no feelin's for him at all?"

"That's what I said" she proclaimed sternly.

"Get the fuck outta here" I said and hung up.

CHAPTER 29

Me and Tammi were talkin' regularly and she was writin' and sendin' photos. I enjoyed her conversation, she inquired about "my girl" so I told her we were "straight" to which she said "y'all can't be straight cause all of a sudden you givin' me all this phone time". I brushed that off, knowin' I still had Tammi. She was goin' through too many failed relationships with dudes and her son's father was still a loser. She was on that police force shit hard too, while remaining street oriented yet classy at the same time but… she was a fucking cop now. Wooowwwwww.

"You gonna send me some sexy shots of you with your badge and gun, while profilin' in your panties for me?" I joked with her.

"I'ma see Sha… I may just do that for you."

✶✶✶✶✶

I can never forget my duty as a civilized man and a righteous man. I must always stand on my square. I'm God all day, every day so what I was doin' to Oceasia was unacceptable and I knew it. I'm supposed to be the sole controller of our universe. It just took me a second to get back on my square. I also had to start actin' my age. I was fuckin' up. I'm a General so before I removed my own stripes and demoted myself, I had to tighten up; had to start showin' and provin' again.

In reality, I didn't need Oceasia for no financial gain. I could get my own currency. I'm a hustler, been one for a long time; I'm known to make things happen so it wasn't like I needed her because she kept funds in my account. I needed her for emotional, mental, spiritual and lyrical reasons. We were on a higher plane of energy. I wanted to manifest force and power through her, help her with her career, let her shine and in the process, I'd shine as well. I loved her for her, you gotta remember when we first started communicatin' it was all mental. We built on lessons, on reality but there was nothin' physical, we wasn't on that level; couldn't be. Oceasia had no idea what I looked like and I didn't know what she looked like either. We were attracted to each other's mind, our vibe began there first so it was just gonna take some time to get back to that first stage; a time where time could not be measured... it just had to happen on its own again.

* * * * *

"Dirt" started fallin' back a lot. Somethin' was goin' on on the outs and like myself he shielded it and kept everyone out. He wasn't comin' out to the yard like he usualy did so I had to sneak up in his block, which was on the other side of the prison's compound. Sometimes he would be in the bed at 12:30 p.m., yeah, he was goin' through somethin'... I guess because he was goin' home within 15 months or so, he was fallin' back more and more. I still went and checked for him. I told him about Tammi and he lit up and laughed.

"You better be careful Sha and don't let the Earth find out."

Dirt just didn't know what I was goin' through and that I didn't care if she found out anything; at that point, I was doing me.

"About time you got at Shorty, she was goin' at you hard body".

I started hanging with True God and Miz more frequent, schemin' on some moves. One afternoon, Miz surprised me by askin' me why I aint runnin' to my unit to call my shorty. He remembered how I used to slide off to the phones to call my earth, leavin' them outside. I told him I was good and spreadin' my wings but everything was still love. I knew he sensed that I was frontin'... just like how I sensed the hate he felt askin' me about my relationship.

* * * * *

282

"This is a call from Federal prison... This is a pre-paid call... You will not be charged for this call... This call is from..."

Oceasia accepted by pressing five.

"PEACE!"

"Bay... I miss you. I need you to call me all the time like before. It's like I'm losin' you. You're changin'."

"Is that so?" I asked sarcastically. "How you expect me to act? You lied to me; sayin' how much you love me, we were workin' on getting' your career on point, you had me makin' all these moves"

I blew air.

"Bay, I never lied to you. I love you and nothin' has changed."

"I know, you just pregnant by another dude, a destroy power at that"

I knew this because she and I did build on this through letters, she wrote me and explained who "Scramz (a nickname for a sucka, a clown, a lame and in this case, Oceasia's baby's father)" was... He was a savage from New Orleans; she was havin' a seed for a savage poison animal eater. Wow!

"Bay... listen to me. I really need to talk to you... this phone thing isn't getting' it... You don't call me like you used to... I know you usin' the other lines to call other people... I can feel your energy and your attitude and tone changes. If you didn't love me you wouldn't call... so listen to me... next week I'm flyin' out there to West Virginia. Raheeme's girl is supposed to call me back and let me know everything. I'm gonna stay with her for the weekend. I'm comin' to see you next weekend... so if you don't want me to come, let me know before I waste this current on the plane ticket and all. I need to see you. Do you want me to come or what?"

---Slience---

"Bay?' she started with the sniffing and cryin'.

"I'm still here" I informed.

"Do you want me to come or what? I got until tomorrow to pay for this ticket."

"I will let you know by tomorrow."

"What?" she scoffed.

I laughed to myself but let her hear me.

"Shakim?"

"What's up?" I inquired...

"You tell me" she snapped.

"You know what's up... I better see you next weekend."

＊＊＊＊＊

    Aww shit!!! I got back on my hard body workout to get extra right for the visit with Oceasia the following weekend. You know I had to get extra on point too. Had to let her see and know that I'm still "like that" and that I'm someone to hold on to forever ever. I had to scream at the cats in laundry to get the new crispy khaki shirt and pants and some new boots. I upped my pull-up and dip workout; stepped up my push-ups and water bags routines too. I had to look my part although, even if I didn't workout at all, I'd still look my part on the day of the visit, I shine heavily, regardless.

＊＊＊＊＊

The following morning, I was on the walkway comin' back from work. I was rushin' to go smoke a cigarette when Big Rah caught up with me.

Peace to the God!!"

"Peace Big Rah, what's good Sun?"

"You! You already know that I'm givin' you a heads up, your Earth Rita got in touch with my wiz Rita and they're comin' through next weekend so they're both gonna be out there reppin' Sun.... You my manz from the heart so I'ma tell my Rita to look out and don't accept no current other than gas money from your Earth... I wanna see you out there shinin'" said Raheeme, he smiled and gave me a pound.

"No doubt Rah... good lookin' out... Yo... peep this though. I'm not tryna let it be known that I'm slidin' out on the "dance floor (visiting room)"; don't need people in my business, nah mean?"

"C'mon Sha... I aint one of these young dudes who just started biddin'. I was in Sing-Sing when you were watchin' Sesame Street singin' along with Big Bird."

We both laughed hysterically. Rah was still stuck in the early eighties, not knowin' that in the mid and late eighties my guns was BARKIN' crazily too.

*****

I felt kind of bad that I was hidin' shit from Rah. That was my manz but how could I tell him that me and my Earth was not on good terms and we were goin' through somethin' because she was pregnant by another dude? Especially after the way I had been biggin' her up and reppin' her to everybody the way I was... My pride wouldn't let me expose her violation as of yet but I knew Rah would know once he seen her, if she was showing. That was on my mind kinda heavy too, I

285

thought to myself "Shit! I'ma be on the dance floor with a pregnant chick... I can't be on no lovey-dovey shit out there. I'm not thirsty for no love, I'm Shakim Bio from Queens." Man, this shit was killin' me.

*****

I could tell Calico had been watchin' my movements because since he moved in the cell with me, he would always be in the cell but when I would come in, he'd get up to leave; I'd stop him, lettin' him know I'm straight and he didn't have to bounce.

"You usually play the cell to write scribes so I'ma give you your space"

"Nah, nah... I'm good Calico"

"Yeah? I notice you aint been scribin' as hard plus you hardly open up the mail you get... what's good?"

"Nothing B... I be playin' the phone hard... that's all"

"Yeah. I see that too... but you aint on the phone wit your girl though."

I turned and asked him...

"Why you say that?"

"The way you used to play the unit to call her... Now things is different, you don't play mail call like that... and that look in your eyes aint the same. Remember, I live in the cell with you Sha."

I smiled and said...

"Nah... I'm good... I'm just bein' entertained by this one chick I know from the town... that's all."

"Who?" Calico asked.

I gave him the spill about Tammi and our history.

"What's good with your girl though?"

"We straight... I just need a little space from her" I reassured.

"The way you was reppin' her and her bein' the rider that she is, you need to focus on her, Sha."

"I'm good Calico. I'm Shakim Bio"

"I know... from Queens"

We both laughed.

*****

I was getting' myself on point for the visit and at the same time, I was thinkin' of what I would say to Oceasia. I had to let her know that I was very disappointed in her and that I had no other choice but to move on and do me... so that meant I was lettin' her go. I went over several scenarios in my mental as to how I was gonna approach and orchestrate the situation. I didn't want to hurt her any more than she already was but I was beyond hurt.

*****

I was still spittin' to Tammi crazily. She had me kinda open on her all over again. I guess it was because I was tryna forget the situation I was in with Oceasia. Now Tammi was sendin' me her new work schedule, demandin' that I call her so she could hear my voice and bug out with me. She was real funny and kept me laughin', especially when she would bring up the females from around her way she swore I was messin' with. She was a very open person and she didn't hide the fact that she was crazy about me even though I was a very street oriented dude and kept my hands into somethin'; still having ties that kept me in tune and correspondin' with other females. Tammi accepted my ways and didn't mind as long as I kept other shorties in line and out of her mix; I was definitely cool with that.

*****

"Shakim Bio... the illest Brooklyn dude from Queens!!" Dirt said as he greeted me with an embrace and pound handshake. "What's going on my dude? ...You workin' out three times a day... What the fuck you on B?" questioned Dirt.

"Nah... I been slackin' a bit and poppin' mad bottles... so I gotta get back, smell me?"

"Yeah, I know that's right but you goin' hard body... what... you getting' ready to hit that dance floor or somethin'?" he asked, looking directly at me.

"Nah Sun... I'm just tryna to get back."

"Get back to what? ...You aint gonna get no bigger!!... Who's comin', that police chick you got? I know you reminded her that you still that dude"

I laughed at Dirt tryna to pick me and fish for information.

"Nah, she aint ready yet... but she will be soon" I smiled.

"Yeah... I know you still got that Jay – Z spit game flow and all that. I know someone is comin' through... Let me find out you sneakin' the Jamican chick... or is it the Earth?"

We started laughin'. Dirt was throwin' his hands up in a fightin' stance, swingin' playful punches in the air; he kept comin' at me with questions...

"C'mon my dude. what is it?"

"Yo… I'ma let you know when it's time Sun… let me do this my way, Shakim Bio-Chemical Wise style."

"No doubt!" he said as he dapped me up. "Whatever you up to, I know it's a plan that's on point!"

I smiled at his comment… only if son knew the real.

$$* * * * *$$

A week came and left that quick, it was almost the weekend… the weekend I had been getting' ready for. I came out the cell after the 4 pm count, skipped the mail call and went straight over to the phones. I dialed Oceasia's number followed by my pac. "Thank you" the automated operator replied and Oceasia's phone started ringin'. After about five rings, Oceasia answered "Hello?" and the recording came on, she quickly accepted by pressin' "five"

"Bay?"

"Peace" I responded.

"Why haven't you called? I thought y'all was locked down or somethin'… I was worryin', thinkin' I'ma fly out there and not be able to see you" she said, soundin' kinda sad.

"I was takin' care of a few things" I kicked.

"It was so important that you couldn't call me? You used to call me every day or at least you tried to."

"Is that so?… I was busy on a few things." I shot back.

"Well will you be busy this weekend? I would like to see you and talk to you."

"Nah, I'm not gonna be busy this weekend." I said, tryna be funny.

"You definitely a trip Shakim… born u truth I truly love you and I know you know this or I would never put up with your bullshit and childish games. I put up with it not because I have to born u truth because I love you and everything about you. My flight leaves tomorrow at the born hour so call me at the God hour. I trust that Rita is good peoples and you don't have me in no savage crib, even though, I would sleep anywhere if it means I get to come see you."

"Ok." I spat.

"That's all I get… a Ok?"

"It sounds good. You know sound travels at the rate of 1,120 feet per second. You spit so you know the sound of music, right? All you need is a beat."

"Yeah, like L.L. I need a beat and you're gonna give it to me. Admit it Shakim, you love me just as much as I love you."

"I will see you when you get here." I responded.

"That sounds like music to my ears, the kind of music I love"

"Aiiight"

"What time Shakim?" she asked.

"The God hour."

"That's my Bay. I love you."

"Peace"

"No Peace… you know what it is"

"Ok then… No peace… war then." I said sarcastically.

"What?" she scoffed.

"I love you too" I finally said.

She started laughin' and I hung up.

*****

That Thursday evening, I was ever ready to make that call. I called several times and couldn't catch Oceasia. I called at 7 p.m. like she asked, then 7:05 p.m., 7:08 p.m., 7:11 p.m. and I called back to back, attempting to catch her before she boarded the plane. By 7:50 p.m., I tried again only to get her voicemail after a few rings. I was semi-buggin', thinkin' "What type of shit is this?" I know Shorty aint playin' no fucking games with a fella." At 8 p.m., I tried again and after several rings, she picked up and accepted the call.

"Peace"

"Peace... what's good?"

"What you want to be good?" she replied.

"I thought you wanted me to call at the God hour."

"I did, I was busy handling a few things" she kicked back.

It was some noise in the background like... a radio.

"Where you at?" I questioned.

"In my skin, where I'm supposed to be."

"Oh yeah? We rockin' like that now?" I asked.

She said somethin' but I couldn't hear her due to the radio or whatever it was.

"Turn the radio down cause I can't hear you" I shouted.

"I aint turnin' nothing down."

"You stay on that bullshit."

"I gotta go... I gotta hang up now." she yelled.

"So why you pressed "five" then if you wanna play games?"

"We ready to take off. I'm on the plane, we on the runway waitin' to take off. I BEEN supposed to turn this phone off!!"

"OH...."

I felt so stupid as I hung up.

*****

Friday morning I was up early. I got my pull-ups and dip game in early and was real vicious before I called Oceasia on the horn. She made it in late last night and I knew she was up waitin' on my call. She was so happy and I was too; we spoke for ten minutes. She had to get ready by takin' a shower and what not because she and Rita was leavin' within the hour to be among the first ones on the visit. I spoke to Rah's wiz Rita and thanked her for showin' love, allowin' my Earth to stay with her. It was all Love on Rita's part so me and Oceasia hung up after sayin' we'll see each other soon.

By breakfast, I went to wait for Big Rah, I stood outside in the smokin' section in front of the unit.

"Yo Shakim... Peace to the God!!"

"Peace"

"You look like you just smoked a cigarette."

"Yeah? I'm about to blaze another one right now too."

"You ready?" asked Rah.

"Born ready my G!!" I responded.

"Well make sure you're on point when they call your name."

"No doubt!"

"See you on the dance floor."

"No question!"

I passed the lit cigarette to Rah and headed back to my unit.

✳✳✳✳✳

By 7:30 am, I was showered; my mouth was extra, extra minty so I had no tobacco on the breath. My head was extra bald and my clothes was on point. I had on the Egyptian must oil scent, my body was on blast and my boots was laced up right. I was on one trillion and what's ill about it was I didn't get dressed all the way until after the C.O. came to my cell door tellin' me I had a visit. Once I was ready, I snatched up the photo tickets and pepper mint candy and was on my way. I strolled down the walkway but I slowed up to see if Raheeme was comin'. I knew they had to have called him by now. Convicts on the yard seen me walkin' down the walkway with no question, they knew where I was headed, lookin' laced up like that. I made it to the west corridor and went toward the visitin' room. Once I got there, I seen Raheeme was already there in front of the mirror adjusting the round framed glasses he only wore on visits. Yeah, son had a special pair just for the dance floor. I greeted him...

Peace!"

"Peace! Yo what took you so long? I been waiting on you like ten minutes... I figured you must not want no V.I. so I journeyed up here myself."

"Word? They just called me... so I was lookin' to see where you were."

I handed the C.O. my ID card, he filled out the log book and listed what I had in my possession, photo tickets and all. The C.O. patted me down and made me and Rah go through a metal detector before handin' back our I.D. cards.

"Have a nice visit... before you sit down, stop by the front desk and hand in your I.D.

"Ok C.O." I responded.

"Yeah Davis... we got you" responded Raheeme as we made it to the steel door.

CHAPTER 30

When we went inside the visiting hall, it was semi-packed. This was my first time getting' a visit at Big Sandy but I noticed all visiting halls was built pretty much the same. I bopped to the head C.O.'s desk and gave her my ID card. I looked around to see where Oceasia was seated, I seen her sittin' down in the middle section of the five row seating area, close to the back... she waved to me.

Big Rah was already headed in Oceasia's direction because his "Wiz" was sittin' two seats over. The seating arrangement was different at this spot, instead of sittin' across from each other with a table between us, we got to sit side by side; this way you could put your arm around your visitor and stay hugged up the whole visit. Shit was lovely! As I walked toward Oceasia, she was cheesin' crazily... as I got closer to where she was sitting, she got up. She was wearing a loose fitting, jean jacket outfit with an oversized blue t-shirt, white and yellow Lacoste sneakers with ankles socks. As she stood there, I could see her stomach sticking out, showin' that she was pregnant. I slowed up and then the whole situation just stopped me in my tracks... I was fucked up in thought... Oceasia saw that I stopped... the smile left my face... the expression that replaced my smile MUST have told over a million different stories... and none of them pleasant.

"Shakim" Oceasia said, lookin' me in my face; her eyes started to water as she said...

"Please don't do this to me... I'm here."

I stood there for another few seconds then started walkin' those last few steps toward her, we embraced... she was holdin' on to me for dear life but the hug I gave her was half-hearted, nowhere near as tight as the one she was givin' me. She lifted her face to kiss me so I pecked her lips. "What?" she asked me... Deep down I knew I was playin' myself... people was starin' at me but I couldn't tongue kiss and hug a pregnant woman, who was carrying the next man's seed.

"Shakim?"

"What's good?"

"Kiss me baby... don't do me like this... please..."

I shut her up by kissin' her deeply, lettin' her taste my tongue then she stopped me so she could suck on my bottom lip.

"I love you Shakim"

"I love you too" I said as we broke our embrace.

I knew she could tell that our kiss was not intense and passionate as it had been in the past. I could feel her tremble as I turned in my seat and asked her...

"How could you do this to me?"

It was already out the bag... Big Rah seen that she was showin', his wiz already knew from when she picked Oceasia up at the airport. Rah was surprised to see this... now he knew what was eatin' me up all this time; why I was drinkin' heavily and smokin' cee i germs. Now he knew... He and his wisdom held hands but was lookin' to see my reaction, makin' it clear to me that Oceasia shared her fears with Rah's wiz Rita... she feared a negative reaction from me.

Do what Baby?"

"Now you wanna play games... if that's what you came here to do I'ma get up and leave you sittin' here by yourself... I can go back to my unit and get my drink on"

I started to get up but she grabbed my arm and stopped me.

"No... wait! Don't leave!"

I turned and looked in her eyes.

"Shakim... I didn't mean for it to happen"

Oceasia's eyes started fillin' with tears again, I had to stop her and tell her to "dry those tears". I didn't want to see her cry or put on a show out there on the visit. She had to regroup and gather herself then she opened up and told me everything. She took me by the hands and while she was playin' and massagin' my inner palms, she explained to me, who the father of the unborn baby was, how it happened and that she wanted me to forgive her. She kept repeatin' that he meant nothin' to her and that he wasn't even a part of her life. I interrupted her...

"But now he is... what you mean he means nothin'? You're carryin' his seed... that means a lot" I quietly barked.

She told me that her gettin' pregnant was a mistake.

"Ma, listen.... you knew things like this can happen when you practice unprotected sex. He coulda gave you a disease or somethin', what the fuck is wrong wit you?"

I was tryin' my best to remain calm and not lose my composure or get loud... I stared at her. She explained to me how bad she wanted a seed, how a seed would complete her and due to my situation I couldn't give her one. She explained how she was told that she could never conceive a child and how this pregnancy and baby was a blessing. I was startin' to think that maybe she was crazy after all; I snatched my hand and turned away from her.

"Shakim... Don't do this... I still love you the same and I want to be with you forever."

"Yeah... but with a baby... somebody else's baby at that" I responded.

She then went into how I really don't love her because I didn't understand what she was goin' through, been through and so on. She said I would've done her dirty if I was out, probably wouldn't give her the time of day. Said I would've been messing with so many wisdoms (women) and how it wasn't fair because I already had two seeds by two different women. She said I was not bein' right and exact and that I was so selfish. I sat there and listened to her go on and on and on...

Oceasia knew I had other wisdoms because I wasn't callin' like I used to and I wasn't bein' supportive. She was comin' at me like I was her baby's daddy, like I was to blame for her bein' pregnant.

The first day of visit we went back and forth, Oceasia wanted me to let her hold my hand, rub her small hands in mine and I knew deep down that she did love me but I knew I couldn't keep her. I had to let her go. I got up to use the bathroom and she thought I wasn't coming back, thought I was gonna leave her sittin' out there. I gave her my "Word is Bond" that I would be back. On my way to the bathroom, I passed Raheeme... I saw the look in his eyes... he looked like he wanted to cry.

*****

I came back from the bathroom with a chess board, checker pieces and a deck of cards. I wanted to have fun with Oceasia, make her smile, laugh and enjoy her company on this visit. I beat her in a few games but she won a few too; she was enjoyin' herself and laughin' her ass off. We played cards for a little while and out of nowhere, she looked at me and said...

"Shakim?"

"Yeah, what's good?"

"When you gonna tell me that you're leavin' me and it's over between us?"

I stared at her, wonderin' how she sensed what I had been tryna figure a way to say but hadn't said yet. I put the cards down and looked to the ground, when I looked back up at her she was tearin' up in the eyes again.

"Ma... let's just enjoy the visits, let's enjoy each other's company right now."

"But I can't... I can't live without you Sha. You are everything to me."

"I hear you" I responded.

"So... you leavin' me? ...is that it? ...You gonna leave me baby?"

I stared at her for a good minute before responding...

"No... I'm not leavin' you. I'm still with you."

*****

On the way back from the visit, Rah waited for me outside with a lit cigarette. We walked in silence for a few minutes before he broke the ice.

"How'd you enjoyed your visit?"

"It was peace" I responded.

Rah passed me the cigarette. I needed a whole one to myself but because I didn't have one on me, half a stogie had to do.

"Shakim... you my manz... I respect you; always know and understand that. I know you're goin' through a lot. I saw it in your ways and actions

299

these past few weeks. Remain strong and always be on your square… that Earth loves you."

"Yeah Rah I know, I know" I replied as I smoked that half of a cigarette like it was the last one in the world.

*****

I stayed inside the unit the rest of that evening. I didn't wanna go out or kick it with anyone at all. I knew word that I was on the dance floor with a pregnant looking chick had spread like a wild forest fire; dudes gossip in prison like crazy!

I wasn't sweating what would be said, I really didn't give a fuck about what someone thought of me and my situation. It was all about what I thought about me and my situation so I prepared myself mentally, for what direction I would take on tomorrow's visit with Oceasia. I had to let her know how I saw things.

*****

The next morning, I got up and did my routine pull-ups, dips and hit the water bag to workout my arms real heavy. The weekend schedule was run different than the workdays in the Feds; they opened up the doors late, more like 6:30 – 6:45 am. I did my workout then jumped on the telephone. After Oceasia picked up and let the recording play half way, she quickly accepted the call.

"Good Morning My God, lover and future husband."

"Peace Queen… what's good?"

"Always you… forever you… I really enjoyed our visit yesterday Bay."

"Yeah, it was peaceful. I was very happy to see you."

"I'm gettin' ready to come see you again now; we'll be there before the born hour."

"Ok then."

"Nine – twelve – twenty one." she said happily.

"True Indeed."

* * * * *

Me and Rah walked up to the west corridor together, he was smoking a "germ" (cigarette) on the way. I didn't want none because I didn't want to smell or taste like cigarette smoke as I did plan on kissin' Oceasia again. I was gonna "go in" because it may be our last time seein' each other. I didn't know for sure but once we made it to the visiting room, we went through the procedures of logging in and bein' pat searched. It was Saturday so the camera man would be in around noon to 2pm but he didn't show up at all the day before plus my mind wasn't right to take any photos. As our ID cards were handed back and allowed into the visiting hall, I stepped to the front desk... it was really crowded to be only almost 9am. I looked around and seen Oceasia sittin' in the back row almost by the vendin' machines. Rah's wisdom was sittin' in the middle row so that meant he wouldn't be able to hear me or see my facial expressions; I needed some one on one with Oceasia without anyone else's antennas bein' up.

Oceasia was smiling and waving to let me know where she was sittin'. I walked in her direction, passing other convicts who were sittin' with their families and loved ones. Oceasia stood up, she was wearing loose fitting black jeans and a pinkish and white polo shirt with a pink collar; her black jacket was on the chair and she had her pink and white Nike "Air Max" sneakers on. She was semi-showin' as her tummy was

301

sticking out a little somethin'. We embraced, I squeezed her gently and she immediately went for my mouth to kiss me. I opened my mouth and passionately French kissed her and she routinely stopped to suck on my bottom lip. She said "Squeeze my ass, Bay" we laughed as I got my squeeze, feels and rub on. I just didn't wanna take advantage of her bein' that she was pregnant... with another man's seed. Her small hands roamed all over my chest as she slipped them under my khaki shirt to feel my skin.

"What you wearing?" she asked.

"You know... your favorite" I responded as she went in for another deep kiss.

We knew we were pushin' the limit but it was overdue. She rested her head on my chest and deeply inhaled. We finally sat down, I put my arm around her and she leaned more into me layin' her head on my shoulder.

"Ooohhh... I'm lovin' this right here!" she exclaimed before stealin' another kiss from my lips.

I seen that she was so happy and needed my comfort so I kept my arm around her and we had fun... sneakin' kisses and talkin' shit to each other.

"You hungry, Bay?" she asked.

"Yeah... but don't get up yet" I gently demanded as we laughed.

During the visit, we built about my case, my seeds, my mom, my sisters, her mom... I didn't want to bring up her music career or the moves we were strivin' to manifest because that was all down the drain... she kept her head on my shoulder and would raise up to turn, look me in my eyes and ask me.

302

"What are you thinking?'

"I'm thinking about you."

"Well… I want you to think about us" she announced as she placed her head back on my shoulder.

"Let me ask you somethin'…."

I had come to the point where I had to speak my mind.

"Yes Bay" she said with inquiring eyes...

"What about your baby's dad? …You can't just forget that he exists. What you gonna do? You gotta have a plan to raise your seed; he's gonna wanna see his child."

"No he isn't… he doesn't care. We are not together… he knows who I want, he knows all about you. He was just there at that moment, Bay. I don't want him, I want you."

I had to really spark Oceasia's brain. I explained to her the sciences of mathematics, of man, woman and child, God and Earth… what drew her to me…. Why I was attracted to her mental first before we took anything to the physical… we never knew what each other looked like… I spoke on how we lost contact and re-linked up; how I opened up to her and allowed her into my world and she allowed me into hers. I reminded her how everything was destroyed but I had to remain a general, stay strong and always stay God. I told her I didn't know how this would work or if it could.

"Shakim"

"I'm listening…."

"I don't doubt us... I know and understand what you're sayin'... but I'm gonna be right here with you as your girl, your wife, your Earth; your everything" she said, wipin' a tear a way.

We remained quiet for a while... just enjoyin' the moment. I told her to go get me some chicken wings and some water. She told me that ever since she'd been restin' her head on me, she'd been following my heart beat and how her heart was in tune with mine. She said we belong to each other then she stole a kiss and jumped up to go get me somethin' to eat.

*****

We ate up a storm and when it was time to take reflections, Oceasia and I acted like we were on a photo shoot... we had fun... I took a lot of close up shots with her so I could have my artist do a portrait of us... but you know how women are... always movin' off of emotions; she swore I had the photograper takin' close ups because I didn't want no photos of her showin' that she was pregnant so she had an attitude when we returned to our seats but It wasn't long before I had her smilin' and laughin' her ass off again.

*****

Oceasia was resting her head on my shoulder while my arm was wrapped around her shoulder. Her hands were roaming and she was feelin' areas where she knew she wasn't supposed to in the visiting room. We were like little kids on that visit, she kept lookin' around to see if the C.O.s, who were positioned in the visitin' room to watch, noticed she was getting' her rubs, feels and kisses on; we had so much fun, I can't front. Eventually, Shorty started playin' with the loose ends of her dreads, tangling with the loose ends like it was somethin' she does when she's nervous or has somethin' heavy on her mental.

"Ma...what's on your mind?"

304

"You"

She gave me a quick peck on the lips then she proceeded...

"I want to ask you somethin' Bay."

"What?"

"Do you know that I really love you... you know that right?"

"I... dun... know!" was my response, knowin' she was easily irritated when I did this.

"See...? Why you gotta do that?"

I started laughin' at her and she playfully smacked me in the face.

"For real Shakim... you know I love you right? I came way out here to see you and talk to you. You mean the world to me. You know this don't you? I will do anything for you."

"What?" I sat up to hear her clearly.

"I said I will do anything for you Shakim. Anything... Ask me... I will show you"

She was still twisting the loose ends of her dreads.

"Anything?" I asked.

"Yeah... Anything... just ask me" she said confidently as she sat up and looked me in the eyes.

All kinds of thoughts was runnin' wild in my mind as I looked at her and then at her stomach where she was carrying that seed... that seed that wasn't mine... wasn't planted by me... I looked back up in her eyes and said...

305

"I thought of something."

"What?" she quickly asked; thirsty for me to tell her what I wanted her to do to prove herself to me.

"Pop one of those little loose dreads off and hand it to me"

I surprised her with my odd request and she obliged, fighting with a dread, finally poppin' it and givin' it to me. I still have that lock of her hair to this very day.

*****

We were given a five minute warning before the end of the visit. This was the time to get the hugs and extra kisses in so like young teenagers, we were at it. She stopped me and looked up at me in my eyes as we stood face to face...

"Bay, I want to ask you somethin' but don't answer me until tomorrow... give me an answer... Do you want me to kill my seed? Think it over... I said I will do anything for you... so tell me do you want me to kill my seed"

She wiped a tear away, kissed me and said...

"I love you Shakim."

"Love you too, see you tomorrow but I'ma call tonight."

"But don't give me an answer over the phone, tell me tomorrow, face to face"

We hugged and kissed once again, not wantin' to let each other go.

*****

Once I got stripped searched, re-dressed and made it out to the compound walkway, I stood around until Rah made it out. He stopped to light a cigarette then greeted me...

"Peace Sha"

"Peace" I responded. "Yo, I had a good one."

"Yeah, I saw you and your Earth havin' a ball back there. I thought you was gonna get butt-ball and get it in up in there"

We both started laughin' out loud but in my mind I thought... "I didn't know it was that obvious."

"Shakim... we really need to build... and it's important."

"Ok... No doubt... let's build"

We slow walked back to the unit even though yard recall was about to be called at any moment.

"You had K.O.S. for a very long time... knowledged 120 lessons."

"One twenty two" I interrupted.

"One twenty two then... You are very swift and I admire you for a lot of reasons... you are a real, sincere and genuine dude"

"True Indeed"

"You know and understand that our Earths are very important, they reflect our light and keep our nation in constant reproduction so it is our duty to keep them in their proper orbit."

"True Indeed Sun... but what are you gettin' at?" I asked.

"Shakim Bio, that Earth really, really loves you. Shorty digs you hard and she wants to be in your life badly. I don't know what you feed her but she is crazy about you... she is truly a blessing to you. I know she fucked up and it hurt you... but it aint nothin' you can't fix and put back in order. You got seeds and you are in here my G. Don't mess that Earth's life up and make her kill her seed, Sha... don't do that."

"Yeah?" I responded.

I knew right then and there, that Oceasia had pre-planned to ask me if I wanted her to abort her pregnancy and that she revealed her thoughts to Rah's wiz before that visit, therefore Rah's wife told him.

"Sha... if she deads that seed and by any means you choose to move on without her... her life will be all messed up cause she will be without you and without the child she always wanted, don't do that to her. She doesn't deserve that. Give her, her chance to produce life... she will love you more."

"Yo... what makes you think I would decide she should kill her seed?"

I had to ask Rah this; I had to see how he viewed me.

"She told my wiz that she loves you so much that she was gonna ask you what you want cause your ways and actions are sayin' somethin' your words aren't... not sayin' you would make her... but she wants and needs to know where you stand on this. I just want you to be very conscious in your decision - making and don't destroy her or that unborn seed's life. She chose you and you're in prison, that should tell you she's really feelin' you. Shorty is not ugly; there are a million cats out there who would love to have her and they can do more for her than you and I put together... because we are in here but she chose why cipher universe... YOU! So do what's right for y'all and let her have that seed."

I was silent as I walked, thinkin' about what Raheeme said. I wasn't hatin' on the unborn seed but I was upset that it wasn't planted by me and it came between what me and Oceasia built or tried to build.

The situation with Oceasia, the baby and all that came with it was testin' me to see what type of man I was. My intention of getting' her down there to see me was to tell her how I felt, let her go and move on with my life... but my plans backfired and I got sucked in deeper as I motioned for Rah to pass me a cee I germ and remained in deep thought.

A voice came over the institution's intercom system, announcing...

<u>YARD RECALL</u>!!   <u>YARD RECALL</u>!!

"Yo Rah, I'ma build with you later my dude. One- One!!"

"Ok Shakim"

We gave each other pounds and I traveled to my unit's door.

*****

I stayed in after count again... me and Calico had our building session; he knew that my Earth came up but I still didn't reveal my situation even though I knew it was probably floatin' around by now. It was all good, I had to deal with it regardless. I stayed in the cell listenin' to the radio and as I mentioned before, Shade 45 was poppin' on Saturdays and it was Saturday. Around 9pm, I called Oceasia to make sure she was good and enjoyin' her stay, she said she was comfortable with Rita and that she was really nice. I knew she was really feelin' her if she told her that she was gonna let me decide her seeds fate. I told her I loved her and that I would call her early tomorrow. We exchanged our words of Love, hung up and I took it in for the night.

*****

The next morning, as soon as the cell doors were opened, I was already ready for my Sunday a.m. workout. I checked my watch, it was 6:37am, I got into beast mode with the pull-ups, dips, and push-ups. I

309

did a light ten sets and went to get some water then dipped over to the phone booths.

I dialed Oceasia's number and my pac digits, after a few rings, she picked up, as soon as the recording started... she accepted.

"Peace Bay"

"Peace Ma, what's good my Beautiful Breathing Diamond?"

"Wow... I haven't heard that name in a minute Bay. I feel great already, we're leavin' in like five minutes to come up there"

"Ok, I will be ready."

"I'm already ready Bay."

"Love you"

"Always do"

Just as we hung up, they called coffee hour to the chow hall. I stepped outside to take a walk and smoke a cigarette.

*****

"Peace to the God!"

"Peace!" I responded to Serious Wisdom.

"I see you finally came out, haven't seen you in a few days."

"Allah is God in the Earth and Heaven, he is just and true and there is no unrighteousness in him but he is not unseen. He is seen and heard everywhere, for he is the all eye seeing"

That response I gave was me showin' my ability to quote the thirty-seventh degree in the one through forty.

310

"True Indeed Shakim Bio, true indeed... I heard you been out there on the Vee, who came up, your sisters or one of your shorties?"

"Now Cipher Sun of Man, my Earth from N.O. came through to see me so we could build and add on."

"Word?" he responded soundin' very surprised.

I was waiting for him to speak on whatever he heard but he switched topics.

"You addin' on at the rally held at the end of this moon?"

"No question... plus I'm bringin' my celly Calico."

"That's peace Sha, I see how he been playin' the law library a lot too."

"Yeah... he realizes that there is no future in these concentration camps, he is waking up now." I spitted.

"Shiiiiit... with a celly like Shakim Bio, he has no other choice"

We laughed at that comment.

* * * * *

On the last day of the three day visit with our earths, me and Big Rah was on our way up to the visiting room. My Khaki wears were extra crisp and I was so sharp and on point you couldn't tell me nothin'. I gave Rah a few extra photo tickets so he could flick it up as well. I didn't want all the shine, I don't mind sharing it. We small talked as we took quick steps on the way. Rah also had to steam a Newport on the way; I couldn't because I didn't want to taste like a Newport when I kissed my Earth. We went through the procedures of loggin' in and we got pat searched... after that, we took our ID cards and made our way through the visiting hall to the front desk... Today was Sunday and it was gonna be jam packed and I was glad to be in the first group of fifteen convicts being let into the visiting room. I saw Oceasia sittin' in the first row but towards the back, I waved at Rah's wiz, who was in the middle row and she waved back as I walked down the middle row towards my Rita (Oceasia).

"I want to thank you again for letting my Rita come down, stay by you and for bringin' her up."

"Oh Shakim, it was nothing... she is such a nice, sweet young lady and she really loves you. I want the best for y'all two."

"Thank you again Rita."

I walked towards my Earth and saw that she was all smiles and glowing. She stood up, wearing light blue jeans with a matching jacket; some cloth green, high top Chuck Taylor sneakers with the thick laces and her dreads were loose but tied up like they'd been for previous two days. As we embraced, I hugged her tight and Oceasia returned an even tighter hug... I could feel the bulge of her stomach against my body as she lifted her head to meet my lips with hers. We kissed like it was no tomorrow; as if each suck and twist of tongue was to keep us alive as we both broke our kiss so she could suck on my bottom lip, she opened her eyes to look deeply into mine.

"I love you Bay."

"I love you too."

We pecked each other's lips again, makin' that wet juicy "smack" sound effect.

"I got a surprise for you Shakim"

She sounded like a little girl.

"What you got for me, Ma?"

She opened up her jacket and I seen she had on a grey t-shirt with a pic my face covering the whole front... I smiled. She took her jacket off so anyone who saw us would see my face on her shirt. We sat down and I put my arm around her, she took my other hand to play with it the same way she'd been doin' for the last two visiting days.

"Today is the last day... of visits... I wish it was all week."

"Me too" I responded.

"I can't wait until you come home, I need you home Sha... you still comin' home to me, Bay?"

It took a minute to think about the question she had just asked me... I looked at her again and started smilin'.

"What you cheesin' 'bout Bay?"

"Just thinkin' about you and what you will be like thirty years from now."

"I'm still gonna be crazy in love with my husband"

She squeezed my hand.

"You comin' home to me?"

"You know I'ma be there" I responded as she turned to give me a kiss.

The C.O. called me and I had to get up and walk over to the one who was standin' on the wall.

"What's good?" I asked.

"You know it's only kissing at the beginning and end of the visit... we already gave y'all the privilege of keeping your arm around your visitor..."

"My Bad C.O."

"Don't let it happen again" he warned.

I walked back to Oceasia.

"What happen Bay?" she asked.

"Can't get caught touchin' and kissin' and all that shit… we good though"

I sat down and wrapped my arm back around my Earth. We had so much fun; spent the whole visit talkin' about everything under the Sun. I kept her laughing and she asked me what I was gonna do with that piece of dread she popped and gave to me. I told her it was in a nice spot and I would hold on to it forever.

"You aint gonna work none of that Jamaican roots on me, are you?"

We laughed it up; I looked to see where the C.O.'s were floatin' around at on the visiting floor. Once I seen the coast was clear, I went for a kiss, which Oceasia submitted to. All throughout the visit we snuck quick kisses, Oceasia would keep look out on the left, I watched the right and when the coast was clear we got nasty with the kisses. I even bit and sucked, leavin' hickey marks all over her neck.

"Oceasia?"

"Yes?"

As she smiled and looked in my eyes, I could feel moisture in the palms of my hand.

"I got an answer to your question."

I felt her tremble.

"I understand Ma... and it wouldn't be fair to you or the unborn seed so I'm not gonna be evil and ask you to kill your seed... you deserve the best of everything and you may never get another chance to be a mother... have your seed."

I looked at her and she was cryin'.

"What's wrong Ma?" I asked.

"You still gonna be with me?"

"Yeah ma, I'ma be right there with you."

She smiled and looked to the left to see if the coast was clear...

"Look and see where Cee Ciphers at cause I want to taste you" she said as we went back to bein' nasty.

*****

We ate and had fun playin' cards, checkers and playin' guessing games. She even started daring me to do certain things, knowin' we was jeopardizing our visit; it was so much fun though. We took photos and even had Big Rah and his wiz Rita jump in some with us. Big Sandy was sweet like that... I gave Rah's wiz a hug for bein' so nice to my Rita. "Rita and Rita", I joked and everybody laughed. Oceasia held on to me as I led the way back to our seats and I felt her hands roamin' all over me.

"Ooooh my Bay got hard muscles everywhere."

"You better quit before you awake the monster muscle up" I playfully warned.

"I'm with that" she said as she laughed and kept feelin' on me.

"Yeah... you know what they say about pregnant power u."

315

"What, what they say Bay?"

"They say it's the best"

We laughed all the way to our seating area.

*****

Oceasia and I were hugged up, havin' a quiet moment, lookin' at all the couples that was hugged up like us... enjoyin' love.

"Shakim"

"What's good, my BBD?"

"Are you gonna help me name the baby?" she asked.

I stopped everything and looked at her; I couldn't believe she was going there.

"What?" I scoffed.

"I asked are you gonna help name the baby?"

This time she had bass in her voice.

I remained quiet.

"If it's a boy, I'm namin' him Shakim."

"<u>NO</u> <u>YOU</u> <u>ARE</u> <u>NOT</u>!" I said sternly.

"Yes I…. am… his name will be Shakim."

"Why would you do that? Why would you name that man's baby after me?"

"Because it is my baby and I'm havin' it and that's what I want" she answered.

316

"So everything is based on what you want?" I asked...

Oceasia remained quiet, after about five minutes, she looked up to me and asked...

"Do you think you will ever love my baby the way you love me?"

"It's gonna take time for this to heal ma"

She squeezed my hand.

"So what are you gonna do if you want other children or if the baby wants brothers or sisters?" I asked.

"I'ma wait for you Shakim. I'm not ever gonna do this again without you, I promise."

"I hear you" I responded.

"My word is always my bond, Bay. The hardest thing I ever had to do in my entire life was tell you that I'm pregnant... knowin' I could lose you. So I'm never endangering US ever again Bay. I can't hurt or lose you, I love and need you."

"I love and need you too." I replied.

"You gonna tell your Ole Earth?"

"Gots to"

"I'ma call her and tell her that I'ma love you until there is no such thing as life."

I squeezed her and smiled.

"I hear you ma."

* * * * *

We ended the visit with more hugs, rubs, squeezes, kisses... real wet sloppy kisses, vows, oaths and promises of loyalty. Her flight was leavin' that night at 9:22pm.

"Thanks for comin' Oceasia."

"I had no other choice." she responded.

"Yes, you did."

"No, I didn't... my life begins and ends with you."

"Now you got a mouth to feed and a seed to raise" I added.

"True Indeed... and I'ma be Mrs. Edwards."

"Proper Earths are covered every day."

"I know, I know, I'm getting' right, Bay."

"Love you."

"Love you more, even more."

CHAPTER 31

The Greatest book I ever read is based on her, titled after her, written by her. It's such a beautiful book; filled with beautiful jewels on the most beautiful woman. She inspires me and challenges me to tackle the greatest force which is Love. Every time I read a page of her thoughts, I get more tangled and in tune with her energy, every page is informative, astonishing, scientifically, terrificibility... see what I mean? ...Got me makin' up words on the spot just to describe the feelin' I feel from absorbing this novel. The more I read, the more I learn about her, the more I want to know her, love her, make her scream, make her cream, make her quake.

I couldn't seem to put this book down. I was addicted to her, she fascinated me. I talked about her all the time, even to those who didn't seem to be listening. I recommend that they order this novel but so far it seems that it's one of a kind, no one was able to find it but me. I got an antique, rarity, prototype. The cover artwork is so original every book should copy its style. The pages are unique, the inks used to print the words are exquisite, the words and thoughts are so swift and changeable that it can shift emotions within multi-seconds. Some chapters are not easy to understand, some are allegorical but it's never a dull or simple moment. This book will make the toughest, coldest man in beast mode become a tame poetical poet... This book is a bestseller without advertisement or commercials; it became an instant classic.

The name of this novel is "Queen Oceasia"

*****

I called Oceasia before she took her flight back to New Orleans and we kicked it for the fifteen minutes; revisiting' the fun we had over the weekend especially Saturday and Sunday. She told me Friday was a day she was so in fear of, she said she didn't know what my reaction was gonna be… but now it was all love. I told her I would call her early the next morning and we blew each other wet sloppy kisses.

"Nine – twelve – twenty one"

"Always"

I rested like a baby that night.

*****

The next morning, I didn't even workout. I called Oceasia and spoke to her for a few minutes. She was dead tired so I told her I would call later that evening. We hung up and I prepared for my job detail and I told Calico about the Earth bein' pregnant… I found it easy to get it off my chest now that she and I talked face to face; Calico remained quiet and understood. Later on, while in the yard, I saw Miz, El, and True God. I had to get back into grind mode to build my current back up cause I wasn't in the mix but I had been hittin' up my stash, spending.

"Shakim Bio!"

Me and True pounded dap to each other and I greeted El and Miz the same.

"Peace… what's goody?" I responded.

"You… Yo I heard you was shinin' on the dance floor this weekend, who was the pregnant shorty?" asked True, who had no regard or respect for how he came at a person.

"That was my Earth from N.O. that came through."

"OH Shit! Word? Damn G! She pregnant?" he asked, shakin' his head.

"My seed's mom did the same thing to master equality… she just cold did a fella….."

I cut True off right then and there, sayin'...

"I don't want to hear that shit"

I didn't feel it was necessary to add on to whatever was floating around, it was what it was already. I know "True" like to get slick and found humor in my situation but I was still winnin', still shinin'. The Earth was still with me.

"Damn Sha, Don't get aggie with me G."

"Just leave it alone then "True"... let's build about getting' this paper!"

That brought a smile to True's face as he gave me his attention and we went to spin the track.

*****

I was lookin' for Dirt; I hadn't seen him in a few days and wanted to build with him. In less than a month, cigarette smokin' was gonna be banned. They banned them in most of the fed spots; I got scribes from convicts in other pens, who told me how the administration had institutional lockdown to search and seize all tobacco products and how the price skyrocketed in the black market world on compounds. It was even bigger than drugs now, I needed to connect with Dirty to see what was what and share this info with him so I sent word for him to come out... but still there was no word from or sighting of Dirt.

As I came in later that morning at like 11 am before chow, I ran to jump on the phones. Oceasia's line kept ringin' so I hung up and dialed Tammi's number. She picked up, let the recording go through and accepted.

"Damn Sha... why I aint hear from you all weekend? I thought you were on lock down... I wrote you like five letters, sexy"

321

I kept it official with Tammi and told her shorty from N.O came through. She didn't want to hear that...

"I know you aint lettin' her back in your square after she did you like that!! I remember you from out here when you had these chicken heads goin' coo-coo over your shit! We were almost an item... What's goin' on Sha, you fallin' off like that?"

I didn't feel I had to justify my gangster to Tammi, I told her I was good and that's what counted.

"Yeah, that's what counts... just make sure you call me every day... I will make sure to be available for you... if you need money or anything... someone to talk to, always know your Tammi is here and I love you for real and I always will."

"I hear you ma" I responded.

*****

After chow, while spinnin' the track, I ran into some of the New York homies. I inquired about Do-Dirt cause I hadn't seen or heard from him. I was told he been chillin' in his cell.

"Tell son to get at me a.s.a.p."

I kept it movin' after dappin' everyone up.

*****

I seen Big Rah and we did our usual hittin' up the law library to do research. We had reserved seats by the law computers Monday through Friday so I did an hour a day.

"Yo Sha, you heard they closin' your unit down to make it a spot for the emotionally stressed?"

"Nah... I aint hear no shit like that and I live in that unit, not you!!"

"Word! Plus they gonna be givin' out tobacco arm patches to help kick smoking' now that we got like three weeks left before we dead on smokin'."

"Yeah... I stopped last night" I enlightened Rah.

"What?"

"Yeah, I gave it up again... I'm no longer stressin', I'm back on my hop."

"Fuck that... I gotta get my smoke on so don't dead on hittin' me with some every now and then" kicked Rah.

"Man... Listen, you might have to get you one of those patches, unless you gonna smoke dried up orange or banana peels"

We started laughin'.

*****

After the four o'clock count I didn't stay around for mail call. I made the recreational move to the yard; once you made that move you was struck on the yard until after dinner was served. I needed the fresh air plus I needed to feel things out since I was getting' back into stackin' my chips up.

*****

Do-Dirt finally came outside and he needed a shave badly. He looked a complete wreck as we met up on the track, dapped up and gave each other a brotherly embrace.

323

"What's good Sun?" I asked him smilin'.

I could see the pain in his eyes and the cold expression on his face.

"Goin' through it right now Sha... word"

We started walkin' towards the picnic tables so we could sit and talk.

"What's up Dirt?" I inquired. "You been inside for a while now... what, this goin' home soon got you noyd or somethin'?"

"Nah Sha, a lot been on my mental... that's all. Yo, I heard you was dancin' (having visits) hard body this weekend that just passed."

"Yeah, Rita came through"

       I explained the situation I was goin' through, told Dirt how I found out and that it caused me to smoke and drink heavily. I opened up, revealin' how Rita's getting' pregnant had me stressed then it opened doors with Tammi and how that was goin'. He took it all in.

"Yo, you a General so you can control that and fix what's needed. Shorty trooped it all the way up these mountains to see you and you never stuck your meat up in her not once, nor did she know you when you was on top of the world... She is ridin' with you while you down and out? Yo, my dude... you doin' right and y'all love each other."

"Word... what's good with you? Wifey still tryna come back in your life?" I asked.

"Sha... word life... I'm goin' through it my dude. Mom is in her very last stages of cancer and can't hold on until I get there, I'ma lose her any day now Sha"

Dirt looked up in the sky and his eyes got moist, he was hurtin' bad.

"Sorry to hear that."

"Yeah, God takin' one life away to give meaning to another one; I'm losin' my mom but your Rita will be bringin' in her seed... that's how life balances".

We remained quiet for a while.

"Yo, I'ma stack this paper... I'm hearin' that this tobacco move gon' be bigger than the crack epidemic in the eighties. So I'm goin' all out Sha, I can't go home broke, I gotta take care of my little sister."

"I hear you Sun... I got kites from cats in other spots sayin' shit is real."

"Like Fifty (Cent), we gotta get rich or die tryin'"

I listened and felt Dirt's pain.

*****

Everything was back to normal on my end. I was back callin' Oceasia and burnin' up my other lines between her and Tammi. Tammi was showin' me that she wanted to play her part as well. I was getting' money again so I told Oceasia that I would reimburse her for what she spent on the trip to see me bein' that she was workin' while pregnant and would soon have to stop so I had the money sent off of my account.

Later that day was full of surprises. First, the unit's counselor called a town hall meeting where he addressed everyone in the unit; informin' us that we had thirty days to relocate to another unit on our own or else we would be sent to units based on the administration's decision; meaning we had to make it happen now or get put somewhere we didn't wanna go. Wow... they was closin' my unit down in order to turn it into a medical unit for emotionally distressed convicts with tobacco withdrawal... I guessed Big Rah would be movin' down there cause he stayed askin' me for cigarettes and I was little over twenty-five packs to the good when I should have had over seventy... Do Dirt was in the hundreds.

Before four o'clock p.m. count, Calico got called to the counselor's office for legal mail. When he came back in the cell for count, he was readin' a stack of legal papers.

"Yo Shakim, they just made a decision on my appeal... my shit got denied"

Calico kicked over the chair in our cell.

"Damn Sun... sorry to hear that" I told him.

"Yeah... they denied me.... man these devils is vicious. I can't win for nothin'... what it means that my appeal was affirmed in part, reversed in part and remanded?" he asked, lookin' confused.

"What? Let me see that shit!"

I took the papers out of his hand.

"Yo Son... you won your appeal in part... you goin' back to court for re-sentencing on the murder cross reference argument. You won that argument Son, you goin' back to court!"

"Word?!!"

"Yeah, they affirmed your drug conspiracy count but reversed the cross murder reference so bein' that your drug count started at a level thirty eight, you know... at that base offense level, you gonna get a number. You may get fifteen – twenty years, if that."

Calico jumped up and down like he just won 100 million dollars, he just gave back a life sentence and I felt proud of him and happy for him.

As the following week came in, I was plottin' and schemin' on various moves to generate currency. My Co-defendant Al Monday was ready to link Rita Books with Lyfe Jennings but that wasn't gonna happen now because she was pregnant and not doin' any songs or studio sessions. I let the scribes from him go unanswered as I thought of other moves.

*****

Big Rah sent word for me to get at him as soon as I could but I was stuck at work. Unbeknownst to me, CNN News was broadcasting an emergency evacuation of the city of New Orleans, their levees was expected to break due to a hurricane that they named Katrina. Katrina was a category five and it was expected to leave the city underwater so people were ordered to leave immediately. As soon as I heard this, I rushed back to the unit. My phone minutes were dead and I didn't revalidate until the first of the month, which was in a few days so I used my other lines to call Oceasia, who wasn't pickin' up that whole morning or day. I called the Boutique only to get the same results... I started to worry. I almost broke my strength and collapsed to a cigarette but I knew I couldn't fall victim to that again so I kept on tryna call.

*****

Upstairs in Raheeme's unit, I was pacin' his cell's floor, worryin' about my Earth. I had my mom callin' her as well, she was worried too. My moms liked Oceasia, even as I expressed my love for her after revealin' that she was pregnant. It was funny because my mom asked me in her rich Jamaican accent "How she do dat ting so? Dat's your chile dat?"

Mom felt my pain too, I had her callin', had Big Rah's wiz Rita callin' but still <u>no answer</u>. Everyone was leavin' messages on her voicemail but <u>no response</u>. I was like "<u>Where my Earth at</u>???"

*****

After watching the news on TV. and callin' Rita (Oceasia) like crazy for two days straight, I went outside to spin the track with Dirt.

327

"Yo God… Mom is gone… I lost her" Dirt said as we spun the track.

"Damn Sun, sorry to hear that"

I stopped to face him.

"It's all good… I gotta stay strong… take care of the household and make sure baby sis stay in school. I gotta provide for her, now I'm the backbone; gotta maintain mom's crib and all. I got big responsibilities and I'm in prison with less than eleven or so month short to the door."

"I feel you on that Dirt."

"Yo, y'all gotta move out of C-one unit by when?" he asked.

"Like two weeks from now" I answered.

"You got a spot yet?"

"Nah, I may go upstairs with Rah."

"Maaan, why don't you move to my unit …A-Four, I'll let you get the bottom bunk Ole head. I don't really fuck with no one in my unit like that. Word life Sha… come through, we can scheme and plot together. I gotta get cream!!!"

Let me think about that Sun" I replied.

"Make that shit happen!!!"

＊＊＊＊＊

August twenty-ninth, two thousand and five

New Orleans was all over the News and it was practically under water; people were drownin' and lyin' dead in the streets. It was a very sad day for America and I couldn't catch Oceasia. I called around on my other lines to see if anyone heard from her. My mom said Oceasia called and was safe, she was headed out west but didn't know where her mom and grandmother were; she promised to call my mom back and I was relieved to know that she was ok.

＊＊＊＊＊

Calico was going to stay in C – one unit since he was goin' back to court within a month or two to get re-sentenced. I went to the counselor and gave him a request form to move to unit A – four. It had to be approved by the unit counselors in both units. A-four counselor approved it but it was up to my counselor to update it in the computer.

"As of tomorrow, you live in unit A – Four, cell 217 with Thomas Singletary."

"Ok counselor" I responded.

'Yeah Edwards, don't bring your ass back over here."

＊＊＊＊＊

Big Rah was glad to hear my Earth was good.

"I'm glad she is straight so you can stop worryin' G… and now you movin' to the other side of the compound with all that tobacco, you should leave me a couple packs Shakim."

"Ah shut your crybaby ass up" I playfully snapped as I threw him a pack.

Calico, Big Rah and a few other convicts helped me move all my property over to the other side of the compound to unit A – Four, which was also on the top floor so once we made it to the building, we had to run up two flights of stairs then the cell Dirt lived was on the second floor so that was another flight of stairs… shit was definitely a workout; carrying boxes after boxes of legal material, then my personal stuff like massive food, clothes, kicks and so on. I noticed that a lot of convicts in

329

the unit didn't know which one of us was "him". After seein' all of the mean mugs and ice grill stares, we made it to Dirt's cell, which was the last one in the corner then we made it back to the first floor so I could give the unit C.O. my bed card. I dapped Calico, Rah and others and told them I would see them after lunch. I looked around and seen convicts lookin' my way but it was all good. As I looked around… shit was crazy… from C-one unit to A – Four Unit… it looked like I left the modest suburbs and moved into the worst projects in America. Word Life B, it was dirty and nasty in that unit; garbage on the floor… it even smelled funny in here. I noticed everybody looked grimy as I made it back upstairs to the cell to straighten up a bit.

Dirt was happy to see me.

"Yo, what's goodie Ole head?"

"You… now move your shit to the top bunk!!" I playfully barked.

CHAPTER 32

The first two days in A – Four was incredible. I was up and about as soon as the doors were opened and so was the rest of the unit. It was like I was living in Vietnam somewhere, shit was very crazy, always loud and the convicts were rowdy. When leavin' the unit, the staircase lights were always out so it was dark spots and the staircases were always crowded; shit was like the projects for real. It seemed like everyone worked out too and a lot of the war head missiles from different cars were housed in A –Four. When I say "cars", I'm not speakin' on vehicles, I'm speakin' on geographical crews reppin' where they're from and N.Y. held it down in A – Four as well. Miz, Big Mike, El, Killa Clap and Dirt lived in the unit and Shakim Bio was added to that list. When I was comin' down the unit stairs on the way to dinner my first night there, I noticed somethin' wasn't right. Everyone was lookin' and actin' shady so I went back upstairs and got strapped up with my sharpened knives then made it back outside, down the stairs. I didn't know what was up but I wasn't gonna be on the menu, unarmed. As I made it down the stairs, I saw that everyone outside had their backs against the wall lookin' crazy. I went over to one of the N.Y. homies named "Silk"...

"Yo, Sun... What's poppin' over here, why y'all lookin' and actin' so shady?"

"Yo Sha, put your back against the wall and fall back" was his answer.

I noticed he was focusin' on somethin', I looked and saw two convicts goin' at it on some 1971 shit. They both had a Rambo lookin' knife taped in one hand and they were holdin' onto a knotted sheet with the other hand, goin' blow for blow on some "Clash of the Titans" shit. I put my back to the wall and watched them go at it, you could tell they were also strapped with body armor which was hard covered books and thick magazines under their clothes. They were goin' at it heavy, until one let go of the tied sheet and dropped to one knee and

331

the aggressor amazingly backed off… instead of takin' advantage, he kicked the down convict in the face and said…

"I better not see you by next move or I'm finish the job!!!!"

I was like "What the fuck? They don't do it like that over there by C-Building, shit is crazy!!!"

*****

I finally caught Oceasia on the phone; we were both happy to hear each other's voice. She told me she lost everything she owned (In Hurricane Katrina), except for what she was able to pack up, which was mostly clothes; all our letters, photos, cards and stuff was destroyed or lost. She was out in Los Angeles, California, living with her aunt and she was very uncomfortable there, she still couldn't locate her mom or grandma. I asked her…

"What can I do for you?"

She said the money I sent off my account reached her in time and was very helpful.

"If you need any more scream at me ma."

I also told her I was gonna build with my Ole Earth and get her to let Oceasia stay with her in Florida for a while. Now that was some real shit… to ask my mom to put up with a female I loved, while she was also pregnant and it wasn't my baby. I mean, if I was goin' all out to do that for her, Oceasia had to know that I truly loved her.

"Nah Bay… I can't do that to your Ole Earth… she is older and needs her space."

"Ma… "momma love" got a big house, she will let you stay. Let me build with her and you call her tomorrow. Ok?"

332

"Ok, Bay… thank you… I love you."

"Love you too."

$$*****$$

I spoke with my ole Earth… she truly understood and said Oceasia was welcome to come stay in the house with her in Florida. Mom had three extra bedrooms and an extra car so she said…

"Tell her she can call me soon."

"Ok mother dearest… love you."

$$*****$$

Yo, I'm dead serious when I tell you this… Unit A – four's shower was so nasty that you couldn't even touch the walls while you takin' a shower. The shower curtain was caked up with so much dirt, grime and who knows what else, you couldn't even hang your towel on it. The first few days, I was goin' back to Unit C – one shower to take showers, true story "B". Then I stole a shower curtain out of C – one shower and took it back to A – Four for my personal use. When other convicts seen how clean that curtain was, they all got together to complain to the showers orderly to get new ones from the unit's counselor. If you live in a nasty environment, you will have a nasty attitude. Shit was lookin' like the south Bronx in 1983, all burnt down and shit. Me and Dirt had our cell lookin' like a penthouse. We were stocked up on everything and were livin' like jailhouse kingpins; Miz was livin' lovely as well. I couldn't see how they lived in that unit lookin' like that outside their cells for so long… No wonder why the unit went to chow last… Where a unit was placed in the rotation to be called to chow was based on a unit inspection, A – four was ALWAYS last and now I knew why.

"Why did Musa have a hard time civilizin' the devil in the year 2000 B.C?

333

Because he was a <u>Savage</u>!!!!

*****

Even though Oceasia was goin' through the hardship of being pregnant and bein' pushed out west, we tried to stay in tune with each other but at the same, time Tammi started steppin' her game up with the letters, cards and photos. She was pushin' the issue of me sendin' her a visiting form. She was on my visiting list once upon a time but I took her off once I thought it wasn't no need for any other female to visit me when Oceasia and I became an item... that was before the pregnancy.

I started getting' familiar with convicts in the unit, they were already used to seein' me on the yard or whatever but now I was livin' in the unit with them and of course they knew I was also a move maker. On top of being a move maker, a brother had "knowledge of self" so they wanted to know me. There was a cat named "Lake", Lake was his last name so everyone called him that; he was from Lexington, Kentucky, brown-skinned with dreads and was a vicious gambler. Lake was makin' his little moves and started comin' around me askin' about K.O.S. so we started havin' building sessions. After a while, he cut his dreads, started brushin' waves into his hair and showin' up to the ciphers the Gods were havin'. Only bad thing was, Lake was too tied up with gambling and getting' into fights over not payin' his debts so I fell back from son. He also lived in my new unit and one day, he came to the cell to talk, at the same time, he was lookin' at all my sneakers.

"Damn Sha, you livin' lovely God!!... Damn... you got the exclusive 1996 Penny Hardaway, Nike Air Zooms!!"

Lake was referring to the grey and white "Hardaways" with the black patent leather patches I had, they were in excellent shape. I rarely wore them cause they were exclusives, everyone was on me for them. I paid eighty dollars for them, copped 'em from my manz Amin from

334

South Philly when I was in U.S.P. Lee County. Do Dirt had the Reebok S. Dot Carter joints, which was exclusives too, sittin' in plastic... so I told Lake to buy the S. Dots from Dirt.

"Nah Sun, I need those Air Zooms"

Lake stayed on me about those sneakers for days so me bein' a hustler and tired of him sweating me, I just threw a number at him.

"Give me four hundred for them!"

"Four hundred? ... what about three fifty?" he asked.

"Bet!"

I couldn't believe that he wanted them so bad that he was willin' to pay three hundred and fifty for them but I put them in a clear plastic bag and told him...

"When the money touches, they yours!"

I gave him my name and I.D number, knowin' he was frontin'.

"Give me a few days Shakim Bio"

"O.K!!"

＊＊＊＊＊

On the phone with Oceasia...

"Ma, let me know if you need anything, I got a little somethin' on my end"

"O.K Bay"

"I love you"

"Love you too"

335

Me and Oceasia were speakin' a lot. I surprised her with a big portrait of us on the visit; I sent it to her Aunt's crib in Cali; she forgot I had that address since I was in U.S.P. Lee County.

*****

Lake surprised me and told me to check my account and the money for the sneakers was there so I handed him the Air Zooms, he was happy as shit. He wore them every day of the week too, he was so happy that he gave me a piece of paper with a name, address and phone number of a female named "Robyn"...

"Sha … I already told her about you, she wants you to call and she is only like two hours away. Her cousin is my girl and she seen you on the visit with a pregnant chick and told her cousin you was cute"

He passed me the info.

CHAPTER 33

I went to call Oceasia and a recording came on sayin' her number was disconnected. I tried again and got the same thing so I wrote to her...

Peace to My Earth,

Today's reality is I am missing you like crazy and trust you did not go out of orbit again. I called and it said your math been disconnected. Get at me and let me know you are alright. Why didn't you call my Ole Earth yet?

Nine – twelve – twenty one

"Yourz"

Shakim Bio

I flew the scribe to her aunt in Cali.

*****

The day came and it was official, no more Tobacco in the Federal System. I repeat, tobacco products were officially banned, even the C.O.'s couldn't have it and just when you thought things would get better, they got worse. Every day you would hear about an armed robbery or cell invasion; convicts were groupin' up, robbin' and tyin' up other convicts for their valuables and tobacco stashes. Tobacco product prices skyrocketed tremendously, exploding from $1.40 for a pack of cigarettes to $250.00 a pack and prices was still rising. A brand new pair of Air Force one sneakers that cost $80.00 in the commissary store couldn't even get you a half a pack of generic cigarettes so some convicts went ape shit and turned into Gorillas as life at Big Sandy U.S.P. got hectic for the weak... even the strong went against the strong.

"Do Dirt" sat back smilin', playin' the waiting game.

*****

Violence was at its peak as convicts were goin' hard on the yard; robberies was an everyday thing but I was still makin' moves and generatin' small money. I still didn't hear from Oceasia but I tried that number daily... it was still disconnected. She never called my Ole Earth and never responded to the scribes I was sendin' regularly either, it was like she just disappeared without a trace. Days turned into weeks and the weeks turned into months... I didn't give up on her but it seemed that she was gone maybe she found a life after Shakim Bio after all.

*****

It was times like these that I really missed Oceasia and just needed to talk to her. I wasn't hearin' from her, not even a quick note to let me know that she was good and safe. I started gettin' upset again because she stayed with the bullshit and she was goin' on seven months pregnant but it was all good. Tammi kept gettin' at me so I started givin' her more and more attention. She made me laugh cause she was goofy and her police job stories were funny because she was the dispatcher who radioed everything in on the "Calling all cars!!... Calling all cars!! Be on the look out for Shakim Bio... he is on the loose!" We used to joke our asses off about that. She always reminded me as to why she gave me her phone number when we first met. She had a man and a son when we first seen each other but after seein' the type of "candy (her words)" I was, she had to know it and try to have it. We bugged out about that and I decided right then to send her the visiting form.

*****

Still no Oceasia... I wasn't understandin' that at all... I flew a scribe to her aunt's crib in Cali and another one to New Orleans and

338

after about two weeks, the letter I sent to N.O. came back. I also got a letter addressed to me from Robyn Mays from Lexington, Kentucky. I opened and read the scribe then I told Dirt about the letter and where she was from.

"Yo, you got shorties checkin' for you and they don't even know you? I told you, you was that dude!!" said Dirt.

I decided to write Robyn back and put her number on my phone to be approved.

*****

I had already sold most of my packs and Dirt was doin' great, gettin' four hundred dollars a pack, and he had the little homies movin' some piece by piece to make extra money; he was jailhouse / prison rich, buyin' all the drinks and weed to party and soak away the pain of losin' his mom but he still stacked his money up and remained on point though. The wolves, vultures and gorillas was out there watchin' and waitin' for a sign of weakness but we let it be known that we were elephants and we started the jungle stampede over here. Question! Why you never seen no wild animal fuck with an elephant? Or why elephants don't follow paths? They knock things down with their trunk and create their own paths and if you are thinkin' they are afraid of mice... come find out!

*****

Me and Robyn was back and forth, scribin' each other, she sent a photo and shorty was a "ten" no question; real cute with an ass like Trina the "diamond princess". Shorty was proper and a tender- roni girl, twenty four years old, in college, working part-time but had that hood feel in her like she was born and raised in those streets. I only called her once a week and I let it be known that I had a girl and that was cool with

339

her so it was cool with me. We wrote more than we spoke on the phone, I sent her a photo and shorty went wild.

*****

By now Robyn was on my visiting list as well as Tammi but I didn't let either of them know that they were approved. I was really trustin' to hear from Oceasia, I always asked my Ole Earth if she called or left word but… Nothin'… I was at mail call hopin' to hear from my Earth but ended up with letters and cards from Tammi and Robyn.

The tobacco prices went to five hundred dollars now but I only had two and a half packs left. Dirt was just gettin' started. He had over two hundred packs because he started storin' and stashin' them way back when the rumor got out that tobacco might be banned in the Federal System. He had that determined mind and a purpose from that point on and was gainin' from it crazily. Envy and animosity was stemmin' from inside our N.Y. car a little somethin' but it didn't stop nothin'. Dirt was goin' home with some bread to do what he had to, he showed as much love as he could but knew he had bigger plans on the streets.

*****

Me and Big Rah stayed in that law library, he was upset that Dirt wasn't givin' him no tobacco to smoke. Rah was on that Brooklyn shit real hard too. One day he told me…

"Yo Shakim… let Dirt know that Big Rah will come down there to his cell and take all his shit… I was in Attica in 1989 wearin' Slick Rick chains, in Sing-Sing and Clinton Maxes when that Blood shit was gettin' Big. I came from the state straight to the Feds. I was beefin' with La-Sun and them from the A-Team, had shoots outs with King Tut and dem… What Dirt think this is!!!! Tell him to send me some cigarettes!!!"

340

*****

"I aint sendin' Rah shit!!" exclaimed Dirt. "I can't support his habit and I aint scared of that 1982 Brooklyn shit either... I was up north before and rocked the bells like L.L!!"

We both busted out laughin'.

"My little sister need school books and it's expensive... and I gotta settle all the bills Mom left. They about to read her will... I'm still hurtin' over that Sha so Rah better fall back if he aint tryin' to get aired out!" snarled Dirt as he gave me one cigarette to give to Rah...

"He better take one pull, put it out and take another pull again later!"

We busted out laughin' again then I went in my stash and added two cigarettes cause Rah was my dude.

CHAPTER 34

Violence was still on the rise in Big Sandy... every morning when we came to the chow hall, it was a different story about who was found tied up with their cell cleared out. Calico finally left to go back to court for re-sentencing, after puttin' down a few cell invasions before he left. A lot of convicts stayed strapped with homemade knives and shanks made out of all kinds of materials from steel, copper, plastic, plexi-glass, heavy duty bolts, nails and they had some ginsju shit too; Rambo lookin' joints without the compass type shit and there were a few swords... shit was crazy but this was Big Candy... I mean U.S.P Big Sandy.

＊＊＊＊＊

I told Robyn that she was good to come up on the approachin' Saturday so we could do a face to face. She was happy and very excited and at this time, Lake owed so much money for gambling debts... the Air Zooms he bought from me for $350... he sold for $50... WOW!

＊＊＊＊＊

Someone got poked up somethin' vicious and that led to an institutional lockdown. We were given a chance to get to the phones to postpone any upcoming visits for the weekend. Robyn was upset but lookin' forward to when the prison raised back up off of lockdown. I took those two weeks of lockdown to rest up from excessive workin' out and catch up on writin' letters and reading.

＊＊＊＊＊

When we came off of lockdown, the prison was on pins and needles but slowly goin' back to normal. The tobacco was movin' and I was still sittin' on my last two packs. Dirt was still strong, doin' his thing and we were livin' it up. Robyn was comin' up to see me in those mountains in a few days so I went and got everything on point and had to go check with Big Rah to make sure his wiz Rita wasn't comin'. I couldn't let her see me out there with another female. Even though I hadn't heard from Oceasia in five months, I still respected her enough to not disrespect her by bein' on a visit with another female while someone she knew was out there seein' it so I made sure the coast was clear.

*****

It was Friday and I was getting' ready for the next day when I would see Robyn in the flesh. The day went by like the rest of the weekdays, smooth. After 4pm count, during mail call, I caught a scribe from Calico sayin' they postponed his sentencing date and pushed it to three more months. I also got a card from Harvey, Louisiana from "Mrs. Edwards (Oceasia)", I immediately opened it. It was a card with the sun smilin' in the sky and her words made my day...

I miss U Shakim. Please give me a minute to get on point. I don't have a phone right now but this is my address.

Love you

9 – 12 - 21

I read the card fifty times and was glad to finally hear somethin' from Oceasia and know that she was good but I was also upset at her and wasn't respondin' back... Fuck that! I had a visit to attend to tomorrow.

*****

The next morning I got up and did my usual routine. I kept the fact that I was goin' on the visit to myself, the only ones who knew was Big Rah, Dirt and Lake knew cause his girl was cousins with Robyn and they were comin' together so he would also be on the visit; I told him to keep it on the low.

343

* * * * *

At about nine fifteen a.m., I was called out to the visit and of course, I came with all the shine and swagger of a real live New Yorker but one who also had K.O.S. When I came into the visiting hall and headed toward the front desk, I took a look around and seen Robyn sittin' in the front row not too far from the front desk. It was all good, I handed my ID to the C.O. and went over to Robyn. She stood up and gave me a nice hug and I squeezed her back... and of course palmed that phat ass like a basketball, she was lovin' that. She had on some skin tight, Baby Phat jeans that looked painted on, some knock-off Manola boots and a nice cream silk shirt as her breasts were poking out. I knew she was puttin' on her best as I kissed her cheek and smelled her scent before breakin' the embrace.

"Robyn... what's goodie ...Ms. Kentucky?"

"You... You look even better in person Shakim. Man let me get another hug. Please!"

We embraced again... I gave her a strong squeeze and of course felt that phatness once again... ok, I admit, I squeezed it twice this time. We were back and forth with the conversation flow and I was learnin' all about her and her future. She was a dancehall queen, meanin' she played the clubs partyin' a lot. She barely made her grades in college but she maintained a job. She asked a lot about my past life and how much time I had left... I was real funny styled with answerin' those kinds of questions. I looked her in her eyes cause she had a very cute face and was getting' a lot of stares from convicts comin' in; she knew she was all that. "I'm tryna be your girl, if not your wife, Sha."

"What? How you gonna do that? I already got a girl and I love her. I already told you that shit Robyn."

"Yeah, you said so but she aint here... I am" she affirmed.

344

"True that."

"And from what I hear, she aint all of that... and must not love you as much as you love her."

"What you mean by that ma?" I asked.

"I heard she came up here pregnant and you know as well as I do that the baby aint yours boo. So fuck that chick, you need to be rockin' with me"

Robyn smiled up a storm not knowin' that she just fucked up, she fucked up real BIG. After about twenty minutes of her tellin' me how she can rep me right, I asked Robyn to get me an orange juice.

"That's all you want baby?" she asked. I said "Yeah".

As she got up to go get my orange juice from the vending machine, Robyn was switchin' that beautiful phat ass all the way; knowin' I was lookin'. I took one last look before I got up and ended the visit... she came back to an empty chair.

*****

There was a lot of fireworks poppin' off comin' from both Oceasia and Tammi. Oceasia was writin' to me but I still wasn't respondin'. I read her letters and seen a lot of them were back dated months ago like she was scribin', datin' and holdin' on to the letters for whatever reason. There were short scribes, long scribes and real short notes... at the same time... Tammi was scribin' me even harder and Do Dirt was getting' a kick out of all of this shit. It was like he had front seats at a soap opera show. For every scribe I received from Oceasia, there were three from Tammi and the cards were overwhelming. At one point, they both sent me the same exact card. Dirt was really laughin' as I sat back readin' letters and respondin' back to Tammi but had Oceasia on the bench. Oceasia still hadn't given me her new number and she

345

wasn't bein' straight forward about why she disappeared for all those months. I was startin' to believe that her seed's father was somehow still in the picture, somewhere in the mix and she didn't want to let me go but he was there momentarily. Somethin' wasn't right and exact but instead of bustin' my brain cellsm tryna figure it out, I kept Tammi in the cut as we got freaky with each other through our letters but no matter how good things seemed to be goin' with us, I still couldn't forget or stop thinkin' about Oceasia. I really loved and cared about her.

I was looking forward to building a future with her and spending the rest of my life with her. Not too many real men can say that they are ready to settle down with that special someone. I was tired of the games and wanted to keep it real and official and out of all the females I had in my life, Oceasia was the one that came into my life at a specific moment and meant something to me. So I wanted to dedicate the rest of my life to loving and sharing my world with her but it seemed life doesn't always work your way.

Tammi always said that this N.O. chick was a substitute cause she wasn't there but could it be that Tammi was a substitute cause Oceasia wasn't there? At the moment, I wasn't tryna go through all that... I was just rollin' with the punches so I kept the cell light on late nights, readin' Oceasia's letters and lookin' for a reason why she was shuttin' me out the way she was. Shorty must not have really known me. Both my seeds mothers wished I was that 'one' they settled down with, even Tammi wanted that as her reality. She was beggin' me to give her the daughter she wanted to complete her family with. She was talkin' about buildin' a future with a fella but I told her I wasn't ready to move on from Oceasia yet... she knew why... everybody who was in ear shot knew why. Oceasia even knew why... that's why she kept scribing me...

*****

346

Christmas came... then New Years... Oceasia was now in her ninth month... she was still pennin' me and was pennin' me as if I was responding to her scribes but I wasn't... it was a one sided thing. She did all the talkin' and I just did the listening through reading. She said she was doin' water painting and was sendin' me photos of her art work. She mentioned how she thought of me constantly and knew I was constantly thinkin' of her. She spoke on how I had a part of her with me, which was a piece of one of her dreads but she didn't have a part of me... it so happened that one of the diamonds fell out of my gold fronts while I was brushin' my teeth and I kept it in a folded piece of paper so I drew a heart with a red pen, taped the diamond inside the heart with clear scotch tape and mailed that to her that night... I didn't write any words or nothin'... but now she had a part of me.

*****

We were goin' through a lot of institutional lockdowns due to the violence in the prison. Everybody had weapons and I mean everybody; it could've been a dispute between two men on the yard, weapons got drawn and a knife fight popped off then the gun towers opened up and warning shots were fired with a powerful shotgun. The recording would come over the yards loud speaker in English, then in Spanish, tellin' the entire rec. yard to lie down on the ground. When security came to secure the area, everyone comin' off the yard would be searched, shirts came off then shoes. What would start off as two convicts getting' into it in the rec yard, would turn into over four hundred knives and shanks found on the ground from convicts throwin'them when the warning shots were fired and everybody was told to lay down; shit was real on top of that mountain.

*****

Oceasia sent me a small card in a very small envelope, when I opened and read it, there was a phone number in there. I smiled but my ego and pride wouldn't allow me to be bothered. Later I called my Ole Earth to see how everything was goin' with her and the household. She said Oceasia called a few times and left a number for me, she made sure I had the number even though I told her I already had it. Somehow, I could be tough on myself and everybody else but I couldn't be tough on Oceasia; I put her new number on my phone list.

*****

When a new number was added to your phone list depended on when you submit the phone sheet. The unit counselor was never really around so it was hard to actually catch him because he never showed up at his schedule. I used to turn my phone sheet in during the noon meal in the chow hall where most, if not all of the prison's administration, everybody from the warden, assistant wardens, captain, Lt's, unit managers, counselors and business office staff would be at the mainline. So that is when I turned my list in and sometimes the new number would be added to my phone that same day. I'm tellin' you Big Sandy was sweet to those who knew how to carry themselves like a real convict and had no flaws in character or paperwork.

*****

A lot of extortion moves was goin' down in Big Sandy. The drug dealers was bein' pressed to be able to continue operation. It was a lot of funny shit goin' on too; dudes even kidnapped this one cat and held him hostage all the way until stand up count and the whole time, he was bein' tortured by havin' his testicles burned with cigarettes to make him give up his stash. We laughed at that story when it was brought to the chow hall tables. They locked up the alleged kidnappers as well as the victim when come to find out, the stash was buried in the mattress he was layin' on while he was tied up. We laughed at that crazy shit too, things were off the hook. To this day, I'm surprised we didn't get locked down over that.

348

*****

I made it back to the unit and went to the phones. I tried Oceasia's new number and the call went through. After like seven rings, she picked up and pressed 'five' after the recording.

"What's up?" I spitted.

"Bay? ...Peace God. I was wonderin' if or when you would call."

"I called now."

"I'm gettin' ready to have this baby... I sent you some pictures of some art I been doin' and...

I cut her off and asked...

"How you been doin' and where you been?"

"I also been callin' your Ole Earth too"

She went on as if I hadn't asked her anything.

"I asked you a question" I snapped.

"I heard you... I heard what you said!!!!" she shouted.

"So what's the answer?"

"Look... I'm out here dealin' with all this hardship and bullshit... you are in there. You can't help me nor will you understand."

"Is that so? You keep leavin' and comin' back whenever you want, do what you want... even came back with a baby and you expect me to go for this shit?"

"Shakim..." she attempted to speak.

I hung up on her. I wasn't tryna hear that shit.

349

$*****$

Many times, I would go outside to get fresh air... bein' so high up on a mountain makes the air real crisp so if you inhale deep, it burned your nostrils type shit. The winters were freezin' cold... (like right now) and the summers were vicious, it felt like the sun was only a few miles away, most people got sun burnt or started shedding dead skin from bein' baked. On this particular day, I was baring the cold temperatures in order to get some piece of mind but my hands started numbing up and I was stuck out there until they called a rec move.

$*****$

I called Oceasia back that night and we spoke about her family. Her mom and the rest of her family was back in the city of New Orleans but Oceasia had an apartment out in Harvey, which was outside of New Orleans. I let her do all the talking, I just listened... she was due to have the baby any day.

"There's somethin' I want to show you to let you know it's just you, Shakim."

"I don't care"

I had to tell her that... I wanted her to hurt the way I was hurtin' due to her runnin' in and out of my life.

"You don't care... how can you say that?" she asked.

"Same way you been showin' me that you don't care... that's how."

"Why you bein' so mean to me?"

"Because you deserve it"

"I know I do... but I'ma send it anyway" (the phone beeped)

"Bay... when you gonna call me back?" she asked.

"I don't know… in a few days…. maybe next week, maybe next month or maybe I will never call you again."

"I love you, Shakim"

I hung up… -

*****

Two days later, I called and someone picked up but it wasn't Oceasia. As the recording came on and stated where the call was from, that the call was prepaid, from where and how to accept the call, I could hear the tone of the button "five" bein' pressed and held down a little bit too long.

"Hello?" asked a female's voice.

"Peace! Is Oceasia there?"

"Hello Shakim… this is Oceasia's mother, Ms. Diane."

"Hello Ms. Diane, how are you?"

"Fine baby… just fine. Oceasia is in the hospital, she had a little girl yesterday." she informed.

"Oh word!! That's peace!" I responded.

"It sure is."

"What did she name her?"

"Evher"

"Ever?"

"Yes, she named her "Evher'"

"Ok, anyway Ms. Diane, tell her I called and will call back in a few days."

"No, no, no... she is expecting you to call back tonight. I'm bringing her, her phone so call her tonight. She is really expecting your call Shakim."

"Ok."

Like mother, like daughter... they seemed to say what they wanna say; it was what it was... I hung up.

✶✶✶✶✶

That day, I got a letter with photos from Oceasia. The letter was backdated like if she wrote it month before she mailed it and there were photos of her baby shower party with it. The scribe read...

Peace 7

I had my baby shower on this day 12/16... Do u know why? No one knows my history better than u. U are my God so u should know the true significance of this day. Tell me in ur response. I got that diamond that came out ur teeth. Even though u don't spray ink to me, I can still feel u and ur connection... I'm vexed that the hurricane destroyed all the cards, photos, and special things u had made me. I'ma carry this diamond with me 4ever

9 – 12 – 21

Mrs. Edwards

It didn't take me but a second to know the significance of December sixteenth; back when Oceasia first opened up to me, she told me that she lost her virginity that day. I looked at her baby shower photos and smiled.

✶✶✶✶✶

I built with Big Rah, told him the Earth had a daughter and named her "Ever".

"That's peace Sun... so now you got you a responsibility to be a father figure to "Ever", you are forever dedicated to that."

"True Indeed."

"Now go tell Dirt to send me over some cee i germs (cigarettes)."

"Fuck outta here!!"

We laughed at that cause Rah was dead serious.

*****

"True God" surprised me by askin' me how my Earth (Oceasia) was doin'. I told him that she had her seed, which was a girl named "Ever".

"That's Peace G!"

I directed the conversation to the show and prove we had comin' up that month and also the current (money) there was to get out there on the compound.

*****

""Ever?... Why would she name her seed that?" asked Dirt. "You gotta show and prove that to me... Bio –Chemical."

"I'ma call her later on tonight so I'll have an answer for you." I responded.

"You gotta show and prove for everything, huh old head?"

"Yeah... I'ma show and prove to you when Tammi comes up here to see a fella."

"You been screamin' that shit for months, you scared of shorty"

We started laughin' again.

I still hadn't let Tammi know she was approved on my visitor list; I wasn't ready to see her yet.

*****

"Peace ma... how you?"

"I'm fine... kinda tired... but I'm fine."

"Congratulations on bringin' life into existence and finally becomin' a mother."

"Thank you Bay..."

"Where's the seed at?"

"They just took her away ten minutes ago."

"What's her whole attribute?" I inquired.

"Evher Salaam Earth" she replied.

"Ever Salaam Earth?"

"Yea... Evher as in E.V.H.E.R ... Salaam as in peace... Earth."

"As in "For Ever Peace on Earth" I added, shinin' light on the meaning.

"Exactly" she responded. "I now have my piece of peace on this Earth bay."

"I hear you... I saw that name "Evher" in one of the paintings."

"You have a great eye Bay."

"Just like, I know why you had your baby shower on that specific date."

"I knew you knew… I still got somethin' to show you" she said.

"What?"

"You'll get it."

"Yeah… sure" I said, bein' smart.

＊＊＊＊＊

As time went by... days turned into weeks... Oceasia and I didn't have much to talk about as she was real busy being a mother; feeding and tending to her daughter "Evher Peace". So when I called, she couldn't stay on the phone long. She was sendin' me photos and I must say Evher Peace was very gorgeous. As I stared at this cute, little baby girl, I felt real bad and ashamed about some of the things I said back when I first found out Oceasia was pregnant. The Baby looked so happy and she was very, very beautiful. I called and apologized for the things I said to her during the early stages of her pregnancy; Oceasia was very quiet and listened… I also complimented her on havin' such a beautiful baby girl.

I could feel Oceasia smilin' through the phone...

"She loves you too Bay."

CHAPTER 35

I was receivin' a lot of photos Young Evher and Oceasia, who had gained a lot of weight in all the right places. Her ass got phatter, her legs and thighs got bigger... she looked even better. Evher did her mother a lot of justice... word! I sat and compared the before and after photos and everything seemed to be goin' ok with us until I got the new Power Paper.

While reading the paper, I saw a section that read "<u>Nation Neonates Evher Salaam Earth born on 01/11/06 @ 11:07 a.m. to Derrick and Oceasia Divine True Earth</u>."

During our phone call a few days later, I asked her what's up with her seed's father Derrick?

"I wanted to tell you about him" she stated.

"Tell me about him... for what?"

"It's somethin' that I gotta tell you Shakim" she pleaded.

"Fuck you and Fuck Derrick" I said...

Then I hung up.

One thing about a lot of incarcerated brothers... if you don't know by now ladies... we sometimes get emotional and it's only because we are vulnerable to certain situations. We are men and have great pride in takin' care of our women and families and controllin' our situations. We are providers and maintainers by nature and bein' in this situation where we are sometimes helpless, fucks with us. A lot of times, you women know this and use it against us... why y'all do the things y'all do? Sayin' it's because we (men) are not there or other made up shit that fucks with us men. Bein' in prison is hard to both people in a relationship so don't look at me like I'm the bad guy. I was goin' through a lot. I know brothers will agree to that.

＊＊＊＊＊

I was still sittin' on my last packs of cigarettes. I had them hid so well that during random cell searches or institutional shake downs, my packs still remained in place. At the time, they were worth twelve hundred for both packs but if I broke them down, I could make about two stacks. I was sittin' on them until they got stale. – FUCK that!!!!!

＊＊＊＊＊

Me and Tammi was burnin' up the phones again. She made me forget my worries as we bugged out about all kinds of shit. I told her about me leaving Robyn on the visit when she went to go get me something to drink but I didn't tell her the real reason why, Tammi found it funny as hell.

"When you gonna let me come see you?" she asked.

"Did you send back your visiting form yet?" I asked, knowin' damn well she already did"

"Yeah, I sent it last year."

"I gotta go scream at my counselor to see what's the hold up."

"Nay Sha Boo Boo, just send me another one."

"Aiight"

"Make sure you drop it tonight so I can get it in a few days, fill it out and priority mail it back to that spot. I'm tryna put my hands down in your pants!!"

"I'ma make sure I do that tonight ma!"

*****

That following day after 4pm count, Dirt was at mail call and brought up my mail. He had an affair goin' on with so many females due to the fact that he was due at a halfway house before Valentine's Day next year. So old flames, new flames and even his ex-wife was poppin' back up in his life. Dirt was gettin' a kick out of what I was goin' through with Oceasia and Tammi; he passed me my mail, which consisted of five letters two from Oceasia and three from Tammi.

"Yo Ole head... let me ask you somethin'"

I stopped what I was doin' to give Dirt my attention.

"You and this chick Tammi got a little history with one another... you knew her when you were on those bricks and all... You bagged Oceasia while you been in and shorty been walkin' dem dogs with you and all... Shorty is crazy about you like she been knew you and you never touched that. If you had to choose one... who would you choose?"

I just looked at him... I was stuck on stupid. He continued...

"You know you will have to choose, right? You can't continue playin' this game with both of them; you're gonna have to let one go. They both investin' time and energy in you and you're in prison!! That means a lot... but you gotta make a choice and choose my dude... word!!"

I stood there shaking my head.

*****

Inside of the envelope Oceasia sent was a copy of a newspaper article. It read "Evacuee from N.O. held for slaying in Texas case" The article was based on a Hurricane Katrina evacuee, accused of allegedly, fatally shooting a man in Texas and how he got caught and he was also on parole in Louisiana for a previous manslaughter conviction. Then I

358

seen his name, his first name was Derrick. In the other envelope was Evher Salaam Earth's birth certificate and a copy of her social security card. Her birth certificate showed where she was born, day, time and to whom but on the father's first and last name, there were x's, showin' there was no name given. This is what Oceasia wanted to show and tell me.

*****

I wasn't callin' Oceasia as much but I was droppin' her a lot of cards and she was still sendin' me cards and photos of Evher; Evher was gettin' big and more beautiful. Things in the unit was "same shit different toilet"... well actually, it was same shit, same toilet... but I around this time, I had to go to "Unit Team", which was when "them people" re-evaluate your file on your progress and tell you about your points and so on. They just made it mandatory that we had to show up or we could receive an incident report so I had to go even though I knew I had nothin' comin'. It was also my first Unit Team hearing since I moved in the nasty A-Four Unit. My Unit Counselor, Unit Case Manager and Unit Manager were all gonna be present. I saw what time I had to be there and that I had to be dressed in my prison Khakis... shit!!!

*****

When I went to "Team", I was surprised by the outcome. They commended me for not catchin' any incident reports, for maintainin' a job detail, at which I got great work reviews and for obtaining over ten educational achievement certificates. Due to my Ohio sentence and conviction, I couldn't go to a medium but I could go to another pen so I asked for a transfer closer to N.Y. or closer to my mom in Florida. They said they could transfer me, if I change my address to my mom's address in FL and it would be submitted... nothing beats a try so I thanked them and left.

359

*****

Spring left, summer was now here and violence was off the hook at Big Sandy. We stayed on lockdown and every time we came off we went right back on. They were now tearin' the prison up, lookin' for any tobacco products. Dirt was still sittin' pretty on about one hundred packs... Me? I still had two packs. We didn't get to enjoy the summer as much due to lockdown and this was the time Oceasia was writin' me, wantin' to come see me. I sent her a nice amount of current from off my account but every time she tried to make plans to come, those plans were thrown off course due to lockdowns. Tammi was also makin' plans to come, I couldn't stall her no more but those back to back lockdowns kept her at bay.

*****

I kept on the low the fact that I might be transferred to Florida; I did this for various reasons. Number one, I was in prison and not everyone was routing for me in that piece. Misery loves company and some wanted me to lose, fail and remain unhappy like they were. Number two, I was gettin' a little money and was gettin' away with it so it made no sense to reveal my hand now, which would only add on to the already obvious animosity... no need to cause drama when everything was fine as it was. Number three, which was number one to me, I owed it to my Ole Earth to make it easier for her. I needed to be housed closer to her so I kept it on a hush as I kept makin' my moves.

Summer was off the hook, well it was a few weeks before summer but the Bloods went against the Jamaicans, Muslims went against the administration, D.C. went against each other, N.C. against Texas, the G.D's (Gangster Disciples) against Florida and robberies on top of robberies went down. N.Y. still remained on top overall but I knew at some point, that we would be tested so I kept an eye out and remained on point as the God bodies checked on one another daily.

My birthday was right around the corner and we were movin' around again. Oceasia wanted to bring Evher to see me and Tammi was plannin' to come. Me and Dirt was gettin' together for my birthday bash and Serious Wisdom was transferrin' to U.S.P Terre Haute in Indiana to be part of a challenge program so we included his goin' away party in my party but as soon as things was comin' along, shots rang out from the gun towers on the yard and everything was shut down...

* * * * *

My physical birthday was peace, even though we were locked down. I still had drinks and smoke and enjoyed my day. A C.O. delivered the mail and I was blessed with cards from my mom, sisters, my aunt, seeds, seed's mothers, my eldest seed's grandma, comrades and associates. Tammi sent me a very nice card, Oceasia sent me a special card and I got my first card from Evher Peace but of course it was addressed and signed by her mom. Inside the card was a reflection of Evher smilin' with her arms open wide while sittin' in her walker. On the bottom of the card it read...

"Happy Birthday – I love u Daddy!!!!"

I could see that Evher was made to be in front of the camera...

* * * * *

WORD is BOND... things could be so crazy because as soon as we got off of lockdown, I went to make a few calls. First, I called Oceasia and her number was disconnected. I hung up and tried again and again... same results. I then went to call the God "Knowledge" cause he was doin' some legwork for me and we needed to build. After callin' around a bit on my other lines, I called my Ole Earth to see how she was doin' and if she heard from Oceasia... she said <u>NO</u>! I didn't know what to think, so I kept it movin'.

*****

Weeks went by and Tammi was playin' her part as the greatest entertainer, even though other wisdoms jumped in and out of the picture. I also caught up with Daymond from FUBU, who revealed that he passed my novel manuscript to a publisher to view and there was new breaking news in my state case. The star witness came forward and recanted his testimony, sayin' he lied about everything in all of our trials. This became a big topic in the newspapers, causin' everyone to contact me due to the fact that I might get my state conviction overturned. Oceasia's physical birthday was comin' up on the thirteenth of July and I still didn't hear from her. I was tired of playin' childish games with her but I still... addressed a few birthday cards to her and mailed them to the Harvey, LA address.

*****

I received a big envelope with "Oceasia Edwards" listed as the sender. There was over twenty photos in the envelope when I opened it... I was open as I looked at them.

"Yo Dirt. Check this out!"

I couldn't believe it... Oceasia sent photos of her cuttin' her dreads. She had them photographed while she cut them. July – seventh – 0 6... she now had the Toni Braxton / Kelis look as she showed off for me in the photos... inside the envelope was also a note.

"How you like my new look?"

9 – 12 – 21

Mrs. Edwards

I'm not gonna lie, she looked even more stunning without the dreads, even though I liked her with them, she was still lookin' proper.

July came and went just as fast. I got two cards from Oceasia as she sent me reflections of her on her Born day. She said all she did was stay home and have a few drinks... she still didn't send me a number to call her though.

*****

There was this one guy from Charlotte, N.C. named "Dog", who used to always come around and ask me if he could jump in and do pull-ups and workout routines with me. I saw nothin' wrong with it, dudes in A – four was used to me but the unit was still nasty. Me and Dog used to build during the workouts and I kept tellin' him that he is a "Dog" spelled backwards but he kept assuring me that he was a vicious dog at that. One morning, we was just kickin' it and I told him that I had a shorty from Queens, N.Y., who was now livin' in Charlotte. He was surprised and asked me if she was comin' down anytime soon. I told him she had been tryin' to travel to see me for months. He said his girl comes through at least once a month. I was like "Word?" He then said "I'll give you my girl's number so they can hook up and travel together." I was like "You got that!"

*****

A couple weeks went by and I was conversating on the phone with Tammi, buggin' out as usual, when she got quiet, too quiet for me.

"Tammi?"

"Yeah, I'm still here Sha."

"What's good ma... why you quiet all of the sudden?"

"I'm just thinkin' Sha... You got a bad hit and you don't deserve that. You so sweet and real, you got a strong mind and you are such a good man. You are everything I'm lookin' for in a man. I love you Sha... Loved

363

you for a very long time and I know you know that... I'm tired of playin' games. I want us to get serious and become an item."

She cold got serious on me that quick.

"I hear you ma... but we can't" I replied.

"I know that you are locked up ...but I'm willin' to do this with you... all the way. I want to be there for you... all the way to the end"

"But that aint it Boo... it's not... it's me... why it can't happen is because I still love shorty."

"What... is you crazy... you still talkin' about that bitch? You love her but keep callin' me? ...She isn't gonna ride with you Shakim. When you gonna wake up and realize that?"

"You don't understand Tammi."

"So you choosin' her over me.... you diggin' that country ass chick over me? I knew you when you was up and when you were down; we been doin' this off and on since ninety-four."

"Yeah I know."

"But you still put her in the same sentence as me... or even above me? Did you even fuck her yet?"

I started laughin' at Tammi's foulness.

"Well I need to come see you... so you can tell me to my face that you want to end what we could have... so you can be with the next bitch!!. I need to see you!!"

* * * * *

I linked up with Dog and passed him Tammi's number to give to his girl and I then gave Tammi his girl's number so they could get together to plan a trip to Kentucky, which was maybe five or six hours away from where they were in Charlotte, North Carolina. I kept the plans of the visit on the low, the only one I was gonna tell was Rah, to make sure his wiz Rita wasn't comin' up that weekend.

"For a few cigarettes, I could make sure she doesn't come"

We fell out laughin'...

By now Raheeme had other convicts, who were lookin' for packs, goin' through him as the middle man and he was makin' fifty dollars a sale and a couple cigarettes from the buyer's end. He was usin' that 1981 Brooklyn game shit and it was workin' lovely as convicts stayed lookin' for Rah to put together a buy for them; after the laugh, he continued...

"But nah, I'ma make sure everything is everything…. my seed "Little Raheeme" and his ole Earth, who still happens to be crazy about me, wants to come see me so I got you Sha Bio"

"I'd hate to see your Earth and Evher come and whip your ass out there on the dance floor"

We dapped up and laughed, Raheeme stayed with the jokes.

I spoke to Tammi… because of her and Dog's girls schedule, they were comin' late Friday. They could do all day Saturday but had to head back to N.C. that night for her to go to work early Sunday and Dog's girl had to go to church Sunday. It was all good, half a visit Friday and all day Saturday was cool so we ended our call and I put things in effect to make sure my wears and appearance was on point.

*****

Everything was normal, it didn't seem like there was any tension on the yard or any drama in the air that could jeopardize the visit or runnin' of the institution. Lockdowns stopped all movements and moves so goin' on lockdown hurt our pockets as well as the prison's... Thursday night, I called to make sure everything was everything with Tammi...

"Yeah we leaving tomorrow so I will be there around noon or 1pm"

"Aiight ma"

We ended our call and I kept the visit on the hush but "Dog" knew the drill. "Dirt" didn't even know that I had a visit comin'; I just moved like I usually moved.

*****

The next morning when I seen Rah, he said his Rita was on her way up there to visit that day, I got shooked.

"Damn Sun... Tammi is on her way today."

Rah laughed his ass off.

"I'm just playin' my G... you scary, shook one... Mobb Deep was talkin' about you in that song"

I laughed it off.

*****

About 1pm, I was called for the visit so I hurriedly took a shower, oiled up, put on some "Issey Miyake" (or however you spell that shit) and got dressed. Dirt was like...

"I knew you was up to somethin'!!"

I made it out to visit to see my long lost Boo... Tammi.

366

CHAPTER 36

When I finally made it out to the visiting hall and to the front desk, I saw that it wasn't packed out there, which was strange for a Friday. Dog was already up there with his girl and little son. I saw Tammi sittin' over across from them and as I walked over to her, she was lookin' like brand new, crispy money. She immediately stood and ran over to me, we embraced, I gave her a real big hug and kissed her lips but I didn't go in ...Nah. she held on to me as I released her from our embrace but still holdin' her hand upward, I twirled her around slowly, like a ballroom dance move so I could get a real good look at her. She was killin' it. Anyone who wasn't from N.Y. could tell she was from New York; she had on some skin tight, black "True Religion" jeans that put her booty on blast! She was rockin' a tight grey t-shirt and some very small timberland boots that were laced up like if they just came out the box. Yeah, Tammi was lookin' so sexy out there with her long hair pulled up in a ponytail, revealing the diamonds studs in her ear. "I see you ma!!" I said as I twirled her around again (hey, we were on the "dance floor", right?) and makin' sure I saw every curve on her very well proportioned, Beyonce-like physique, she basked in the spot light and showed out...

"N.O. (Oceasia) aint got nothin' on this!" she boasted.

"Yeah... I hear you" I replied.

We embraced again and made it over to our seats.

"Damn Sha, you still look good... you look even better now that you gained some weight with your skinny ass"

 We laughed it up.

"How was your trip?"

As Tammi explained the long drive up from Charlotte, we bugged out. You would never believe that she was supposed to be a police officer or a nerd in school cause she could get classy, then ghetto up in that visiting hall... man, we laughed it up. We missed the camera man cause he came so late but it was cool. We had all day tomorrow... I put my arm around her and we talked about the old times of me bein' in N.Y. callin' her for late night booty calls, which she turned down repeatedly. We spoke on N.Y. and the difference of Charlotte compared to home (NY). We also spoke about her teenage son, who was wildin' out crazily. We had fun as two hours flew by and it was time to end our visit.

"Maan... I brought all this change and you didn't want nothin'?"

She played like she had an attitude.

"Nah... I'm cool... tomorrow I'ma eat up a storm."

"But I want to walk over to the vending machine so you can get a good look at this sexy ass and mean walk but I got you tomorrow"

She giggled cause she was referring to when I told her how I got a good look at Robyn's ass before I left her stranded in the visiting room but made sure to get a real good glimpse so I could have memories when I jerked off.

"You crazy Tammi."

"For you... I'm anything."

We embraced... I gave her a soft kiss and ended our visit.

"Tomorrow ma!"

"Yeah, I'ma be here early... so early, you'll think I slept in the parkin' lot."

I waved over to Dog's girl, sayin' bye-bye, I looked back at Tammi and said...

"Aiight ma... I'ma call later tonight."

*****

When I made it back to the unit and stopped at the B.E.T TV for a second to see Lyfe Jennings new video "S.E.X", I thought of Oceasia when I saw the chick who made the song with him singin' the hook. I shook my head and made it to my cell.

*****

"Yo Dun... who came to see the Ole head?" asked Dirt as soon as I went in our cell.

Dirt had a full bottle of White Lightening and he pointed to a full, twenty ounce bottle over on my locker.

"My boo Tammi came through today".

"What? You got her to come up... you sure you aint pennin' Jay Z's shit for him? Your flow is forever so incredible" he said, lifting up his bottle to bang (one some "Cheers" or "Salutes" shit) with the one Dirt put on my locker for me and I was now holdin'.

"A toast my dude."

"A toast for what?" I asked.

"To Realness... You a General for real... You got everyone smellin' your style. You got Tammi up in these mountains. I knew you was gonna make a choice... so what you gon' tell her... is it her or is it the Earth Rita Book (Oceasia)?"

Well if Dirt knew, that made ONE of us, cause after seein' Tammi, lookin' the way she did and vibin' with her on the visit, I STILL aint know who to choose my damn self...

*****

That night I renewed my history by goin' over One-Twenty in my mind. It's a habit I've had since about 1982 – 83. I repeatedly go over the lessons in my mind but first I relax, then work myself up to where I'm all hyped up, only to relax again... so, that night, I sat back doin' the "One" mentally.

*****

The next morning, I was up early and as soon as the doors were opened, I was off to doin' pull-ups. After about twelve sets, I was off to the showers. Me and Tammi didn't speak on my decision on the visit much and our conversation on the phone last night was a flirting, sexy conversation like we just met one another type thing; somethin' she started so I made her finish but today there was gonna be no playin'. I had to tell her that I made up my mind and I was gonna go and get my Earth back. I stayed under the steamin' hot water but made sure not to touch the walls.

*****

t was almost ten minutes after eight when I was called to the visit. I grabbed my photo tickets and shot up to the visiting area. After loggin' in and gettin' pat searched, I was allowed in the visiting hall. I came in like I was makin' a grand appearance, I walked to the front desk to check in and saw Tammi sittin' to the far left in the front. I guess she liked bein' up front so she could strut and show me that sexy ass walk on her way to the vending machine; I made my way to her. She stood up

370

and was more aggressive then yesterday, she grabbed me by my shirt and pulled me towards her, her lips met my lips.

As we kissed, she went to tongue kiss me but I pulled back. She then attempted to bite down on my bottom lip as soon as I opened my mouth to say somethin' and she slipped her tongue in, takin' her kiss, which I allowed as I felt her hand in my pants, grabbin' my manhood. I wrapped my arms around her to hide our activity as she gently stroked me while we kissed. We broke the kiss and she took her hand out my pants but I still embraced her. I looked around to see Dog's girl peepin' us with a smile on her face.

Tammi had on a blue and pink "Apple bottom" jean outfit that accommodated that nice shapely phatness she carried behind her with pride. She was rockin' some brand new, crispy, custom-made white and pink air force ones and she was rockin' them well. Her hair was hangin' loose but styled up as her diamond studs stood out; gleaming.

"What's good Boo?" I asked while holdin' her still.

"I want to always be your Boo"

She looked so sad.

We sat down, I wrapped my arm around her and we sat in silence for at least twenty minutes enjoyin' each other's presence... until she broke the peace.

"Tell me Sha... what is it about her that you don't see in me..."

I then looked up to the ceiling and a smile came across my face.

"She was made for me ma, she understands me, she knows me..."

"How? ... She don't know you!!" Tammi cut in. "You don't even know her like that!! I can't understand why she can't find her a man but want one in prison, one she met while he is in prison..."

371

Tammi was upset; it was written all over her face and noticeable in the tone of her voice.

"Listen Tammi... You know and understand that I am God body... me and you don't stand on the same principles nor do you understand my struggle"

I removed my arm from around her and turned to look into her eyes.

"You knew me when I was bein' destructive... When I was a destroyer and not the universal builder that I really am and am supposed to be showin'... You were in a relationship and seen the bad boy that I was, you weren't seeing the God in me. Shorty sees the God in me, not the bad boy... she knows it exists but that's not what got us together. It's a fine mist not seen by the physical, naked eye but only the mind can detect. She saw the beauty of my mind before she ever saw my face. She saw the thoughts that my mind manifested and she was able to comprehend and relate. It was beyond physical or material... it was Supreme Mathematics."

"But she did you dirty... and had a baby on your Sha" Tammi reminded me.

"Yeah... she did that but I understand. Love is the highest elevation of understanding. Love is not a fuck feelin' when one is sexin'. Love is more than an emotional state, even though one may fall a victim to emotions. Hell is the trick, sometimes you gotta go through hell to make it to heaven to get right. Right is to be right and exact."

Tammi looked at me and said...

"That was real deep... but why not me?"

"My mind says a lot of things because of the position I'm in... I'm in prison so my flesh is weak. If a shorty wants to give me some pussy..."

I pointed to a bad bodied, out of shape, white, female C.O. "I would only fall a victim because of my situation but my heart wouldn't be in it. My heart is with her... I know you and a lot of people may feel she did me wrong but I did a lot of people wrong in my life... I sold crack to whoever... then I supplied crews, destroyed families, communities... I shot guns and abused women with my destructive power so that which she did is small... I still love her..."

Tammi was crying.

"That's the kind of love I want, Shakim... that kind of love... I don't think she deserves it or... you"

"She knows it only exists with me... Shorty is at peace and happiness when she is with me. I make her smile without even sayin' anything; she melts and lets it be known who I am to her Tammi."

"I hate her and I don't even know her" she admitted.

"Why?" I asked.

"Because... I'm not her"

We sat quietly for a while.

Tammi then turned to me and with power and a voice full of emotion, she sang Anita Baker's "Sweet Love". I didn't even know shorty could sing... Then she sang Mary J's "Reminisce", one of my favorites... I hugged her and just listened...

After she was done... again, we sat quietly...

"I know you will make her happy Shakim, she just doesn't know how lucky she is."

"True that" I agreed.

373

"I just wanna enjoy the day with you... just act like she doesn't exist for one day... ok?"

"Ok."

We kicked it about life and her son, who was actin' grown; smokin' weed with her brother and other things then. After chatting it up, she asked me...

"Are you hungry yet?"

"Yeah... snatch me up some chicken wings and some orange juice."

"What else Boo?"

"Snatch me up a few wings... Let me see that mean walk ma, put a little pep in that step, fashion model runaway style"

We laughed and she got up and remembering what I told her I did to Robyn, she asked...

"You're not gonna let me come back to an empty seat is you... huh?"

"Hell no... never"

Tammi looked at me then smiled and strutted like she was on a Paris runway. All eyes was on her and she killed it by squattin' down and bussin' open her legs to get the food out of the vending machine. She put on a show for a fella, I was sure gonna miss her but I had an Earth and I knew she needed me.

*****

Tammi and I took some incredible photos, we even took one kissing. I needed to have them to look at and remember what I gave up to keep my Earth. At the end of the visit, I tongued Tammi down viciously, she cried for a few as I gave her a good bye hug.

"Shakim, you will be back. I can't wait until she breaks your heart and sends you runnin' back."

"You gonna wait for me?" I asked.

"Of course" she responded.

"Don't hold your breath… You'll kill yourself Tammi."

"I love you Shakim."

"Thank you for comin'"

We embraced one more time… then I let her go…

Deep down, I know I did the right thing. I couldn't keep stringin' Tammi along and playin' with her emotions like that. She told me a very long time ago that if she had to choose between me and any man including her child's father… she would choose me, hands down… Well I had to choose and I chose Oceasia… we shared the same culture and all we had to do now was rebuild our foundation, a foundation that included Evher Peace Earth.

*****

I sat down and scribed Oceasia a letter. I had to go back to the very thing that got Oceasia's attention from the first scribes I ever sent her. I had to take her back to the foundation, wake up that element that sparked back when all I intended to do with my letters was commend her for her strength and courage. My ink sprayed…

CHAPTER 37

Peace My Earth

I'm hopin' my thoughts find you and the young Earth in the ultimate sphere of strength and safety. I remain True and Living God. Positive Education Always Corrects Errors. I'm scribing you in honor, to show my appreciation for you and to let you know that you are truly cherished by me. You seen something special in me that a lot of people didn't. You saw the God in me even though I am in prison with a lot of time and you still chose to stay and deal with me when any other female would have moved on. You have strong endurance, being able to put up with my nonsense but overall, I feel our good times outweigh the bad we went through.

I'm sorry for acting other than myself and not being the God that I'm supposed to be. I am here anytime you need me... you know how to get at me. Close your eyes and feel my positive energy. We share the same heart... it beats on the same accord. No sense in tryna stop its beating or breaking it now, killing us and what we got... life.

We belong together – Mariah Carey

Word is Bond and Bond is Life

9 – 12 – 21

PS – Kiss Young Evher Peace for me

*****

From then on, I made it my duty to get back in tune with the Earth Oceasia and she started back with the cards and photos. She flew me reflections of what she and Evher wore on her physical birthday. She told me stories through photos, no words at all... then she sent me photos of the portrait of us that I sent to Cali and one with the heart I drew with the diamond taped in the middle. We were gettin' back on track and layin' a new, stronger foundation.

*****

Things was still in order and I was doin' what I could in the law library. Tammi was still writin' me and I called her once to thank her for travelin' to visit me. She welcomed me and said she would always remember me and thanked me for bein' real; we ended the call on a good note.

*****

A lot of stabbings was takin' place, one even resulted in a convict's death so we were locked down for several weeks. I used those weeks to reconnect with my street team and let them know that it was time to get the novel back on track. The copyright registration certificate came back lettin' me know it was on file and by then, I found that much of my team moved on to other things. The Hype was gone… what was to be the next big thing was now a stack of typed up paper in my cell, while Ethan Brown's "Queens Reigns Supreme" told another story and my story… remained stacked in my locker.

I'm not the type of convict to cry about lockdowns or bein' in the SHU. I don't stop every staff member who walks by to complain or anything. I roll with whatever punches are thrown so as Dirt was standin' by the door, tellin' me about one of his stick up escapades, we were so into the story that when the unit's case manager showed up at our door, Dirt turned around to face her with his menacing ice grill stare through the door.

"What's up?" Dirt asked.

"Nothing…. making sure everything is OK" said the unit's female case manager.

377

"We good up in here"

Dirt turned his back on her and started to go back to tellin' his story with all the theatrics like she wasn't even there. She knocked on the window of the cell door.

"Edwards, are you Ok?"

"Yeah. I'm good" I answered from the chair I was sittin' in.

"By the way" she said, giving me the "thumbs up" with a big smile on her face.

Not understanding her gesture... I don't have no secrets or nothin' that I keep under lids when it comes to communicatin' with administration staff or C.O.s so I wasn't feelin' no thumbs up like we were cool and the gang. Shorty wasn't givin' me no pussy or bringin' nothin' in for me so I had to straighten this out immediately.

"Excuse me, Ms.Tompkins... why you comin' at me with the "thumbs up" signal? What's that all about?" I inquired.

"OH... I didn't know if you wanted your business out in the open about what you asked for at "team"... your transfer to Coleman, Florida? It's been approved."

I know I must have looked like I just got busted eatin' a ham sandwich during Ramadan...

"Oh yeah?... Shakim Bio tryna sneak out on the low?" shouted Dirt so the whole unit heard him.

*****

We came back off of lockdown and I told Big Rah and the God bodies that I was approved to be transferred to U.S.P. Coleman in Florida. Some understood my reasons for wanting to leave, some didn't.

I wanted to be closer to the Ole Earth (mom) and enjoy her company before it was too late. I didn't care what others thought, I had to do me.

Mom was comin' to see me in a few weeks too. Actually, it was my mom, my baby sister and my two nieces. I told my sister but told her to keep it hush, hush because I wanted to surprise mom. In the meantime, I started gettin' all new stuff to take with me to U.S.P. Coleman... new sweats, sneakers, Timbs... everything had to be new so I got on that right away bein' that I didn't know when they were gonna call me to pack out and be transferred. This was the first time I was ever bein' transferred to a facility of my choice. A few brothers was hatin'... but I kept it movin'.

*****

Right out of nowhere, another murder happened and that laid us down (locked us down) again with mom and family on the way ... Damn!!!

*****

Me and Oceasia was flowin' back and forth through letters but I didn't reveal to her that I was gettin' ready to be transferred at any moment because I didn't want her to accidentally mention it to my Ole Earth, which could happen even though at the time, they were playin' phone tag with each other. Oceasia was also switchin' cell phone numbers to the point that as soon as she sent a number to me and I got it approved on my list, the number was no longer good. She was usin' bootleg burn out phones and she never understood why I didn't tell her that I was leavin' Big Sandy.

*****

We came off of lockdown two weeks later and the Ole Earth and family were comin' back from a trip in Virginia so they were only able to do a one day visit with me, which was still peace. We enjoyed each other's company and I reminded baby sis not to let mom know I was comin' to Florida.

*****

"Do Dirt" gave me a pack of cigarettes to "do me" with... he was still strong so I sold both my packs for eight hundred dollars, took the pack from Dirt with plans of splittin' it with the homies who didn't have much and the other half would go to Big Rah. I was heavy on food and sneakers but could only pack two pairs of sneakers so I planned on leavin' a lot of stuff to the Gods. I gave them first pick on everything.

*****

The day came when I was on the call out to pack out, after I packed out and gave away all my extras to the Gods; I said my goodbyes and good luck to others. Me, "Born Sun" and Big Rah kicked it all day until after count. I built with Brother Mahardee and Brother Means from D.C. then me and Rah pollied for the rest of the evening until yard recall at 8:30pm.

We gave our last pound and embrace...

"PEACE to the God!! I told him.

I wished him the best on his case and everything, thanked him for his realness and brotherhood.

"Make sure you do the Earth right, her and young Evher" he said as I gave him a photo of Oceasia, young Evher and an envelope.

"I'ma make sure to put this in my family Album" he said.

"True Indeed."

"Stay in touch Shakim Bio"

Big Rah looked like he was gonna cry as I walked in the direction of A – units. He opened up the envelope and saw the half of a pack of cigarettes I left him. I heard him scream...

"Tell Do Dirt, I'ma let him live cause of you!!"

I laughed all the way back to the unit.

*****

That night, Dirt threw me a goin' away party so I got drunk and kicked it with him and a few real convicts we associated with like "Mike Mumbles" and Black Jerry from Baltimore, "Spanish Vee" from Bronx. I smoked some trees and drunk a bottle of Lightening.

 "Florida, here come Shakim Bio!!"

By ten o'clock lock in, I was gettin' my salutes, pounds, embraces and nods.

 I was leavin' U.S.P. Big Sandy

*****

The next morning at 5am, I was taken to R and D to dress out and be shackled and cuffed up and put on the bus.

I was taken to U.S.P. Atlanta and processed there. I sat there for two and a half weeks in the SHU. I did Christmas and New Years there while communicating with the convicts I knew from previous run-ins on previous transfers and I was networking with new convicts. There was a lot of good lookin' female C.O.s down in that piece too.

 January fifth, I was put on the bus headed to Coleman U.S.P #2 in Florida.

*****

I arrived at U.S.P Coleman -2 on January 5, 2007. This was the first institution I'd been designated to, where it was mostly run by Black staff. Even the warden was black and there were quite a few females workin' there too. To me, Coleman was like a college campus compared to the penitentiaries I was used to. The structure was completely different, it was six, two story buildings with two parts splittin' them so it was two units per building. Everything was clean, the air was different and the grass was green; Coleman, Florida was beautiful. I was thinking, "Isn't Disney World in Florida?" I was in Disney World compared to the spots I had been in and the weather was extra beautiful.

I met the Gods immediately.

"PEACE!! I come in the divine righteous name of Shakim Bio-Chemical Wise."

"PEACE God! I already know of you Sha. My attribute is High Priest AB-God P.H.D. Allah"

"P.H.D?" I asked.

"Yes, true indeed... it's Power to Heal the Dumb" he informed.

AB God was a slim older God, a brown seed with long dreads put up in a Rasta type crown with the tassel. God even had the universal flag pinned to it."

"PEACE God! I'm Wise Understanding Allah form Norfolk, Victory Allah"

"PEACE Original man. I'm Glorious Divine Allah"

Divine was an older, Panamanian God from Brooklyn, who I'd heard the back in the day stories about. I met all the Gods and bumped into a lot of brothers who I knew from another spots. I even bumped into Siddiq (former cellmate) again, who was eighteen months short of goin' home; everything was everything.

＊＊＊＊＊

I surprised my Ole Earth when I called cause she hadn't heard from me and assumed that Big Sandy was on lockdown again; she worried so she was happy to hear my voice. She said Oceasia had been callin' her daily, askin' for me because the mail she sent to me in Big Sandy was bein' sent back "return to sender". I was smilin' to myself. I told the Ole Earth that I need to see her a.s.a.p. like right away. She said she couldn't plan a trip to come back to Kentucky so soon. I played with her for a few minutes, tellin' her she must come a.s.a.p., until she got upset sayin' she couldn't make no plans to come to Kentucky. She just left there... I told her...

"Surprise...   ...I'm in Florida!!!"

From there she had been comin' at least two to three times a moon. Everything was Love, she always told me that Oceasia been callin'.

＊＊＊＊＊

I'd been in Florida over a month and a half when I went to mail call and I received a big manila envelope. I looked and it said "Mrs. Edwards" on the return address. It was numerous Valentine's Day and other cards that was mailed to me at Big Sandy that were sent back to her bein' that I was no longer there so she put them all in one envelope and mailed them to me. I knew she was mad!! Enclosed was a letter, it read...

Peace My 12,

It's been a long time since I've had the chance to tell u how much I love u and hear u tell me how much u love me! I miss u, I miss pressin "5".

I miss hearing ur voice. I miss seein' "Mrs Edwards" on envelopes in my mail box. I miss holdin' ur handwriting (smiling). I miss knowin' how ur day was, etc. etc. etc... I miss US! U.n.I. Mind 2 Mind, Love with no beginning or ending. The kind U only find once in a lifetime, worth the wait – no mystery – Just true soul mates, together, forever, for real... U forget? U hold the master key, as a matter of fact, the only key that's actually able to unlock/lock down my heart and vice versa, of course I remember when U ripped open ur chest (I stole) to give (ur heart) U forget? This Love is 'til Death!! Regardless of whom or what. It may seem like it's on face value – but looks are deceiving – my love for u is the supreme 20. Word is Bond!! And what's understood don't need to be explained – seen? Shit is so real... There's no denying Supreme Mathematics, it always adds up... mind does detect mind cause I always think about u everyday, as always, I know u think about me - I feel u still… We are connected – meant 2 be – it's bigger than us physically – Do u realize we fell in love before we ever even met in person? We're meant 2 b – Do u remember when we first met thru a scribe, then lost contact and then the way we hooked back up and was instantly bonded to each other? It was like we been knew each other, been dating, been fuckin and everything else – We were totally comfortable beyond the naked eye – we're attached by a fine mist – its science!! U forgot? I swear, sometimes u act like a build power for real. U be buggin' out easily to think in the wrong direction… Good thing I'm able to understand thru that and separate and preserve the best part for myself. It takes a certain type female to deal with u and I'm her, N_____a, u met ur match… How I know? Cause I'm the same way. A lot of N___az can't/don't know how to deal with me. U got it all – personality, strength, sensitivity, aggression, loyalty, equality, positivity, knowledge, wisdom, understanding, million dollar looks, skills, drive, motivation, attitude, arrogance, courage, affection, bangin' body, confidence and that's just to name a few – Did I mention A Heart? A great big humongous, genuine heart that is very fragile. Warning, handle with care :) ...Just like sugar melts easy. That's why u are my sweetheart that always kept in a cool dry place.

Answer this ...Do u honestly feel like I don't love u or want any dealing wit u? Well, why would I hunt ur Ole Earth down to get ur new address and give her my new mathematics and geographical after u didn't give it to me or even let me know u moved yourself? Why would I even go thru that if u meant nothing to me? – That doesn't add up. I just need u to do the knowledge. Have some understanding, work wit me! We're both in a difficult situation, trust me, lovin' a man in jail isn't easy B.U.T. I deal with it the best I can because love u, not cause I want to. Especially now since I have Evher. Of course things have changed, #1. I don't have the same amount of me time I had before. #2. I don't have the same extra money as before. I am a totally changed person now, my priorities have changed as well as my responsibilities, my hobbies, my interests, my thoughts. EVERYTHING... my whole world. Does that mean I don't love u the same anymore? Shakim, u still give me butterflies in my stomach. I still get a rush just thinkin' about u. I still read those old letters U sent me, even the ones where u said a lot of fucked up shit to me. Evher exists now. Get over it and realize u have to share me wit her. Did u know I don't even write or perform songs anymore? I don't know what to say anymore, my timing is off and I'm focused on being the greatest parent, not the greatest rapper. This is my first seed so I'm completely inexperienced but paying close attention to everything. I have no choice, especially being a single parent. I have to carry a double load and I'm still learnin' with a lot still to be learned. I have to do this right the first time cause I don't get no second chances. I'm trying to feed her the right foods and I'm supervising her at all times cause my family eat and live totally different so I'm struggling with motherhood as well as enjoying every minute of it.

So what did u do wit all my kytes and pictures when u moved? I gotta go now B.U.T I'll be back shortly. I wanna send u some pictures so u can see how big she's getting and I will as soon as I get this computer together.

9 – 12 – 21

Love u 4 Evher Peace

The official Mrs. Edwards – still

PS – There's no such thing as Divorce!

*****

Getting married" by Nas.

That was a very powerful song with ill lyrics... "Nas is one of the best whoever did it", I thought to myself as I smiled, listening to that song while gettin' ready for a visit...

Guess who came?

You already know... as they called me out for V.I.

*****

"I'm a movement by myself...

But I'm a force when we're together

Mommy... I'm good all by myself

But Baby you... you make me better"

"Make Me Better"

Fabolous Featuring NeYo

As I came out and saw Oceasia with her new hair style, mommy was lookin' like Taraji P. Henson for real... she ran to me and we kissed and hugged and held on to each other. Finally we were back together.

I looked to see a little girl standin' there lookin' like a little version of Oceasia... I called her name...

"Evher"

She looked up at me.

"Come here ma." She acted like she didn't wanna come.

"Evher... come hug and kiss Shakim" Oceasia said to her daughter.

Evher shook her head "NO" and all I could do was smile at her. She was beautiful... she stayed away from me though. Me and Oceasia sat down across from each other but there was no table in between us, we were sittin' knee to knee. Evher ran up and looked at me, I opened my arms and she jumped up on me, climbed in my lap, wrapped her arms around my neck and kissed my face. She wasn't even two years old yet and was already digging the God.

* * * * *

Oceasia Divine True Earth still writes for the Five Percenter Newspaper. Evher Peace Earth is now a young model, who has an agent and manager and she's not even in the first grade yet... oh and she already knows her Supreme Mathematics.

I, Shakim Bio-Chemical Wise, am still at war for my freedom. During the years of my incarceration, I have obtained my G.E.D and over 50 educational achievement certificates, I founded Mikahs 7 Publishing from behind these concrete and steel prison walls and I still and will always show and prove.

Oceasia and I are still together, goin' strong and planning to be married.

Below is a Mikahs 7 Publishing teaser for

Shakim Bio's

"The Omega Jon Christ -

The Last Illest "

You always hear about brothers gettin' shot up, robbed or killed out of town. I heard about the stories every day. I lost so many close comrades and associates to that unwanted option, sometimes you don't believe it could happen to you. Until one day you get caught slippin'...

I been playin' these Baltimore clubs for a couple months. I'm gettin' too "laxed" out here. I'm even leavin' the burner in the car instead of tryna figure a way to get it in the public spots I hung out in. I'm lettin' these niggahs rock me... to sleep.

I'm drinkin' heavily but that's nothin' new, I always do. I'm havin' a good time too, not knowin' I'm bein' watched... watched real closely. My manz taps me and says "let's go". Even though the nights is live up in here, the feelin' is kind of uncomfortable, probably because we so far from home and we stay in beef... we be in more shit than flies do... Plus we aint deep like we usually are but I'm a live nigga by myself nigga.

We goin' out the door, which leads into a hallway that takes you to the front door. There's people comin' in and people goin' out...

there's no stoppin' because people are pushin' both ways to... I'm so used to this though... that's why I aint see them behind us.

Once we hit outside, they made their move, guns were drawn. "Yeah? What's up now big mouth niggah from New York?" He is up on me too close. I still go hard "Fuck it. We struggle... it's too many of them... 4 or 5 of them... I'm gettin' hit in the head with steel, 4 or 5 times but I'm still fightin' back... I can't give up... Blood is everywhere... I keep swingin' but it aint lookin' too good for me. They are on me... Somehow I break loose... I'm tryna run... They all start firing... People are screamin', runnin' and tramplin' over each other to get away, to find cover...these niggahs was aimin' straight at me... about 20 or more shots was fired...

I'm bleedin' from my head, nose, mouth, eyes, ears... I can't see. I'm just runnin' or... tryna run... I hear the shots... It's like the club's speakers beatin' bass into my back... it's so close... They are chasin' me... shootin' ... everybody's screamin'...

Damn, all those shots missed me... yeah, All of 'em.

But I was left with a head full of stitches, my face was swollen for weeks and I learned a valuable lesson...

These out of town niggahs aint playin' at all... So Sha Bio can't play either... Game don't stop son. I gotta get some Get back!!

N. Why (NY). 'til I die

"I'm wanted Dead or Alive...

I stalk the New York sidewalks all the girls hawk / but I don't stop to talk / I keep steppin' with a 9 on my waistline / Got 16 shots and I'ma waste mine/ never fess / cause I dress wit a bulletproof vest / try to test / I'ma leave a Bloody ass mess!"

"Wanted Dead or Alive"

- Kool G Rap

The Omega Jon Christ – The Last Illest

I don't shoot guns no more... I shoot ink!

"Shakim's Hood" blog / interviews available on gorillaconvict.com

Made in the USA
Columbia, SC
20 September 2020

21220648R00222